Irish Rebel / Rose

**Praise for #1 *New York Times* and *USA TODAY*
bestselling author**

NORA
ROBERTS

"Characters that touch the heart, stories that intrigue,
romance that sizzles—Nora Roberts has mastered it all."
—*Rendezvous*

"With clear-eyed, concise vision and a sure pen, Roberts
nails her characters and settings with awesome precision,
drawing readers into a vividly rendered world of family-
centered warmth and unquestionable magic."
—*Library Journal*

"Roberts' bestselling novels are some of the best
in the romance genre. They are thoughtfully plotted,
well-written stories featuring fascinating characters."
—*USA TODAY*

"You can't bottle wish fulfillment, but Nora Roberts
certainly knows how to put it on the page..."
—*New York Times*

"Roberts has a warm feel for her characters
and an eye for the evocative detail."
—*Chicago Tribune*

Dear Reader,

In *Irish Hearts,* Nora Roberts evokes the magic of Ireland, the fire of the Irish spirit and the power of the American dream.

For Adelia Cunane in *Irish Thoroughbred,* that dream is to be given a chance. She may be a small woman with a hot temper and prickly pride, but she knows that she can train champion horses for Royal Meadows stables…if she could get the devilish owner, Travis Grant, out of her stables—and out of her thoughts. But Travis sees more than Royal Meadows' destiny in Adelia. He sees his own.

Irish Rose features Adelia's cousin, Erin McKinnon. Erin follows Adelia to America and can immediately see why Adelia wanted to stay in this idyllic place, though she's hardly as impressed by Burke Logan, the owner of the farm beside Royal Meadows. He's arrogant and infuriating and far too rich. She's feisty and stubborn and far too independent. This relationship has forever written all over it….

And don't miss the follow-up volume, *Irish Dreams,* containing the story of Adelia and Travis's daughter, as well as the story of enigmatic Irish painter Colin Sullivan, available in September 2011.

Happy reading!

The Editors,
Silhouette Books

NORA ROBERTS

Irish Hearts

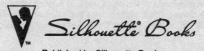

Published by Silhouette Books
America's Publisher of Contemporary Romance

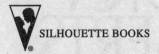

SILHOUETTE BOOKS

IRISH HEARTS

ISBN-13: 978-0-373-28150-3

Copyright © 2011 by Harlequin Books S.A.

The publisher acknowledges the copyright holder of the individual works as follows:

IRISH THOROUGHBRED
Copyright © 1981 by Nora Roberts

IRISH ROSE
Copyright © 1988 by Nora Roberts

Visit Silhouette Books at www.Harlequin.com

Printed in U.S.A.

CONTENTS

IRISH THOROUGHBRED

Chapter One

Adelia Cunnane stared out the window without seeing the magic layer of clouds. Some formed into mountains, others glaciers, flattening and thinning into an ice-encrusted lake; but, for one experiencing her first air journey, she found the view uninspiring. Her mind was crowded with doubts and uncertainties that merged with a strong pang of homesickness for a small farm in Ireland. But both farm and Ireland were now very far away, and every minute that crawled by brought her closer to America and strangers. She knew, with a sigh of frustration, that nothing in her life had ever prepared her properly to cope with either.

Her parents had been killed in a lorry accident, leaving her an orphan at the tender age of ten. In the weeks that followed her parents' death, Adelia had drifted though a fog of shock, turning inward to ward off the agony of separation, the strange and terrifying feeling of desertion.

Slowly, a wall had been constructed around the pain, and she had thrown herself into the work of the farm with an adult's dedication.

Her father's sister, Lettie Cunnane, had taken over both child and farm, running both with a firm hand. Although never unkind, neither had she been affectionate: she had possessed little patience or understanding for the unpredictable, often tempestuous child.

The farm had been the only common ground between them, and woman and child had built their relationship with the dark, fertile soil and the hours of labor it required. They had lived and worked together for nearly thirteen years; then Lettie had suffered a paralyzing stroke, and Adelia had been forced to divide her time between the duties of the farm and caring for an invalid's needs. Days and nights had merged together as she waged the determined battle to shoulder the increasing responsibility.

Her enemies had been the lack of time and the lack of money. When, after six long months, she was again left alone, Adelia was near the point of exhausted desperation. Her aunt was gone, and though she had worked unceasingly, the farm had had to be sold for taxes.

She had written to her only remaining relative, her father's elder brother, Padrick, who had emigrated to America twenty years previously, informing him of his sister's death. His answer had been immediate, the letter warm and loving, asking her to join him. The last sentence of the missive was a simple, gentle command: "Come to America; your home is with me now."

So she had packed her few belongings; sold or given away what could not be taken with her, and said goodbye to Skibbereen and the only home she had ever known....

A sudden movement of the plane jolted Adelia back

from memory. She sat back against the cushions of her seat, fingering the small gold cross she always wore around her neck. There was nothing left for her in Ireland, she told herself, fighting against the flutters of her stomach. Everything she had loved there was dead, and Padrick Cunnane was the only family she had left, the only link with what she had once had. She pushed back a surge of sudden, unaccustomed fear. America, Ireland— what difference did it make? Her shoulders moved restlessly. She would manage. Hadn't she always managed? She was determined not to be a burden to her uncle, the vague, shadowy man she knew only from letters, whom she had last seen when barely three. There would be work for her, she reasoned, perhaps on the horse farm her uncle had written of so often over the years. Her ability to work with animals was innate, and she had absorbed a varied knowledge of medicine through her experiences, her skill being such that she had often been called on to aid in a difficult calving or stitch up a rent hide. She was strong, despite her diminutive stature—and, she reminded herself with an unconscious squaring of shoulders, she was a Cunnane.

Surely, she told herself with more confidence, there would be a place for her at Royal Meadows where her uncle worked as trainer for the Thoroughbred racing stock. There'd be no fields needing plowing, no cows needing milking, but she'd earn her bread and butter if she had to work as a scullery maid. She wondered suddenly, with a small frown, if they had scullery maids in America.

The plane touched down, and Adelia disembarked and entered the Dulles terminal in Virginia, where she found herself gaping in confusion, fascinated by the scene, confused by the babble of foreign tongues, the odd mixture of people. Her eyes lingered over an East Indian family in full native dress. She turned to observe two teenagers in faded denims strolling by hand in hand, followed by a scurrying middle-aged businessman clutching a leather briefcase.

Later, standing in the lobby, she looked around hoping to see a familiar face. Everyone rushing and hurrying, she thought. A body could be trampled and never seen again....

"Dee, little Dee!" A man hurried toward her, a stockily built, compact man with a full thatch of curling gray hair, and she caught a glimpse of eyes as bright and blue as her father's before she was enveloped in a warm, crushing hug. The thought occurred to her that it had been a lifetime since anyone had held her so close.

"Little Dee, I would have known you anywhere." He pulled back and studied her face, eyes misty, smile tender. "It's like looking into Kate's face again—it's the image of your mother you are."

He continued to stare at her while she searched for her voice, his gaze taking in the deep, rich auburn hair falling in gleaming waves to her shoulders, the large, deep green of thickly lashed eyes, the tip-tilted nose and full mouth which Aunt Lettie had described as impudent, the face now of a startled pixie.

"What a beautiful sight you are," he said at last on a sigh of pure pleasure.

"Uncle Padrick?" she asked, finding a multitude of questions and emotions racing through her.

"And who else would you be thinking I might be?" He looked down at her with those well-remembered eyes, filled with love and laughter, and doubts, fears, and questions vanished in a wave of joy.

"Uncle Paddy," she whispered as she flung her arms around his neck.

As they drove along the highway from the airport, Adelia stared about her in fresh amazement. Never had she seen so many cars, and all flying by at an outrageous speed. Everything moved so fast, and the noise, she marveled silently, the noise was enough to wake the dead. Shaking her head, she began to bombard her uncle with questions.

How far was it they were going? Did everyone drive so fast in America? How many horses were at Royal Meadows? When could she see them? Questions buzzed in her mind and through her lips, and Paddy answered them tolerantly, finding the soft lilt of her voice as sweet as a summer breeze.

"Where is it I'll be working?"

He removed his eyes from the road a moment and glanced at her. "There's no need for you to be working, Dee."

"Oh, but Uncle Paddy, I must," she disagreed, turning to face him. "I could work with the horses; I've a way with animals."

Thick gray brows drew together in a doubtful frown. "I didn't bring you all this way to be putting you to work." Before she could protest, he went on. "And I don't know what Travis would be thinking about me hiring my own niece."

"Oh, but I'd do anything." She brushed back masses of chestnut hair. "Groom the horses, muck out the stalls, cart hay—it doesn't matter." Unknowingly, she used her eyes in an outrageous manner. "Please, Uncle Paddy, it's crazy I'd be in a week, not having some sort of work to do."

Her eyes won the small battle, and Paddy squeezed her hand. "We'll see."

So engrossed had she been in their conversation and the fascinating stream of traffic that she had lost all track of time. When Paddy pulled into a drive and halted the car, Adelia gazed about her with new wonder.

"Royal Meadows, Dee," he announced with a sweeping gesture of his hand. "Your new home."

The entrance to the long, winding drive was flanked by two tall stone pillars, and bushes studded with the promise of flowering buds continued along its path as far as she could see. The grass was brilliantly green over softly rolling hills, and horses grazed lazily in the distance.

"The finest horse farm in all of Maryland, sure as faith," Paddy added with possessive pride as he proceeded along the curving drive. "And—in Padrick Cunnane's opinion—the finest in the whole of America."

The car rounded a bend in the drive, and Adelia caught her breath as the main house came into view. An immense structure, or so it seemed to her, with three magnificent stories of old and muted stone. Dozens of windows winked in the gleaming sun like large, clear eyes. Wide and boldly glistening, they were a sharp contrast to the stone's mellowness. Skirting the top two stories were balconies, the design of wrought iron as intricate and delicate as the finest lace. The house stood on a gently sloping lawn of close-cropped green, graced with bushes and stately trees just awakening from their winter sleep.

"Beautiful, isn't it, Dee?"

"Aye," she agreed, awed by its size and elegance. "The grandest house I've ever seen."

"Well, our house isn't so grand as this." He turned the car left as the drive forked past the stone building. "But it's a fine place, and I hope you'll be happy there."

Adelia turned her attention to her uncle with a smile that transformed her face into a work of art. "I'll be happy, Uncle Paddy, as long as you're with me." Letting impulse guide her movements, she leaned over and kissed his cheek.

"Ah, Dee, I'm glad you're here." He took her hand in a firm grip. "You've brought the spring with you."

The car came to a halt, and Adelia turned to look out the front window, her mouth falling open at what greeted her eyes. An oval track commanded her view, and across from it stood a large white building, which Paddy identified as the stables. Fences and paddocks checkerboarded the area and the scent of hay and horses drifted through the air.

In solemn amazement she gazed about, and the thought sped through her brain that she had not moved from one farm to another but from one world to another. At home, the farm had meant the earth, with its blessings and curses, a small barn in constant need of repair, a strip of pasture. Here, the space alone made her eyes widen, so much space to belong to one man. But as well as space, she recognized the efficiency and the order in fresh white buildings and split-rail fences. In the distance, where the hills began their soft roll, she saw mares grazing while their foals frolicked with the joy of spring and youth.

Travis Grant, she mused, recalling the name of the owner from Paddy's letters. *Travis Grant* knows how to care for what he owns....

"There's my house." Now Paddy pointed out the opposite window. "Our house now."

Following his direction, she let out a cry of pleasure. The first story of the building was a large white garage, which she learned later serviced the trailers and trucks used for transporting the Thoroughbreds. Atop this was a stone structure, nearly twice as large as the farmhouse in which she had spent her life. It was a miniature replica of the main house, with the same native stonework and glistening windows graced with balconies.

"Come inside, Dee. Get a look at your new home."

He led her down a narrow, crushed stone path and up the stairs to the front door, opening it wide and nudging her ahead of him.

A bright, cozy room welcomed her, with pale green walls and a shining oak floor. A brightly checked sofa and matching chair invited her to sit in front of the raised hearth when the weather was cool, or contemplate rambling hills through wide, sheer-draped windows.

"Oh, Uncle Paddy!" She sighed, making an inadequate but expressive movement of her hands.

"Come, Dee, I'll show you the rest."

He led her through the house, her wide eyes growing larger with each new discovery, from the kitchen, with its sunny yellow fixtures and spotless counters, to the bath, where creamy ivory tiles made her dream of languishing for hours in hot, soapy water.

"This is your room, darlin'."

He opened the door across from the bath, and Adelia stepped inside. It was not an overly large room, but to her inexperienced eyes it was huge indeed. The walls were painted a robin's-egg blue, and sheer white curtains billowed and swayed at two opened windows. The soft blue and white was repeated in the flower print of the bedspread, and a fluffy white rug lay on the wooden floor. The mirror over the maple dresser reflected the expression of stunned pleasure on her face. The knowledge that the room was to be hers brought unaccustomed tears to her eyes. Blinking them away, she turned and threw her arms around her uncle's neck.

Later, they strolled across the lawn toward the stables. Adelia had changed from the dress she had worn for the trip and was now clad in her more customary attire of jeans and cotton shirt, with her auburn curls pulled up and covered by a faded blue hat. She had convinced her uncle that rest was not what she needed, and that seeing the horses was what she wanted above all else. With her face glowing and eyes pleading, Paddy would have found it impossible to deny her anything.

Approaching the stables, they spotted a small group gathered around a chestnut Thoroughbred. The raised voices reached uncle and niece before their presence was noted.

"And what might be the problem here?" Paddy demanded.

"Paddy, glad you're back," a tall, husky man greeted him with obvious relief. "Majesty just had one of his spells. Gave Tom a bad kick."

Paddy transferred his attention to a small, spare young man seated on the ground, nursing his thigh and muttering.

"How bad is it, lad? Did you break anything?"

"Naw, nothing broke." Disgust was more evident than pain in both voice and face. "But I don't guess I'll be riding for a couple of days." Looking over at the dark chestnut, he shook his head with a mixture of resentment and reluctant amusement. "That horse may be the fastest thing on four legs, but he's meaner than a stomped-on cat."

"His eyes aren't mean," Adelia commented, and several pairs of eyes focused on her for the first time.

"This is Adelia, my niece. Dee, this is Hank Manners, assistant trainer. Tom Buckley, on the ground there, is an exercise boy, and George Johnson and Stan Beall, grooms." After the introductions had been completed, Adelia quickly turned her attention back to the horse.

"They don't understand you, do they? Ah, but you're a fine fellow."

"Miss," Hank cautioned as she lifted a hand to stroke his muzzle, "I wouldn't do that. He's not in the best of moods to begin with, and he doesn't take to strangers."

"Ooch, but it's not strangers we'll be for long." Smiling, she stroked the length of his strong muzzle, and Majesty blew from wide nostrils.

"Paddy," Hank began in cautious warning, but the other man lifted a hand to silence him.

"A fine, beautiful horse you are. I've never seen another to compare with you, and that's the truth of it." She continued to speak as she ran her hands over his smooth neck and side. "You're built for running—strong, long legs and a fine, wide chest." Her hands moved over him freely as the horse remained still, ears at attention. She fondled his nose before resting her cheek against his neck. "I bet you're lonely for someone to talk to."

"I'll be switched." Hank observed Adelia's confident handling of the frisky colt and shook his head. "He's never let anyone do that before, not even you, Paddy."

"Animals have feelings as well, Mr. Manners." She brought her face from the Thoroughbred's neck and turned around. "He wants some pampering."

"Well, little lady, you certainly seem to have a way with him." He gave her a grin expressive of both amusement and admiration before turning his attention to Paddy. "He still needs to be exercised. I'll give Steve a call."

"Uncle Paddy." Adelia grabbed his arm on impulse, eyes shining with excitement. "I can do it. Let me take him out."

"I don't think a little lady like you could handle a big

fire-breather like Majesty," Hank put in before Paddy could speak, and Adelia drew herself up to the full of her five feet two inches and tilted her chin.

"There's nothing on four legs I can't ride."

"Is Travis back yet?" Paddy concealed his smile and addressed Hank.

"No." He eyed Paddy through narrowed lids. "You're not thinking of letting her take him out?"

"I'd say she's about the right size—couldn't weigh over a hundred pounds." He gave his niece a thorough survey, one hand rubbing his chin.

"Paddy." Hank's hand descended on his shoulder, only to be ignored.

"You're a Cunnane, aren't you, lass? If you say you can handle him, then by the saints you can." Adelia beamed at her uncle and told him firmly she was indeed a Cunnane.

"God knows what the boss is going to say when he finds out," Hank muttered, finding himself against a solid wall of family alliance.

"Just leave Travis to me," Paddy answered with calm authority.

With a shrug of his shoulders and another incoherent mutter, Hank resigned himself to Paddy's loss of common sense.

"Once around the track, Dee," her uncle instructed. "Pace him to what you can handle; I can see from the look of him he wants his head."

Pulling her cap lower, she nodded, watching the well-trimmed hooves paw the ground in impatience. With an easy vault she was in the saddle, and as Hank opened the wide gate she took Majesty onto the dirt track. Leaning forward, she whispered in his ear as he sidestepped and strained to be off.

"Ready, Dee?" Paddy called. As an afterthought, he pulled out his stopwatch.

"Aye, we're ready." Straightening, she took a deep breath.

"Go!" he shouted, and horse and rider lunged down the track.

Crouching low over the Thoroughbred's neck, she urged him on to the speed for which he thirsted. The wind beat against her face, stinging her eyes, as they tore over the dirt at a pace she had never experienced, never imagined, but somehow had craved. It was a wild, exhilarating adventure; both horse and rider revelled in the unbridled sensation as they sped as one around the oval track, sun, wind, and speed their companions. She laughed and shouted to her partner, a new sense of freedom liberating her from the concerns and worries that had been a part of her life for so long. For a few short moments she was riding the clouds, away from pressure, away from responsibility, in a glorious haven that returned her to carefree childhood. When they came to the end of the run, she slowed the horse gradually to a halt and flung her arms around his gleaming neck.

"I'll be a son of a gun!" Hank said in simple astonishment.

"What were you expecting?" Paddy questioned, feeling as proud as a peacock with two tails. "She's a Cunnane." He held out the stopwatch for Hank to see. "Not a bad time either." With a final smile, he strutted over as Adelia slipped to the ground.

"Oh, Uncle Paddy!" Her eyes gleamed like emeralds against her flushed face, and she pulled off her cap, flourishing it in excitement. "He's the grandest horse in the world. It was like riding Pegasus himself!"

"That was nice riding, little lady." Hank extended his

hand, shaking his head in admiration both for her ability and for the gleaming hair that now spilled over her shoulders.

"Thank you, Mr. Manners." She accepted his hand with a smile.

"Hank."

She grinned. "Hank."

"Well, Adelia Cunnane." Paddy slipped his arm around her shoulders. "Royal Meadows just hired another exercise boy. You've got yourself a job."

Lying in her bed that night, Adelia stared wide-eyed at the ceiling. So many things had happened, in so short a time, that her mind refused to relax and allow her body rest.

After her ride on the Thoroughbred, she had been taken through the stables, introduced to more hands and more horses, shown into a tackroom that contained more leather than she had ever seen in one place at one time, and exposed to more people and more things than she believed she had ever been exposed to in her life. And all in the course of one day.

Paddy had prepared their dinner, firmly refusing assistance, and she had merely watched as he bustled around the kitchen. The stove, she decided, had more to do with magic than technology. And a machine that washed and dried the dishes at a touch of a button—marvels! Hearing abut such things and reading about them was one matter, but seeing them with your own eyes…it was easier to believe in the Pooka and the little people. When, with a sigh, she said as much to her uncle, he threw back his head and laughed until tears flowed down his cheeks, then enveloped her in a hug as crushing as the one he had greeted her with at the airport.

They had eaten at the small dinette set by the kitchen window, and she had answered all his questions about Skibbereen. The meal was full of talking and laughing, and Paddy's eyes twinkled continually at her colorful descriptions and outrageous stories. She elaborated here and there, her hands working with her words, brows raising over guileless eyes as she stretched truth into an obvious exaggeration. Her uncle had noticed the faint shadows under them, however, and urged her to retire early, overcoming her protests with the deft suggestion that she had need to be fresh in the morning.

So Adelia had obeyed, drawing a steaming tub and wallowing in unfamiliar luxury for what she knew Aunt Lettie would have considered a sinful amount of time. When at last she lay between the cool, fresh sheets, she found it impossible to relax. Her mind was full, crowded with new sensations, new images; and her body, so used to complete exhaustion before sleep, was unable to cope with the lack of physical exertion. Easing out of bed, she exchanged her nightdress for jeans and shirt and, piling her hair once more under the absurd cap, slipped noiselessly from the sleeping house.

The night was clear, cool and quiet, a vague breeze sweetening the air, only the bright, insistent call of a whippoorwill breaking the stillness. The light of the half moon guided her toward the stables as she strolled without thought of destination over the smooth new grass. The stillness, the familiar scent of animals, reminded her of home, and suddenly she felt a contentment and peace she had not even known she had lived without.

Hesitating outside the door of the large white stables, she debated whether she dare enter and spend the last of her evening with the horses. Having decided there was no harm in it, she was reaching out for the handle when an iron grip closed around her arm and whirled her around, and she was lifted off her feet for a moment like a rag doll.

"Just what do you think you're doing? And how did you get in here?"

She stared wordlessly at the owner of the harsh, angry voice, a vague shadow silhouetted in the dim moonlight, looming over her like an avenging giant. She searched for her own voice, but the combination of shock and pain had stolen it. Her words slipped down her throat as she felt herself being dragged into the building.

"Here, let's have a look at you," the voice growled as its owner switched on the lights. He spun her around, dislodging her cap, and the glory of her hair escaped its confinement to form a fiery cascade down her back.

"What the...you're a girl!" He released his firm hold and Adelia stepped back and began to give him both sides of her Irish tongue.

"Sure and it's observant you are to be noticing that—" She rubbed her arm vigorously while her green eyes glared up at her astonished assailant. "And who are you to come around grabbing innocent people and crushing their bones? A great, hulking bully you are, sneaking up on a body and dragging and pulling them about! A horse-whipping is what you're deserving for scaring the life from me and nearly breaking my arm in the process—"

"You may be pint-sized, but you're packed with dynamite," the man observed, obviously amused. He wondered as he looked over her softly rounded shape how he could have mistaken her for a boy. "From your accent I could make a guess that you're little Dee, Paddy's niece."

"I'm Adelia Cunnane, but it's not your little Dee I am." She regarded him with unconcealed resentment. "And it's not me who's having the accent. It's you!"

He threw back his head and roared with laughter, increasing Adelia's fury. "Oh, I am glad to have made you so happy." Folding her arms across her chest, she tossed her head, rich dark curls swinging wildly. "And who in the world are you, I'd like to know?"

"I'm Travis," he answered, still grinning. "Travis Grant."

Chapter Two

It was Adelia's turn to gape at her companion. As the mists of fury cleared from her eyes, she saw him clearly for the first time. He was tall and powerfully built, and the sleeves of his shirt were carelessly rolled above his elbows, revealing deeply tanned, muscular arms. He had chiseled features, clear and sharp, and his eyes were so blue against the brown of his skin that they startled the casual onlooker. His hair was rich and full, thick black curls in a disarming disarray to his collar, and the mouth that continued to grin at her was well formed, showing strong white teeth.

This was the man she was to work for, this was the man she needed to impress, Adelia's brain registered numbly, and she had just raked him clean with her furious tongue. "Jakers," she whispered, shutting her eyes a moment, and wishing she could disappear in a puff of smoke.

"I'm sorry we met under such, uh…" he hesitated,

his mouth twitching again "...confusing circumstances, Adelia. Paddy's been on top of the world since he made arrangements to bring you over from Ireland."

"I didn't expect to be meeting you till tomorrow, Mr. Grant." She clung desperately to pride and kept her voice even. "Uncle Paddy said you wouldn't be back."

"I didn't expect to find a half-pint fairy invading my stables," Travis returned, grinning once again.

Adelia straightened her spine and threw him a haughty look. "I couldn't sleep, so I came for a walk. I was thinking I might look in on Majesty."

"Majesty's a very high-strung animal," Travis admonished, his gaze roaming over her from top to bottom. "You'd best keep a respectable distance."

"And how will I be doing that?" she demanded imperiously, disconcerted by his masculine appraisal. "I'm to be exercising him regularly."

"The devil you are!" His eyes rose to hers and narrowed. "If you think I'd let a slip of a thing like you on my prize colt, you've lost your senses."

"I've already been on your prize colt." Anger returned, and her head tossed with it. "I rode around your track on him in fine time."

"I don't believe it." He took a step toward her, and her head was forced to tilt still further. "Paddy wouldn't let you up on Majesty."

"I'm not in the habit of lying, Mr. Grant," Adelia retorted with great dignity. "The boy, Tom, got a kick for his trouble, so I rode Majesty instead."

"You rode Majesty?" Travis repeated in slow, even tones.

"That I did," she agreed, then, noting the anger hardening the blue eyes, sped on. "He's a beauty, rides like the wind, but he's not bad-tempered. He wouldn't have

been kicking Tom if the boy had understood him better."
She was speaking rapidly, not giving Travis an opportunity to comment. "The poor thing just needed someone to talk to him, someone to show him he was loved and appreciated."

"And you can talk to horses?" Travis's lips curved on the question.

"Aye," she agreed, unaware of the mocking gleam that lit his eyes. "Anyone can if they've a mind to. I know animals, Mr. Grant. I worked with the vet back in Skibbereen, and I know a bit about healing as well. I would never do anything to bring harm to Majesty or any of your other horses. Uncle Paddy trusted me; you mustn't be angry with him."

He said nothing to this, only took his time studying her as her extraordinary eyes unknowingly employed their power. As his silence and intense regard continued, she felt a small tingle of fear, mixed with another sensation, strange and foreign, that she was unable to decipher.

"Mr. Grant," she began, swallowing pride to plead. "Please, give me a chance—a fortnight, no more." She took a deep breath and moistened her lips. "If you don't want me after that, just tell me, and I'll abide by your decision. I'll tell Uncle Paddy I'm not happy with the job, that I want to be doing something else."

"Why would you do that?" His head tilted as if to gain a new perspective.

"It's what I'd have to do," she returned with a shrug and a push at her tumbled hair. "Otherwise I'd be putting him in the middle. He's devoted to you and to this place—I know that from the letters he wrote me—but he's taken me on as his responsibility now. If I told him you had fired me, his loyalties would be torn in two. I'll not be the cause of that. Will you give me a two-week trial, Mr. Grant?" *Pride goeth before destruction,* she quoted silently, trying to remember Aunt Lettie's lectures on humility.

She stood, determined not to squirm under his silent contemplation, wishing he would not look at her as if he could read the thoughts running through her brain.

"All right, Adelia," he said at length. "You'll have your two-week trial, just between us."

A brilliant smile lit her face and she extended her hand. "Thank you, Mr. Grant. I'm grateful to you."

He accepted her hand, but his returning smile faded, a frown replacing it as he turned her palm up and examined it. Her hand was exquisitely small, fingers long and tapering, but it was rough and calloused from years of the abuse of labor. The continued contact was sending odd tingles through her body, and she looked down helplessly at the hand under his critical scrutiny.

"Is something the matter?" she asked in a voice she barely recognized.

He raised his eyes and looked into hers with an expression she could not fathom. "It's a crime for such a tiny hand to be as hard and rough as any ditchdigger's."

Unaccountably stung by his softly spoken words, she jerked her hand away, holding it behind her back. "I'm sorry they're not as soft as a lily, Mr. Grant. But it's not lady's hands I'll be needing for the job I'm doing for you. If you'll excuse me now, I'll be going in."

She moved past him quickly, and he watched her run like a rabbit across the grass and out of sight.

Birdcalls broke the night's slumber, and Adelia woke with the sun. She dressed quickly, happy with the anticipation of beginning her job, a job which was to her more of a magic wish granted than labor. She was sure she could prove herself to Travis Grant. A new home, a new life, a new beginning; she stared out at the infant sun and knew it would bring nothing but wonders.

The scent of frying bacon led Paddy to the kitchen, and he stood for a moment watching her movements while she remained unaware of his presence. She was humming an old tune he remembered from childhood, and she seemed to him the essence of shining, unspoiled youth.

"Sure and it's the most beautiful sight these old eyes have awakened to in many a year."

She turned to him, her smile dimming the sunlight into insignificance. "Good morning to you, Uncle Paddy. It's a fine, beautiful day."

While they were eating, Adelia casually mentioned that she had met Travis Grant the previous night during her nocturnal wanderings.

"I was hoping to introduce you myself this morning." He took a bit of crisp bacon and raised his brows. "What did you think of him?"

She tactfully kept her opinion to herself and answered with a move of her shoulders. "I'm sure he's a fine, good man, Uncle Paddy, but I wasn't with him long enough to make judgments." *Big, arrogant bully,* her mind added. "But I did tell him about Tom's accident, and that I'd been taken on as an exercise boy."

"Did you, now?" A slow smile formed as he added jam to his bread. "And what did he say to that?"

"He's smart enough to trust Padrick Cunnane's opinion." Her fingers crossed under the table, and she wondered if she had earned another black mark in Aunt Lettie's often mentioned Record Book of the Angels.

A short time later, Adelia stood in front of Majesty, rubbing his muzzle and holding an intimate conversation, unaware her actions were being observed by a pair of deep blue eyes.

"Morning, Paddy. I hear you've taken on a new hand."

Paddy broke off his conversation with Hank and greeted the tall, lean man. "Good morning to you, Travis. Dee told me she met you last night."

"Did she?" His lips curved as he continued to regard woman and horse.

"Wait till you see that little lady ride," Hank put in, shaking his head. "Could have knocked me over with a feather."

Travis inclined his head. "We'll soon see." He moved to where Adelia still stood speaking softly to the large Thoroughbred. "Hello again, half-pint. Does your friend ever answer you?"

She whirled, caught off guard, and regarded his amusement with indignation. "Aye, that he does, Mr. Grant, in his own way." She brushed past him to mount, and Travis stopped her with a hand on her wrist.

"Good Lord, did I do that?" He ran a finger over the dark smudge of bruises on her arm, and Adelia followed his glance before raising her eyes to his.

"That you did."

His eyes narrowed a moment, his fingers still light on her wrist. "We'll have to be more careful with you in the future, won't we, little Dee?"

"Not the first bruising I've had, nor likely to be the last, but you'll not be having any more occasion to be grabbing at me, Mr. Grant." With this, she swung herself astride Majesty and rode him onto the track. At Paddy's signal, the pair sprinted forward and galloped around the oval in a clean, steady rhythm.

"You wouldn't have been thinking I'd lost my senses hiring my niece, now would you, lad?"

"I'll admit when she told me she'd been hired I had a moment of doubt about your sanity," Travis answered, keeping his eyes on the small woman glued to the speeding horse. "But I've always trusted your judgment, Paddy; you've never let me down."

Later that morning Adelia worked in the stables, insisting over Paddy's objections that she assist in the grooming of some of the horses. A sound behind her caused her to turn her head, and she encountered two small boys, one the mirror image of the other. She closed her eyes in mock alarm.

"Saints preserve us, sure and it's losing my mind I am! I'm seeing double."

The boys collapsed into giggles and spoke in unison. "We're twins."

"Is that the truth?" She breathed a deep sigh of relief. "Well, I'm glad to know it. I was afraid a spell had been put on me."

"You talk just like Paddy," one boy observed, eyeing her with unrestrained curiosity.

"Do I, now?" She smiled down at their identical faces. The boys were about eight, she hazarded, dark as gypsies, with snapping brown eyes. "The reason for that may be I'm his niece, Adelia Cunnane, just arrived from Ireland."

Two faced creased in two doubtful frowns. "He calls you little Dee, but you're not little, you're all grown up," one boy complained, the other nodding in agreement.

"That I am, as far as I ever will be, I'm afraid. But I was just a wee babe when I last saw Uncle Paddy, and I never did grow very tall, so I'm little Dee to him. And what might your names be?" she questioned, putting down the currycomb that she had been using.

"Mark and Mike," they announced, again in one voice.

"Don't be telling me who's who," she commanded, narrowing dark green eyes. "I'll guess; I'm mighty good at guessing." She circled them as they resumed giggling. "You'd be Mark, and you'd be Mike," she pronounced, placing a hand on each head. Two pair of eyes stared at her in amazement.

"How did you know?" Mark demanded.

"I'm Irish," she stated simply, controlling a grin. "There's many of us from Ireland who's fey."

"Fey—what's that?" Mike chimed in, eyes wide and curious.

"That means I have strange, secret powers," Adelia claimed with a dramatic sweep of her hand. The two boys looked at each other and back at Adelia, suitably impressed.

"Mark, Mike." A woman entered the stables and shook her head in despair. "I should have know the pair of you would be here."

Adelia stared at the newcomer, stunned by her beauty and elegance. She was tall and slender, clad in a simple but, to Adelia's untrained eye, overwhelmingly beautiful outfit of dark blue slacks and white silk blouse. Black, silky hair curled back from her face. Soft, rose-tinted lips and a classic straight nose led to a pair of heavily lashed deep blue eyes that Adelia identified as Travis's.

"I hope they haven't been bothering you." The woman peered down in indulgent exasperation. "They're impossible to keep track of."

"No, missus," Adelia said, wondering if there had ever been a lovelier woman. "They're fine lads. We've just been getting acquainted."

"You must be Paddy's niece, Adelia." The generous mouth curved in a smile.

"Aye, missus." Adelia managed a smile of her own and wondered what it would be like to be as graceful as a willow limb.

"I'm Trish Collins, Travis's sister." She extended her hand, and Adelia gaped at it in horror. After Travis's words of the previous night she was self-conscious about the state of her hands, and her mind began to work swiftly.

How could she put her hard, rough hand into such a lovely soft one! Yet there was no way out without being pointedly rude, so, wiping her palm on her jeans, she joined it with the one Trish offered. The other woman had noted Adelia's hesitation and concluded the reason for it when their hands met, but she made no comment.

At that moment, Travis entered the building, along with Paddy and a small, spare man Adelia did not recognize.

"Paddy!" The twins launched themselves at the stocky figure.

"Well, if it isn't Tweedledee and Tweedledum. And what mischief have you been up to this fine day?"

"We came to meet Dee," Mark announced. "She guessed which one of us was which."

"She's fey," Mike added soberly.

Paddy nodded, equally grave, his eyes twinkling as they met Adelia's over the two small heads. "Aye, that's a fact. There's been many a Cunnane who's had the sight."

"Adelia Cunnane—" Travis made introductions, a light smile playing over his mouth "—Dr. Robert Loman, our vet."

"Pleased to meet you, Doctor," Adelia greeted him, strategically keeping her hands behind her back.

"Rob's come to look over Solomy," Paddy explained. "She'll be foaling soon."

The pixie face lit with pleasure, and, looking down at her, Travis raised his brows. "Would you like to see her, Adelia?"

"Very much." She beamed him a smile, previous animosity forgotten.

"She's foaling quite late," Travis commented as the group walked down the long length of stalls. "A Thoroughbred's official birthday is January the first, and normally we breed with that in mind. We just acquired Solomy six months ago, and of course she was already in foal. She's from a good line, and the stud she was bred to is by the same sire as Majesty."

"Then you must have big hopes for the foal," Adelia returned, thinking of Majesty's style and speed.

"I think," he said with a smile, "you could safely say we had hopes for this foal." Placing a hand on her shoulder, he turned her toward an enclosure. "Adelia," Travis said with amused formality, "meet Solomy."

She sighed with delight at the animal, a dark, gleaming bay mare with a mane of flowing black silk. Running her hand down the stark flash of white on the forehead, she looked into dark, intelligent eyes.

"You're a fine, beautiful lady." The caressing of the smooth hide was met with a whinny of approval.

"I suppose you'd like a closer look," Travis observed, opening the stall door and gesturing for her to enter.

She preceded him and the vet into the stall, carrying on a low conversation with Solomy as she explored the swollen belly, probing with gentle, capable fingers. After a few moments she stopped and turned concerned eyes to Travis's laughing ones.

"The foal's turned wrong."

The blue eyes lost their laughter and studied her intently.

"Quite right, Miss Cunnane," Robert Loman agreed with a professional nod. "A quick diagnosis." Entering the stall, he too ran hands over the mare's belly. "We're hoping the foal will turn before she's full term."

"But you're not thinking it's likely; her time's almost here."

"No, we're not." He turned back to her, faintly surprised and greatly curious as to her knowledge. "We have to deal with the possibility of a breech. Have you had any training?"

"More doing than training." She shrugged, uncomfortable at having the attention focused on her. "I worked with a vet back in Ireland. I've done some birthings and some stitching and splinting."

She stepped out of the stall to stand beside Paddy, watching as the vet proceeded with his work. Paddy's arm slipped around her shoulders, and she rested her head against him.

"I hate to think what a hard time she'll be having. We had a mare that carried breech once, and I had to turn the babe." She sighed with the memory. "I can still see her poor, trusting eyes on me. How I hated to hurt her."

"You turned a foal by yourself?" Travis demanded, drawing her attention from the past. "That's a difficult enough job for a full-grown man, let alone a little thing like you."

She bristled, bringing herself up to the full of her meager height. "It may be that I'm small, Mr. Grant, but I'm strong enough to do what needs to be done." She glared up at him, her pride under attack, and stuck out her chin. "I'll tell you this: for all our difference in size, I can work the day through with you!"

Stifling a snort of laughter, Paddy focused on a spot on the ceiling as Travis regarded her indignation with cool, steady eyes. After a moment, she turned and began to walk toward the front of the building.

"Did you really see a horse being born, Dee?" The twins tagged after her full of excitement.

"Many a time, and cows and pigs and the like." She took a small hand in each of hers and continued over the concrete floor. "There was a time I birthed twin lambs, and that was the prettiest sight…"

Travis continued to stare after her as her voice trailed off in the distance.

The next few days passed easily for Adelia as she became accustomed to a new life and new surroundings. On the occasions she spoke to Travis, she continually struggled to hold back the tongue he seemed to have a habit of provoking. He stirred strange feelings in her, feelings she could neither comprehend nor prevent, and her defense against them took shape in a quick retort and flashing eyes. Though she gave herself nightly lectures on the evils of temper, when confronted with him during the daylight hours her vow of restraint slipped through her fingers.

She found herself watching him once as he strode toward the stables, his blue denim work shirt straining over broad shoulders as he moved over the grass. He seemed to eat up the ground with a careless vitality. There was a strange pull at her heart, and she sighed, then bit her lip in annoyance. It was only that he was such a fine, strongly built man, she told herself, lean and powerful. She dismounted from the Thoroughbred she had been exercising and rubbed his neck vigorously. She had always admired strength and power, the same way she admired this strong, well-proportioned animal. Everyone she had met held Travis Grant in great respect and admiration. When he gave an order, it was carried out without question. Only Paddy, it seemed, had the right to advise or question.

But she was Adelia Cunnane, she reminded herself, and no man would get the better of her. She would not play peasant to his squire and pull her forelock when he passed by. She did her job, and did it well. He would have no cause to complain in that field. But she would speak her piece if she'd a mind to, and the devil take him if he didn't like it!

Late each afternoon, Adelia visited Solomy. She was sure the mare would deliver any day, and, knowing the birth would be a difficult one, she spent her visits comforting the mare and gaining her confidence.

"Soon you'll be having a fine, strong son or daughter," Adelia told her as she closed the stall door after her visit. "I'd like to take you and the babe and bundle you off with me. What do you think himself would do about that?"

"He might be tempted to have you hanged for horse thieving."

She spun around, her eyes encountering Travis's powerful form resting idly against the next stall. "It's a bad habit you have of sneaking up and scaring a body to death," she snapped at him, assuming that the uneven beat of her heart was the result of surprise.

"I do happen to own this place, Adelia," he returned in low, calm tones that only increased her agitation.

"That's a fact I'm not likely to forget. There's no need to remind me." She tilted her chin in defiance of him and the continuing flutter of her stomach, knowing she should guard her words, and knowing the power to do so was beyond her. "I give you your day's work but maybe you think I'm forgetting my place. Should I be bobbing a curtsy, Mr. Grant?"

"You impudent little wench," Travis muttered, straightening from his relaxed position. "I'm getting a bit weary of being stabbed by that sharp tongue of yours."

"Well, it's sorry I am about that. The best advice I can give is that you not be conversing with me."

"That's the best idea you've had." He grabbed her around the waist, lifting her a foot off the ground as their eyes warred with each other. "I've been wanting to do this since the first time you slashed at me with your sharp Irish tongue."

He crushed her mouth with his, cutting off a heated retort. Too surprised by his action to resist immediately, Adelia began to experience unfamiliar and disturbing sensations, a heat and weakness that she might feel on a day spent working in the field. His hands were like steel around her small waist, holding her body suspended in the air while his lips assaulted hers, entering her mouth with his tongue in a kiss that was both devastating and totally foreign to any she had ever known.

Pressed hard against him, lips joined, she felt his warmth, his essence, seeping into her, demanding and receiving her merging. She could feel the authority in the arms that held her, taste the knowledge on the lips that claimed hers, and body and mind surrendered to both. Unable to combat the turbulence of the unexplored, she felt it whirl her like a cyclone, spinning her toward the sun until the heat threatened to become fire.

And as each of her senses were assaulted and conquered, he continued to explore her mouth, feasting on it as a man who knew a woman's flavor. He took, and she knew nothing of the richness of the banquet she gave him, warm and ripe and fresh.

After a lifetime, he released her, dropping her back to the ground as she stared at him mutely, eyes huge with confusion.

"Well, half-pint, this is the first time I've seen you at a loss for words." He mocked her openly, the lips that had just conquered hers lifted in a smug, satisfied smile.

His taunt broke the strange hold over her mind and tongue, and her eyes lit with molten green fire. "You son of the devil," she began in a rich explosion, and what followed was a raging stream of Irish curses and dire predictions delivered in so strong an accent that it was nearly impossible to comprehend the words.

When her imagination had at last run dry, and she could only stand staring at him breathlessly, he threw back his head and laughed until she thought he would burst.

"Oh, Dee, you're a fabulous sight when you're breathing fire!" He took no trouble to hide his amusement, an infuriating grin glued to his face. "The madder you get, the thicker the brogue. I'm going to have to provoke you more often."

"I'm giving you warning," she returned in an ominous voice, which only widened the grin. "If you ever molest me again, it's more than my tongue you'll be feeling."

Lifting her head, she strode out of the stables, clutching the last threads of her dignity around her.

She said nothing to Paddy about her scene with Travis, and instead banged around the kitchen as she prepared dinner, muttering incoherent sentences about great arrogant beasts and strong-arm bullies. Her fury with Travis was intermingled with fury with herself. The fact that his touch had brought both excitement and unexplained pleasure angered her further, and she berated herself for the uncontrollable attraction she felt for him.

Chapter Three

By the next day, Adelia's anger had faded. She was not given to prolonged periods of ill humor; rather, she exploded like a burst of flame, simmered, then slowly cooled down. There remained, however, a disturbing new awareness, an awareness both of herself and the unfamiliar longings of womanhood, and of the frustrating, attractive man who had released them.

She managed to avoid any face-to-face contact with Travis during the morning, going about her duties in the normal fashion while she kept a cautious eye alert for his approach. Duties complete, she strolled back for her daily visit with Solomy. Instead of leaning over the low barrier to greet her, as was Solomy's habit, Adelia found her lying on her side in the hay, breathing heavily.

"By all the saints and apostles!" Rushing inside, she knelt beside the raggedly breathing mare. "Your time's come, darlin'," she crooned, running her hands over the large mounded belly. "Just rest easy now. I'll be back." Springing up, she sped from the stables.

She spotted Tom in the far paddock and, cupping her hands, shouted. "Solomy's time's here. Get Travis—call the vet. Be quick!" Without waiting for an answer, she ran back inside to comfort the laboring horse.

She was murmuring and stroking the sweating hide when Travis and Paddy joined her. Soft words and gentle hands had calmed the mare, whose deep brown eyes were riveted on Adelia's dark green ones.

Travis knelt beside her, his hand joining hers on the gleaming skin, and though Adelia spoke to him, her eyes never left the mare's.

"The foal's still the wrong way; it must be turned, and quickly. Where's Dr. Loman?"

"He's had an emergency—can't be here for half an hour." His voice was clipped, his own attention on Solomy.

She turned her head and captured his gaze. "Mr. Grant, I'm telling you she doesn't have that long. The foal has to be turned now, or we'll lose them both. I can do it; I've done it before. It's God's truth, Mr. Grant, she hasn't much time."

They stared at each other for a long moment, Adelia's eyes wide and pleading, his narrowed and intense. Solomy let out an agonizing whinny as a new contraction began.

"There, my love." Adelia switched her attention back to the mare, murmuring words of comfort.

"All right," Travis agreed, a long breath escaping through his teeth. "But I'll turn it. Paddy, call in some of the men to hold her down."

"No!" Adelia's protest caused the mare to start, and she spoke quietly again, using hands and voice to soothe.

"You'll not bring a bunch of bruisers in here forcing her down and frightening her." Again she raised her eyes to Travis's and spoke with calm assurance. "She'll hold for me; I know how."

"Travis," Paddy intervened as he started to speak. "Dee knows what she's about." Nodding, Travis moved off to scrub his hands and arms.

"Have a care," she warned as he prepared to begin. "The babe's hooves will be sharp, and the womb can close on your hand quickly." Taking a deep breath, she lay her cheek against the mare's, hands circling the damp flesh in a steady rhythm as she began to croon in quiet Gaelic.

The mare shivered as Travis entered her, but remained still listening to Adelia's comforting voice.

The air seemed to grow closer, heavy with Solomy's breathing and the mystical beauty of the ancient tongue Adelia murmured. It brought a heavy warmth to the spring afternoon, isolating them from all but the struggle for life.

"I've got him," Travis announced, sweat running unheeded down his face. His breath came quickly, and he muttered a steady stream of soft curses, but Adelia heard nothing, giving herself over to the mare. "It's done." He rested back on his heels, turning his attention to the woman at his side. She gave no sign to him, only continued her slow, rhythmic crooning, hands gently caressing, face buried in the mare's neck.

"Here it comes," Paddy cried, and she turned her head to watch the miracle of birth. When the foal finally emerged into the world, both woman and horse sighed and shuddered.

"It's a fine, strong son you have, Solomy. Ah, sure, and there's no more beautiful sight in the world than an innocent new life!"

She turned her glowing face to Travis and gave him a

smile that rivaled the sun. Their eyes met, and the look deepened until it seemed to Adelia that time had stopped. She felt herself being drawn into fathoms of dark blue, unable to breathe or speak, as if some invisible shield had descended, insulating them from all but each other.

Can love come in an instant? her numbed brain demanded. Or has it been there forever? The answer was forestalled as Robert Loman arrived, shattering the magic that had held her suspended.

She stood up quickly as the vet began to question Travis on the colt's delivery. A wave of giddiness washed over her as she rose, and she sank her teeth into her lower lip to combat the weakness. Keeping the mare calm had been an enormous strain, almost as if she had experienced each pang of labor, and the unexpected rush of emotion when Travis had held her eyes had left her drained and dizzy.

"What is it, Dee?" Paddy's voice was full of concern as he took her arm.

"Nothing." She placed her palm to her spinning head. "Just a bit of a headache."

"Take her home," Travis commanded, regarding her closely. Her eyes were bright and enormous against her pallor, and she appeared suddenly small and helpless. Rising, he moved toward her, and she stepped back, terrified he would touch her.

"There's no need." She kept her voice calm and even. "I'll just go up and have a wash. I'm fine, Uncle Paddy." She smiled into his frowning face, avoiding Travis's at all costs. "Don't you worry." Stepping from the stall, she moved quickly from the building, filling her lungs with fresh, clean air.

That evening found Adelia quiet and pensive. She was unused to confusion and uncertainty, characteristically knowing what needed to be done and doing it. Her life had always been basic, the fundamental existence of meeting demands as they came. There had been no room for indecision or clouded reasoning in a world that was essentially black or white.

She lingered in the kitchen after dinner, reasoning with herself with firm common sense. The foaling had been difficult, the strain emptying her body of its strength, and the sight of the new colt had fogged her brain. These were the reasons she had reacted so strongly to Travis. She could hardly be in love with him; she barely knew him, and what she did know was not altogether to her taste. He was too big, too strong, too self-confident, and too arrogant. He reminded her of a feudal lord, and Adelia was too Irish to have any liking for landed gentry.

However, after her work was done and self-analysis complete, she remained oddly weary and disturbed. Sitting down on the floor at Paddy's feet, she laid her head in his lap with a deep sigh.

"Little Dee," he murmured, stroking the thick auburn curls. "You're working too hard."

"What nonsense," she disagreed, snuggling deeper into the still newness of comfort. "I haven't worked a full day since I arrived. The day would not nearly be over yet if I was back on the farm."

"Was it hard for you, lass?" he asked, thinking she might now be ready to talk of it.

Again Adelia sighed, moving her shoulders restlessly. "I wouldn't say hard, Uncle Paddy, but everything changed after Mother and Da died."

"Poor little Dee, such a wee thing to be losing so much."

"I thought my world had ended when they died," she whispered, hardly aware she was speaking aloud. "I'm thinking I died myself for a time, so angry and frightened I was, then numb, feeling nothing. But I began remembering how they were together. No two people could have loved each other more. Such a fine, full loving they had, even a child could see it."

So engrossed were the man and woman in the words being spoken that neither heard the sound of feet climbing the stairs. Travis halted in his action of knocking, dropping his hand as he watched the poignant picture, and Adelia's words drifted through the screen.

"The only thing I could give them was the farm, and it was all I had left of them. Poor Aunt Lettie, she worked so hard, and I was a constant cross for her to bear." She laughed as memory flickered through her mind. "She never could understand why I had to ride so fast. 'Sure and it's your neck you'll be breaking,' she used to call after me, shaking her fist. 'Who'll be helping with the plowing if you bash in your head on the road?' Then when I'd have one of my rages and go off shouting and cursing—and it's often, I'm afraid I did just that—she'd cross herself and start praying for my doomed soul.

"Jakers, but we worked." With a long breath she shut her eyes. "But it was too much for one woman and a half-grown girl, and not enough money to hire help, and none to be made without it. Do you know how it is, Uncle Paddy, when you see the thing you need, but the closer you get the further away it is? Always moving away from you, always just out of your reach. Sometimes, when I look back, I can't tell one day from the rest. Then Aunt Lettie had that stroke, and how she hated to be lying there helpless day after day."

"Why did you never let me know how things were?" Paddy questioned, looking down at her dark head. "I could have helped you—sent you money, or come back myself."

She raised her head and smiled at him. "Aye, that's just what you would have done, and to what good? Throwing your money away, taking yourself from the life you'd chosen...I'd not have had that for a minute, and neither would Aunt Lettie, or Mother and Da. The farm's gone, just as they are, and so is Ireland. Now I have you, I'm not needing another thing."

Looking into his eyes, seeing the concern and regret written there, she wished suddenly she had kept her own counsel. "How is it, Padrick Cunnane, that a fine, handsome man like yourself never took a wife?" Her grin turned impish, and devils danced in her eyes. "There must have been dozens of ladies willing. Have you never found a woman to love?"

He touched her cheek, giving her a wistful smile. "Aye, lass, that I did, but she chose your father."

Deep green eyes filled with surprise that melted into sympathy. "Oh, Uncle Paddy!" She flung her arms around him, and Travis turned from the door and walked silently down the stairs.

The next morning the air seemed to sigh with spring, whispering promises of flowers and cool, leafy trees. To Adelia it brought memories of other springs. Spring was the time the earth asked to be replenished and grew pregnant with new life. Her world had always revolved around the earth, its gifts and hardships, its demands and promises.

From the balcony of Paddy's house she surveyed the land that was Travis's. It seemed to stretch on and on with the easy, gentle roll of a calm sea. Green and brown waves were dotted, not with boats, but with finely sculptured Thoroughbreds. It ran through her mind that she had no conception of what lay over the last hill. This land was still a stranger. From the moment of her arrival in America she had seen little else but what belonged to Travis Grant.

Over the pure, sweet air floated an occasional whinny or the quick call of a bird. But for this, there was silence. There was no strident call of rooster announcing the new day, no fields turned up waiting to receive seed, no weeds demanding uprooting. All at once homesickness washed over her so intensely that she could only shut her eyes and weather the storm.

So much is gone, she thought, and her hands hugged her elbows as if in comfort. I'll never be able to go back, never see the farm again. Sighing, she opened her eyes and tried to shake off the melancholy. There's nothing to be done about it; the bridges are burned. This is home now, and if it's not really mine, it's the closest I'll come.

"Where are you, lass?"

Adelia started slightly as Paddy's arm slipped around her; then she sighed again and rested against his shoulder. "Back on the farm, I suppose. Thinking about spring planting."

"It's a day for it, isn't it? That air's cool, and the sun's warm." He gave her shoulder a small squeeze, then clucked his tongue as if in regret. "I've got to go into town today. It's a pity."

"A pity?"

"I was hoping to get some seeds in around the walkway. Thought I might make a flower bed in front of the house too." He shook his head and sighed. "Just don't know when I'll find the time."

"Oh, I'll do it, Uncle Paddy. I've plenty of time." Drawing away, she looked at him with such innocent acceptance of his trumped-up excuse that he nearly broke into a grin.

"Little Dee, I couldn't ask you to do all that on your day off." He creased his face into doubtful lines and patted her cheek. "No, it's too much. I'll get to it as soon as I find a bit of time."

"Uncle Paddy, don't be silly. I'd love to do it." Her smile was blooming again, chasing the clouds from her eyes. "Just show me what you want done."

"Well…" He permitted her to argue a few more minutes before allowing himself to be persuaded.

Armed with a myriad of seed packs and a small spade, Adelia stood on the patch of lawn surrounding Paddy's house and mentally mapped out her landscaping. Petunias along the walk, asters and marigolds against the house, impatiens for the border. And sweet peas, she thought with a smile, for the trellis she had asked Paddy to buy. In the fall, she decided, I'll plant bulbs, as many as the ground will hold. Daffodils and tulips. Satisfied with her planning, she began to turn the earth.

The sun grew warmer, and her sleeves were soon pushed past her elbows. In the distance she could hear the sounds of men and horses going through their daily routine: a shout, laughter, the thud of hooves on dirt. But soon, lost in her planting, she drifted apart. Softly, she began to sing a song remembered from childhood, the words soothing and familiar. The scent of fresh earth eased the ache with which she had awakened.

A shadow fell across her. Twisting her head, she dropped the spade nervously as Travis looked down at her.

"I've made you stop. I'm sorry."

He seemed impossibly tall as he stood over her. She

craned her neck and squinted against the sun. It glowed in an aura around his head, and for one fanciful moment she thought he looked like a knight on his way to vanquish dragons.

"No, you just startled me." Picking up the spade, Adelia told herself she was a fool and began to work again.

"I didn't mean the planting." He crouched down beside her, his shoulder brushing hers. "I mean the song. It sounded very old and very sad."

"Aye, it's both." She inched away, carefully patting soil over seeds. "A lot of Gaelic songs are old and sad."

Folding his legs under him, he sat easily on the grass and watched her. "What's it about?"

"Oh, love, of course. The saddest songs are always about love." She lifted her head to smile at him. His face was close, his mouth a breath away. The spade hung suspended in her hand as she only stared, wondering what she would do if the whisper of space was gone and his mouth found hers.

"Is love always sad, Adelia?" His voice was as soft as the breeze that danced around them.

"I don't know. I..." She felt the weakness growing stronger and tore her eyes from his. "We were talking about songs."

"So we were," Travis murmured, then brushed back the hair that curtained her face. She swallowed and began digging with renewed interest. "I never thanked you properly for your help yesterday with Solomy."

"Oh, well..." Moving her shoulders, she kept her eyes on the ground. "I didn't do that much. I'm just glad Solomy and the foal are well. Do you like flowers, Mr. Grant?" she asked, needing to change the subject.

"Yes, I like flowers. What are you planting?" His voice was casual as he lifted a package of seeds.

"All different kinds," she told him, this time able to raise her head and smile. "They'll be a lovely sight by summer. Your soil's rich, Mr. Grant; it wants to give." She squeezed a handful of earth, then held it out in her palm.

"You'd know more about that than I." Taking her fingertips, he studied the soil in her hand. "You're the farmer."

"I was," she amended and tried to free her hand.

"I'm afraid I don't know much about planting—vegetables or flowers." He ignored her attempts to pull her fingers away and brought his eyes to hers. "I suppose it's a gift."

"It just takes time and effort, like anything else. Here." Concluding that if she gave him something to do, her hand would be released, she held out some seeds. "Just drop a few in and cover them up. Don't crowd them," she instructed as he obeyed. "They want room to spread. Now you cover them up and let nature take over." Smiling, she absently brushed a hand across her cheek. "No matter what you do, nature has the last word in any case. A farmer knows that here the same way a farmer knows that in Ireland."

"So, now that I've put them in," he concluded with a grin, "I just sit back and watch them grow."

"Well," she said, tilting her head and giving him a sober stare, "there might be a thing or two more, like watering or weeding. These seeds will take quick, and the flowers will pop up before you know it. I'm putting in sweet peas there." She pointed across the lawn, forgetting that she still held the soil in her other hand. "When the breeze comes up at night, the scent will drift through the windows. There's something special about sweet peas. They start off so small, but they'll just keep climbing as long as there's something to hold on to. There should be a rosebush," she murmured almost to herself. "When the scents mingle together, it's like nothing else on earth. Red roses, just starting to open up."

"Are you homesick, Dee?" The question was low and gentle, but her head whipped back around in surprise.

"I…" Shrugging, she bent her face to her work again, uncomfortable that he had read her emotions so clearly.

"It's quite natural." He lifted her chin with his hand until their eyes met again. "It's not easy to leave behind everything you've ever known."

"No." Moving her shoulders again, she turned away and began to spread marigold seeds. "But I made the choice, and it truly was what I wanted. It's what I want," she amended with more firmness. "I can't say I've been unhappy a moment since I got off the plane. I can't go back, and I don't really know if I'd want to if I could. I've a new life now." Tossing back her hair, she smiled at him. "I like it here. The people, the work, the horses, the land." Her hand made a wide, encompassing gesture. "You've a beautiful home, Mr. Grant; anyone could be happy here."

He brushed a trace of dirt from her cheek and returned her smile. "I'm glad you think so, but it's your home too."

"You're a generous man, Mr. Grant." She kept her gaze level with his, but her smile was suddenly sad and sweet. "There's not many who'd say that and mean it, and I'm grateful to you. But for better or worse, the farm was mine." Sighing, she traced a finger through the soil. "It was mine…."

Late the next morning when Adelia turned one of the Thoroughbreds she had been exercising over to a groom,

Trish Collins approached her with a friendly smile. "Hello, Adelia. How are you settling in?"

"Fine, missus, and good morning to you." She regarded Trish's dark beauty with fresh admiration. "And where are the lads this morning?"

"In school, but they'll be here tomorrow. They're half crazy to get a look at the new foal."

"A beautiful sight he is."

"Yes, I've just had a peek at him. Travis told me how marvelous you were with the mare."

Her mouth dropped open a moment, surprised and inordinately pleased that Travis should have praised her. "I was glad to help, missus. Solomy did all the work."

"Call me Trish," she requested with a shake of her head. "Missus makes me feel old and crotchety."

"Oh, no, missus, you're not old at all," she blurted out, horrified.

"I wouldn't like to think so. Travis and I won't be thirty-one until October." Trish laughed at the stricken face.

"So you're twins as well," Adelia concluded, feeling more at ease. "I suppose that's why I saw your brother's eyes the first time I met you."

"Yes, we do bear a strong resemblance to each other, which is why I constantly tell him how handsome he is." She smiled at Adelia's light, musical laugh. "Am I holding you up? Are you busy?"

"No, missus." At the raised brow, she amended, "No, Trish. I was about to take my break and fix a cup of tea. Would you like one?"

"Yes, thank you, I would."

They paused at the top of the stairs to the garage house as Adelia bent to pick up a long, narrow white box. "Now what might this be?"

"Flowers would be my guess," Trish concluded, indicating the printed name of a local florist.

"What would they be doing here?" She frowned down at the box as they stepped inside. "Someone must have left them at the wrong house."

"You might open them and find out," Trish suggested, amused by the frown of concentration. "As your name's on the box, they just might be for you."

Auburn curls danced as she shook her head and chuckled. "Now who'd be sending me flowers?" Setting the box on a table, she opened the lid and gave a small cry of pleasure. "Oh, just look! Have you ever seen such a sight?" The box was filled with long-stemmed roses, deep blood red, their half-closed petals soft as velvet to her hesitant fingers. Lifting one out, she held it under her nose. "Ah," she breathed and passed the bloom to Trish. "Straight from heaven." Then, shrugging, she returned to practical matters. "Who could they be for?"

"There should be a card."

Locating the small white note, Adelia read it silently, and her green eyes widened as she read the words a second time. She brought her gaze from the slip of paper to meet an openly curious regard. "They're for me." Her voice mirrored disbelief as she handed Trish the card. "Your brother sent them to thank me for helping with Solomy."

"'Dee, to thank you for your help with the new foal. Travis,'" Trish read aloud, and added under her breath, "You certainly wax poetic on occasion, brother."

"In my whole life," Adelia murmured, touching a silky petal, "no one has ever given me flowers."

Trish looked over quickly, observing the shimmering eyes and the stunned pleasure passing over Adelia's features. Pushing tears back, Adelia spoke on a sigh. "This was a lovely thing for your brother to do. I had a rosebush at home—red roses they were too. My mother planted it." She smiled, feeling incredibly happy. "It makes them that much more special."

Later, they walked back to the stables. As they drew near, Travis and Paddy emerged from the building, and the Irishman greeted them both with a beaming smile.

"Travis, we've died and gone to heaven. Sure and it's two angels coming to greet us."

"Uncle Paddy." Adelia tweaked his cheek. "Living in America hasn't lessened your gift for blarney." Looking up at the man who towered above the rest of them, she treated him to the pure, honest smile of a child. "I want to thank you for the flowers, Mr. Grant. They're lovely."

"I'm glad you liked them," he answered, enjoying the smile. "It was little enough after what you did."

"Here's something more for you, Dee." Paddy reached into his pocket and withdrew a piece of paper. "Your first week's wages."

"Oh," Adelia said with a grin. "It's the first time I've been paid in money for doing anything." She frowned at the check, confused, and Travis's brows rose in amusement at her expression.

"Is something wrong with it, Adelia?"

"Yes…no…I…" she stumbled and brought her eyes to Paddy.

"You're wondering what it is in pounds," he concluded, grinning merrily.

"I don't think I figured it right," she answered, embarrassed under Travis's gaze.

Chuckling, he did some mental arithmetic and told her. Confusion changed to astonishment and something close to terror.

"What would I be doing with that kind of money?"

"First time anyone around here complained about being overpaid," Travis commented and received a baleful glance.

"Here." Adelia turned her attention back to her uncle and held the check out to him. "You take it."

"Now, why would I be doing that, Dee? It's your money; you earned it."

"But I've never had so much money at one time in my whole life." She sent him a pleading look. "What will I do with it?"

"Go out and buy some of those female trappings and folderol," he suggested vaguely, waving his hand, then pushing the check back at her. "Treat yourself to something. The good Lord knows it's about time."

"But, Uncle Paddy—"

"Why don't you buy yourself a dress, Dee?" Travis inserted with a grin. "I'm curious to see if you've got legs under those jeans."

Adelia's head snapped up, and she eyed Travis with a dangerous gleam. "Aye, I've legs, Mr. Grant, and I've been told a time or two it's not a trial to look at them. But you'll not have to be worrying yourself; it's not dresses I need to tend your horses."

His grin only widened as he gave a negligent shrug. "It doesn't matter to me if you want to be taken for a boy."

Her wrath increased as he had meant it to, and her eyes fired sharp green daggers. "There's only one who ever made that mistake, he being an ill-mannered, bad-tempered brute of a man without a brain working in his empty head."

"Shopping's a marvelous idea," Trish broke in, deciding it was time to play peacemaker. "As a matter of fact, Travis—" she smiled and fluttered her lashes "—Dee's taking the rest of the day off so we can do just that."

"Oh, really?" he returned dryly, folding his arms across his chest.

"Yes, *really*. Come on, Dee."

"But I haven't finished...."

Trish linked her arm through the still protesting Adelia's and propelled her to a late-model compact. Before she had time to think things through, Adelia had an account at a local bank, a checkbook, and more cash than her apprehensive brain could comprehend.

"Now—" Trish backed the compact from its parking space "—we're going shopping."

"But what will I buy?" She stared at Trish's clear profile in complete consternation.

Stopping at a red light, Trish turned to her anxious face. "When's the last time you bought something for yourself for the fun of it? Have you ever bought something because you wanted it instead of just needing it?" The light changed, and as she joined the flow of traffic she sighed at Adelia's blank expression. "Don't misunderstand. I'm not saying people should just throw their money away, but it's high time you did something for yourself." Glancing at Adelia's furrowed brow, she smiled and shook her head. "You can afford to slow down, Dee, take a day off, buy something foolish, stretch your wings, take a breath." She grinned as Adelia merely stared at her. "The sky will not fall if Adelia Cunnane takes time off to have some fun."

No one was more surprised than Adelia when, in fact, she did have fun. The large mall fascinated her with its various small specialty shops and large department stores. There were more clothes than she had ever seen, in colors and soft materials that had her staring and touching in frank admiration.

While Adelia gazed around her, Trish examined

garments critically, going from rack to rack, dismissing dozens of dresses, skirts and blouses, occasionally removing an item and hanging it over her arm. Finding herself in a changing room, Adelia could only stare at the garments Trish had placed on a hook. Then, taking a deep breath, she stripped off her shirt and jeans and slipped on a soft jersey dress in muted shades of green.

The silky material felt strange and wonderful to her skin, clinging to gentle curves and falling gracefully below her knees. She gaped at the stranger in the mirror, her hand seeking the cross at her throat to assure herself that she was still the same person.

"Dee," Trish called from outside the curtain, "have you got one on yet?"

"Aye," she answered slowly, and Trish pulled the curtain aside, smiling in triumph at the reflection in the full-length mirror.

"I knew that dress was you the minute I saw it."

"It doesn't feel like me," Adelia mumbled, then turned to face Trish directly. "It's beautiful, but what would I do with so grand a dress? I exercise horses. I work in a stable—"

"Dee," Trish interrupted firmly. "Whatever your occupation, you're still a human being; you're still a woman, an exceptionally beautiful woman." Adelia's eyes widened, and her mouth opened to protest, but before the words could be uttered Trish took her by the shoulders and turned her to face her reflection. "Look at yourself, really look," she ordered in no-nonsense terms, then shifted to gentler tones. "There'll be times when you'll want only to be a woman; this dress is for those times. Now," she said with practical authority as she released her, "try something else on."

For the rest of the afternoon Adelia allowed Trish to

take command. For the first time in more than a decade, she permitted someone else to make all the decisions, and somehow she found she was having fun. They halted in front of a cosmetics counter, and Trish began spraying scents until Adelia grumbled in protest.

"This." Trish selected one of the bottles she had sampled. "Light and delicate, with just a touch of spirit." Paying for the cologne, she handed the package to Adelia. "A present."

"Oh, but I can't!"

"Yes, you can. Friends get pleasure from giving presents. Now, that marvelous skin of yours doesn't need any help, but I think we'll accent your eyes—and some lipstick, nothing too dramatic." She stopped and laughed. "I'm bullying you, aren't I?"

"Aye," Adelia agreed, feeling caught up in a genial whirlwind and finding she liked it.

"Well, you needed it," Trish said firmly. "Is there anything else you want?"

She hesitated, then blurted out quickly. "Something for my hands. Your brother said I've hands like a ditchdigger's."

"That man!" she exclaimed in disgust. "He's the epitome of tact and diplomacy."

"Trish, hello!"

Adelia turned to see a flash of amazing silver-blond hair before Trish was enveloped in an exuberant embrace. Adelia's first startled impression was of lavish curls and musky scent.

"I'm so glad to see you, darling." A high, bubbly voice drifted with the scent. "It's been weeks."

"Hello, Laura." With an affectionate smile, Trish disentangled herself. "It's good to see you too. Laura Bowers—Adelia Cunnane."

"How do you do, Mistress Bowers." The greeting was returned with a flash of beautiful white teeth before Laura's attention returned to Trish.

"Darling, how is that fabulous brother of yours?"

"Fabulous," Trish returned, giving Adelia a quick grin of mischief.

"Don't tell me he's not pining after Margot?" Laura sighed and gave a flutter of extensive lashes. "I was so hoping to offer him my comfort. Not even a tear or two to be dried?"

"He seems to be bearing up under the strain," Trish returned. Hearing the unexpected sarcasm, Adelia glanced at her in surprise.

"Oh, well, if he doesn't need comfort," Laura continued, obviously not affected by Trish's tone, "he's still at loose ends, so to speak. If dear Margot overplayed her hand by whisking off to Europe, I for one am not above volunteering to fill the gap. Heard from her lately?"

"Not a peep."

"Well, then, I'll take it that no news is good news." She gave Trish a wink and tossed her brilliant curls. "Such a gorgeous man. Do you know Travis, Adelaide?"

"Adelia," Trish corrected before Adelia could do so herself. "Yes, Dee knows Travis very well."

"Charming man," Laura bubbled. "Now that Margot's out of the picture, at least temporarily, I'll just have to give him a ring. Do tell him I'll call, won't you?" With another flurry of curls, she pecked both of Trish's cheeks. "I hate to, darling, but I simply must run. Don't forget to give Travis my very best. So nice to have met you, Amanda."

Adelia opened her mouth, then closed it again as Laura scurried off in a wave of musk.

"Sorry, Amanda." Trish grinned and patted Adelia's

cheek. "Laura's really very sweet and basically kind, but she's a bit short of brains."

"She has such beautiful hair." Tearing her gaze from Laura's retreating coiffure, Adelia turned back to Trish. "I've never seen hair that color before. She must be very proud of it."

Trish laughed until she was forced to wipe away tears as Adelia looked on in puzzlement. "Oh, Dee, I adore you! Come on, we'll get that hand cream; then I'll buy you a cup of tea."

Waiting patiently while her mentor weighed the pros and cons of various lotions, Adelia reflected on Laura Bowers's conversation. *Margot,* she repeated, nibbling absently on her bottom lip. Who is this Margot, and what is she to Travis? For a moment she struggled with the urge to ask Trish outright, then, remembering her manner, she kept silent. *Perhaps he's in love with her.* This thought brought such a sharp, unexpected pain that she nearly gasped aloud. *But he's not,* a part of her insisted. If Travis Grant were ever to love a woman, he would never let her go. He would go to the ends of the earth to bring her back. Unless, of course, *he had been rejected.* His pride would never allow him to pursue a woman who had refused him. But who would ever refuse such a man? *It's not my concern,* she told herself fiercely, forcing herself to concentrate on Trish's detailed description of various hand lotions.

At last Trish was satisfied. Adelia was suitably outfitted and had all the cosmetics that Trish thought were necessary. Laden with parcels, the two women headed back to the car. For once, Adelia was reduced to silence. She sat bolt upright on the front seat as Trish drove swiftly over the winding country roads. She was even too excited to enjoy the rolling hills and the horses grazing in the meadows, now softly outlined by the sinking afternoon sun.

Paddy was there to open the door when Adelia burst in with her new treasures.

"Little Dee, you're looking as happy as the first time you rode Majesty round the track," he said, observing her flushed, happy face.

"This was nearly as exciting, Uncle Paddy." She laughed and stepped through the doorway. "Never have I seen so many clothes, so many people. Do you know, I think everyone in America is in a constant hurry, driving, rushing through the stores—nothing ever seems to move slowly. This place Trish took me was amazing—all these shops in one big building, and it had fountains, right inside." She sighed, then shrugged and grinned. "I know I should be ashamed for squandering money the way I did, but I'm not. I had a fine time."

"It was due time, lass, due time." He kissed her cheek as they entered the living room.

"Well, Paddy, she's lost her innocence." Travis rose from an armchair and grinned down at Adelia and her packages. "Trish corrupted her. I knew I shouldn't have let that sister of mine get hold of her."

"Your sister is a wonderful lady, Mr. Grant." Adelia tossed back her head to meet his eyes, chestnut curls falling back from her face. "She has a sweet and generous soul, and a good deal more in the way of manners than some I could name."

His brow lifted, and he glanced over her head to look at Paddy as the older man struggled not to grin. "It appears Trish has a champion, and one I don't think I care to challenge." He shifted his gaze back to Adelia's irate face. "At least," he added with a slow, enigmatic smile, "not today...."

Chapter Four

Saturday dawned sunny and unseasonably warm. The trees were now in full leaf, and the air carried the sweet scent of flowers as spring approached midterm. Adelia sang happily as she groomed Fortune, a sturdy three-year-old colt who listened with approval to her high, lilting voice as she brushed him.

"Dee! Dee!" She whirled around to see Mark and Mike scurrying into the stables. "Mom said we could come down and see you, and the new foal too."

"Good day to you, gentlemen; it's pleased I am to have you visiting me."

"Will you show us the foal?" Mike demanded, and she smiled at his enthusiasm.

"That I will, Master Michael, as soon as I've finished with my friend here. Now." She set down the brush and reached a hand into her back pocket. "Where is it that I put that hoof pick?" Her pockets were empty, and she searched the ground, frowning. "It's the little people at work again."

"We didn't take it," Mark objected.

"People are always blaming kids for everything," Mike complained righteously.

"Oh, but it's not children I'm speaking of," Adelia corrected. "It's leprechauns."

"Leprechauns?" the twins chorused. "What's a leprechaun?"

"Could it be you're telling me you've never heard of leprechauns?" She asked in amazement. The boys shook their identical heads, and she folded her arms across her chest. "Well, your education's sadly lacking, lads. It's a sorry thing to remain ignorant of the little people."

"Tell us, Dee," they demanded, pulling at her hands in excitement.

"That I will." She hauled herself up to sit on a bench as the two boys squatted on the floor at her feet. "Now, the leprechaun is a strange fellow, his father being an evil spirit and his mother a fairy fallen from grace. By nature he's a mischief-maker. He only grows to be about three feet high, no matter how old he happens to be. Some say he likes to be riding on sheep or goats, so a man knows, if his stock is tired and weary of a morning, that the little people have been up to their tricks and using them for some errand where they didn't want to travel on foot. They can be lazy when they've a mind to.

"They love to be making mischief about the house as well. Why, a leprechaun'll make a pot boil over on the stove, or keep it from boiling at all, as his whim suits him. Or he'll steal the bacon or toss the furniture about for the sheer love of the confusion. Other times he'll drink his fill of the milk or poteen and fill up the bottle with water.

"Now," she continued, her eyes bright with excitement

as the two boys clung to her words, "to catch a leprechaun would bring certain fortune to the one who had the wit to hold him. The only time you can catch him is when he's sitting down, and he never sits unless his brogues want mending. He's forever running about so that he wears them out, and when he feels his feet on the ground, he sits behind a hedge or in the tall grass of a meadow and takes them off to mend them. Then—" she lowered her voice to a dramatic whisper, and the two heads inched forward "—you creep up, quiet as a cat, and grab him tight in your arms." She flung her arms around an imaginary leprechaun and shouted, "'Give me your gold,' you say. 'I've got no gold,' says he."

Releasing her invisible captive, she gave the boys a roguish smile. "Now, there's gold by the ton, and that's the truth of it, and he can tell you where it's to be found, but he won't till you make him. Now, some try choking him or threatening him, but, whatever you do, you mustn't for a moment take your eyes from him. If you do that, he's gone in a flash, and you'll not be seeing him again. The scheming devil has a pocketful of tricks for getting away, and he can charm the birds from the trees if he's a mind to. But if you hold your ground and keep your eye on him, his gold is yours, and your fortune's made."

"Did you ever see a leprechaun, Dee?" Mark asked, bouncing with excitement.

"By the saints, I thought I did, a time or two." She nodded sagely. "But I never got close enough before they had vanished, quick as you please. So—" she jumped from the bench and tousled two dark heads "—unless I'm finding me one who's traveled to America, I'll have to be working for my living." She picked up a hoof pick from the bench. "And that's what I'm doing now, or I'll be fired for laziness and be begging for pennies."

"We wouldn't let it come to that, would we, boys?"

Adelia spun around, her color rising as she met Travis's mocking smile. The thumping in her heart she attributed to surprise, and she was forced to swallow nervously before speaking.

"It's a habit you're making of creeping up on a body and frightening the wits from them, Mr. Grant."

"Maybe I mistook you for a leprechaun, Dee." His grin was annoying, but she refused to be baited and bent to lift Fortune's hoof.

He led the twins down to visit the new foal, and she set down the horse's leg and watched his broad back retreat down the passage.

Why did he always send her into a flutter? She wondered. Why did her pulses begin to race at a speed that rivaled Majesty's whenever she looked up and met those surprisingly blue eyes? She leaned her cheek against Fortune's sturdy neck and sighed. She'd lost, she conceded. She'd lost the battle, and though she fought against it, she was in love with Travis Grant. It was impossible, she admitted. Nothing could ever develop between the owner of Royal Meadows and an insignificant stablehand.

"Besides," she whispered to the understanding colt, "he's an arrogant brute of a man, and I don't believe I like him one little bit." Hearing the boys approach, she bent quickly and lifted another hoof for cleaning.

"Run along outside, boys. I want a word with Dee." At Travis's command, the twins scrambled past, chattering and exclaiming over the foal. She set down the horse's leg and straightened to face him, the color fading from her cheeks.

Blast my cursed tongue, she thought in desperate condemnation. Aunt Lettie told me a thousand times where my temper would take me.

"I—have I done something wrong, Mr. Grant?" She stammered slightly and bit her lip in frustration.

"No, Dee," he answered, slowly searching her troubled face. "Did you think I was going to fire you?" His voice was oddly gentle, and she felt a tremor at the unfamiliar tone.

"You did say I could have a fortnight, and I've a few days left before—"

"There's no need for a trial," he interrupted. "I've already decided to keep you on."

"Oh, thank you, Mr. Grant," she began, overcome with relief. "I'm grateful to you."

"Your way with horses is quite phenomenal, a strange sort of empathy." He stroked Fortune's flank, then fixed his eyes on her again. "It would be impossible to complain about your work, except that there's too much of it. I don't want to hear about you cleaning tack at ten o'clock at night anymore."

"Oh, well…" Turning back to the bench, Adelia gave intense concentration to placing the hoof pick in its proper spot. "I just—"

"Don't argue, and don't do it again," he commanded, and she felt his hands descend to her shoulders. "You know, you seem to split your time between working and arguing. We'll have to see if we can find another outlet for all that energy."

"I don't argue, exactly. Well, perhaps sometimes." She shrugged and wished she had the courage to turn and face him. The decision was taken out of her hands as she found herself being turned, then lifted until she once again sat on the bench.

"Perhaps sometimes," Travis agreed, and she found it disconcerting that his smile was so close, his hands still circling her waist.

"Mr. Grant," she began, then swallowed as he reached up to pluck her cap from her hair, freeing the rich cloud of auburn. "Mr. Grant, I've work to do."

"Mmm." His comment was absent as he became involved with the winding of curls around his fingers. "I've always had a fondness for chestnuts." Grinning, he gave her hair a firm tug until her face lifted to his. "A very particular fondness."

"Would you like to check my teeth?" Seeking a defence against a swift wave of longing, Adelia stiffened and sent him what she hoped was a lethal glare. His burst of unrestrained laughter caused the glare to light with green fire, and she struggled to slide from the bench.

"Oh, no." He held her still with minimum effort. "You should realize by now that I find it impossible to restrain myself when you start spitting fire."

He took her mouth quickly, one hand still tangled in her hair, the other slipping under her shirt to claim the smooth skin of her back. She found her second trip through the storm no less devastating than the first, and while her will melted under its force, her senses sharpened. The scent of leather, horses and masculinity rose and surrounded her, a strange, intoxicating scent she knew she would always associate with him. She could feel his strength as he plunged her deeper into the kiss, demanding every drop of sweetness from her mouth. Hard and seeking, his lips parted hers, his tongue teasing hers into mobility until she was pliant and yielding against him.

For the first time she felt the pain and demand of womanhood, the slow ache growing in the center of her being and spreading to encompass her entirely, until there was nothing but the need and the man who could assuage it. She heard a soft moan as her lips were freed, not aware it was her own weak protest at liberation, and her lids opened slowly to reveal eyes dark and slumberous with desire.

"I find," Travis commented in a low, lazy voice, "that is a more productive use of time than arguing."

Adelia watched his eyes drop to the lips still warm from his and felt his hand tighten on her hair. It relaxed slowly, and a smile moved across his face as his eyes rose to hers. "It also appears to be the only way to shut you up for any amount of time."

He dropped her cap back on her head, then traced her cheek with his finger. "I find Irish tempers have definite advantages."

He strode away, and Adelia contemplated his long, graceful stride in confusion, reaching up one hand to press the cheek his finger had touched.

Pushing away a puzzle she could not solve, she spent the rest of the day in a state of euphoria. She was staying. She had found her place on the mammoth horse farm, and an uncle who wanted as well as needed her, and a job that was a dream realized. And at least, she thought happily, she would be close to Travis, seeing him almost daily, feeding her need on the sight of his tall, powerful form, on a few snatched words of conversation. That was enough for the present, and the future was something to be faced when it arrived....

Long after her uncle had retired, Adelia remained wide awake. She had tried to relax with a book, but her spirits were too high for sitting idly, and she closed it and slipped outside.

She decided to walk to the stables, promising herself she would not touch one bridle but merely look in on the horses. The night remained warm; the sky blanketed with stars, so clear and vivid that she reached up, imagining she could pluck one from the soft, black curtain. At peace with the world, she meandered toward the large white building.

Entering, she switched on a low light to dispel the unrelieved darkness. She had gone no more than twenty feet when a soft moaning sound caught her attention, and she whirled in the direction of an empty stall. A man lay in a crumpled heap, and she caught her breath in alarm.

"Merciful heavens!" She hurried in and bent over him. "What's happened? Oh!" she uttered in disgust and stood, hands on hips. "You are drunk, George Johnson, and a pitiful sight indeed. You smell like a poteen factory. What do you mean drinking yourself into such a state and lying about in the stables?"

"So, it's pretty little Dee," George mumbled thickly, hauling himself into a half-sitting position. "Did you come for a visit? Come to share my bottle?"

Adelia had found herself avoiding the groom. She had often found his eyes on her, and his leering smile had caused her to recoil instinctively. Now, however, she was angry and disgusted, and she took no pains to hide it.

"No, I'll not be sharing a bottle with the likes of you—I've no patience for drunken sods. Haul yourself up and be on your way. You've no business in here with your mind fuddled with whiskey."

"Giving orders now, little Dee?" He struggled to his feet and faced her. "Too good to drink with me?" He raked her from head to foot with bleary eyes, pausing on the swell of her breast and moistening his lips. "Maybe you don't want to drink when there's more interesting things to do." He grabbed her shoulders and closed his mouth over hers, the strong smell of whiskey assaulting her senses as she pushed against him.

"You filthy pig of a man!" she spat, infuriated that he

had touched her. "You great, sniveling, drunken buzzard, don't you ever put your hands on me again. You guzzling serpent, I'll kick you into next week if you touch me again." She ranted at him until he grabbed her with such force that her breath caught in her throat.

"I'll do more than touch you." His hand clamped over her mouth, and he pushed her down roughly in the straw-filled stall. She fought in wild fury, kicking and scratching as his hands began to bruise her body, choking back the sickness that rose as his lips violated hers. Her blouse ripped away from the shoulder, the sound exploding in her ear. Anger gave way to terror, and she struggled more violently. Her nails dug into his arms, tearing his skin, and as he cursed with pain and raised his head, her scream pierced the still night.

A hand slapped hard across her cheek, numbing her face as he closed his palm over her mouth again. She continued to thrash out as his free hand captured her breast and moved over her with cruel purpose. Her strength was ebbing, and she realized she was helpless against the violation that was to come. He was tugging at her jeans, his drunkenness causing his fingers to fumble at the snap. The hand over her mouth was depriving her of air, and a foggy dimness floated in front of her eyes.

Please, somebody, help me, she prayed desperately as nausea swamped her. Suddenly, she was released from his crushing weight. She heard a muffled curse and the soft thud of flesh on flesh. Crawling to the stall's opening, she breathed deep to force back the queasiness. *Travis,* she thought dizzily, as she made out his powerful figure in the dimly lit stable.

He was beating the smaller man with a ruthless determination, knocking him to the floor with crushing blows, only to drag him up again by the shirtfront and send him sprawling once more. George offered no resistance; indeed he could not, she realized as her mind cleared, he was already unconscious. Still, Travis's fist pounded, pulling the man up on his watery legs again and again. He's killing him, she thought suddenly, and sprang to her feet, running toward them.

"No, Travis, you're killing him!" She grabbed the hard, muscular arm. "For the love of God, Travis—you're killing him!"

He jerked back, and for a moment she feared he would brush her off like a fly and finish the man who now lay in a motionless heap on the stable floor. As he turned to face her, Adelia stepped away, frightened by his expression of rage. His face seemed to be carved from granite, his eyes steely blue and penetrating as he stared at her. She trembled at the strong, harsh mask and offered up a silent prayer that she would never have that deadly fury directed at her.

"Are you all right?" His voice was clipped, his eyes boring into hers.

"Aye." She swallowed convulsively, dropping her eyes from his stare. "Oh, Travis, your hands!" Without thought, she took them in her own. "They're bleeding; you'll have to tend to them. I have some salve that's—"

"Damn it, Dee." He yanked his hands away from hers, taking her by the shoulders and tilting her head back so her eyes once more met the icy fury in his. He surveyed the torn blouse, the bruises already in evidence on the creamy skin, the rich hair tousled around her pale face. "How badly did he hurt you?" His voice was low and uneven.

Dee struggled to keep her own voice calm and not give way to the hysteria bubbling below the surface. "Not badly—he just frightened me. He only hit me once." His face suffused with color, dark and angry at her words, his hands tightening uncontrollably on her shoulders. "Is he alive?" she asked, her voice barely audible. Travis let out a long breath, released her, and turned to study the crumpled form.

"Yes, more's the pity. Heaven knows he wouldn't have been if you hadn't intervened. The police will see to him now."

"No!" Her cry of protest brought Travis's attention back to her.

"Adelia…" he began slowly. "The man tried to rape you, don't you understand?"

"I know very well what his intentions were." She hugged herself to control the spasmodic trembling assailing her. "But we can't call the police." She rushed on as Travis made to protest. "I don't want Uncle Paddy to know about this. I won't have him worrying and upset because of me. I'm not hurt, and I won't have Uncle Paddy upset—I tell you, I won't!" Her voice rose, and he slipped a gentle arm around her shoulders.

"All right, Dee, all right," he soothed, tightening his grip around her shuddering frame. "I'll call a couple of men and have him taken off the property. No police." He began to lead her from the stables. "Come on, I'll take you home."

The room began to lurch sickeningly as a roaring sound filled her brain, the dim light ebbing until she could barely see. "Travis." Her voice sounded strange and far away over the deafening roar in her head. "I'm sorry, but I'm going to faint." As she spoke, the darkness closed in and swallowed her.

Adelia opened her eyes slowly, experimentally. There was something cool and wonderful on her forehead, and someone was stroking her cheek and speaking her name. She sighed and closed her eyes again, enjoying the new sensation of pampering. Before opening them once more to focus on her surroundings.

The room was lit with a warm glow, the walls a cool, soft ivory trimmed with carved dark wood. She made out a wingbacked chair and a dark mahogany table on which stood an antique globed lamp that softly lit the room. Her eyes traveled over to the man who knelt beside her and rested on Travis's face.

"I'm in the main house," she stated matter-of-factly, and his expression of concern was transformed into an amused smile.

"Leave it to you not to say the usual 'Where am I?'" He removed the wet cloth from her head and sat down beside her on the long sofa. "I don't know anyone else who could calmly announce she was sorry, she was going to faint, and then proceed to do so."

"I've never fainted before in my life," she told him, mystified. "I'm sure I don't like it."

"Well, your color's better now. I've never seen anyone go so white. You scared the daylights out of me."

"I'm sorry." She gave him a weak smile and sat up. "It was a foolish thing to do, and—" She stopped suddenly as her hand went to her throat, only to find the cross that always hung there missing. "My cross," she stammered, looking down to where her hand rested. "I must have lost it in the stables. I've got to go find it." He pushed her back firmly as she attempted to rise.

"You're in no shape to go out there now, Dee," he began, but she cut him off, struggling against his hold.

"I've got to find it. It can't be gone." Her color had drained again, and he pushed her back on the sofa.

"Dee, for heaven's sake, you'll fall flat on your face."

"Let me go. I can't lose it."

He tried to keep his words soothing, feeling helpless against her rising hysteria. He had seen her flaming angry and deeply moved, but never incoherently desperate, and he struggled to hold both her and his own temper in check. "Dee," he said shortly, giving her a small shake. "Get a grip on yourself. It's just a cross."

"It was my mother's. I've got to have it—it's all I have left of her. It's all I have." She was trembling violently, and he drew her into the warm circle of his arms and began the ageless comfort of rocking.

"I'll find it for you, don't worry. I'll go back and find it tonight."

Resting against his strong shoulder, she felt strangely content, and both panic and the threatened tears dissolved. "Do you promise?"

"Yes, Dee, I promise." He rubbed his cheek against the silk curtain of her hair, and she wondered suddenly what it was about a man that made it so good to be held by one—or was it just one man? Sighing, she allowed herself another moment's luxury pressed against him.

"I'm all right now, Mr. Grant." She drew herself away as far as his arms would permit. "I'm sorry I acted like that."

"You don't have to be sorry, Dee." His hand lifted to brush back the full, thick waves that tumbled around her face. "And it was Travis before; let's leave it at that. I rather like the way you say it."

She felt her pulse respond to his soft words and gentle touch, her awareness of him growing until she thought her veins would burst from the pressure.

"I—Is it that you're implying I have an accent?" Her brows lifted in mock censure as a defense against the suddenly dangerous atmosphere.

"No. I'm the one with the accent."

His smile drew one of her own, but the innocent intimacy only heightened her confusion, and she felt her color rise in an unaccustomed blush, her lashes sweeping down like fragile shutters. He grinned at the uncharacteristic shyness before he rose and moved to a small bar across the room.

"I think you could use a drink before I take you home." He lifted a crystal decanter. "Some brandy?"

"Brandy's a stranger to me, but perhaps if you've some Irish…" She sat up straighter, grateful for the distance between them.

"I'd be hard pressed not to with Paddy as my trainer," he commented, pouring a small measure of whiskey into a glass. "Here." He walked back to her and offered the glass. "This should steady you and keep you from falling into my arms again."

She took the glass and downed its contents without a shudder as Travis watched with uplifted brows. He looked down at the empty glass she handed him before bursting into gales of laughter.

"And what would you be finding so funny?" Tilting her head, she regarded him with curious eyes.

"That a half-pint like you could down two fingers of whiskey as though it were a cup of tea."

"Aye, well, it comes with the blood, I suppose. I'm not one that drinks often, but when I do I can handle my liquor—which is more than can be said of that slimy pig of a groom." He turned back to set the empty glass on the bar so that she was unaware of the hardening of his features. "Travis…" she said, hesitating over his name, and he turned, relaxing his face into calm lines. "I'm grateful to you for what you did." Standing, she moved until she stood in front of him. "I'm owing you, Travis, though God Himself knows how I'll ever repay you."

His eyes were intense for a moment, brooding over the face she turned up to his; then his features relaxed into a smile, and he ran his finger down her cheek. "Perhaps one day I'll call in the debt."

The sun streamed onto the kitchen table as Adelia removed the postbreakfast clutter. She was grateful Paddy had noticed nothing amiss, having been fast asleep when, late and disheveled, she had arrived back home. He had greeted her that morning with his usual cheery smile, and she had mirrored it, firmly blocking the memory of her night's encounter from her mind. Hearing footsteps approach the kitchen, she closed the door on the dishwasher.

"I'm just coming, Uncle Paddy. I've got the buttons all figured out now. It's amazing how—Oh!" She stopped as she turned and saw Travis leaning against the doorway. "Good morning." She pushed at her hair as her thought processes skidded to a halt.

"How are you?" He walked toward her, eyes traveling in an intense survey.

"I'm f-fine, just f-fine," she stammered, and despised herself. Will I always behave like this when he comes on me unexpectedly? she demanded of herself, and determinedly offered a slight smile. His hand cupped her chin, and Adelia held very still as he searched her face.

"Are you sure?"

She nodded; then, realizing she had been holding her breath, she let it out slowly. "I'm fine, really." Her eyes traveled past him, and he read her concern easily.

"Paddy's already gone. I told him I needed to speak

with you for a minute." Releasing her chin, Travis reached into his pocket and pulled out her cross and chain.

"Oh, you found it!" Her face lifted to his, illuminating the room more brilliantly than the sun. "Thank you, Travis, for troubling. It means a great deal to me."

"There's no need to thank me, Dee, and it wasn't a question of troubling." He tucked a strand of hair behind her ear in a gentle gesture that threatened to dissolve her knees. "The clasp is broken. I'll have it repaired for you."

"You don't have to do that. I can—"

"I said I'll have it repaired." His voice was firm, and her brows drew together at the underlying anger in his tone. Letting out a long breath, he slipped the cross back into his pocket, then carefully framed her face with his hands. "Adelia, I'm responsible for what happened last night. No, don't argue," he commanded as her mouth opened to contradict. "What happens to you—to the people who work for me—" he amended, "is my responsibility. I wanted you to know I'd found your cross, so you wouldn't worry. I'll have the chain repaired and get it back to you as soon as possible."

"All right," she murmured, finding currents of pleasure brushing along her skin as his hands continued to cup her face as if it were something fragile and precious.

He smiled, and his thumb traced her lips with a teasing lightness. "At times, Dee, you can be surprisingly docile. Then, just when I think you've been halter broke, you start bucking again."

Drawing away, Adelia straightened her shoulders. "I'm not a mare to be pulled about on a lead line."

Smile became grin. Travis tousled her hair before taking her hand and pulling her from the room. "Maybe you'll find it depends who's holding the line."

* * *

The days passed slowly for Adelia as the two main men in her life were absent for a time. Paddy had accompanied Majesty to Florida in preparation for the Flamingo Stakes. She found, for one who had always taken her own self-sufficiency for granted, that the nights grew longer without Paddy's company. The house seemed large and quiet and empty. Alone in the evening, she reflected how easily a heart could be lost to another. In less time than it takes for the moon to go from full glory to a sliver of light, love had swept over her, leaving her vulnerable. Love for Paddy, a sweet, full warmth of belonging, and love for Travis, an aching, spreading need.

She built a fire, though the spring air was kind through opened windows, and curled up in front of its company, her head resting on the arm of her chair. Paddy would be home the next day, and she found the knowledge comforting, for with his presence there would not be so many hours alone, so many hours to think. Travis would not leave her thoughts or her heart, and seeing him daily brought as much torment as it did delight.

As the fire grew soft and low in the grate, her mind drifted to him, her lashes fluttering down to conceal her dreams, her hair falling in a curtain against her cheek.

"Dee." She stirred in the twilight world of dreams, sighing as a hand brushed through her hair. "Dee, wake up."

Lids opened slowly, and eyes misted with sleep focused on Travis. Her hand lifted to touch his cheek before fantasy was completely dimmed. "Oh." Dropping her hand, she struggled to sit up, pushing back her hair to look up at him. "Travis." She felt fresh color warm her sleep-flushed cheeks and pulled the neck of her faded blue robe closer together. "I must have fallen asleep."

"If I could have understood how anyone could be comfortable in that position, I would have left you alone." Smiling, he moved from his crouched position to sit on the arm where her cheek had rested.

Desperately aware of his nearness, Adelia pushed far into the corner of the chair, her hands clasped in her lap. "I was just thinking that Uncle Paddy would be home tomorrow," she said with partial honesty.

"Yes. I'd like to have gone with him, but I just couldn't get away." He laid a finger under her chin and lifted it. The dying power of the fire danced in her hair. "You've missed him."

"Aye." Her smile spread as her eyes traveled over his face. "And Majesty as well." His smile answered hers, and as the moment grew long, she felt the need to abort the contact. "I'm sorry Majesty didn't win his race." Her fingers smoothed the skirts of her robe.

"Hmm?" His hands were exploring the flickers of light in her hair, and she repeated her statement in a rush of words.

"Oh well, he placed and made a good run. Winning takes time, Dee." With a laugh, Travis ruffled her hair. "Time, patience and strategy... Look, I have something for you." Reaching into his pocket, he drew out her cross. "I didn't have the opportunity to give it to you earlier today."

"Oh, Travis, thank you." She lifted her face again to smile. "It means a great deal."

"I know." Instead of handing it to her, Travis opened the clasp and slipped the chain around her neck. His fingers on her skin were warm and gentle, and Adelia lowered her eyes, struggling not to tremble. "Better?" he asked when the clasp was secured, and she nodded, swallowing before the words would come.

"Much better, thank you, Travis."

He studied her bent head a moment; then, taking her hand, he pulled her to her feet. "Come on, close the door behind me and go to bed. You're tired." Reaching the door, he paused, one hand on the knob. "You look like a child." Her chestnut hair hung loose and heavy over the shoulders of her robe, and he ran a hand down the length of it. "A child can't be bundled off to bed without a good-night kiss," he said softly. Before she could step away, his hand had circled her neck, his mouth lowering to linger on her cheek while her lips parted in hunger. Her hunger was to go unsatisfied, for his mouth barely brushed her other cheek. As in a dream, she watched him straighten, then turn to leave, closing the door gently behind him.…

With Paddy's return, Royal Meadows threw itself into preparing Majesty for the Bluegrass Stakes. The race was a preliminary for the most prestigious race in the country, the Kentucky Derby. Majesty's record was impressive, and his good showing in Florida had hopes running high for his next venture on the track.

Adelia leaned on the fence surrounding the track, chin resting on crossed arms, as Steve Parker, the young jockey, raced Majesty around the large oval. There had been an immediate liking between her and the small man, an easy rapport born of a mutual love of horses. She watched their progress around the track, enjoying their fluid harmony.

Pushing the button on the stopwatch he was holding, Paddy let out a loud whoop of approval before he handed it to Travis. "If he runs like that in Kentucky, there's not another horse will come within five lengths of him at the finish. He holds the turns like a lover."

"Aye, and he runs for the sheer love of it," Adelia

murmured, sighing as Steve brought the colt toward them in a slow walk.

"Let's hope he loves it as much in Kentucky," Travis put in and sauntered over to speak to his jockey.

"Are you excited about your first race, little Dee?" Paddy asked, ruffling her hair.

"You might say I'm a bit excited," she returned with a grin. "My eyes will be glued to the television; not even a ton of dynamite could blast me away."

"Television?" Paddy repeated, the skin crinkling around his eyes as he narrowed them. "What's put it in your mind about television? You'll be coming with us."

"Coming with you?" She stared back in confusion.

"Of course, Adelia." She spun around at Travis's voice, her eyes making contact with his hard chest before she tilted her head back to meet his calm, controlled gaze.

"Now why would I be doing that?"

"Because," he answered evenly, "I say so."

"Is that the way of it?" she demanded, infuriated by the tone of command in his voice. "Well, if it's a groom you need, there's others who've been here longer. Stan or Tom deserves to go more than me."

"But, Dee," Steve protested with a wide grin as he joined them, "you're much prettier than those two. I'd rather look at you—you'll give me inspiration."

"Inspiration, is it?" she returned, amused by the compliment. "You're mad as a hatter." She turned to Travis again, shifting her eye level by several long inches. "I think you'd best take one of the men," she began, but he cut her off, narrowing his eyes and grabbing her hand.

"Excuse us," he called over his shoulder as he began to stride off, dragging Adelia in his wake. When at last he stopped some distance away, she rounded on him furiously.

"What the devil do you mean racing off like that and carting me behind you?" she panted, outraged. "Your legs are almost as long as my whole body, and I had to fair run to keep up with you."

She glared up at him, a picture of righteous indignation.

"I prefer to argue in private, Adelia," Travis said coolly, meeting her mutinous face with nonchalant command. "I run Royal Meadows and I give the orders." Even through her own anger, Adelia could see the signs of temper held in check; his eyes hard and direct, he was suddenly the essence of the master. "I will not have you countermanding my orders privately, and most certainly not publicly." His words annoyed her further simply because she knew he was right. "You're going to have to get it through that stubborn head of yours that you are no longer in solitary control of what is to be done. Now, I believe the issue here is your presence in Kentucky," he went on calmly, his face expressionless.

"I was telling you—"

"I'm telling you," he interrupted imperiously. "You're going."

Her eyes flashed at the order. Why, she thought, if it's God's pleasure for me not to be forever bursting with temper did He give me such a demanding one?

"Majesty responds better to you than anyone else," Travis went on. "I want you tending to him." Anger receded slowly at his words, and she dropped her eyes, staring at the ground while she considered his statement. "You'll come to Kentucky because it suits me to have you there, and I'm accustomed to having what suits me." His smile spread in a rapid change of mood as her head snapped up with fresh anger. His hands claimed her waist, then trailed slowly upward, resting on the sides of her firm young breasts as her anger faded into confusion. Lingering, his thumbs caressed in a slow circle, then trailed once in a lazy arch over the subtle curves, pausing at their fullness before moving to rest under their soft swell. Her lips parted, but she found no strength to protest against the unfamiliar intimacy, her body responding to his touch, eclipsing her will. She felt herself rising from the ground, and her hands went to his shoulders automatically to compensate for the loss of gravity.

"Put me down." The order emerged as a trembling whisper, and his smile grew wider before his mouth lowered.

"In a minute."

His mouth was dominant and sure, and her fingers dug into his shoulders as the force of the kiss held her in its prison. With a final flash of lucidity, she knew she could never fight Travis on these terms. Then all was lost in the dark demand of need.

"Steve's right," he murmured, his teeth nibbling at her lip and sending shooting sparks of flame through her veins. "You are prettier than Tom or Stan."

With a final hard, brief kiss, he dropped her back to the ground, to stride away with casual arrogance, whistling the first few bars of "My Wild Irish Rose." Adelia stood gaping after him, trembling with a confusing mixture of indignation and longing.

Chapter Five

Adelia found herself on a plane for the second time in her life. This plane, however, was vastly different from the crowded economy section of the passenger jet in which she had traveled over the Atlantic. Now she was passing over the relatively short distance between Maryland and Kentucky in the lush comfort of Travis's specially equipped private jet. Adelia's attitude during this flight was also a marked variation from her first. She stared, mesmerized, from the window, fascinated by the topography of far-distant West Virginia.

She looked down on patchworks of green and umber dotted by small houses, toy-train cities and gray ribbons of roads snaking and winding to connect them. There were rivers and pine-topped mountains, their colors soft from her eagle view, and she thought with pleasure that the world was indeed a wondrous place. Engrossed in her new discoveries, she did not notice when Travis sat next to her.

"Enjoying the view, Dee?" he asked at length, smiling at the way she pressed her forehead to the glass like a child at a bakery window. She started at his voice, then turned her head to face him, pushing back the chestnut curls that spilled over her face at the movement.

"Merciful heavens, you're forever surprising me. You move like the wind through a willow."

"Sorry. I'll practice stomping." He grinned and shifted in his seat to regard her more directly. "I've often thought you move like one of those fairies Ireland's so famous for, or maybe one of your leprechauns."

"Oh, well, it can't be both. A leprechaun's not considered a fit associate for a reputable fairy."

"Only a disreputable fairy," he returned, amused at the sobriety of her statement.

"Aye, and for the most part they're on their good behavior, hoping to be readmitted to Paradise on the last day."

"Tossed out, were they?"

"When Satan was rebelling, they stood back from the fighting, not wanting to take sides till they knew how it would end. But since that was their only offense, they were banished to earth instead of tossed into the pit with the rebels."

"Seems fair," Travis concluded with a nod. "As I recall, they have the rather awesome power to turn one into a dog or a pig or something equally undesirable, but are normally disposed to good deeds if treated with the proper respect."

"That's right," she agreed. "How did you know that?"

"Paddy saw to the holes in my education." He leaned over her, smiling, and she pressed back into the cushions, green eyes growing wide. "Relax." His voice tightened in annoyance. "I'm not going to eat you." He fastened the seat belt around her waist and leaned back. "We'll be landing in a minute."

"So soon?" She controlled her voice to casualness while the beating of her heart vibrated in her ears.

"That's right," he answered, matching her tone as he secured his own belt. "You've been staring down at Kentucky for some time now."

With amazing organization and economy of movement, the plane was landed, Majesty was unloaded, and transferred to a waiting van, and the travelers were on their way to Churchill Downs.

Adelia's impression of Louisville was vague. Her mind was in the back of the van with Majesty. She worried that he might be frightened and confused by the strange sights and long transport. When she voiced her concern, she was rewarded with a deep, full laugh from Travis. The ominous gleam in her eye was ignored as, chuckling, he informed her that Majesty was a seasoned traveler and took it in his stride.

Her irritation had faded by the time the van reached the extensive stables at Churchill Downs. Travis immediately confirmed the arrangements that had been made for Majesty's stall space and feed.

Travis Grant was well known and highly respected in racing circles. Adelia noted that he was greeted with warmth by the men and women milling around the stable area. He stood head and shoulders above the group, exuding power and a virile masculinity which, she observed with a rude stab of jealousy, was obviously appreciated by the women who greeted him. Infuriated with herself for her own weakness, Adelia turned sharply back to Majesty and led the gleaming colt into his stall.

Time passed swiftly as she tended to the animal's needs, brushing and soothing as she kept up a flow of one-sided chatter. As she was completing her duties, she heard loud footsteps approaching and turned around to see who was causing the din.

"Loud enough?" Travis grinned at her with unexpected boyishness.

"Aye," she agreed and gave him a solemn nod. "You sounded like a herd of great African elephants. You're a funny man, Travis," she commented, tilting her head to the side and studying him.

"Am I, Dee? How?"

"There's times you're like the local squire tossing orders about, and the steel in your eyes could freeze a man in his tracks. Then I think you're a hard man. But then sometimes..." Faltering, she shrugged and turned back to Majesty.

"Don't stop now." Deliberately, he turned her back to face him, a faint smile playing on his mouth. "You've intrigued me."

She was uncomfortable now and wishing with a full heart that she would learn to think before speaking. But Travis ignored her expression of embarrassment, hands light but firm on her shoulders, eyes demanding her elaboration.

"Sometimes... I've seen you laughing and talking with the men, or carting one of the twins about on your shoulders. And I see the way it is between you and Uncle Paddy, and the way you treat your horses. I think then maybe there's a gentle side, and maybe you're not so hard, after all." She finished in a rush, wishing she had never started, and turned back to give Majesty unnecessary additional attention with the brush.

"That's very interesting," he commented, taking the brush from her hand and continuing the grooming himself. "She's spoiling you," he addressed Majesty, running an affectionate hand along his flank. "She'd stand in here rubbing you down for the next hour if I let her."

She tore her eyes from Travis's fingers as they stroked the rich chestnut hide. "I don't spoil him; it was just love and care I was giving. We all need that from time to time."

He turned his head and met her eyes with a long, level look. "Yes, we all need that from time to time."

That night, awake in the unfamiliar hotel room, Adelia tossed and turned, ultimately rolling over and pounding her innocent pillow. Love was decidedly uncomfortable, unpredictable and unwelcome. Sighing, she hugged the pillow she had just beaten, determined to erase incredibly blue eyes from her dreams.

The next morning Adelia had her first real look at Churchill Downs. Leading Majesty from the stables, she stopped as she came to the track, her companion waiting with calm indulgence as she stared in open amazement.

The grounds were enormous, the wide mile-and-a-quarter track encircling a grass field bordered by fences and graced with well-shaped shrubs and flower beds of brilliant color. Moving her eyes over the vast expanse of stands, she wondered somewhat whimsically who would be left to tend to the outside world when they were filled with people. The tops of the stands were roofed, crowned with spires, she noted.

"Something wrong, Dee?" Her observations were interrupted by Travis's question, and she jumped in surprise. "Sorry," he said without bothering to conceal a grin. "Forgot to stomp."

"I should be getting used to it by now." She sighed and began to lead Majesty along once more. "What a grand place this is." Her hand swept in an expressive arch as he fell into step beside her.

"It's one of my favorites. The architecture's basically the same as it was when it was built over a hundred years ago. And, as you well know, it's the most famous track of all because it is here that the Derby is run. And the Derby, everyone remembers. On the first Saturday in May, this ribbon of track is gold, and for a few minutes the world stops, and it's only the race." He turned to her with a smile. "It all comes down to the challenge at the turn for home, when the goal is still a quarter of a mile away. Since 1875 the best horses have run here, and the best horses have won here. It's not only the classic race, it's a breeders' race, and there isn't anyone in the States who wouldn't rather produce a winner in this than in any other contest. The winner of a Derby becomes the horse to beat for the rest of the season; the magic stays with him. And this," he continued, giving Majesty a friendly slap on the flank, "is one who likes to win."

"Aye, that he does," she agreed, giving Majesty an indulgent smile. "And he's not shy about his own capabilities. He's feeling pretty sure of himself. He wants the Bluegrass Stakes out of the way so he can move on to the Derby."

"Does he?" The corner of his mouth tilted as Majesty nuzzled Adelia's shoulder. "And how do you feel?" His finger touched her cheek, and she turned to face him. "Do you want the prep race out of the way so you can dive into the Derby?"

"I'm not ready for the first one yet." Adelia shrugged, nearly stumbling as Majesty's head nudged at her back. "It's him that's in the hurry. But I like the looks of this place." Again, she encompassed Churchill Downs with a sweep of the hand. "I like knowing it hasn't changed much in all these years." She began to walk again, at Majesty's urging. "Never did I think to see such a place."

"There are other tracks that are perhaps more eye-catching," he commented, following her fascinated gaze. "At Hialeah in Florida, they have hundreds of pink flamingos in the center-field lake."

Stopping, she turned to him with wide eyes. "I should like to see that."

"I'm sure you will," he murmured, twining his fingers in the ends of her long, silky waves. Then, pulling the brim of her cap down over her eyes, he repeated in a lighter tone, "Yes, Dee, I'm sure you will."

The week moved swiftly, hours crammed with duties and activities. Most of Adelia's time was given to Majesty's care, talking and fondling as much as grooming and seeing to his more practical needs. She spent much of her free time with Steve Parker, teasing him about his girlfriends or watching from the rail as he accustomed Majesty to the track. Other times she spent with Paddy, discussing the Thoroughbred's qualities and the style of the other colts who would compete in the qualifying race.

"The colt that wins is automatically eligible for the Derby," he informed her, giving Majesty a thorough examination as she watched from the stall door. "Of course, Travis nominated this fellow right after he was born, the same way he's entered Solomy's foal, and kept up with the nomination as he got older. He knows when he's got a winner. Travis is a man who keeps one eye on the future."

"He's good with the horses," Adelia commented. The obvious pride and affection in Paddy's voice warmed her.

"You can see he cares for them; it's not just a matter of the money they'll bring him."

"Aye, he cares," Paddy agreed, giving Majesty an affectionate slap on the flank. "And he's fierce on the matter of using painkillers or drugs as others have been known to do. If one of Travis's horses isn't up for the race, he doesn't run and that's that. Of course, money's not a problem with Travis, but it wouldn't make any difference if it was, because that's the man he is. Now, he has a practical side as well." He moved from the stall to join Adelia and slipped an arm around her shoulder. "Investments—and he's mighty crafty about them. He knows how to take a purse or the sale of a foal and turn it into more. He's got the touch," Paddy added with a wise nod. "And a time or two, he's stretched my pennies for me, though not on as grand a scale as his. Travis takes care of his own." Squeezing her shoulder, Paddy led Adelia out into the flash of sunlight. She remained silent, thinking of this new aspect of the man she loved.

The sky was overcast on the day of the Bluegrass Stakes. The air was heavy. Lead-gray clouds lay thick as a blanket overhead. Tension seemed to start at Adelia's brow and spread down to her toes; the stillness of the air weighed like a stone at the nape of her neck. To take her thoughts off the coming race she kept both hands and mind busy. Glancing up she saw Travis enter the building. She smiled as he approached.

"I believe that, if you could, you'd get into the silks and ride him today."

"The truth of it is," she began, finding the ease of his smile soothing, "I think I'd be less terrified that way. But I don't think Steve would care for it."

"No." The syllable was accompanied by a slow, grave

nod. "I don't think he would. Come up to the stands with me. Paddy'll take over now."

"Oh, but—" Her objection was neatly cut off as he captured her arm and propelled her to the door. "Wait!" she cried and pivoted to run swiftly back to Majesty, throwing her arms around his neck and whispering in his ear.

When she rejoined Travis, he stared down at her, both amused and frankly curious. "What did you tell him?"

She gave him a mysterious smile for an answer. As they approached the stands, she dug into her back pocket and thrust some bills into his hands. "Will you place a wager for me? I don't know how to go about it."

"A wager?" he repeated, looking down at the two dollars in his hand. Looking up, his features were entirely too serious. "Who do you want to bet on?"

"Majesty, of course." She frowned at the question, her expression lightening as she recalled some of the terms she had heard tossed around the stables. "To win...on the nose."

To his credit, Travis's features remained grave. "I see. Well, let's see...his odds are five to two at the moment." Brows drawn, he studied the odds board. "Now, number three there is ten to one, but that's not too long for a gambler. Number six is two to one; that's rather conservative."

"I don't know about all that," she interrupted with a frustrated wave of her hand. "It's just all a bunch of numbers."

"Adelia." He said her name slowly, giving her a small pat on the shoulder. "One must never bet unless one knows the odds." Ignoring her, he glanced back up at the flashing numbers. "It's three to one on number two, a nice safe choice for win, place or show. It's eight to five on number one."

"Travis, you're making my head spin with all of this. I just want to—"

"And fifteen to one on number five." He looked down at the two crumpled bills. "You could amass a small fortune if that one came in."

"It's not for the money." Her breath came out in one impatient huff. "It's for the luck."

"Ah, I see," he returned with a solemn nod before the grin escaped and spread. "Irish luck is not to be scoffed at."

Though she scowled quite fiercely for a moment, he slipped his arm over her shoulders and led her to the two-dollar window.

Before long, she was standing next to him and gaping openly at the masses of people filling the stands. The enormous stadium would hold one hundred and twenty-five thousand, Travis had informed her, and to her astonished eyes there seemed to be no less than that. Several people greeted Travis, and she felt an occasional twinge of discomfort as eyes often passed over her in speculation. Embarrassment was soon eclipsed by excitement as post time approached. She watched the horses step onto the track, her eyes immediately focusing on Majesty and the rider in brilliant red and gold silks on his back. As Majesty's name was announced, Adelia closed her eyes, finding the combination of excitement and nerves nearly overpowering.

"He looked ready," Travis commented casually, then laughed as she jolted at his words. "Relax, Dee, it's just another race."

"I'll never be easy about it if I see a hundred," she

vowed. "Oh, here comes Uncle Paddy. Is it going to start?"

For answer, he pointed, and she watched the horses being loaded into the starting gate. Her hand clutched at the cross at her neck, and she felt Travis's arm slip over her shoulder as the bell sounded and ten powerful forms lunged forward.

It seemed to her a mass of flying hooves and thunderous noise, the pack clinging together in one speeding block. Still, her eyes were glued on Majesty as though he were racing alone. Her hand reached up of its own accord to grasp the one on her shoulder, tightening as she urged the colt to greater speed. Steadily he moved forward, as if following her remote-control command, persistently passing one, then another, until he emerged alone from the field. Suddenly the long legs increased their stride, streaking across the dirt track until his competitors were left with the sight of his massive hindquarters as he lunged under the wire.

Travis's arm encircled her, and Adelia found herself crushed to his hard chest, sandwiched between his lean body and her uncle's stocky frame. It was like being caught fast between two unmoving, loving walls, and she found the sensation torturously wonderful, a heady mixture of scents and textures. Her uncle's voice was raised in excitement in her ear, and her head was snuggled, as if it belonged, against Travis's chest. Majesty's win, she decided, closing her eyes, was the best present she had ever had.

Every man, woman and child in Louisville ate, slept and breathed the Kentucky Derby. As the days dwindled, the very air seemed to shimmer with anticipation. Adelia saw Travis sporadically. Their conversations revolved around the colt, the only personal aspect of their relation-ship being the abstracted pat on the head he would give her from time to time. She began to think that quarreling with him had had its advantages, and she relieved her frustrations by spending more time with Majesty.

"You're a fine, great horse," she told him, holding his muzzle and looking into his intelligent eyes. "But you mustn't let all of this go to your head. You've a job to do come Saturday, and it's a big one. Now, I'm going out for a few minutes, and I want you to rest yourself, then perhaps we'll see about a currying."

Satisfied with Majesty's silent agreement, Adelia stepped out of the stables into the bright May sun and found herself surrounded by reporters.

"Are you the groom in charge of Royal Meadows' Maj-esty?" The question was fired out by one of the people who suddenly cut her off from the rest of the world with a wall of bodies. The sensation was disconcerting, and she was thinking wistfully of the dim solitude of the stables when she heard another voice.

"You don't see many grooms that look like this one."

She rounded on the man who had spoken, squinting against the sun to see more clearly. "Is that the truth, now?" she demanded, discomfort replaced by annoyance. "I thought red hair was common enough in America."

The group roared with laughter, and the man at whom her remark had been directed responded with a good-natured grin. Questions were fired at her, and for a few moments she surrendered to the pressure and answered, valiantly attempting to keep one query separate from the next.

"By the saints!" She threw up her hands in dismay, shaking her head. "You're all speaking in a muddle." Pushing the brim of her cap back from her head, she took a deep breath. "If it's more information you're wanting, you'd best ask Mr. Grant or Majesty's trainer." She pushed through them with determination, turning when she felt a hand on her arm and finding herself facing the reporter who had made the personal observation.

"Miss Cunnane, sorry if we were a little rough on you." He smiled with considerable charm, and Adelia found herself smiling back.

"No harm was done."

"I'm Jack Gordon. Maybe you'd let me make it up to you by taking you out to dinner tonight."

She was both surprised and flattered by the invitation, gaining the pure feminine pleasure of having an attractive man pay her specific attention. He was, however, a stranger, and she was opening her mouth to decline when a voice sounded behind her.

"Sorry, my groom's off limits."

She whirled around to see Travis watching them, blue eyes cool and direct. Fury bubbled inside her, reflecting plainly in her flashing eyes.

"Don't you have some work to do, Adelia?" he asked with an imperial lift of brows. The eyes that met his told him without words what she thought of his question before she wheeled around and stalked to the stables.

Some fifteen minutes later, Travis disengaged himself from the avid reporters and joined her. She watched as he strode toward her, hands carelessly thrust in the pockets of slim-fitting jeans.

"Don't you know better than to make dates with strange men, Adelia?" His tone was deliberate, superior, and infuriating.

"My personal life is my own affair," she raged at him. "You've no right to interfere."

"As long as you're in my employ and responsible for my horses, your life is my affair."

"Aye, Master Grant," she tossed back , undaunted by the narrowing of his eyes. "I'll be certain to ask your permission before I take my next breath." Her foot stomped in temper. "I didn't arrive on this earth yesterday. I can take care of myself."

"Were you taking care of yourself in the stables a couple of weeks ago?" She paled at this and turned away. With a muttered curse, he turned her around to face him. "Dee, I'm sorry. That wasn't fair."

"No, it wasn't." She jerked away, eyes bright with angry tears. "But it doesn't surprise me you'd be saying it. You've a habit of putting me in my place, Master Grant, and I've been reminded there's work to be done. So be off with you and let me be about it." Removing her cap, she dropped a curtsy. "If it please Your Honor."

"I've had just about enough, you green-eyed witch," he muttered, taking a step toward her. "I'd like to haul you over my knee for the spanking you deserve, but I'll get more out of this sort of punishment."

He had her crushed against him with a speed that allowed her only a short gasp of protest before his mouth descended, hard, then demanding, then possessing, in rapid succession. When he lifted his mouth, she felt him drawing her soul through her eyes.

"I'm not going to make a habit of this," he muttered and took her lips again, his fingers tangling in her hair, then moving over her back until she thought she would perish from the heat.

Feather-light tremors followed the trail of his hand along her spine, touching her with an exquisite fear. She felt the pressure of his arms bending her back, his mouth hard on hers, demanding not response but submission. She became aware of her own slightness, a fragility she had never known was part of her, as his strength overpowered even the thought of struggle. Lucidity drifted from her, leaving only the feel of a hard body and a demanding mouth which took from her until even breathing was impossible.

Drawing away, Travis held Dee steady as she staggered. He stood a moment looking down thoughtfully into her flushed face. "You know, Dee," he said at length, his voice as calm and unperturbed as she was ruffled and confused, "you're too little to possess such a dangerous temper."

Flicking a friendly finger down her nose, he strode out into the sunshine.

The day of the Derby was an advertisement for spring, warm with a soft, scented breeze under a clear, cloudless sky. The perfection of the weather meant nothing to Adelia, whose nerves were so tightly coiled that it could have easily been midwinter. Seeing Travis several times during the morning and early afternoon, she was both envious and annoyed by his calm, easygoing manner while she remained a massive bundle of quivering nerves. Between the lingering sensation of her last encounter with him and the prospect of the race, she found functioning at even borderline normality an effort. Waiting through the preliminary races was sheer torture.

She found herself beside Travis in the stands, thinking that if the race did not begin soon she would have to be carted away and locked up until it was over.

"Here." Adelia glanced down at the glass he offered before raising her eyes to his.

"What is it?"

"A mint julep." Taking her hand, he placed the glass

in it and curled her fingers around it. "Drink it," he commanded, then smiled at the frown she gave it. "The purpose is twofold. One, it's traditional, and you can keep the glass to remember your first Derby. And two," he continued, grinning, "you need something to calm your nerves; I'm afraid you're going to keel over."

"So am I," she admitted and sipped gingerly from the glass. "Travis, I would swear there are more people here than the last time. Where do they all come from?"

"Everywhere," he returned easily, following her fascinated gaze. "The Run for the Roses is the most important race of the season."

"Why do they call it that?" she asked, finding the combination of conversation and mint julep soothing.

"The winner's draped with a blanket of red roses in the Winner's Circle, and the jockey gets an armful. So," he concluded and lifted his own glass, "it's the Run for the Roses."

"That's nice," she approved, lifting the brim of her cap further on her head. "Majesty will like red roses."

"I'm sure he'll be crazy about them," Travis agreed with suspicious sobriety, and Adelia's dignified retort was interrupted by the first strains of "My Old Kentucky Home."

"Oh, Travis, the parade's starting!" She fastened her eyes on Majesty and the small man on his back, clad in colorful red and gold silks. The others with their brilliant contrasts of blues and greens and yellows paled before her eyes. To her there was not another animal to compare in power and beauty with Travis's Thoroughbred colt—and, judging by the way Majesty pranced, he agreed completely.

"Saints preserve us, Uncle Paddy," she murmured as

he appeared at her side. "My heart's pounding so I'm sure it'll burst. I don't think I'm made for this."

Her eyes never left Majesty's form as he was loaded into the gate. Her senses swam with the blare of the trumpets and the roar of the crowd. With a swiftness that took her breath away, the doors were released and the horses sprang forward in a turbulent herd.

Her eyes followed the colt as he galloped with steady assurance around the track. She was not even aware that as the bell had rung she had grabbed Travis's hand in a viselike grip, squeezing tighter as each heart-pounding second passed. The air shivered with the voice of the crowd, individual calls and shouts melding into one trembling roar. She rode every inch of the track on Majesty's back, feeling the rush of wind on her face and the strong rhythm of the colt's gait under her.

As they rounded the second turn, Steve brought Majesty to the inside rail, and the colt took his head and left the field with long, smooth strides. The gap between the chestnut and his nearest competitor widened with what appeared to be effortless ease as he streaked down the back stretch into the home stretch and under the wire more than four lengths in the lead.

Without hesitation, Adelia threw herself into Travis's arms, clinging with a joy which she could only express physically by babbling incoherent and self-interrupted sentences to both him and her uncle, who was improvising an enthusiastic jig beside her.

"Come on." Travis tossed an arm around Paddy's shoulders. "We've got to get down to the Winner's Circle before the crowd's too thick."

"I'll wait for you." Adelia pulled back, stooping to retrieve her dislodged cap. "I don't like all those reporters staring and snapping and jumping all over me with their questions. I'll wait on the outside and take Majesty along when it's over."

"All right," Travis agreed. "But tonight, we celebrate. What do you say, Paddy?"

"I say I've just acquired a strong yearning for champagne." The two men grinned at each other.

That evening, Adelia stared at the reflection in the full-length mirror of her room. Her hair lay full and lush on her shoulders, shining like newly minted copper against the muted greens of her dress.

"Well, Adelia Cunnane, look at you." She smiled with satisfaction into the mirror. "There's not a one back in Skibbereen who'd be knowing you in such a dress, and that's the truth of it." A knock sounded at her door, and she plucked her key from the dresser. "I'm coming, Uncle Paddy."

Opening the door with a dazzling smile, she was not greeted by her merry-faced uncle but by an incredibly attractive Travis in a dark dinner suit, the white silk of his shirt startling against his deep tan. They stood silently for a moment as his gaze roamed over her, from shining hair and deep green eyes to the soft, rounded curves outlined by the clinging jersey. His gaze rose to her face again, but still he did not smile.

"Well, Adelia, you're astonishingly beautiful."

Her eyes widened at the compliment, and she searched for something suitable to say. "Thank you," she finally managed. "I thought you'd be Uncle Paddy."

His eyes continued to hold her in the doorway, and she moistened her lips with the tip of her tongue in an innocently inviting gesture. "Paddy's meeting us downstairs with Steve."

The single-minded intensity with which she was being

studied was rapidly stripping her of all composure, and her words tumbled out quickly. "We'd best be joining them—they'll be waiting."

Travis merely nodded, a slight inclination of his head, and she took a step toward him, only to stop nervously when he made no move to let her pass. Raising her eyes from his shirtfront to his face, she opened her mouth to speak, only to find her mind a vacuum. He gazed down at her for another unnerving moment, then held up a single red rose, placing it in her hand.

"Majesty sent it. He says you're fond of red roses."

"Oh." He was not smiling with the whimsy of his words, and her mind fidgeted for something to ease the sudden awareness, the physical strength of his gaze. "I didn't know you talked to horses."

"I'm learning," he answered simply, and ran a finger over her bare shoulder. "My teacher's an expert."

She dropped her eyes to the bloom in her hand, thinking that twice in her life she had been given flowers, and both times they had come from Travis, both times they had been red roses. She smiled, knowing she would never again see a red rose without thinking of him. That was a gift more precious than jewels. Open and innocent, her smile lifted for him.

"Thank you, Travis, for bringing it to me." On impulse, she rose to her toes and kissed his cheek.

He stared down at her, and for a moment Adelia thought she saw some hesitation, some indecision, flicker in his eyes before his features relaxed into a smile.

"You're welcome, Dee. Bring it along—it suits you." Taking the key from her hand, he placed it in his pocket and led her to the elevator.

The celebration dinner was a new experience for Adelia. The elegant restaurant, the unaccustomed dishes and her first encounter with champagne combined to give her a glowing sense of unreality. The tension brought on by the few moments alone with Travis was dispelled by his casually friendly attitude during the meal. It was almost as though the awareness that had passed between them had never taken place. The evening drifted by in a haze of happiness.

The following week, however, found her back in Maryland in jeans and cap, busily fulfilling her duties and thrusting elegant meals and fancy dresses from her mind. Long hours of grooming, exercising and training filled the days, giving her little time to dwell on the strange new emotions Travis had aroused. She avoided the reporters who were often hovering around the track and stables, not wishing to be cornered again and bombarded with questions. At night, however, she was less successful in avoiding the dreams that assaulted her awakened senses.

Days passed into weeks, and although Adelia gave all the Thoroughbreds love and attention, she continued to dote on Majesty.

"Don't forget yourself just because you've had your picture in some fancy magazines," she admonished him, failing to keep her voice stern as she completed his grooming.

Paddy strolled into the stables and laid a hand on her shoulder. "Keeping him in line, are you, little Dee? Don't want him too big for his breeches, do we?"

"That we don't." Turning, she smiled at her uncle, then studied him carefully. "You look tired, Uncle Paddy. Aren't you feeling well?"

"I'm fine, Dee, just fine." He patted her rosy cheek and winked at her. "I think I'll sleep for a week when the Belmont's come and gone."

"You've earned a rest; you've been working hard and long. You're a bit pale. Are you sure—"

"Now, don't fuss," he interrupted with a good-natured scowl. "Nothing worse than a fussing woman. Just be keeping your mind on this lad here." He patted Majesty's side. "Don't you worry about Paddy Cunnane."

She let this pass, vowing silently to keep her eye on him. "Uncle Paddy, is the Belmont important?"

"Every race is important, darlin', and this is one of the top. Now, this fellow here, with that barrel of a chest"— he inclined his head toward Majesty and winked again— "he'll do well there. It's a long race, a mile and a half, and that's what he was bred for. A distance runner, and one of the finest. Not like Fortune, mind you; he's a sprinter and can beat almost anything at a shorter distance. Travis is smart enough to breed horses with both distance and sprinting in mind. That's why he put Fortune in the Preakness at Pimlico, and he was second by half a length. And that's just fine. But this one's for the Belmont." He shook Majesty's head lightly by the muzzle. "And so are you," he added, giving Adelia a pat on the head.

"Me? Am I going as well?"

"That's right. Hasn't Travis told you?"

"Well, no. I haven't seen much of him since we got back from Kentucky."

"He's been busy."

Her answer was absent as she considered the wisdom of attempting to refuse. Recalling the result of her previous attempt, Adelia thought New York might be a fine place to visit.

Belmont Park, on Long Island, was alive with reporters. Adelia managed to stay in the background the majority of the time, and when cornered she escaped as soon as possible. She was unaware of the speculation about her and her relationship with the owner of Royal Meadows' Majesty. The casual attire of jeans and shirt did nothing to conceal the appeal of her beauty, and her reluctance to speak with the press added a mystery that acted as a meaty bone to the hungry pack of reporters. At times she felt hounded and wished she had stood firm and refused to come. Then she would see Travis as he moved toward the stables, hands in pockets, hair ruffled by the breeze. She would admit, though it brought little comfort, that she would have gone mad had she been left behind.

Newspapers and nagging reporters were not in Adelia's thoughts as she joined Travis for the third time in the crowded stands. She noticed, with some discomfort, that Belmont and its occupants were more sophisticated than Churchill Downs. There, size had been offset by an old-world charm, the soft, lazy accent of Louisville. Somehow, Belmont seemed more vast, more intimidating, and beside the sophistication of the elegantly groomed women who occupied the stands and clubhouse, Adelia felt inadequate and naïve.

Silly, she told herself and straightened her shoulders. I can't be like them, and they're certainly taking no notice of me, in any case. Most of these fine ladies can't keep their eyes off Travis. I suppose these are the kind of ladies he sees at his country club, or takes out for a quiet dinner. Depression threatened to settle over her like a black cloud, but she took a deep breath and blew it away.

Adelia had lectured herself that by this time she should be accustomed to the tension and the crush of people, but as post time drew closer she found the familiar anxiety and undeniable excitement capture her. She could find neither words nor ability to speak, and stood gripping the rail with both hands as Majesty strutted to the starting gate. He was impatient, she observed, sidestepping and lifting his front legs in small, nervous prancing steps as Steve struggled to control him, urging him forward into his place in the starting gate.

"I'll have to bring you to the track more often, Dee." Travis gave her shoulder a small squeeze. "In a couple of months, you'll be a veteran."

"I'll never be a veteran, I'm afraid, because each time it seems like the first. I can hardly bear it."

"I'm going to keep bringing you in any case," he informed her, tangling his fingers for a moment in the ends of her hair. "You bring the excitement back. I believe I'd been taking it for granted."

She turned to him, nonplussed by the gentle tone of his voice, and had opened her mouth to speak when the bell shrilled with the roar of the crowd. Brilliant silks were now a soft blur as Thoroughbreds thundered around the track. After the first turn the field dispersed, transforming from a single mound of speeding legs to a zigzagging cluster of gleaming bodies. To Adelia, Majesty seemed to weave his way through them like a fiery comet, passing one after another until he bore down on the leader. Then, as if a switch had been flicked, came the power, the lengthening of stride, the rippling of muscles, the steady increase of his lead, until Majesty flew down the home stretch, capturing the coveted Belmont with power and style.

The crowd went wild, cheering and shouting with one deafening voice. Adelia's feet left the ground as Travis lifted her, swinging her in circles as she clung to his neck. He continued to hold her as Paddy's arms came around them both, drawing them all together in joy and excitement. The words shouted were senseless to her, and she told herself later that it was the temporary insanity of the moment that had caused her to meet Travis's lips with hers. Even on later reflection, she was unclear who had initiated the kiss, but she knew she had responded. She had flung her arms around his neck, and the thrill that had coursed through her had eclipsed even the rushing flurry of the race. When her feet touched the ground, and Travis lifted his mouth from hers, her head was still spinning with light and color, her body trembling with the backlash of emotion, the tidal wave of sensation. She could do no more than stare up at him. For a moment, it was the same as the day the foal had been born, and the crowded, noisy stands of Belmont Park faded into a solitary, private world. She was oblivious to the throng and the curious stares, aware only of his arms around her, and the feeling that she was slowly, helplessly, drowning in his eyes.

"We'd best be going down, lad." Paddy made a business of clearing his throat before he laid a hand on Travis's shoulder. Her knees weakened as his eyes left hers to meet her uncle's. She felt the sudden dizziness and disorientation of one who had been awakened from a dream too quickly.

"Yes." Travis grinned, the quick-spreading grin of a boy. "Let's go congratulate the winner. Come on." Spinning Adelia around, he began to lead her away.

"I'm not going down there," she objected, making a futile attempt to hold her ground.

"Yes, you are," he disagreed, not bothering to glance back at her. "I let you have your way before, not this time. You're coming down to help Majesty accept his flowers, white carnations this time, and one's for you."

Her sputtering objections and attempts to disentangle herself went unheeded, and she found herself in the Winner's Circle with the others.

There were microphones and the flash of lights, and she faded into the background as far as possible. She was still shaken by the intensity of need that had flowed through her in Travis's embrace, a strong, wild desire to belong to him completely. It was like being assailed with an unquenchable thirst, and the sensation terrified her. Her morals were deeply rooted, a melding of religious and personal beliefs. She knew, however, that her longing for Travis, her love for him, made her weak, and any resistance would melt as quickly as springtime snow if he pressed his advantage.

She must stay away from him, she determined, avoid situations where they would be alone and she would be vulnerable to his experience and her frailty. As she glanced over at his tall, lean frame, their eyes locked, and she trembled. Her lashes swept down, and she realized helplessly what a rabbit feels when cornered by a strong, sleek fox.

Chapter Six

Back at the hotel, Adelia accompanied Paddy to his room, having no wish to be alone with her thoughts. Travis walked down the carpeted hall with them, pausing at the doorway as they slipped through.

"I've made reservations for us." His teeth flashed in a grin. "Steve's doing his own celebrating with a little lady who's been dogging his footsteps since the Derby."

"Ah, Travis." Paddy sat down heavily on the bed. "You'll have to do without this tired old man. I'm weary to the bone." He gave a smile and a shake of his head. "I've had all the excitement I can stand for today. I'll play lord of the manor and have my dinner in bed like royalty."

"Uncle Paddy." Adelia moved closer, dropping a hand on his brow. "You're not feeling well. I'll stay with you."

"Go on with you." He made a dismissing gesture with

his hand. "Fussing like your grandmother used to. It's
tired I am, not sick. The next thing I know you'll be
pouring some strange remedy down my throat or threatening me with a poultice." He glanced up at Travis with
a long-suffering sigh. "She's a worrisome bundle, lad.
Take her off my hands and give these old bones a rest."

With a nod of masculine understanding, Travis turned
to Adelia. "Be ready in forty-five minutes," he stated
simply. "I don't like to be late."

"'Do this, do that,'" she fumed, throwing up her hands.
"Never a 'will you' or 'may I.' I'm not in the stables now,
Travis Grant, and I don't fancy being ordered about." She
tossed back her fiery curls and folded her arms across her
chest.

Travis raised a quizzical eyebrow before he moved to
the door. "Wear that green thing, Dee. I like it." He closed
the door against any possible further outbursts.

Dee was ready at the appointed time, having been
cajoled by her uncle to leave him and celebrate Majesty's
victory. Telling herself she was only going out with the
arrogant brute for Paddy's sake, she zipped herself into
the green dress as a knock sounded at her door. Muttering disjointedly about the devil's own spawn, she swung
open the door and glared.

"Good evening, Adelia," he greeted her, obviously un-
concerned by her warlike stance. "You're looking lovely.
Are you ready?"

She glowered at him for another moment, wishing
she had something handy to throw at him. Tilting her
chin, she stepped into the hall, closing the door with force
behind her.

She clung to her stubborn silence as the taxi drove
through surging traffic, but Travis remained unperturbed,

chatting amiably and pointing out various spots of interest. He was making it very difficult for her to keep her anger on the boil.

Defiance wavered as they entered the restaurant, grander than she could ever have imagined. Wide-eyed, she gazed around her at the sophisticated patrons in their evening dress. She allowed herself to be led unresisting to a quiet corner table, greatly impressed by the elegance of the maître d'. Softly lit and situated for privacy, the table sat high above the throbbing city, the lights blinking and speeding below a direct contrast to their quiet seclusion. She glanced up as their waiter requested her choice of cocktail, then looked across at Travis with a helpless shake of her head. Smiling, he ordered champagne.

"It's a shame we couldn't bring Majesty with us," she commented, then grinned, animosity forgotten. "He did all the work, and we're drinking the champagne."

"I very much doubt he'd appreciate it even if we took him back a bottle. For a royal steed, he has the taste of a peasant. So—" he paused, allowing his finger to rub gently over her hand as it rested on the cloth "—it's up to us to drink to his victory. Did you know, Adelia, the candlelight scatters gold through your eyes?"

Surprised by his sudden observation, she merely stared, greatly relieved when the arrival of the champagne saved her from inventing a response.

"Shall we have a toast, Dee?"

Lifting the slender-stemmed glass, she smiled, more at ease. "To Majesty, the winner of the Belmont Stakes."

His lips curved as he copied her gesture. "To winning."

"Hungry?" he asked after an interlude of quiet conversation. "What's your pleasure?"

"Well, it won't be mutton and potatoes," she murmured

absently, sighing at the strange workings of the world that had shifted her into a new life. Her attention came to a full stop as she glanced over the menu, her eyes lifting to his, wide and astonished.

"Is something wrong?"

"It's robbery, sure as faith; there's not another word for it!"

He leaned forward, taking both her hands in his and grinning at her anxious expression. "Are you sure there's no Scots blood in you?" Adelia opened her mouth to retort, highly insulted, but he raised her hands to his lips, causing the words to die before they were born. "Don't get your Irish up, Dee." He smiled over their joined hands. "And overlook the prices. I'm able to deal with them."

She shook her head. "I can't look at it again—it makes my head spin. I'll have what you have."

Chuckling, he ordered the meal and more wine as his hands held hers captive. When they were once more alone, he turned her hands over, examining her palms, ignoring the sharp jerk she made to release herself.

"You're taking better care of them," he murmured, rubbing his thumb over her skin.

"Aye," she retorted, embarrassed and resentful. "They're not quite as bad as a ditchdigger's these days."

He raised his eyes to hers, watching her a moment without speaking. "I offended you that night. I'm sorry." His gentle tone tilted her balance, and she felt the familiar weakness flowing into her.

"It doesn't matter," she stammered and shrugged and tugged at her hands again. He ignored both verbal and physical protests.

"You have fascinating hands. I've made quite a study of them. Small, exquisite, and totally capable—the three rarely go together. Capable Adelia," he murmured before his eyes fastened on hers again with an intensity that caught her off guard. "You had a bad time on that farm, didn't you?"

"I—no. No, we got along."

"Got along?" he repeated, and she felt his eyes searching her face for the words she was not saying.

"We did what needed to be done." She spoke lightly, not sure what it was he wanted from her. "Aunt Lettie was a strong, stubborn woman, and not one to be beaten easily. I often thought it strange how little she was like Da," she continued, her expression drifting into introspection. "And now I see how little she was like Uncle Paddy, for all she was their sister. Perhaps it was the demands of having to take on me and the farm that left her so little time for the gentler things. Such small things: a kiss goodnight, a word of affection…a child can starve with a full plate."

She brought herself back with a shake of the head, surprised by her own words and uneasy under his glance. She groped for some way to turn the subject. "I only had the farm to concern me; she had the farm and me, and I think I was more trouble than the farm." She smiled, willing him to lighten his features with one of his own. "She told me a time or two I had too loose a grip on my temper, but, of course, I've tightened the hold now."

"Have you?" At last the smile curved his mouth.

"Oh, aye." She gave him a solemn and guileless nod. "I'm a very mild sort of person."

The smile spread to a grin as their meal was set before them. As they ate, conversation drifted into generalities, an easy flow of words, as undemanding and soothing as the wine that accompanied the food.

"Come," he said suddenly and rose. "Dance with me."

Before she could voice agreement or protest, she found herself being led to the dance floor and enfolded in his all too familiar arms. Her first stiffness at the contact melted as she relaxed against him, surrendering herself to his movements and the quiet music. Surely, she decided, allowing both mind and body to float, everyone's entitled to a taste of heaven. Tonight I'm taking mine. Tomorrow will come, all too soon.

The night was magic, as if a fairy had granted her a wish, and the very briefness of it heightened her senses. She tucked all the sights and sensations into a corner of her mind to be treasured and sighed over when day broke the spell.

It was late when they stepped into the warm night, and though Adelia's eyes were heavy, she wished the evening were just beginning. Clinging to the last enchanted minutes, she made no objection when Travis drew her close to his side in the cab.

"Tired, Dee?" he murmured, his lips brushing the top of her head so lightly she was not sure she hadn't imagined it.

"No," she said on a sigh, thinking how right her head felt cushioned against his shoulder.

He laughed softly, his voice slow and warm, and his fingers stroked through the silk of her hair until her mind drifted into the world of half-dreams.

"Dee?" She heard her name but, loath to rouse herself from the heavenly comfort, she made a small murmur of protest. "We're back," Travis announced, lifting her chin with his finger.

"Back?" Her heavy lids opened, and she stared at the face so close to hers, dreams and reality mixed into confusion.

"At the hotel," he explained, brushing tumbled hair back from her face.

"Oh." She sat up, realizing the dream was over.

He was silent on the elevator ride to their floor, and Adelia used the time to regain her grip on reality. They moved to her door, and Travis removed her key from his pocket to unlock it as she raised her head to thank him. The smile she meant to accompany her thanks faded as she met his eyes. The concentrated, steady look caused her to step backward, only to find herself trapped against the doorframe, while he closed the distance without seeming to move at all. His hand slipped beneath the curtain of her hair, while he caressed her neck in a slow, lazy motion. They gazed silently at each other; then, very slowly, he lowered his head and pressed his mouth to hers in a kiss that was as soft as a summer breeze, unlike the others he had given and ultimately more devastating. She clung to the lapels of his jacket, trying to steady her world, but soon gave up all such efforts and moved her arms to encircle his neck, rising on her toes to meet him demand for demand.

His lips moved to trail along her face, brushing easily along cheeks and closed lids as if savoring the taste. Trembling heat was replaced by a new and poignant languor, a weak giddiness induced by a far more potent potion than champagne. Her hands moved to tangle in his hair as her body melted to his, submitting to whatever he would ask, willing to give whatever he would take.

She felt his hunger when his mouth took hers again, the hardness of his body as he pressed her more urgently against him, and with a moan of pleasure at the new demand, she drew him yet closer. The longing to be possessed, insistent and clamorous, raged through her like fire. She strained against him, her heart throbbing and echoing in her ears as she felt him devour what was offered, then demand more.

Abruptly he released her mouth, his hand moving to brush against her cheek and linger a moment, and she closed her eyes again, inviting his lips to claim hers.

"Good night, Dee," he murmured, and, giving her a nudge into the room, he closed the door between them.

Adelia stared at the smooth, empty panel, bringing her hands to burning cheeks. Stunned both by her unprecedented actions and by the sudden rejection, she found it impossible to move. She had offered, and he had refused. Even in her inexperience, she knew her willingness could not have been mistaken for anything other than full surrender. But he had not wanted her, not completely. Her own standards had dissolved in his arms, but he had walked away and left her alone. And how else could it be? she asked herself, shutting eyes tight on threatening moisture. I could never be anything to him but a groom for his horses. Someone who amuses him from time to time. He was only being kind to me, trying to show me a pleasant evening. She trembled once. *I should be content with that and stop searching for what can never be mine.* Glancing down at the soft folds of her dress, Adelia reminded herself she was not Cinderella, and in any case it was long past midnight.

They boarded the plane the next morning in a warm, light drizzle. Again, reporters hounded them. Adelia scurried up the ramp, leaving the men to deal with them. Shaking raindrops from her hair and her cream-colored skirt, she pressed her face to a window and watched Travis disengage himself from the press.

During the flight, she skimmed through a magazine, reluctant to enter into conversation. Travis's attitude toward her that morning had been casual, friendly, and vaguely preoccupied, and the stirring need in her that lingered from their previous evening made it a strain for her to mirror his mood.

When he disappeared into the forward cabin with Steve, she let out a deep breath and began to pace the lounge. What am I to do? she asked herself desperately. How can I control the way he makes me feel? I'll be making a fool of myself over him; he's bound to see the way I love him. Then he'll be feeling sorry for me, and I couldn't stand that. I'll just have to find a way to keep more distance between us.

Her gaze wandered over to her uncle, all thoughts of her problem fleeing her mind as she observed the unhealthy cast to his normally ruddy skin.

"Uncle Paddy." She moved to him, cupping his face in her hands and studying him carefully. "You're not well. What is it?"

"Nothing, Dee." The strain in his voice drew her brows together. "I'm just tired."

"You're like ice." She knelt down in front of him so that their faces were level. "You see a doctor the minute we get home. It won't be long now. I'll fetch you a cover and a cup of tea."

"Now, Dee, I'm just feeling my age." He stopped and grimaced in pain.

"What is it?" she demanded, hands already searching to comfort. "Where are you hurting?"

"Just a twinge." The words came out in jerks before he began to gasp for air.

"Uncle Paddy! Merciful heaven, Uncle Paddy!" She clutched at him as he collapsed, falling forward out of the chair and into her arms.

She was not even aware that she shouted for Travis

over and over, desperately, helplessly, as she lowered her uncle onto the floor. But suddenly he was there, brushing her hands aside, his head lowering to the stocky chest.

"Tell John to radio ahead for an ambulance," he called to Steve over his shoulder, his hands beginning to push in a steady rhythm on Paddy's chest. "He's had a heart attack."

With a moan, Adelia clutched Paddy's hand to her own heart as if to transfer her strength. "Travis, in the name of heaven—Travis, is he dying? Oh, please, he can't be dying."

"Stop it," he commanded sharply, the words as effective as a slap. "Pull yourself together. I can't deal with this and hysterics as well."

One breath came and went quickly, then she took several more, deep and steady, her hand clutching and unclutching convulsively over Paddy's. Slowly the hysteria was buried under a wall of control, and she began to stroke her uncle's head and speak in soft, reassuring tones, though she knew he probably couldn't hear her.

Seconds dragged and minutes crawled with Travis continually monitoring the unconscious man's pulse, only Adelia's murmurs breaking the silence. She felt the change in the plane's speed and the loss of altitude, heard the whine of the landing gear and felt the jerk of wheels on ground, but her flow of words continued, and she kept her uncle's hand firmly in hers.

She watched through a haze of unreality as paramedics worked on him before transferring him to the waiting ambulance. As she made to join them, Travis took her arm, telling her they would follow in the car. She went without protest, her mind and heart encased in the numbing ice of fear.

She responded only in vague monosyllables to his

attempts at consolation, and after a glance at her pale, waxen features, he concentrated on weaving through the traffic toward the hospital.

The long wait began in a small, cheerless lounge scattered with ancient magazines which some read to pass the time and others stared at in desperation. Adelia did neither, but sat, still as a stone, her hands gripped together in her lap, neither moving nor speaking as Travis paced the room like a caged tiger. Her mind was screaming in protest, searching for the power to pray as fear devoured her. Her control was tight, stretching at the seams like an ill-fitting coat as the minutes passed.

When at last a white-coated figure approached, Travis whirled and advanced on him. "You're Padrick Cunnane's family?" the doctor asked, glancing from the tall, powerful man to the small, pale woman.

"Yes." His answer was curt as he too glanced at Adelia. "What's going on? How is he?"

"He suffered a coronary—not a massive attack. He is conscious now, but his condition is aggravated by anxiety over someone named Dee."

Adelia brought her head up. "I'm Dee. Is he going to die?"

The doctor studied the pale, composed features and took a step closer to her. "We're doing all we can to stabilize his condition, but his own anxiety is a factor in his recovery. His concern is focused on you. I'm going to let you see him. You must do nothing to upset him; persuade him to relax." He turned back to the dark man whose eyes were fixed on the woman. "Are you Travis?" At his nod, the doctor continued. "He wants to see you too. Come with me."

Travis took Adelia's hand and lifted her from the chair, leading her after the retreating white coat.

"Five minutes," the doctor cautioned, and led them into the Cardiac Care Unit.

Her hand tightened in Travis's as she saw her uncle in the hospital bed, wires and tubes joining him to machines that whirled and buzzed. He was pale and drawn and suddenly old, and her mind screamed in revolt as she struggled for control.

"Dee." The voice was weak and unsteady, and she moved close to take his hand in hers.

"Uncle Paddy." Kissing the hand, she held it to her cheek. "Everything's going to be fine. They'll be taking good care of you, and soon you'll be home again."

"I want a priest, Dee."

"All right, don't worry." A cold hand gripped and squeezed her heart, and she felt the trembling start in her knees but forced it away.

"It's you I'm worried for. You can't be left all alone again, not again." His voice was rasping, and she soothed and murmured. "Travis…is Travis here?" He continued to fret, and she turned, fear shining from her eyes.

"Right here, Paddy." He moved to stand next to Adelia.

"You've got to take care of her for me, Travis. I'm giving her to you. She'll be all alone again if anything happens to me. Such a wee thing she is and so young. It's been too hard for her…. I should have been there for her before. I was going to make it up to her." He made a feeble gesture with his free hand. "I want your word you'll be taking care of her. I can trust you, Travis, with what's mine."

"I'll take care of her; you have my word." His answer was calm and steady, his hand closing over the two that were joined. "You don't have to worry about Dee. I'm going to marry her."

The relaxation in the taut face was visible, his breathing slowing. "You take care of my little Dee, then. I want to see the two of you married. Will you bring a priest here, and let me see it done?"

"I'll arrange it, but you'll have to relax and rest. Let the doctors do their job. Dee and I will be married right here this afternoon. All I need is a judge to sign a waiver of the two-day waiting period."

"Aye, I'll rest till you come back. Till you come back, Dee." She forced her lips into a smile and placed a kiss on his brow before she followed the doctor and Travis from the room. She whirled on him as soon as the door closed behind them.

"Not here," Travis commanded, gripping her arm. "Is there somewhere private we can talk?" he asked the doctor in calm tones. After directing them to an office, the doctor closed the door and discreetly left them alone.

Chapter Seven

Adelia jerked out of Travis's hold as the door shut, fear and despair bubbling into fury. "How could you do that? How could you tell Uncle Paddy you were going to marry me? How could you lie to him that way?"

"I didn't lie, Adelia," Travis returned evenly. "I have every intention of marrying you."

"What are you thinking of, saying such things?" she continued as if he had not spoken. "It's cruel, with him lying there sick and helpless and trusting you. You had no right to make such a promise. You'll break his heart, you—"

"Get hold of yourself," Travis commanded, taking her shoulders and administering a brisk shake. "I told him what he needed to hear, and by God you'll do what he wants if it helps save him."

"I'll not be a party to such a cruel lie."

The grip on her shoulders increased, but she was

beyond physical pain. "Doesn't he mean anything to you? Are you so selfish and hardheaded that you can't make a small sacrifice to help him?" She flinched as if he had struck her and turned blindly away, her hands gripping the back of a chair. "We'll stand in that room this afternoon, and we'll be married, and you'll make him believe it's what you want. When we know he's strong enough, you can get a divorce and end it."

She drew her hands over her eyes, pain washing over her in turbulent waves. *Uncle Paddy lying there half dead—Travis telling me we're marrying and divorcing in the same breath. Oh, I need someone to tell me what to do,* she thought frantically.

To be his wife, to belong to him—she'd wanted it so badly that she hadn't even dared to think of it, and now he was telling her that it was going to happen, that it *had* to happen. She was hurt beyond words. It would have been easier to go through life without him than to be his wife for an hour without his love. *Divorce*—he had said it so easily. He was talking of divorce before he had even put the ring on her finger. Taking a deep breath, she tried to force herself to think clearly, but she was too overcome by the bleak realization that he was not talking of a real marriage, a marriage of love, that he didn't want her for herself, but rather for her uncle's sake. There must be another way. There had to be another way. She swallowed painfully to steady her voice, "I'm Catholic. I can't get a divorce," she said dully.

"An annulment, then."

She stared at him in horrified silence, "An annulment?"

"Yes, an annulment. It should not be any problem if the marriage isn't consummated. It will simply be a matter of a little paperwork." He spoke in calm, businesslike tones, and her hands tightened on the chair as she attempted to fight her way through to reason. "For Pete's sake, Dee," he said impatiently, "can't you go through the motions of a ceremony for Paddy's sake? It won't cost you anything. It could make the difference between his living and dying."

He took her shoulders again, spinning her around, checking his anger as he studied the transparent glow to her skin, the fear in her eyes that stared back at him. He could feel the trembling begin under his hands and watched as she shut her eyes and tried to stem it. He muttered an oath, then drew her against him and wrapped his arms around her. "I'm sorry, Dee. Shouting at you is hardly going to make it any easier, is it? Come on, sit down." Leading her to a sofa, he sat beside her, keeping her close inside his arms. "You've been hanging on to control for too long; have a good cry. Then we'll talk."

"No, I don't cry. I never cry. It doesn't help." She held herself rigid in his grasp, but he continued to hold her close. "Please, let me go." She felt her control slipping and struggled against the arms that would not give way. "I have to think. If I just knew what to do…" Her breath came in short gasps, the trembling no longer controllable, and her hands clutched at his shirtfront to keep from falling. "Travis, I'm so afraid."

She burst into violent sobs, and his arms tightened around her. Once the tears escaped, she could not stop them. Held in check for more than a dozen lonely years, they now flowed freely down her face pressed into Travis's chest. He kept silent, one hand stroking her hair, and let the storm run its course.

The sobs lost their force, subsiding to soft whimpering,

until she lay quiet in his arms, empty and spent. She gave one long, shuddering sigh. "I'll do whatever you think has to be done."

How Travis arranged the paperwork so quickly, she never questioned. She had been too numb to deal with technicalities. The only stand she had made was to refuse to leave the hospital even for a quick rest or a meal. Determinedly, she had planted herself in the waiting room and refused to budge.

She signed her name on the license where she was told, greeted the slender young priest who would make her Travis's wife, and accepted a handful of flowers from a friendly nurse who claimed a woman couldn't be a bride without a bouquet. She smiled at this, a small, frozen smile that hurt her cheeks, knowing she was not really a bride. Legally she would bear the name of the man she loved, but the vows they would exchange would mean nothing to him. The words and motions were only a charade to bring comfort to a sick man.

They stood side by side in the stark room, surrounded by machines, the air heavy with the smell of medicine, and became husband and wife. Adelia repeated the priest's words in a calm, clear voice and looked blankly at the signet ring Travis slipped on her finger before closing her fist over it. It hung loose on her finger and lay like a stone on her heart. In less than ten minutes it was all over, and she accepted his light, brief kiss without demur.

Adelia Cunnane Grant bent over and kissed her uncle's brow. He smiled up at her, his eyes lighting with a suggestion of their usual merriment. She knew in that instant that Travis had been right.

"Little Dee," he murmured, seeking her hand and

clinging to it. "You'll be happy now. Travis is a good man."

She forced a smile and patted his cheek. "Aye, Uncle Paddy. You'll rest now, and we'll be able to bring you home soon."

"I'll rest," he agreed, and his eyes raised above her head to meet Travis's. "Treat her with care, lad…she's a Thoroughbred."

They drove home in silence. The sun broke through patches of clouds to filter on the road. Adelia watched the play of light and kept her mind a blank. Pulling up in front of the main house, Travis broke the heavy silence.

"I called ahead and informed my housekeeper of the wedding. She'll have prepared your room by now. Your things have been brought over."

She frowned. "I'm not—"

"For the time being," he cut in, his eyes narrowing, "you are my wife, and as such you will live in my house. We'll keep separate bedrooms," he added in a tone that caused her mouth to shut quickly. "We will, however, maintain the outward appearance of a married couple. There is no reason for the present that anyone other than you and I know of this arrangement. Explanations now would only complicate matters."

"I see. You're right, of course."

He sighed at the strain in her voice and went on in gentler tones. "I'll make it as easy on you as possible, Dee. I only ask that you play your part; otherwise you'll be free to do as you please. There'll be no need for you to work."

"I can't work with the horses?" Adelia broke in, eyes widening in dismay. "But, Travis—"

"Adelia, listen to me." He cupped her face in his hand. "You can do as you like. You don't even know what that means, do you?" His brows drew together at her blank, bewildered face. "If you want to work with the horses, you're free to do so, but not as my employee, as my wife. You can spend your time lounging around the country club or cleaning out stalls—it's up to you."

"All right." Slowly, she unclenched the fists that were tight in her lap. "I'll do my best to make it easy on you as well. I know you were right to do this for Uncle Paddy, and I'm grateful to you."

He stared at her for another moment, then shrugged and slipped from the car.

When they entered the house, a plump, gray-haired woman bustled into the hall to greet them, wiping her hands on a full, white apron.

"Hannah, this is Adelia, my wife."

Warm hazel eyes inspected Adelia and smiled in approval. "Welcome, Mrs. Grant. It's about time a lovely young thing lured my Travis to the altar." Adelia murmured something she hoped was appropriate. "I'm sorry to hear about Paddy; we're all fond of him." The treacherous tears started again, and Adelia closed her eyes against them. "Oh, the poor thing's dead on her feet. Travis, take her up; the room's ready for her."

She started the climb up the staircase, which seemed to take on the proportions of Mount Olympus. Without a word, Travis swept her into his arms and carried her up the remaining steps and down a long, carpeted hallway. Entering a bedroom, he crossed the floor and laid her on a huge four-poster bed.

"I'm sorry." She lifted her hand and dropped it again. There seemed to be nothing further to say.

He sat next to her and brushed the hair from her cheeks.

"Adelia, when will you learn weakness is not always a

flaw? Darned Irish stubbornness," he muttered, frowning down at her. "I'd swear nothing else kept you on your feet this long. There hasn't been a whisper of color in your cheeks for the past six hours."

She stared up at him, wanting to pull him down to her and feel the comfort of his warmth. He turned abruptly and moved to a large cherrywood wardrobe.

"I don't know where Hannah put your night clothes." Pulling open the double doors, he exposed the meager contents. "Good heavens, is this all you have?"

She tried to snap at him, but found gathering the strength too great an effort. Moving over to a mirrored triple dresser, he began opening drawers, muttering and swearing, and she lay back and watched him, too weary to be embarrassed that he should handle her clothes with such familiarity.

He pulled out a plain, high-necked cotton gown and, after a brief disparaging scrutiny, brought it to her. "Tomorrow, for heaven's sake, go shopping and buy some clothes."

"Don't you order me about, Travis Grant." She sat up, unable to keep quiet any longer, and snapped at him with a ghost of her usual spirit.

He stared down at her without expression. "While we're married, Adelia, we'll be expected to socialize, and you'll have to dress properly. We'll see to it tomorrow. Now, can you manage to change by yourself, or do you need some help?"

Snatching the gown from his hands, she spoke stiffly. "I can manage very well."

"Good. Change and get some rest. You won't do Paddy any good if you make yourself ill." Without waiting for her reply, he turned and strode from the room, shutting the door behind him.

Too tired to appreciate the beauty of the light, airy room, she slipped off the skirt and blouse which had served as her wedding dress and pulled the cotton nightgown over her head. Folding down the mint-green spread, she crawled between the smooth sheets and fell instantly into the deep, dreamless sleep of exhaustion.

The birds woke her, as was their habit, chattering and chirping outside the window. Opening her eyes, she focused on the unfamiliar surroundings and remembered. She relaxed the fist that had remained tight over her wedding ring throughout the night, while her eyes made a slow survey of the room. She had thought her bedroom in the garage house large, but she estimated this would hold two rooms that size. The walls were muted green-and-white striped paper, trimmed with dark woodwork. The furniture was cherry, both the large wardrobe and dresser in which Travis had rummaged the evening before, and a small writing desk, two night tables and a small pie-crust table which served a tufted-back chair. On the small table was a vase bursting with fresh flowers. Their scent drifted to her as she sat up in bed, hugging her knees close. She sighed as she gazed at the tall French windows which led to the balcony, thinking she had never seen such a lovely room. *How happy I could be here if only Uncle Paddy was well, and Travis...* She tried to clear her mind of such negative thoughts. Thrusting back the covers, she jumped out of bed.

After showering and dressing in her only remaining skirt, she ventured downstairs, hoping she could locate the kitchen in the strange house which was now her home.

"Good morning, Dee." Travis appeared from a room off the downstairs hall which she later learned was his office. "Feeling better?"

"Aye," she answered, suddenly shy and uncertain in front of the man who was her husband. "I don't know when I've slept so long."

"You were exhausted." She kept herself still as he lifted her chin and examined her face like a parent seeking to find signs of ill health in a child. "Your color's back," he said at length and smiled.

"I'm fine." She managed to remain passive as his hand continued to hold her chin. "I was wondering if I could call the hospital…and see if Uncle Paddy—" Her hands fluttered, then clung together in front of her.

"I've already called; his condition has stabilized." His hands moved to rest on her shoulders. "He spent a peaceful night."

A tremor passed through her. She shut her eyes and buried her face against Travis's chest. After a moment, she felt his arms encircle her lightly. "Oh, Travis, I thought he was going to die. I was afraid we would lose him."

He held her away until she tilted her head to look up at him. "He's going to be all right, with a little time and care, and no worries." His features relaxed. "Of course, when he gets home, he'll have to slow down. We'll have to bully him into it."

"Aye." Her smile was like the stars through the clouds. "But there's two of us."

"So there are," he murmured, then tousled her hair. "I imagine you're starving. I couldn't wake you for dinner last night."

"I feel like I haven't eaten in a week." With a sigh, she pushed at the hair he had just ruffled. "If you'll show me the kitchen, I'll start breakfast."

"Hannah's seeing to it," he informed her, taking her arm and leading her into a large dining room. Noticing the expression on her face, he whispered confidentially in her ear as he pulled out a chair, "Don't worry, I've been eating her cooking all my life."

"Oh, I didn't mean—I meant no disrespect. It's only that I'm not used to having someone fix my meals." Her expression bordered on horror, and he leaned back in his chair and laughed.

"Don't look so stricken, Dee. Hannah will think I'm beating you already."

"Well, I wouldn't want you to think that I meant…" She fumbled for something to say which would release her from her awkwardness. "The room you gave me is lovely. I want to thank you."

"I'm glad you like it."

At his careless response, she was grateful for Hannah's entrance with a steaming breakfast platter.

"Good morning, Mrs. Grant. I hope you're feeling better after a good night's rest." She set the platter on the table and Adelia smiled up at her.

"Thank you, I feel fine." She was careful not to start at her new title.

"Hungry though, I'll be bound." Nodding, she studied the pixielike face. "Travis told me you ate next to nothing yesterday, so I'll expect you to do full justice to your breakfast."

"You should be warned, Dee, not to trifle with Hannah," Travis put in from across the table. "She can be ferocious. Personally, she terrifies me."

"Don't you listen to his nonsense, Mrs. Grant." She sent Travis a scowl before giving her attention back to Adelia. "You'll be busy for a while with Paddy in the hospital, but once you're settled, you let me know how you want things done. For now, if it's agreeable, I'll just plan your meals around your visits to the hospital."

"I—whatever you think best."

"We'll have plenty of time to talk about it," the house-keeper concluded. "Now, you get to your breakfast while it's hot." With this she bustled from the room.

Adelia listened to Travis's breakfast conversation, answering only when it was required, while she slowly took in her surroundings. The dining room was large with dark wainscoting and elegantly patterned wallpaper. The furniture was heavy, gleaming oak. Everywhere was the glow of silver and glimmer of crystal.

"Travis," she said suddenly, and his brows rose in acknowledgment as he sipped his coffee. "I don't fit into all this. I haven't the way or the experience to know what's expected of me. I don't want to be an embarrassment to you, and I'm mortally afraid I'll do or say something horrible, and—"

"Adelia." The one word stopped her rambling. She saw from his expression that she had already made a mistake. From the way his face was set, she waited for him to rant at her, but when he spoke, his voice was calm and precise. "You will not embarrass me, you could not embarrass me. Relax and be what you are, that's what's expected of you."

They lapsed into silence. Adelia toyed with the remainder of her eggs. "By the way," Travis began, and she raised her eyes and saw he was smiling, "you've had your picture in the paper."

"My picture?"

"Yes." His smile widened at her frowning expression. "Two pictures, as a matter of fact. There's one of you and Steve with the two of you sitting on the paddock fence, and there's one of you and me taken after the Belmont Stakes."

Color flooded her cheeks as she realized the contents

of the second picture. "I don't know why they kept following me around with their cameras and their pencils."

"I can't imagine," Travis returned, his lips curving again. "It appears that the press has had a splendid time speculating about the romances of my attractive groom...."

Her eyes widened, and the color ebbed and flowed again. "Are you meaning... Oh, what a passel of nonsense! Steve and I are friends, and you and I..." She faltered, sputtered and fell into excruciating silence.

"Married, Adelia, is what we are, friends or not." With what she thought was a very odd smile, he drained his coffee and rose. "I don't suppose it will sound like such a passel of nonsense to the press when our current relationship is leaked to them. I can keep it out of the papers for a while, but we'll have to deal with it sooner or later.... I take it you're done since you've been playing with your fork for the last ten minutes." Securing her arm, he brought her to her feet. "Now, if you'll take that frown off your face, I'll drive you to the hospital."

Any anxiety Adelia still harbored was dispelled by the appearance of her uncle. The color in his cheeks, which had appeared a ghastly gray the day before, was now closer to his normal, ruddy hue. His eyes twinkled as Travis brought her into the room. His voice was weak rather than booming, but steady and unforced. When he complained about being hooked up to blasted, noisy machines, her concern melted into laughter, and, kissing the hand she held in hers, she felt the last vestige of tension dissolve.

After a short visit, Travis drew her into the hall. "You won't be able to stay too long this time. The doctor says he tires easily and needs his rest. That, and seeing you, is the best medicine he can get."

"I won't tire him, Travis," she promised. "He's looking so much better, I can hardly believe my eyes. I'll only stay a little while more. As soon as I see he's tiring, I'll go."

He looked down at her smiling face, his fingers tangling absently with the ends of her hair. "I have to get back now, but Trish will be along soon to take you shopping." His hand dropped, and he stared past her as if suddenly preoccupied. "She'll know best what you need, and if you like she can bring you back here for a while longer this afternoon."

"It's kind of you to be doing all this, Travis." She touched his arm to bring his attention back to her. "I don't know how to repay you for all that you've done already."

"It's nothing." He shrugged off her thanks and, drawing out his wallet, handed her some bills. "I've made arrangements for you to charge whatever you need. Trish will be there to see to the details, but you'll need some cash as well."

"But, Travis, it's so much, I can't…"

"Don't argue, just take it." He closed her hands over the bills in a final, impatient gesture. "Give it to Trish to hold for you, and for heaven's sake, Dee," he added with exasperation, "buy yourself a purse. I'll see you this evening."

He strode down the long corridor, leaving Adelia staring after him.

Chapter Eight

When Trish arrived she greeted Paddy with an affectionate kiss and told him firmly that anyone could see he was
faking and enjoying being the center of attention. After
a brief visit, she hurried Adelia out into the corridor and
hugged her with enthusiasm.

"I'm so happy about you and Travis." Her eyes shone
with affection. Adelia began to feel the first weight of
guilt. "Now I have the little sister I always wanted."
Adelia was treated to yet another hug. "Jerry sends his
best." She referred to her husband, her face wreathed in
smiles. "The twins went wild when I told them that Dee
was now their aunt. They claim that makes them Irish
and soon they'll be fey, too."

Adelia responded with smiles and agreeable murmurs,
hating herself for the deception and wishing with all her
heart that she could confide in the woman whom she felt

was a true friend. But she had given Travis her word and she would keep it.

Hooking her arm through Adelia's, Trish began to stroll toward the elevator. "Travis has given me firm instructions to see that you buy a complete wardrobe." She grinned with obvious pleasure as the elevator began its slow descent to the ground floor. "Of course I told him that I would be more than happy to follow orders and spend his money with abandon."

"He said you should hold this for me."

Dee handed Trish the wad of bills, which she accepted and placed absently in her tan leather bag. "This is going to be fun."

Adelia smiled faintly.

If Adelia was under the impression that this shopping expedition would follow along the lines of her first, she was soon enlightened to the contrary. Trish ignored department stores for the more exclusive shops. Adelia began to feel as if she were caught in the backlash of a tropical storm. She was whirled through shops while Trish made selections, dismissed or accepted articles with a nod or murmur to the sales clerks. Purchases mounted into an alarming mountain, leaving Adelia dizzy and confused.

Evening dresses that shimmered and flowed, sportswear Adelia considered suitable for royalty, soft, cobwebby lingerie that seemed too fragile to be real; all were tried on, inspected thoroughly by Trish's critical eye, then approved or rejected. Italian shoes and handbags, French scarves and negligees were included with a nod for foreign craftsmanship.

"Trish, surely Travis didn't mean for me to buy all this," Adelia objected, looking uneasily at the stacks of boxes and bags. "One person couldn't live long enough to wear all those clothes."

"You'd be surprised," Trish murmured absently as she surveyed a long, sweeping evening gown in brilliant green silk. "You'll be doing a lot of traveling, and there are parties and official functions…" Her voice trailed off as she held the gown in front of Adelia and narrowed her eyes in consideration. "Travis was very specific. He told me to see to it that you have everything necessary and to ignore the arguments you were sure to give me. That is precisely what I'm doing. Here." She thrust the gown into Adelia's hands. "Go try this on. Green is your color."

"We can't buy anything else," Adelia stated flatly, attempting to hold her ground. "There'll be no room in the car for us when the packages are put in."

"Then, little sister, we'll hire a van." Giving her a shove into the dressing room, Trish gave her attention to a white linen blouse.

Late that afternoon, Adelia stared at the packages that lay piled high on her bed. With a weary sigh, she turned and left the room. Hannah greeted her as she stood in the downstairs hall, unsure whether she should stay in the house or seek out Travis at the stables.

"Mrs. Grant, how's Paddy?"

"He's looking just wonderful. I left him only an hour ago."

"You poor thing, you look all in."

"I've been shopping. I think cleaning out the entire stable would be less of a chore."

Hannah chuckled. "A cup of tea is what you need. Just sit down and I'll bring you one."

"Hannah." She stopped the plump woman before she could bustle away. "Could I…would you mind if I came into the kitchen and had one with you?" She made a small, helpless gesture with her hands. "I'm not used to being waited on."

The round face brightened, and a motherly arm slipped around Adelia's waist. "Just you come with me, missy. We'll have a nice cup of tea and a little chat."

It was there Travis found them together an hour later. He stood in the doorway watching in amused amazement as Adelia and Hannah worked on dinner preparations, chattering like lifelong partners.

"Well, well, well, a miracle in this day and age." Two heads turned toward him as he gave his brief, charming grin. "I never thought I'd live to see the day when you'd let anyone work in your kitchen, Hannah." He glanced from his housekeeper to the small woman at her side. "What kind of Irish charm did you use on her, Dee?"

"Just her charming self, you young rascal," Hannah stated with great dignity. "Now, missy—" she removed the vegetable parer from Adelia's hand "—you just run along now and keep that man out from under my feet. He's always been a nuisance in the kitchen."

Travis grinned again, serenely unperturbed. "Come out on the terrace, Dee," he invited and captured her hand. "It's too nice to stay indoors."

He led her out through wide French doors and onto the smooth stone surface of the terrace. The sweet scent of plants and flowers filled the June evening. The sun still cast a warm golden light, scattering shadows on the stone.

"So, Dee," he began, seating her in a striped cushioned chair and dropping down in an identical one across from her, "did you get everything you needed?"

"Everything?" she repeated. She closed her eyes and shuddered. "Never in my life have I ever seen so many clothes, much less put them on. Trying on this, taking off that." Opening her eyes again, she met his wide smile with a look of disdain. "You won't be smiling when you have to build another room to hold them all. Your sister is a stubborn woman, Travis Grant. She just kept tossing things at me and shoving me into dressing rooms. I couldn't make her listen to reason."

"I thought Trish might be helpful."

"Helpful?" She gave a long-suffering sigh. "I felt like I was being blown about by a whirlwind. Packages growing like a great mountain, and Trish smiling and finding something else. She had a fine time," she added, mystified.

"Yes, I imagine she did. I don't see her having much trouble filling out your wardrobe." He smiled at the picture and leaned back in his chair.

"Travis," she began after a small pause, "whatever will I do with all those things?"

"You might try wearing them," he suggested. "It's the usual procedure."

"That's fine for a time. I understand I can't go about in my old clothes with things as they are now. But after, when…" She stumbled and searched for the right words. "When things are back as they were before, I—"

"The clothes are yours, Adelia," he interrupted with a quick gesture of his hand. "You'll keep them whatever happens. I certainly have no use for them." Rising, he paced the length of the terrace and stared out over the smooth expanse of lawn.

Adelia sat silently, concerned by his anger and bewildered over how she had caused it. She stood and approached him, laying a tentative hand on his arm. "I'm sorry, Travis. That sounded ungrateful; I didn't mean it to. Everything's happening so fast. I don't want to take advantage of what you're doing for me."

"One can hardly call it taking advantage when it's like pulling teeth to get you to accept anything." His shoulders moved and he turned to face her. "Adelia," he said with a sigh somewhere between impatience and amusement, "you are so artless."

She did not question the ambiguity of his words, so relieved was she that his anger had faded and he was smiling at her again.

"I have something for you." Reaching into his pocket, he drew out a small box. "My signet ring was fine in an emergency, but it looks big enough to fit on your wrist."

"Oh." She found nothing else to say as she opened the box and found a small band studded with winking diamonds and glowing emeralds.

He removed the large, masculine ring from her finger and replaced it with the jeweled wedding band. "I'd say that suits a bit better."

"It fits," she murmured inadequately, overcome with the longing to throw her arms around him and cry out her love.

"I've studied those hands enough to make an educated guess as to your ring size." He spoke lightly and, dropping her hand, moved back to his chair.

Swallowing the obstruction in her throat, she followed him. "Travis." She stood in front of his chair, feeling the strangeness of looking down at him. "Travis, you're doing all the giving, and I have nothing for you. I want to… Is there nothing I can do for you? Is there nothing you want from me?"

He met her eyes with a long, unfathomable stare until she thought he would not speak at all. "For now, Dee," he said at length, "the best thing you can do for me is to accept what's given and not question it."

She sighed at his answer. "All right, Travis, if it pleasures you."

He stood and took her hand, a finger running over her wedding band. "Yes, it pleasures me. Come inside and we'll eat, and I'll tell you how Majesty sulked for you today."

The next two weeks passed quickly, Adelia's days full between the hospital and the stables. Paddy was moved into a regular hospital room. No longer attached to machines, he improved daily, complaining vigorously about being stuck in bed and poked with needles. The easy friendliness of the men at the stables and the soothing routine of riding and grooming brought a sense of normalcy back to Adelia's life, and at times she almost forgot she was Mrs. Travis Grant.

Travis was kind and casually affectionate, speaking of Paddy's recovery and on the general topic of horses when they took meals together. He left Adelia free to pursue whatever project she chose, making no demands, his attitude tolerant, generous and distant. She was aware of a subtle change in their relationship, and she found it did not please her. He never raised his voice or criticized, and he never touched her in any way unless strictly necessary. She wished fervently that he would yell at her or shake her, or do something to lose his cool, composed manner. Their relationship was now far less personal than it had been when they had been employer and employee.

She was returning to the house one afternoon, wondering if Travis had returned from a business appointment, when she stopped and gaped at a large, dirty gray mound of fur exploring a bed of marigolds. After a careful study, she concluded that under the grubby fur was a dog of rather alarming size.

"I wouldn't do that if I were you," she said in a quiet voice that had the dog's head jerking up. "Now, don't be running off. I won't hurt you." The dog hesitated, eyeing her warily, and she kept the distance between them and continued to speak. "It's just that I've seen Travis's gardener—a terrifying man he is. And one that wouldn't take kindly to anyone digging at his flowers." She crouched down, and they studied each other eye to eye. "Are you lost, then, or just roaming? I can see by your eyes you're hungry. I've been hungry myself a time or two. Wait here," she ordered and stood. "I'll fetch you something."

Entering the kitchen, she commandeered a large hunk of roast beef. The whine of the vacuum cleaner was audible from the living room, and, deciding it would be foolish to disturb Hannah and vowing to apologize to her after the deed was done, Adelia slipped back outside.

"It's prime beef, my lad, and from the looks of you, you've not seen its kind before." She placed the offering on the grass and stepped back a few paces.

He came forward slowly at first, eyes shifting from the beef to his benefactor until either his confidence or his hunger grew, and he threw himself on the unexpected meal. She watched him polish off what would have fed three hungry men, finding enormous pleasure in his appetite.

"Well, now, you've made a pig of yourself, and that's the truth, and you don't look a bit ashamed." She grinned and watched the long tail thump in agreement. "Pleased with yourself, are you?" Before she could move, she found herself flat on her back, trapped under a hundred pounds of appreciation, her face being drenched by a large wet tongue. "Get off me, you great hairy brute!" Laughing, she pushed to no avail and tried to turn her face from the moisture. "Surely there's not a rib that's not cracked, and it's God's truth you've not had a bath since the day you were born."

After much pleading and wriggling, she managed to release herself, staggered to her feet, and surveyed the damage. Her shirt and jeans were covered with dirt, her arms smeared with it. She pushed at her disordered hair and stared down at the dog that sat at her feet, his tongue hanging out in adoration.

"We'll both be needing a bath now. Well—" She let out a deep breath, tilted her head, and considered. "You wait here, and I'll see what can be done about you. It might be best if you were cleaned up a bit before I introduce you."

On the way back to the house, she paused on the terrace to brush at the dirt that covered her.

"Dee, what happened? Were you thrown? Are you hurt?" Travis rushed to her, his hands claiming her shoulders, then moving to stroke her face. She shook her head, thrown off balance by the frantic tone of his voice.

"No, I'm not hurt. Travis, you mustn't touch me— you'll get your suit filthy." She tried to take a step away, only to be caught closer.

"The devil with the suit!" His voice was edged with anger as he pressed her against him, one hand cradling her head.

The small intimacy after so many days of impersonal distance swamped her with pleasure, and her arms encircled his waist before she could lecture herself on the wisdom of the action. She felt his lips tarry in her hair, and she thought, with a brief flash of joy, that if she could only have this much of him from time to time, she would be content.

Suddenly, one hand gripped her shoulder while the other tilted her face back, and she saw temper flame in his face. "What in heaven's name have you done to yourself?"

"I haven't done anything to myself," she said with a show of dignity, shaking off his hand. "We've company." She gestured to the lawn.

His eyes moved past her, narrowed, then returned. "Adelia, what in the name of heaven is *that?*"

"It's a dog, Travis, though I wasn't sure myself at first. The poor thing was half starving. That's why—" she paused and braced herself for the confession "—that's why I gave him the roast beef."

"You fed him?" Travis asked in low, even tones.

"Surely you wouldn't begrudge the poor thing a bit of food. I—"

"I don't care a whit about the food, Adelia." He shook her briefly. "Don't you have any more sense than to fool with a strange dog? You could have been bitten."

Straightening, she glared at the censure in his voice. "I know what I'm about, and I was careful. He needed food, so I gave it to him—the same as I'd give it to anyone who needed it. And as for that, he hasn't a thought in his head about biting anyone." Glancing over, she watched the dog's tail begin to thump the ground again. "There—" she pointed triumphantly "—you see."

"I see it appears you've made another conquest. Now," he said, and turned her firmly to face him directly. "Just how did you get in this condition?"

"Oh, well." She looked up at Travis, back to the dog, and back to Travis again. "You see, after he'd finished eating, he was overcome with gratitude, and he—well, he forgot himself for a minute and knocked me down and sort of thanked me in his way. He's a bit dirty—as you can see."

"He knocked you down?" Travis repeated, incredulously.

At his tone, Adelia hurried on. "He's very affectionate, and he didn't mean any harm. Really, Travis, don't be angry with him. See how pretty he is, sitting there now." She glanced over at the dog and saw he was smart enough to blink soulful eyes in Travis's direction. "I told him to wait, and that's just what he's doing. He only wants a bit of affection."

Travis turned back and gave Adelia a long look. "I'm getting the impression you intend to keep him."

"Well, I don't know about keeping him, exactly." She dropped her eyes from him, stared at a spot of dirt on Travis's jacket, and brushed it away.

"What's his name?"

"Finnegan," she responded immediately, then, seeing she had fallen into the trap, looked up frowning.

"Finnegan?" Travis repeated with a sober nod. "How did you come by that."

"He reminds me of Father Finnegan back in Skibbereen, oversized and clumsy but with much inner dignity."

"I see." He moved over, crouched down, and inspected Finnegan. To Adelia's relief, the dog remembered his manners.

When Travis returned to her, she moistened her lips and launched into her campaign. "I'll take care of him, Travis; he won't be any trouble. I won't let him come in the house and get in Hannah's way."

"There's no need to use your eyes, Adelia." At her bewildered frown, he laughed and tugged her hair. "Lord help the world if you ever realize what you're doing. You're perfectly free to keep him if that's what you want."

"Oh, I do! Thank you, Travis—"

"There are, however, two conditions," he interrupted before she could finish being grateful. "One, that you teach him not to knock you down; he's every bit as big as you are. And two, that he has a bath." He glanced over at Finnegan and shook his head. "Or several baths."

"I think I'm due for one myself." She brushed again without success at the clinging dirt, then lifted her face with a smile. The smile wavered as she found Travis looking down at her strangely.

"You know, Dee, I'm tempted to stuff you in my pocket where I won't have to worry about you."

"I'm small," she agreed, finding it suddenly difficult to breathe, "but I think I'm rather too big for that."

"Your size is intimidating."

She frowned, wondering what he could find intimidating about a bare five feet two. His hand wandered through her hair, gently for a moment; then, tousling it with casual friendliness, he added, "I believe it would be easier if you didn't continually look fifteen instead of twenty-three…. I guess I had better change my clothes before I give you a hand bathing that mountain."

As her marriage approached its third week, Adelia sat in her uncle's hospital room, smiling at him as he spoke with excitement of his discharge scheduled for the following day.

"Anyone would think they'd been torturing you and starving you to death, Uncle Paddy."

"Oh, no, it's a fine place, with good and kind people," he protested. "But a hospital's for the sick and never have I felt better in my life."

"You are better, and it makes me happier than I can say. But—" she paused and gave him a stern look "—you've still got to rest for a while and do as the doctors tell you. You're coming home to stay with Travis and me for a few days, till you can get by on your own."

"Now, Dee, I can't do that," Paddy objected, patting her hand. "You two should be off on your honeymoon, not worrying about the likes of me."

With a great deal of self-control, she managed not to wince at the word *honeymoon* and went on in calm but firm tones. "You'll be coming back with us, and that's the end of it. I didn't even have to ask—Travis suggested it himself."

Lying back against the pillows, Paddy smiled. "Aye, he would. Travis is a fine man."

"That he is," Adelia agreed with a sigh. She forced a bright smile and continued. "He's fond of you, Uncle Paddy. I knew as soon as I saw the two of you together."

"Aye," he murmured. "Travis and I go back a long way. Just a lad he was when I came to work for his father. Poor motherless child, so solemn and straight he was."

Adelia's mind wandered as she tried to picture Travis as a small boy, wondering if he was tall even then.

"Stuart Grant was a hard man," Paddy went on. "He ran the lad harder than the horses he raised. Trish he left to Hannah, barely showing the girl a passing interest, but the boy he wanted molded in his image. Always giving orders, with never a kind word or a dab of affection.

"I found myself taking the lad in, telling him stories and making games out of the work we did." He grinned, lost in memory. "'Paddy's Shadow,' the hands called him, 'cause he took to following me about whenever his father wasn't there. He worked hard, and he knew the horses even then. A fine, good lad he was, but the old man couldn't see it. Always finding fault. I wondered sometimes when he grew older why he didn't lay the old man out, goodness knows he was big enough, and the temper was there. But he took the abuse the old man handed him and only looked at him with his eyes so cold." Paddy paused and let out a long breath.

"Travis was away at college when the old man passed on…that would be about ten years ago. He stood there looking down at the grave, and I went over and laid my hand on his shoulder. 'I'm sorry about your father, lad,' says I, and he turned and looked down at me. 'He was never my father, Paddy,' says he, just as calm as you please. 'You've been my father since I was ten years old. If you hadn't been there, I'd have left a long time ago and never looked back.'"

The room was suddenly silent. Adelia gripped the hand that lay in hers tighter as Paddy's eyes grew moist with memory. "And now the two of you are together, I couldn't have wished it any better."

"You'll stay with him, Uncle Paddy, always, no matter what? You'll promise me that?"

He turned to her, surprised by the urgency in her tone. "Of course, little Dee. Where else would I be going?"

Chapter Nine

The following evening, after Paddy was comfortably settled into his room in the main house, Travis announced plans for a party.

"It's expected after Majesty's win, but with Paddy's heart attack it's had to be postponed." He swirled a glass of after-dinner brandy, his eyes sweeping over her, resting for a moment on her hair shimmering on the shoulders of her Nile blue dress. "Our marriage has, of course, leaked to the press, and it will seem odd if we don't have some sort of gathering where you can meet some of my friends and business associates."

"Aye," Adelia agreed, unconsciously nibbling on her lip as she turned to gaze out the window. "And so they can get a look at me."

"That too," he answered in solemn tones. "Don't worry, Dee: as long as you don't trip over your feet and fall on your face you should get by fairly well."

She whirled around to rage at him that she wasn't exactly a clumsy fool, but his good-natured grin stopped her. "Thank you very much, Master Grant." She smiled back at him. "It's a great comfort you are to me."

She gasped out loud at the length of the list Travis gave her for the projected reception. There couldn't be less than a hundred, she estimated, staring at the paper.

"You've nothing to worry about," he assured her. "Hannah will handle the details. You're only expected to make polite conversation."

The attempt at reassurance hurt her pride. "I'll have you know I'm not a complete cabbagehead, Travis Grant. I'm well capable of helping Hannah, and I won't be making a fool of myself in front of your fancy friends."

"You're the one who said she was afraid of making a fool of herself, not me," Travis reminded her reasonably.

"It's not what I said that matters," she concluded with her own brand of logic. "It's what I'm saying." Tossing her head, she turned and stalked into the kitchen.

Despite her proud claims, Adelia found herself terrified on the evening of the party. There had been no time for nervousness in the days before; she had been too busy with plans and preparations. But now, alone in her room, with only the prospect of dressing ahead of her, she began to feel the first flutter of anxiety.

She chose the green silk gown that Trish had insisted she buy and slipped it carefully over her head. Its classic lines accentuated her softly rounded figure; its deeply scooped neckline revealed a teasing hint of her firm breasts. The silk glowed against the creamy health of her skin. She arranged her hair on top of her head, trying for a more sophisticated style, but gave up in disgust and allowed it to fall loose and full to her shoulders, a fiery auburn waterfall.

Voices were audible in the living room as she descended the stairs. She took several deep breaths before joining Travis and Paddy.

Travis broke off what he had been saying as she entered the room. He rose from his chair. She sought his eyes for approval, but found them strangely veiled and unreadable. She wished that she had chosen one of the other gowns that now hung in the large cherry wardrobe.

"Ah, now, isn't that a beautiful sight, lad?" Paddy said, surveying Adelia with uninhibited pride. "Why, there won't be another woman here tonight will hold a candle to my little Dee. It's a lucky man you are, Travis."

"Uncle Paddy." She smiled and moved to kiss his cheek. "What wonderful blarney. But don't stop—I need it. I have to be honest and say I'm scared witless."

"There's no need for that, Dee." Taking her hand, Travis turned her toward him. "You'll have them eating out of your hand. You look incredible." He smiled at her, his free hand brushing through her hair briefly before he turned away to replenish his drink.

Love me, Travis, her mind shouted suddenly. *I'd give the world and more if you'd only love me half as much as I love you.*

As he turned back, his eyes captured hers. He paused, unreadable emotion flickering over his face. "Dee?" he began, his voice questioning, but before she could speak the doorbell pealed and their guests began to arrive.

It was infinitely easier than Adelia had imagined. After the first wave of guests, she felt her tension dissolve and met the few speculative glances with characteristic boldness. The house was soon filled with people and chatter and laughter and the chink of glasses. It was apparent that

Travis was well liked and respected by his associates, and his choice of bride met with acceptance and approval, if not immediately, then shortly after exposure to Adelia's natural, honest charm.

One sleekly coiffured woman who had cornered Adelia halted Travis as he passed. "Travis, your wife is refreshing and charming and more than likely too good for you." She smiled with the privilege of old friendship. "I believe it would be a treat just to listen to her read the telephone directory. Such a marvelous accent."

"Careful, Carla," Travis admonished, slipping an arm around Adelia's shoulder in the casual way she had missed in the past few weeks. "Dee claims we're the ones with the accent—and for all her sweet looks, her temper is not to be trifled with."

"Travis, darling!" The trio turned, and Adelia caught a glimpse of swirling white as the owner of the voice embraced her husband. "I just got back in town, darling, and heard about your little party. I hope you don't mind."

"Of course not, Margot. It's always a pleasure to see you." He turned, and Adelia noted that he didn't dislodge the red-tipped hand from his arm. "Margot Winters—my wife, Adelia."

Margot turned, and Adelia nearly gasped aloud. She was staring right at the most beautiful woman she had ever seen. Tall and slender, she was elegantly draped in a cool white sheath. Ash-gold hair curled softly around an oval face. Her skin was the color of rich cream. Long-lashed gray eyes, as clear and cool as a mountain lake, looked over and beyond Adelia.

"Why, Travis, she's adorable." The gray eyes focused now on Adelia, making her feel small and inadequate. "But she's little more than a child, barely out of the schoolroom." The sweet tone was patently patronizing.

"I'm allowed up with the grown-ups now and again," Adelia said evenly, her chin tilting to meet Margot's gaze. "I hung up my book strap some time back."

"My," Margot observed over Carla's chuckle. "You're Irish, aren't you?"

"Aye." The quicksilver temper began its swift rise. "As Paddy's pig. Tell me, Mistress Winters, what are you?"

"Dee." Trish spoke from behind, laying a hand on Adelia's arm. "Will you come out here for a minute? I need you to help me."

Adelia was pulled out on the terrace, and after she had shut the doors, Trish dissolved into a fit of laughter. "Oh, Dee," she managed between giggles. "How I would have loved to have left you there and watched you lay into her! I just didn't think it was quite the right time. Oh…" She wiped at her eyes. "Did you see Carla? I thought she was going to explode! She kept choking on her drink and trying to keep a straight face. I wouldn't have missed that for the world! How Travis could ever have been involved with that woman is beyond me! She's a cold-blooded snob."

"Travis and Margo Winters?" Adelia asked, attempting to keep her voice casual.

"Oh, yes, I thought you knew." Trish gave a deep sigh, wiped her eyes again, and grimaced. "I don't really think he was ever serious about her—I give him more credit than that. She would have given one of her Tiffany baubles to have him look at her the way he looks at you." Trish smiled, and Adelia made a valiant effort to respond. "They had this big blowup a few months ago. It seems she resented all the time he spent with the horses." She gave a snort of disgust and straightened her skirts. "She wanted him to sit back and let others do all the work while he spent his time entertaining her. She gave

him some kind of ultimatum and took off for Europe in
a cloud of expensive French perfume." Trish laughed in
pure delight. "Her little ploy failed miserably, and now
her nose is out of joint. Instead of pining for her, Travis
is happily married to you." She linked her arm with her
sister-in-law's.

"Aye," Adelia murmured. "Now he's married to me...."
Her tone was melancholy, and Trish glanced at her sharply,
but Dee refused to meet her eyes.

Paddy moved back to his own house a few days
later, and Adelia missed his presence keenly. He found
Finnegan a congenial companion, and the dog divided
his time between them. He would accompany Paddy as
he grumbled inside for his afternoon rest, and Adelia was
never quite sure whether Finnegan's motives were duty
or laziness.

Travis made no mention of Margot Winters or Adelia's
comments to her, and she found their relationship drifting
away again until she felt more like his ward than his wife.
When they attended social functions, he treated her with
the warm attentiveness expected of a newly married husband; but once they were alone again in their own home,
he was distant, showing her only the casual affection he
might give to a favored cousin.

The depression and frustration this caused in her Adelia
hid with apparent success, responding as she believed he
desired and maintaining the same casualness he directed
toward her. Rarely did her temper flare, and she was
aware his was under strict control. At times she imagined
they were only polite puppets pulled on invisible strings.
Desperately she wondered how long they could go on.

One afternoon, as July brought summer's throbbing
heat to the air, Adelia answered the summons of the bell

and found herself confronted with the elegantly clad form of Margot Winters. Her finely penciled brows lifted at Adelia's attire of jeans and shirt. She glided over the threshold without invitation.

"Good afternoon to you, Mistress Winters." Adelia greeted her, determined to act the part of hostess. "Please come in and sit down. Travis is down at the stables, but I'll be glad to send for him."

"That's not necessary, Adelia." Margot strolled into the living room and seated herself in a wingbacked chair as if she belonged there. "I came to have a little chat with you. Hannah—" she glanced over at the housekeeper, who had entered behind Adelia "—I'll have some tea."

Hannah looked pointedly at Adelia, who merely nodded and moved to join her uninvited guest.

"I shall come straight to the point," Margot began, sitting back and linking her fingers together in an imperious gesture. "I'm sure you're aware that Travis and I were about to be married before we had a slight disagreement a few months ago."

"Is that the truth of it?" Adelia asked with apparently idle interest.

"Yes, it was common knowledge," Margot stated with a regal wave of her hand. "I thought to teach Travis a lesson by going to Europe and giving him time to think things through. He's a very stubborn man." She gave Adelia a small knowing smile. "When I saw the picture of him in the paper kissing this little ragamuffin, I thought nothing of it. The press will blow these things out of proportion. But when I heard he'd actually married some little stablehand—" she shivered delicately "—I knew it was time to come back and set things straight."

"And may the stablehand ask how you mean to do that?"

"When this little interlude is finished, Travis and I can proceed as planned."

"And by interlude I suppose you're meaning my marriage?" Adelia inquired, her voice lowering to an ominous level.

"Well, of course." Slender shoulders moved at the inevitable. "Just look at you. It's obvious Travis only married you to bring me back. You can't possibly hope to hold him for very long. You haven't the breeding or style that's necessary to move in society."

Straightening her spine, Adelia hid her pain with dignity. "I'm telling you this as a fact, Mistress Winters: you had nothing to do with the reason that Travis and I were married. It's true I haven't your elegance or manner of speaking, but there's one thing I have you're lacking. I've Travis's ring on my finger, and you'll be having a good long wait before you can add his name to yours."

Hannah entered bearing a tea tray, and Adelia rose and turned to her. "Mistress Winters won't be staying for tea after all, Hannah. She was just leaving."

"Play the lady of the house while you can," Margot advised, rising and gliding past Adelia's stiff form. "You'll be back in the stables sooner than you think." When the door closed with a sharp bang, Adelia let out a deep breath.

"She's got her nerve coming here and talking that way," an irate Hannah sputtered.

"We'll be paying her no mind." She patted the housekeeper's arm. "And we'll keep this visit between the two of us, Hannah."

"If that's the way you want it, missy," Hannah agreed with obvious reluctance.

"Aye," she replied, staring off into space. "That's the way I want it."

* * *

Adelia's nerves remained on edge for several days and showed all too plainly in increased temper. The atmosphere in the house went from a near-stagnant calm to volatile motion. Travis greeted her change in attitude with absent tolerance that changed to strained patience.

She paced the living room after dinner one evening while he sat on the sofa and brooded over his brandy.

"I'm going to take Finnegan and go for a walk," she announced suddenly, unable to bear the silence between them any longer.

"Do as you like," he answered with a shrug.

"'Do as you like.'" She whirled and snapped at him, nerves as tight as an overwound watch. "It's sick to death I am of hearing you say that. I will not do as I like. I don't want to do as I like."

"Do you hear what you just said?" he demanded, setting down his brandy and staring at her. "That is the most ridiculous statement I have ever heard."

"It's not ridiculous. It's perfectly clear if you had the sense to understand it."

"What's gotten into you? You make more sense when you mutter in Gaelic."

"Nothing," she returned shortly. "There's not a thing wrong with me."

"Then stop behaving like a shrew. I'm tired of putting up with your foul temper."

"A shrew, am I?" Her color rose.

"Precisely," he agreed with infuriating calm.

"Well, if you're tired of listening to me, I'll keep well out of your way." Storming from the room, she flew past an astonished Hannah, out the back door, and into the warm summer night.

She awoke the next morning ashamed, disgusted and

contrite. She had spent an uneasy night struggling with the aftermath of temper and the realization that not only had she been unreasonable, she had made a fool of herself as well. One was as difficult to take as the other.

Travis has done nothing to deserve the way I've been treating him, she decided, pulling on her working uniform of jeans and shirt and hurrying downstairs. She determined to apologize and make a study of being as sweet and mild a wife as any man could want.

Hannah informed her that Travis had breakfasted early and gone out, so Adelia sat down in solitary misery, unable to ease her conscience.

She worked hard in the stables that morning, doing self-imposed penance for her faults. And as morning melted into early afternoon, the manual labor began to erase the depression she carried with her.

"Dee." Travis spoke from outside the tackroom where she was busily hanging bridles. "Come out here. I want to show you something."

"Travis." She ran after him as he strode away. "Travis." Catching up to him, she tugged on his arm in an attempt to make him slow his pace. "I'm sorry, Travis. I'm sorry for the way I've been behaving, and for raging at you last night when I had no cause to. I know I've been mean and spiteful and no fun to have around, but if you'll forgive me, I'll… What are you smiling like that for?"

The smile spread to a grin. "You apologize just as emphatically as you rage. It's fascinating. Now, forget it, half-pint." He ruffled her hair and slipped an arm around her shoulders. "Everyone has their black moods. Look," he said simply and pointed.

She gave a cry of pleasure at the glossy chestnut mare prancing around inside the paddock fence. Moving over, she stood on the first rung of fence and scanned the strong, clean lines. "Oh, Travis, she's beautiful—the most beautiful horse I've ever seen!"

"You say that about all of them."

She smiled at him, then back at the horse with a deep sigh of pleasure. "Aye, and it's always true. Who will you breed her with?"

"That's not up to me. She's yours."

Adelia turned wide, unbelieving eyes to his. "Mine?"

"I had thought to give her to you next month for your birthday, but"—he shrugged and brushed a lock of hair from her face—"I thought your spirits needed a lift, so she's yours a bit early."

She shook her head, the still unfamiliar tears filling her eyes. "But after the way I've been acting, you should have been beating me instead of buying me a present."

"The thought entered my mind last night, but this seemed a better solution."

"Oh, Travis!" She flung herself into his arms without restraint. "No one's ever given me such a grand present, and I don't deserve it." She drew her face from his cheek and pressed her lips to his. His arms tightened around her, the kiss changing from one of gratitude to one of smoldering passion, and she offered herself, lips parting and bones melting. "Travis," she murmured as his face lifted, his cheek brushing hers.

He set her away from him abruptly. "You'd better get acquainted with your mare, Dee. I'll see you at dinner."

She watched him stride away, biting her lip to prevent herself from calling him back. Finnegan bounded over, and she swallowed the tears of rejection, burying her face in his fur. "I don't have any appeal for him," she told her sympathetic companion. "And I don't know how to go about making him see me as a woman—much less a wife."

Chapter Ten

Adelia woke to a blinding flash of lightning and a burst of thunder. The room glowed with brief intensity as the sky was broken with spiderwebs of light, and the wind moaned like a man mourning.

Tossing back the covers, she rose from the bed and threw open the French doors leading to her balcony to let the storm enter the room. The hands of the wind pulled at her hair and whipped the soft material of her thin nightgown, molding it against her. Rain fell in torrents like angry tears from the heavens, and she raised her arms wide, laughing in sheer delight at the raging elements.

"Dee?" She turned her head and saw Travis silhouetted in the doorway. "I thought you might be frightened. The electricity's out, and the storm's loud enough to wake the dead."

"Aye," she agreed triumphantly. "It's wonderful!"

"So much for finding you shaking with fear under the covers," he returned with a dry smile and stepped back.

"Oh, Travis, come look!" she cried as another bolt of lightning illuminated the murky sky and was followed by a deafening roar of thunder.

He watched her slimness outlined against the blackness, the fullness of her hair flying riotously around her bare shoulders. He opened his mouth to speak, but Adelia cried out again.

"Oh, come, just look at it!" Taking a deep breath, he moved to join her. "It's so wild, so strong and powerful and free!" She lifted her face to feel the full force of the wind on her cheeks. "It's angry as the devil and doesn't give a hoot what anyone thinks. Listen to the wind, screaming like a banshee! Oooh, but I love a storm that blows free!"

She turned and found his eyes on her. Lightning flooded the room, and she saw the naked desire darkening his unblinking blue stare. Her smile faded. Her heart pounded in her ears, drowning out the turbulence of the storm as he pulled her against him and crushed her lips in a violent, hungry kiss.

Her arms clutched around his waist as they fused together, and she felt the need in him she had not known existed and knew a moment's delirious pleasure that it was for her. Fire ignited fire. Her response was abandoned and uninhibited. His mouth ravished hers, hard and bruising, and she opened under the pressure like a flower to the sun. His hand slid to her shoulders, and the soft material of her nightgown sighed to the floor. Her hands fumbled with the belt of his robe until no barrier of silk came between them. With a swift, desperate gesture, he lifted her and carried her to the bed.

The passionate violence of the storm paled against the turbulence of their lovemaking. His lips moved over hers slowly, his hands roaming with gentle experience over her trembling body, releasing her desire while he kept his own in check. When he made her his, she surrendered, drawing her pleasure from the gift she gave.

Later, she slept in the warm circle of his arms, the deep, peaceful sleep of one who has been lost and searching and finally found home....

Sunlight streamed warm and loving on Adelia's face, and she opened her eyes. Travis's face lay close to hers, and she studied it thoroughly and sighed, her love nearly bursting her heart. His breathing was slow and even, the deep blue of his eyes hidden by lowered lids and lashes which seemed incredibly long and thick against the strongly masculine face. Her hand lifted and stroked the dark curls away from his forehead, and she snuggled closer, murmuring his name.

His eyes opened at her movements and smiled into hers. "Hello," he said simply as his arm tightened around her waist. "Do you always look this beautiful first thing in the morning?"

"I don't know," she answered. "It's the first time I've ever woken with a man on my pillow." She rolled on top of him and peered down at his face critically. "You're not a hard sight on the eyes either." Grinning, she rubbed a hand over his chin. "Though it's a fact you're needing a shave."

He tugged the hair that fell streaming from her head to his shoulders and brought her face down, claiming her lips. After a moment she lay her head in the curve of his shoulder, sighing with absolute contentment as he caressed her back with slow, idle movements. "Travis," she said curiously, "that clock says it's after ten."

He twisted to see for himself and groaned. "That's what it says."

"But it can't be," Adelia objected, raising herself up in indignation. "Why, never in my life have I slept as late as that!"

"Well, you did this time." He grinned. "Even you can't argue the day back."

"I'll pretend I didn't see it," she decided and snuggled against his warmth.

"As much as I'd like to do the same, I have an appointment, and I'm already going to be late." He kissed her again, rolling her over, and she clung to him, moving her hands over the rippling muscles of his back. "I've got to go." His lips tarried a moment at the curve of her neck before he disentangled himself. He rose and slipped on his robe, turning back to gaze at her slim form, scantily covered by rumpled sheets. "If you stay there for a couple of hours, I'll be back."

"You could stay now and be a bit later for your appointment," she suggested with a smile as she sat up, clutching the sheet to her breast.

"Don't tempt me." Moving over, he kissed her brow. "I'll be back as soon as I can."

When the door closed behind him, she lay back with a blissful sigh and stretched. *I'm truly his wife now,* she thought, closing her eyes as memories of the previous night ran through her mind. *I'm a married woman, and Travis is my husband. But he never said he loved me.* She sighed and shook her head. *He said he needed me, and that's enough for now. I'll make him love me in time. I'll make our marriage work, and he'll not be thinking of ending it. I'll make him so happy he'll think he's found heaven.*

She jumped from the bed, full of confidence, and danced into the adjoining bathroom to shower.

Later, she paused halfway down the stairs, her face lighting with pleasure as she heard Travis's voice coming from the living room. Before she could begin the rapid descent she had intended, another voice floated to her, and she stopped, the smile fading as she recognized Margot Winters's voice raised in exasperation.

"Travis, you know very well I never meant those things I said before I left. I only went away so that you'd miss me and come after me."

"Did you expect me to drop everything and run off to Europe chasing you, Margot?" Adelia heard the slight amusement in his tone and bit her lip.

"Oh, darling, I know it was foolish." The voice became low and seductive. "I never meant to hurt you. I'm so terribly sorry. I know you married that little groom to make me jealous."

"Is that so?" The answer was calm, and Adelia's hand tightened on the banister at his cool, dispassionate discussion of her.

"Of course, darling, and it worked beautifully. Now all you have to do is arrange for a quick divorce and give her a nice little settlement, and we'll get things back to normal."

"That may be difficult, Margot. Adelia's Catholic; she'd never divorce me." Her stomach lurched at the easy remark, and she wrapped her arms around herself to ward off the sharp, piercing stab of pain.

"Well, then, darling, you'll just have to divorce her."

"On what grounds?" Travis's voice sounded reasonable.

"For heaven's sake, Travis." The feminine voice rose in annoyance. "You can arrange something. Give her some money. She'll do what you want."

Adelia could stand no more. Covering her ears with her hands, she ran up the carpeted stairs and into her room.

Oh, 'tis a fool you are, Adelia Cunnane, she berated herself, leaning against her door. *He doesn't love you and he never will. Your marriage was just make-believe all along.* She dashed away the tears and straightened her shoulders. Now's the time to end it, she decided firmly. Uncle Paddy's strong enough, and I can't go on this way any longer.

She packed only her old clothes and those bought with her own earnings in the well-battered case she had carried from Ireland, then sat at the writing desk and penned notes to her uncle and husband.

Please understand, Uncle Paddy, she pleaded, placing the two envelopes on the smooth surface of the desk. *I can't be going on with this anymore. I can't stay here so close to Travis, not now, not after all that's happened.*

She slipped downstairs and, taking a deep breath, walked outside to await her taxi.

The airport was as busy as it had been on her arrival, throngs of people rushing around her and shaking her confidence. For a moment she felt achingly lost and alone. Sighting the ticket counter, she drew herself up and headed toward it. A hand gripped her arm and spun her around. She dropped her case to the tiled floor with a thud.

"What do you think you're doing?" she began indignantly, stopping openmouthed as she looked up into Travis's furious face.

"That's precisely what I wanted to ask you," he tossed

back, his eyes boring into hers with a hard blue light. "Where do you think you're going?"

"To Ireland, back to Skibbereen."

"Are you stupid enough to think I'd let you get on that plane without a word?" he demanded, his grip on her arm increasing.

She winced at his bruising fingers but answered evenly, "I left you a note."

"I saw your note," he hissed between his teeth. "It's a good thing I got back early, or I'd be chasing you across the Atlantic."

"There's no need for you to be chasing me anywhere," Adelia insisted, pulling at her arm as the circulation began to slow down. "You're breaking my arm, Travis Grant. Take your hand off me."

"You're lucky it's not your neck," he muttered, and, lifting her case with his free hand, he began to pull her after him.

"I'm not going with you—I'm going back to Ireland."

"You are coming with me," he corrected. "And you can walk on your own two feet, or I'll cart you out like a sack of Irish potatoes."

"A sack of Irish potatoes, is it?" she spat at him, but as he towered over her, formidable and powerful, she tossed her head and went on calmly. "Aye, I'll walk, Master Grant. There'll be other planes."

Muttering an oath, he strode purposefully out to his waiting car, towing her with him. He opened the door and gave her a none too gentle shove inside. "You've got a lot of explaining to do, Adelia," he said as he started the engine. She opened her mouth to retort, but he cut her off with a deadly look. "Save it until we get home. I have no desire to commit murder publicly."

She remained silent on the drive home, stubbornly staring out the side window. Pulling up in front of the large stone house, Travis got out of the car, slamming his door with such force Adelia was amazed that the glass remained intact. He pulled Adelia out and dragged her inside.

"We're not to be disturbed," he announced to a gaping Hannah as he hauled Adelia up the staircase. Pushing her into her room, he slammed the door and locked it. "Now, let's hear it."

"I've an earful for you, Travis Grant," she raged. "You great thundering blackguard, I'm sick to death of your shoving me and pushing me and tearing my arms from my sockets. I warn you, you black-hearted son of the devil, you'll not be battering me about any longer unless you've a mind to have a few bruises of your own!"

"If you've finished," he returned evenly, "I'd like to see you use that double-edged tongue of yours for an explanation."

"I've no need to explain a blessed thing to the likes of you." Her eyes glittered bright green in her furious face. "I told you plain in the note: I want nothing from you. I've my pride, if nothing else."

"Yes, you and your Irish pride," Travis growled, stepping forward and taking her by the shoulders. "I'd like to strangle you with your pride. What was all that about divorce and annulments?"

"I thought my wording clear enough." She jerked away and backed up. "I said that, as an annulment was no longer possible, I was leaving and you'd be free to divorce me. I wanted none of your money and would pay you back for what I took with me."

"And you expect me to accept that?" he shouted at her, and she backed up another step. "Just calmly read your little note and go from marriage to divorce in one easy step?"

"Don't you shout at me," she snapped back. "It was agreed when we started that this marriage was only for Uncle Paddy, and we'd have an annulment when he was better. Now that can't be, so you'll have to divorce me. I'm not able to do it myself."

"You can talk of annulments and divorce after last night?" he threw back bitterly. "I thought it meant something to you."

"I can speak of it? I can speak of it?" she roared, out of control. "You dare say that to me? The devil take you, Travis Grant, for your hypocrisy! You'd no more than left the bed when you spoke of divorcing me with your fine lady. Give me money to buy me off, will you? You low, sneaking buzzard! I would rather die than touch one penny of your money, you low-lying snake!"

"Dee, is that why you left?" Travis demanded, shaking her as she resorted to Gaelic curses.

"Aye." Her small fists beat uselessly at his chest. "Take your hands off me, you cursed brute. I'll not wait around to be bought off like some cheap fancy lady."

He picked her up bodily, tucking her like a football under his arm, and ignoring the flailing fists, laid her gently on the bed.

"So it's back to bed again, is it? I'll not lie in this bed with the likes of you again. A curse on you, Travis Grant!"

"Be quiet, you little fool." Travis captured her mouth, shutting off the stream of Gaelic, and held it until her furious struggles lost their force. "Did you think I'd let you go after all I've been through to get you?" He cut off her reply with another breathtaking kiss. "Now, you little spitfire, keep your mouth shut and listen. Margot came here this morning without invitation. She brought up the subject of divorce, not I. In the first place—Keep still," he warned as she squirmed beside him, "or I'll have to get tough." He demonstrated by closing his mouth over hers until, for a moment, her struggles lost their force.

"In the first place," he began again, "I had never considered marrying her; any plans in that direction were her own. We had a fairly compatible relationship for a while—Adelia, *hold still*. You're going to hurt yourself." He shifted his weight, took both of her wrists in his hand, and held them over her head. "She got it into her head that I should marry her and give up my work here, with some crazy notion about traveling the world and living in high style. I told her she was out of her mind, and she took off for Europe, telling me it was her or the horses." He grinned down at Adelia's flushed face. "The horses won, hands down. She got it stuck in that small brain of hers that I married you to spite her, and when she came here this morning going on about divorce and settlements, I let her ramble, curious to see how big a fool she'd make of herself."

He took Adelia's chin in his free hand and held her head still. "Now, if you had listened to the entire conversation, you would have heard me tell her that I had no intention of divorcing a wife I loved, now, or any time within the next thousand years."

"You said that?" All struggles stopped.

"Or words to that effect. The meaning was clear."

"I—well, you might have told your wife you loved her. It would have saved a great deal of trouble."

"How could I tell her I loved her five minutes after she raged at me, standing there looking like an outraged urchin?" He brushed her curls aside to kiss the creamy skin of her throat. "My first thought was to gentle you so you could stand the sight of me and go from there. Did you really think I took you to Kentucky and New York just for Majesty?" His lips explored her smooth skin. "I didn't dare let you out of my sight; someone might have come along and snatched you away. I decided to wear you down slowly." His mouth moved over her face with slow, lingering kisses. "I thought I was making some headway, but Paddy's heart attack changed everything. I felt the best way to help him was to assure him of your welfare, so I railroaded you into marriage with the promise of an annulment. Of course—" his free hand began fresh explorations "—I never intended to give you one."

"Let go of my hands," she demanded, and he raised his head and shook it.

"Not if I have to keep you here for the next twenty years."

"You thick-brained idiot, couldn't you see how I was dying for loving you? Let go of my hands, blast your eyes, and kiss me."

She pulled his head to hers with her freed hands, and buried her face in the strong column of his neck.

"It appears," he murmured in her scented hair, "we've wasted a great deal of time."

"You seemed so far away. All those weeks you never even touched me. You never even said you loved me last night."

"I didn't dare touch you. I wanted you so much it was driving me mad. If I had told you I loved you last night—and how I wanted to!—you might have thought I said it just to keep you in bed."

"I won't think that now, Travis. Let me hear you say it. I've been needing to hear you say it for such a long time."

He obliged her, telling her over and over until his lips sought hers and told her silently.

"Travis," she finally whispered against his ear. "I'm wondering if you could arrange another thunderstorm?"

* * * * *

IRISH ROSE

Chapter One

Her name was Erin, like her country. And like her country, she was a maze of contradictions—rebellion and poetry, passion and moodiness. She was strong enough to fight for her beliefs, stubborn enough to fight on after a cause was lost, and generous enough to give whatever she had. She was a woman with soft skin and a tough mind. She had sweet dreams and towering ambitions.

Her name was Erin, Erin McKinnon, and she was nervous as a cat.

It was true that this was only the third time in her life she'd been in the airport at Cork. Or any airport, for that matter. Still, it wasn't the crowds or the noise that made her jumpy. The fact was, she liked hearing the announcements of planes coming and going. She liked thinking about all the people going places.

London, New York, Paris. Through the thick glass she could watch the big sleek planes rise up, nose first, and imagine their destinations. Perhaps one day she'd board one herself and experience that stomach-fluttering anticipation as the plane climbed up and up.

She shook her head. It wasn't a plane going up that had her nervous now, but one coming in. And it was due any minute. Erin caught herself before she dragged a hand through her hair. It wouldn't do a bit of good to be poking and pulling at herself. After thirty seconds more, she shifted her bag from hand to hand, then tugged at her jacket. She didn't want to look disheveled or tense... or poor, she added as she ran a hand down her skirt to smooth it.

Thank God her mother was so clever with a needle. The deep blue of the skirt and matching jacket was flattering to her pale complexion. The cut and style were perhaps a bit conservative for Erin's taste, but the color did match her eyes. She wanted to look competent, capable, and had even managed to tame her unruly hair into a tidy coil of dark red. The style made her look older, she thought. She hoped it made her look sophisticated, too.

She'd toned down the dusting of freckles and had deepened the color of her lips. Eye makeup had been applied with a careful hand, and she wore Nanny's old and lovely gold crescents at her ears.

The last thing she wanted was to look plain and dowdy. The poor relation. Even the echo of the phrase in her head caused her teeth to clench. Pity, even sympathy, were emotions she wanted none of. She was a McKinnon, and perhaps fortune hadn't smiled on her as it had her cousin, but she was determined to make her own way.

Here they were, she thought, and had to swallow a ball of nerves in her throat. Erin watched the plane that had brought them from Curragh taxi toward the gate— the small, sleek plane people of wealth and power could afford to charter. She could imagine what it would be like to sit inside, to drink champagne or nibble on something exotic. Imagination had always been hers in quantity. All she'd lacked was the means to make what she could imagine come true.

An elderly woman stepped off the plane first, leading a small girl by the hand. The woman had cloud-white hair and a solid, sturdy build. Beside her, the little girl looked like a pixie, carrot-topped and compact. The moment they'd stepped to the ground, a boy of five or six leaped off after them.

Even through the thick glass, Erin could all but hear the woman's scolding. She snatched his hand with her free one, and he flashed her a wicked grin. Erin felt immediate kinship. If she'd gauged the age right, that would be Brendon, Adelia's oldest. The girl who held the woman's hand and clutched a battered doll in the other would be Keeley, younger by a year or so.

The man came next, the man Erin recognized as Travis Grant. Her cousin's husband of seven years, owner of Thoroughbreds and master of Royal Meadows. He was tall and broad-shouldered and was laughing down at his son, who waited impatiently on the tarmac. The smile was nice, she thought, the kind that made a woman look twice without being sure whether to relax or brace herself. Erin had met him once, briefly, when he'd brought his wife back to Ireland four years before. Quietly domineering, she'd thought then. The kind of man a woman could depend on, as long as she could stand toe-to-toe with him.

On his hip he carried another child, a boy with hair as dark and thick as his father's. He was grinning, too, but not down at his brother and sister. His face was tilted up toward the sky from which he'd just come. Travis handed him down, then turned and held out a hand.

As Adelia stepped through the opening, the sun struck her hair with arrows of light. The rich chestnut shone around her face and shoulders. She, too, was laughing. Even with the distance, Erin could see the glow. She was a small woman. When Travis caught her by the waist and lifted her to the ground, she didn't reach his shoulder. He kept his arm around her, Erin noticed, not so much possessive as protective of her and perhaps of the child that was growing inside her.

While Erin watched, Adelia tilted her face, touched a hand to her husband's cheek and kissed him. Not like a long-time wife, Erin thought, but like a lover.

A little ripple of envy moved through her. Erin didn't try to avoid it. She never attempted to avoid any of her feelings, but let them come, let them race to the limit, whatever the consequences.

And why shouldn't she envy Dee? Erin asked herself. Adelia Cunnane, the little orphan from Skibbereen, had not only pulled herself up by the bootstraps but had tugged hard enough to land on top of the pile. More power to her, Erin thought. She intended to do the same herself.

Erin squared her shoulders and started to step forward as another figure emerged from the plane. Another servant, she thought, then took a long, thorough look. No, this man would serve no one.

He leaped lightly to the ground with a slim, unlit cigar clamped between his teeth. Slowly, even warily, he looked around. As a cat might, she thought, a cat that had just leaped from cliff to cliff. She couldn't see his eyes, for he wore tinted glasses, but she had the quick impression that they would be sharp, intense and not entirely comfortable to look into.

He was as tall as Travis but leaner, sparer. Tough. The adjective came to her as she pursed her lips and continued to stare. He bent down to speak to one of the children, and the move was lazy but not careless. His dark hair was straight and long enough to hang over the collar of his denim shirt. He wore boots and faded jeans, but she rejected the idea that he was a farmer. He didn't look like a man who tilled the soil but like one who owned it.

What was a man like this doing traveling with her cousin's family? Another relative? she wondered, and shifted uncomfortably. It didn't matter who he was. Erin checked the pins in her hair, found two loose, and shoved them into place. If he was some relation of Travis Grant's, then that was fine.

But he didn't look like kin of her cousin's husband. The coloring might be similar, but any resemblance ended there. The stranger had a raw-boned, sharp-edged look to him. She remembered the picture books in catechism class, and the drawings of Satan.

"Better to rule in hell than to serve in heaven."

Yes… For the first time, a smile moved on her lips. He looked like a man who'd have similar sentiments. Taking a deep breath, Erin moved forward to greet her family.

The boy Brendon came first, barreling through the doorway with one shoe untied and eyes alight with curiosity. The white-haired woman came in behind him, moving with surprising speed.

"Stand still, you scamp. I'm not going to lose track of you again."

"I just want to see, Hannah." There was a laugh in his voice and no contrition at all when she caught his hand in hers.

"You'll see soon enough. No need to worry your mother to death. Keeley, you stay close now."

"I will." The little girl looked around as avidly as her brother, but seemed more content to stay in the same place. Then she spotted Erin. "There she is. That's our cousin Erin. Just like the picture." Without a hint of reserve, the girl crossed over and smiled. "You're our cousin Erin, aren't you? I'm Keeley. Momma said you'd be waiting for us."

"Aye, I'm Erin." Charmed, Erin bent down to catch the little girl's chin in her hand. Nerves vanished into genuine pleasure. "And the last time I saw you, you were just a wee thing, all bundled in a blanket against the rain and bawling fit to wake the dead."

Keeley's eyes widened. "She talks just like Momma," she announced. "Hannah, come see. She talks just like Momma."

"Miss McKinnon." Hannah kept one hand firmly on Brendon's shoulder and offered the other. "It's nice to meet you. I'm Hannah Blakely, your cousin's housekeeper."

Housekeeper, Erin thought as she put her hand in Hannah's weathered one. The Cunnanes she'd known might have been housekeepers, but they'd never had one. "Welcome to Ireland. And you'd be Brendon."

"I've been to Ireland before," he said importantly. "But this time I flew the plane."

"Did you now?" She saw her cousin in him, the pixie-like features and deep green eyes. He'd be a handful, she thought, as her mother claimed Adelia had always been. "Well, you're all grown up since I saw you last."

"I'm the oldest. Brady's the baby now."

"Erin?" She glanced over in time to see Adelia rush forward. Even heavy with child she moved lightly. And when she wound her arms around Erin, there was strength in them. The recognition came strongly—family to family, roots to roots. "Oh, Erin, it's so good to be back, so good to see you. Let me look at you."

She hadn't changed a bit, Erin thought. Adelia would be nearly thirty now, but she looked years younger. Her complexion was smooth and flawless, glowing against the glossy mane of hair she still wore long and loose. The pleasure in her face was so real, so vital, that Erin felt it seeping through her own reserve.

"You look wonderful, Dee. America's been good for you."

"And the prettiest girl in Skibbereen's become a beautiful woman. Oh, Erin." She kissed both her cousin's cheeks, laughed and kissed them again. "You look like home." With Erin's hand still held tightly in hers, she turned. "You remember Travis."

"Of course. It's good to see you again."

"You've grown up in four years." He kissed her cheek in turn. "You didn't meet Brady the last time."

"No, I didn't." The child kept an arm around his father's neck and eyed Erin owlishly. "Faith, he's the image of you. It's a handsome boy you are, Cousin Brady."

Brady smiled, then turned to bury his face in his father's neck.

"And shy," Adelia commented, stroking a hand down his hair. "Unlike his da. Erin, it's so kind of you to offer to meet us and take us to the inn."

"We don't often get visitors. I've got the minibus. You know from the last time you came that renting a car is tricky, so I'll be leaving it with you while you're here." While she spoke, Erin felt an itch at the base of her neck, a tingle, or a warning. Deliberately she turned and stared back at the lean-faced man she'd seen step off the plane.

"Erin, this is Burke." Adelia placed a hand on her

skirt at the stirrings within her womb. "Burke Logan, my cousin, Erin McKinnon."

"Mr. Logan," Erin said with a slight nod, determined not to flinch at her own reflection in his mirrored glasses.

"Miss McKinnon." He smiled slowly, then clamped his cigar between his teeth again.

She still couldn't see his eyes but had the uneasy feeling that the glasses were no barrier to what he saw. "I'm sure you're tired," she said to Adelia, but kept her gaze stubbornly on Burke's. "The bus is right out front. I'll take you out, then we'll deal with the luggage."

Burke kept himself just a little apart as they walked through the small terminal. He preferred it that way, the better to observe and figure angles. Just now, he was figuring Erin McKinnon.

A tidy little package, he mused, watching the way her long, athletic legs moved beneath her conservative skirt. Neat as a pin and nervous as a filly at the starting gate. Just what kind of race did she intend to run? he wondered.

He knew snatches of the background from conversations on the trip from the States and from Curragh to this little spot on the map. The McKinnons and Cunnanes weren't first cousins. As near as could be figured, Adelia's mother and the mother of the very interesting Erin McKinnon had been third cousins who had grown up on neighboring farms.

Burke smiled as Erin looked uneasily over her shoulder in his direction. If Adelia Cunnane Grant figured that made her and the McKinnons family, he wouldn't argue. For himself, he spent more time avoiding family connections than searching them out.

If he didn't stop staring at her like that, he was going

to get a piece of her mind, Erin told herself as she slid the van into gear. The luggage was loaded, the children chattering, and she had to keep her wits about her to navigate out of the airport.

She could see him in the rearview mirror, legs spread out in the narrow aisle, one arm tossed over the worn seat—and his eyes on her. Try as she might, she couldn't concentrate on Adelia's questions about her family.

As she wound the van onto the road, she listened with half an ear and gave her cousin the best answers she could. Everyone was fine. The farm was doing well enough. As she began to relax behind the wheel, she dug deep for bits and pieces of gossip. Still, he kept staring at her.

Let him, then, she decided. The man obviously had the manners of a plow mule and was no concern of hers. Stubbornly avoiding another glance in the rearview mirror, she jabbed another loose pin back in her hair.

She had questions of her own. Erin expertly avoided the worst of the bumps on the road and trained her eyes straight ahead. The first of them would be who the hell was this Burke Logan. Still, she smiled on cue and assured her cousin again that her family was fit and fine.

"So Cullen's not married yet."

"Cullen?" Despite her determination, Erin's gaze had drifted back to the mirror and Burke. She cursed herself. "No. Much to my mother's regret, he's still single. He goes into Dublin now and again to sing his songs and play." She hit a rough patch that sent the van vibrating. "I'm sorry."

"It's all right."

Turning her head, she studied Adelia with genuine concern. "Are you sure? I'm wondering if you should be traveling at all."

"I'm healthy as one of Travis's horses." In a habitual

gesture, Adelia put a hand on her rounded belly. "And I've months to go before they're born."

"They?"

"Twins this time." The smile lit up her face. "I've been hoping."

"Twins," Erin repeated under her breath, not sure whether she should be amazed or amused.

Adelia shifted into a more comfortable position. Glancing back, she saw that her two youngest were dozing and that Brendon was putting up a courageous, if failing, battle to keep his eyes open. "I've always wanted a big family like yours."

Erin grinned at her as the van putted into the village. "It looks like you're going to match it. And may the sweet Lord have mercy on you."

With a chuckle, Adelia shifted again to absorb the sights and sounds of the village she remembered from childhood.

The small buildings were still neat, if a bit rough around the edges. Patches of grass were deep and green, shimmering against dark brown dirt. The sign on the village pub, the Shamrock, creaked and groaned in a breeze that tasted of rain from the sea.

She could almost smell it, and remembered it easily. Here the cliffs were sheer and towering, slicing down to a wild sea. She could remember the times she'd stood on the rock watching the fishing boats, seeing them come in with their day's catch to dry their nets and cool dry throats at the pub.

The talk here was of fishing and farming, of babies and sweethearts.

It was home. Adelia rested a hand against the open window and looked out. It was home—a way of life, a place she'd never been able to close out of her heart.

There was a wagon filled with hay, its color no brighter, its scent no sweeter than that of the hay in her own stables in America. But this was Ireland, and her heart had never stopped looking back here.

"It hasn't changed."

Erin eased the vehicle to a stop and glanced around. She knew every square inch of the village, and every farm for a hundred miles around. In truth, she'd never known anything else. "Did you expect it would? Nothing ever changes here."

"There's O'Donnelly's, the dry goods." Dee stepped out of the van. Foolishly she wanted to have her feet on the ground of her youth. She wanted to fill her lungs with the air of Skibbereen. "Is he still there?"

"The old goat will die behind the counter, still counting his last pence."

With a laugh, Dee took Brady from Travis and cuddled him as he yawned and settled against her shoulder. "Aye, then he hasn't changed, either. Travis, you see the church there. We'd come in every Sunday for mass. Old Father Finnegan would drone on and on. Does he still, Erin?"

Erin slipped the keys of the van in the pocket of her purse. "He died, Dee, better than a year ago." Because the light went out of her cousin's eyes, Erin lifted a hand to her cheek. "He was more than eighty, if you remember, and died quietly in his sleep."

Life went on, she knew, and people passed out of it whether you wanted them to or not. Dee glanced back at the church. It would never seem exactly the same again. "He buried Mother and Da. I can't forget how kind he was to me."

"We've a young priest now," Erin began briskly. "Sent from Cork. A hell-raiser he is, and not a soul sleeps through one of his sermons. Put the fear of God into

Michael Ryan, so the man comes sober to mass every Sunday morning." She turned to help with the luggage and slammed solidly into Burke. He put a hand on her shoulder as if to steady her, but it lingered too long.

"I beg your pardon."

She couldn't stop her chin from tilting forward or her eyes from spitting at him. He only smiled. "My fault." Grabbing two hefty cases, he swung them out of the van. "Why don't you take Dee and the kids in, Travis? I'll deal with this."

Normally Travis wouldn't have left another with the bulk of the work, but he knew his wife's strength was flagging. He also knew she was stubborn, and the only way to get her into bed for a nap was to put her there himself.

"Thanks. I'll take care of checking in. Erin, we'll see you and your family tonight?"

"They'll be here." On impulse, she kissed Dee's cheek. "You'll rest now. Otherwise Mother will fuss and drive you mad. That I can promise."

"Do you have to go now? Couldn't you come in?"

"I've some things to see to. Go on now, or your children will be asleep in the street. I'll see you soon."

Over Brandon's protest, Hannah bundled them inside. Erin turned to grip another pair of cases by the handles and began unloading. It passed through her mind that expensive clothes must weigh more when she found herself facing Burke again.

"There's just a few more," she muttered, and deliberately breezed by him.

Inside, the inn was dim but far from quiet. The excitement of having visitors from America had kept the small staff on their toes all week. Wood had been polished, floors had been scrubbed. Even now old Mrs. Malloy was leading Dee up the stairs and keeping up a solid stream of reminiscence. The children were cooed over, and hot tea and soda bread were offered. Deciding she'd left her charges in good hands, Erin walked outside again.

The day was cool and clear. The early clouds had long since been blown away by the westerly wind so that the light, as it often was in Ireland, was luminescent and pearly. Erin took a moment to study the village that had so fascinated her cousin. It was ordinary, slow, quiet, filled with workingmen and women and often smelling of fish. From almost any point in town you could see the small harbor where the boats came in with their daily catch. The storefronts were kept neat. That was a matter of pride. The doors were left unlocked. That was a matter of custom.

There was no one there who didn't know her, no one she didn't know. Whatever secrets there were were never secrets for long, but were passed out like small treasures to be savored and sighed over.

God, she wanted to see something else before her life was done. She wanted to see big cities where life whirled by, fast and hot and anonymous. She wanted to walk down a street where no one knew who she was and no one cared. Just once, just once in her life, she wanted to do something wild and impulsive that wouldn't echo back to her on the tongues of family and neighbors. Just once.

The van door slammed and jolted her back to reality. Again she found herself looking at Burke Logan. "They're all settled, then?" she asked, struggling to be polite.

"Looks like." He leaned back against the van. With his ankles crossed, he pulled out a lighter and lit his cigar. He never smoked around Adelia out of respect for her condition. His eyes never left Erin's. "Not much family resemblance between you and Mrs. Grant, is there?"

It was the first time he'd spoken more than two words at a time. Erin noted that his accent wasn't like Travis's. His words came more slowly, as if he saw no reason to hurry them. "There's the hair," he continued when Erin didn't speak. "But hers is more like Travis's prize chestnut colt, and yours—" he took another puff as he deliberated "—yours is something like the mahogany stand in my bedroom." He grinned, the cigar still clamped between his teeth. "I thought it was mighty pretty when I bought it."

"That's a lovely thought, Mr. Logan, but I'm not a horse or a table." Reaching into her pocket, she held out the keys. "I'll be leaving these with you, then."

Instead of taking them, he simply closed his hand over hers, cradling the keys between them. His palm was hard and rough as the rocks in the cliffs that dropped toward the sea. He enjoyed the way she held her ground, the way she lifted her brow, more in disdain than offense.

"Is there something else you're wanting, Mr. Logan?"

"I'll give you a lift," he said simply.

"It's not necessary." She clenched her teeth and nodded as two of the town's busiest gossips passed behind her. The evening news would have Erin McKinnon holding hands with a stranger in the street, sure as faith. "I've only to ask for a ride home to get one."

"You've got one already." With his hand still on hers, he pushed away from the van. "I told Travis I'd see to it." After releasing her hand, he gestured toward the door. "Don't worry, I've nearly got the hang on driving on the wrong side of the road."

"It's you who drive on the wrong side." After only a

brief hesitation, Erin climbed in. The day was passing her by, and she'd have to make every minute count just to catch up.

Burke settled behind the wheel and turned the key in the ignition. "You're losing your pins," he said mildly.

Erin reached behind her and shoved them into place as he drove out of the village. "You'll take the left fork when you come to it. After that it's only four or five kilometers." Erin folded her hands, deciding she'd granted him enough conversation.

"Pretty country," Burke commented, glancing out at the green, windswept hills. There were blackthorns, bent a bit from the continual stream of the westerly breeze. Heather grew in a soft purple cloud, while in the distance the mountains rose dark and eerie in the light. "You're close to the sea."

"Close enough."

"Don't you like Americans?"

With her hands still folded primly, she turned to look at him. "I don't like men who stare at me."

Burke tapped his cigar ash out the window. "That would narrow the field considerably."

"The men I know have manners, Mr. Logan."

He liked the way she said his name, with just a hint of spit in it. "Too bad. I was taught to take a good long look at something that interested me."

"I'm sure you consider that a compliment."

"Just an observation. This the fork?"

"Aye." She drew a long breath, knowing she had no reason to set her temper loose and every reason to hold it. "Do you work for Travis?"

"No." He grinned as the van shimmied over ruts. "You might say Travis and I are associates." He liked the smell here, the rich wet scent of Ireland and the warm earthy scent of the woman beside him. "I own the farm that borders his."

"You race horses?" She lifted a brow again, compelled to study him.

"At the moment."

Erin's lips pursed as she considered. She could picture him at the track, with the noise and the smells of the horses. Try as she might, she couldn't put him behind a desk, balancing accounts and ledgers. "Travis's farm is quite successful."

His lips curved again. "Is that your way of asking about mine?"

Her chin angled as she looked away. "It's certainly none of my concern."

"No, it's not. But I do well enough. I wasn't born into it like Travis, but I find it suits me—for now. They'd take you back with them if you asked."

At first it didn't sink in. Then her lips parted in surprise as she turned to him again.

"I recognize a restless soul when I see one." Burke blew out smoke so that it trailed through the window and disappeared. "You're straining at the bit to get out of this little smudge on the map. Though if you ask me, it has its charm."

"No one asked you."

"True enough, but it's hard not to notice when you stand on the curb and look around as though you wished the whole village to hell."

"That's not true." The guilt rose in her because for a moment, just a moment, she'd come close to wishing it so.

"All right, we'll alter that to you wishing yourself anywhere else. I know the feeling, Irish."

"You don't know what I feel. You don't know me at all."

"Better than you think," he murmured. "Feeling trapped, stifled, smothered?" She said nothing this time. "Looking at the same space you saw the day you were born and wondering if it's the last thing you'll see before you die? Wondering why you don't walk out, stick out your thumb and head whichever way the wind's blowing? How old are you, Erin McKinnon?"

What he was saying hit too close to the bone for comfort. "I'm twenty-five, and what of it?"

"I was five years younger when I stuck my thumb out." He turned to her, but again she saw only her own reflection. "Can't say I ever regretted it."

"Well, it's happy I am for you, Mr. Logan. Now, if you'll slow down, the lane's there. Just pull to the side. I can walk from here."

"Suit yourself." When he stopped the van, he put a hand on her arm before she could climb out. He wasn't sure why he'd offered to drive her or why he'd started this line of conversation. He was following a hunch, as he had for most of his life. "I know ambition when I see it because it looks back at me out of the mirror most mornings. Some consider it a sin. I've always thought of it as a blessing."

What was it about him that made her throat dry up and her nerves stretch? "Have you a point, Mr. Logan?"

"I like your looks, Erin. I'd hate to see them wrinkled up with discontent." He grinned again and tipped an invisible hat. "Top of the morning to you."

Unsure whether she was running from him or her own demons, Erin got out of the van, slammed the door, and hurried down the lane.

Chapter Two

She had a great deal to think about. Erin sat through dinner at the inn, with her family talking on top of each other, with laughter rolling into laughter. Voices were raised to be heard over the clatter of tableware, the scrape of chair legs, the occasional shout. Scents were a mixture of good hot food and whiskey. The lights had been turned up high in celebration. The group filled Mrs. Malloy's dining room at the inn, but wasn't so very much bigger than a Sunday supper at the farm.

Erin ate little herself, not because one of her brothers seemed to interrupt constantly to have her pass this or that, but because she couldn't stop thinking about what Burke had said to her that afternoon.

She *was* dissatisfied, though she didn't like the idea that a stranger could see it as easily as her family had always overlooked it. Years before she'd convinced herself it wasn't wrong to be so. How could it be wrong to feel what was so natural? True, she'd been taught that envy was a sin, but…

Damn it all, she wasn't a saint and wouldn't choose to be one. The envy she felt for Dee sitting cozily beside her husband felt healthy, not sinful. After all, it wasn't as if she wished her cousin didn't have; it was only that she wished she had as well. She doubted a body burned in hell for wishes. But she didn't think they grew wings for them, either.

In truth, she was glad the Grants had come back to visit. For a few days she could listen to their stories of America and picture it. She could ask questions and imagine the big stone house Dee lived in now and almost catch glimpses of the excitement and power of the racing world. When they left again, everything would settle back to routine.

But not forever, Erin promised herself. No, not forever. In a year, maybe two, she would have saved enough, and then it would be off to Dublin. She'd get a job in some big office and have a flat of her own. Of her very own. No one was going to stop her.

Her lips started to curve at the thought, but then her gaze met Burke's across the table. He wasn't wearing those concealing glasses now. She almost wished he was. They'd been disturbing, but not nearly as disturbing as his eyes—dark gray, intense eyes. A wolf would have eyes like that, smoky and patient and cunning. He had no business looking at her like that, she thought, then stubbornly stared right back at him.

The noise and confusion of the table continued around them, but she lost track of it. Was it the amusement in his eyes that drew her, or the arrogance? Perhaps it was because both added up to a peculiar kind of knowledge. She wasn't sure, but she felt something for him at that moment, something she knew she shouldn't feel and was even more certain she'd regret.

An Irish rose, Burke thought. He wasn't sure he'd ever seen one, but was certain they would have thorns, thick ones with sharp edges. An Irish rose, a wild rose, wouldn't be fragile or require careful handling. It would be sturdy, strong and stubborn enough to grow through briers. It was a flower he thought he could respect.

He liked her family. They would be called salt of the earth, he supposed. Simple, but not simple-minded. Apparently their farm did well enough, as long as they worked seven days a week. Mary McKinnon had a dressmaking business on the side, but seemed more interested in discussing children with Dee than fashion. The brothers were fair, except for the oldest, Cullen, who had the looks of a Black Irish warrior and the voice of a poet. Unless Burke missed his guess, Erin had her softest spot there. Throughout the meal he watched her, curious to see what other soft spots he might discover.

By the time dinner was over, Burke was glad he'd let Travis talk him into an extra few days in Ireland. The trip had been profitable, the visit to the track at Curragh educational, and now it seemed it was time to mix business with a little pleasure.

"You'll play for us, won't you, Cullen?" Adelia was already reaching across the table to grip Erin's oldest brother's hand. "For old times' sake."

"He'll take little enough persuading," Mary McKinnon put in. "You'd best clear a space." She gestured to her two youngest sons. "It's only fitting that we dance off a meal like that."

"I just happen to have my pipe." Cullen reached in his vest pocket and drew out the slim reed. He stood, a big man with broad shoulders and lean hips. The fingers of his workingman's hands slid over the holes as he lifted the instrument to his lips.

It surprised Burke that such a big, rough-looking man could make such delicate music. He settled back in his chair, savored the kick of his Irish whiskey and watched.

Mary McKinnon placed her hand in her youngest son's and, without seeming to move at all, set her feet in time to the music. It seemed a very restrained dance to Burke, with a complicated pattern of heels and toes and shuffles. Then the pace began to pick up—slowly, almost unnoticeably. The others were keeping time with their hands or occasional hoots. When he glanced at Erin, she was standing with a hand on her father's shoulder and smiling as he hadn't seen her smile before.

Something shimmered a bit inside him—shimmered, then strained, then quieted, all in the space of two heartbeats.

"She still moves like a girl," Matthew McKinnon said of his wife.

"And she's still beautiful." Erin watched her mother whirl in her son's arms, then spin with a flare of skirt and a flash of leg.

"Can you keep up?"

With a laugh that was only slightly wistful, Erin shook her head. "I've never been able to."

"Come now." Her father slid an arm around her waist. "My money's on you."

Before she could protest, Matthew had spun her out. His grin was broad as he held her hand high and picked up the rhythm of the timeless folk dance she'd been taught as soon as she could walk. The pipe music was cheerful and challenging. Caught up in it and her family's enthusiasm,

Erin began to move instinctively. She put her hands on her hips and tossed up her chin.

"Can you manage it?"

Adelia looked up at her eighteen-year-old cousin. "Can I manage it?" she repeated with her eyes narrowed. "The day hasn't come when I can't manage a jig, boyo."

Travis started to protest as she joined her cousins on the floor, but then he subsided. If there was one thing his Dee knew, it was her own strength. The depth of it continued to surprise him. "Quite a group, aren't they?" he murmured to Burke.

"They're all of that." He drew out a cigar, but his eyes remained on Erin. "I take it you don't jig."

With a chuckle, Travis leaned back against the wall. "Dee's tried to teach me and labeled me hopeless. I'm inclined to believe you have to be born to it." He saw Brendon go out to take his place as his mother's partner. His mother's son, Travis thought with a ripple of pride. Of all their children, Brendon was the most strong-willed and hardheaded. "She needed this more than I realized."

Burke managed to tear his eyes from Erin long enough to study Travis's profile. "Most people get homesick now and again."

"She's only come back twice in seven years." Travis watched her now, her cheeks pink with pleasure, her eyes laughing down at Brendon as he copied her moves. "It's not enough. You know, she'll take you to the wall in an argument—half the time an argument no sane man can understand. But she never complains, and she never asks."

For a moment Burke said nothing. It still surprised him after four years that his friendship with Travis had become so close, so quickly. He'd never considered himself the kind of man to make friends, and in truth had never wanted the responsibility of one. He'd spent almost half his thirty-two years on his own, needing no one. Wanting no one. With the Grants, it had just happened.

"I don't know much about women." At Travis's slow smile, Burke corrected himself. "Wives. But I'd say yours is happy, whether she's here or in the States. The fact is, Travis, if she loved you less I might have made a play for her myself."

Travis continued to watch her as his mind played back the years. "The first time I saw her I thought she was a boy."

Burke drew the cigar out of his mouth. "You're joking."

"It was dark."

"A poor excuse."

His chuckle was warm and easy as he looked back. "She seemed to think so, too. Nearly took my head off. I think I fell for her then and there." He heard her laugh and looked over as she shook her head and stepped away from the dancers. She came to him, hands outstretched. The jeweled ring he'd put on her finger years before still glimmered.

"I could go for hours," she claimed, a little breathlessly. "But these two have had enough." With her free hands, she covered her babies. "Are you going to try it, Burke?"

"Not on your life."

She laughed again and put a hand on his arm with the simple generosity he'd never quite gotten used to. "If a man doesn't make a fool of himself now and again, he's not living." She took a couple of deep, steadying breaths, but couldn't keep her foot from tapping. "Oh, it's like magic when Cullen plays and all the more magic to be here, hearing it." She brought Travis's hand to her lips, then rested her cheek on it. "Mary McKinnon can still outdance anyone in the county, but Erin's wonderful, too, isn't she?"

Burke took a long sip of whiskey. "It's not a hardship to watch her."

Laughing again, Adelia rested her head against her husband's arm. "I suppose as her elder cousin I should warn her about your reputation with women."

Burke swirled the whiskey in his glass and gave her a bland look. "What reputation is that?"

With her head still nestled against Travis, she smiled up at him. "Oh, I hear things, Mr. Logan. Fascinating things. The racing world's a tight little group, you know. I've heard murmurs that a man not only has to watch his daughters but his wife when you're about."

"If I was interested in another man's wife, you'd be the first to know." He took her hand and brought it to his lips. Her eyes laughed at him.

"Travis, I think Burke's flirting with me."

"Apparently," he agreed, and kissed the top of her head.

"A warning, Mr. Logan. It's easy enough to flirt with a woman who's five months along with twins and who knows you're a scoundrel. But mind your step. The Irish are a clever lot." She stood on her toes and kissed his cheek. "If you keep staring at her like that, Matthew McKinnon's going to load his shotgun."

He glanced back as Erin stepped away from the group. "No law against looking."

"There should be when it comes to you." She snuggled against Travis again. "Looks like Erin's going outside for a breath of air." When Burke merely lifted a brow, she smiled. "You'd probably like to light that cigar, maybe take a little walk in the night air yourself."

"As a matter of fact, I would." He nodded to her, then sauntered to the door.

"Were you warning him off or egging him on?" Travis wanted to know.

"Just enjoying the view, love." She turned her mouth up for a kiss.

Erin drew her jacket tightly around her. Nights were coldest in February, but she didn't mind now. The air was bracing and the moon half-full. She was glad her father had pressured her to dance. It seemed too seldom now that there was time for small celebrations. There was so much work to be done, and not as many hands to do it now that Frank had married and started his own family. And within a year she expected Sean to marry the Hennessy girl. With Cullen more interested in his music than milking, that left only Joe and Brian. And herself.

The family was growing, but at the same time spreading out. The farm had to survive. Erin knew that was indisputable. Her father would simply wither away without it. Just as she knew she would wither away if she stayed much longer. The only solution was to find a way to ensure both.

She hugged herself with her arms to ward off the wind. It brought with it the scent of Mrs. Malloy's wild roses and rhododendrons. She wouldn't think of it now. In a short time the Grants would be gone and her own yearnings for more would fade a bit. When the time was right, something would happen. She looked up at the moon and smiled. Hadn't she promised herself that she'd make something happen?

She heard the scrape and flare of a lighter and braced herself.

"Nice night."

She didn't turn. The little jolt to her system teased her. No, she hadn't wanted him to come out, she told herself. Why should she? Since he had, she would hold her own. "It's a bit cold."

"You look warm enough." She wouldn't give an inch. It only gave him the pleasure of taking it from her. "I liked the dancing."

She turned to walk slowly away from the inn. It didn't surprise her when he fell into step beside her. "You're missing it."

"You stopped." The end of his cigar grew bright and red as he took another puff. "Your brother has a gift."

"Aye." She listened now as the music turned from jaunty to sad. "He wrote this one. Hearing it's like hearing a heart break." Music like this always made her long, and fear, and wonder what it would be like to feel so strongly about another. "Are you a music lover, Mr. Logan?"

"When the tune's right." This one was a waltz, a slow, weepy one. On impulse he slipped his arms around her and picked up the time.

"What are you doing?"

"Dancing," he said simply.

"A man's supposed to ask." But she didn't pull away, and her steps matched his easily. The motion and the music made her smile. She turned her face up to his. The grass was soft beneath her feet, the moonlight sweet. "You don't look like the kind of man who can waltz."

"One of my few cultural accomplishments." She fit nicely into his arms, slender but not fragile, soft but not malleable. "And it seems to be a night for dancing."

She said nothing for a moment. There was magic here, starlight, roses and sad music. The flutter in her stomach, the warmth along her skin, warned her that a woman took chances waltzing under the night sky with a stranger. But still she moved with him.

"The tune's changed," she murmured, and drew out of his arms, relieved, regretful that he didn't keep her there. She turned once again to walk. "Why did you come here?"

"To look at horses. I bought a pair in Kildare." He took a puff on his cigar. He'd yet to realize himself what his horses and farm had come to mean to him. "There's no match for the Thoroughbreds at the Irish National Stud. You pay for them, God knows, but I've never minded putting my money on a winner."

"So you came to buy horses." It interested her, though she didn't want it to.

"And to watch a few races. Ever been to Curragh?"

"No." She glanced up at the moon again. Curragh, Kilkenny, Kildare, all of them might have been as far away as the white slash in the sky. "You won't find Thoroughbreds here in Skibbereen."

"No?" He smiled at her in the moonlight, and the smile made her uneasy. "Then let's say I'm just along for the ride. It's my first time in Ireland."

"And what do you think of it?" She stopped now, unwilling to pass out of the range of the music.

"I've found it beautiful and contradictory."

"With a name like Logan, you'd have some Irish in you."

Unsmiling, he glanced down at his cigar. "It's possible."

"Probable," she said lightly. "You know, you said you were a neighbor of Travis's, but you don't sound like him. Your accent."

"Accent?" His mood changed again with a grin.

"I guess if you want to call it that it comes from the West."

"The West?" It took her a moment. "The American West? Cowboys?"

This time he laughed, a full, rich laugh, so that she was distracted enough not to protest when his hand touched her cheek. "We don't carry six-guns as a rule these days."

Her feathers were ruffled. "You don't have to make fun of me."

"Was I?" Because her skin had felt so cool and so smooth, he touched it again. "And what would you say if I asked you about leprechauns and banshees?"

She had to smile. "I'd say the last to have seen a leprechaun in these parts was Michael Ryan after a pint of Irish."

"You don't believe in legends, Erin?" He stepped closer so that he could see the moonlight reflected in her eyes like light in a lake.

"No." She didn't step back. It wasn't her nature to retreat, even when she felt the warning shiver race up her spine. Whether you won or went down in defeat, it was best to do it with feet firmly planted. "I believe in what I can see and touch. The rest is for dreamers."

"Pity," he murmured, though he had always felt the same. "Life's a bit softer the other way."

"I've never wanted softness."

"Then what?" He touched a finger to the hair that curled at her cheekbones.

"I have to go back." It wasn't a retreat, she told herself. She felt cold all at once, cold to the bone. But even as she started to turn, he closed a hand over her arm. She looked at him, eyes clear, not so much angry as assessing. "You'll excuse me, Mr. Logan. The wind's up."

"I noticed. You didn't answer my question."

"No, because it's no concern of yours. Don't," she said when his fingers closed lightly over her chin, but she didn't jerk away.

"I'm interested. When a man meets someone he recognizes, he's interested."

"We don't know each other." But she understood him. When he'd brought his arms around her in the waltz, she'd known him. There was something, something in both of them that mirrored back. Whatever it was had her heart beating hard now and her skin chilling. "And if it's rude I have to be, then I'll say it plain. I don't care to know you."

"Do you usually have such a strong reaction to a stranger?"

She tossed her head, but his fingers stayed in place. "The only reaction I'm having at the moment is annoyance." Which was one of the biggest lies she could remember telling. She'd already looked at his mouth and wondered what it would be like to be kissed by him. "I'm sure you think I should be flattered that you're willing to spend time with me. But I'm not a silly farm girl who kisses a man because there's a moon and music."

He lifted a brow. "Erin, if I'd intended to kiss you, I'd have done so already. I never waste time—with a woman."

She felt abruptly as foolish as she'd claimed not to be. Damn it, she would have kissed him, and she knew he was well aware of it. "Well, you're wasting mine now. I'll say good-night."

Why hadn't he kissed her? Burke asked himself as he watched her rush back to the inn. He'd wanted to badly. He'd imagined it clearly. For a moment, when the moonlight had fallen over her face and her face had lifted to his, he'd all but tasted her.

But he hadn't kissed her. Something had warned him that it would take only that to change the order of things for both of them. He wasn't ready for it. He wasn't sure he could avoid it.

Taking a last puff, he sent the cigar in an arch into the night. He'd come to Ireland for horses. He'd be better off being content with that. But he was a man on whom contentment rarely sat easily.

She'd come late on purpose. Erin rolled her bike to the kitchen entrance of the inn and parked it. She knew it was prideful, but she simply didn't want Dee to know she worked there. It wasn't the paperwork and bookkeeping that bothered her. That made her feel accomplished. It was her kitchen duties she preferred to keep to herself.

Mrs. Malloy had promised not to mention it. But she tut-tutted about it. Erin shrugged that off as she entered the kitchen. Let her tut-tut, as long as that was all she let out of her mouth.

Dee and her family were visiting in town through the morning. That had given Erin time to clear up her chores at home, then ride leisurely from the farm to handle the breakfast dishes and the daily cleaning. Since the books were in order, she'd be able to take a few hours that afternoon to drive out to the farm where her cousin had grown up.

It wasn't being deceitful, she told herself as she filled the big sink with water. And if it was, it couldn't be helped. She wouldn't have Dee feeling sorry for her. She was working for the money; it was as simple as that. Once enough was made, she could move on to that office position in Cork or Dublin. By the saints, the only dishes she'd have to clean then would be her own.

She started to hum as she scrubbed the inn's serviceable plates. She'd learned young when there was work to be done to make the best of it, because as sure as the sun rose it would be there again tomorrow.

She looked out the window as she worked, across the field where she'd walked with Burke the night before. Where she'd danced with him. In the moonlight, she thought, then caught herself. Foolishness. He was just a man dallying with what was available. She might not be traveled or have seen big cities, but she wasn't naive.

If she'd felt anything in those few minutes alone with him, it had been the novelty. He was different, but that didn't make him special. And it certainly didn't warrant her thinking of him in broad daylight with her arms up to the elbows in soapy water.

She heard the door open behind her and began to scrub faster. "I know I'm late, Mrs. Malloy, but I'll have it cleared up before lunch."

"She's at the market, fussing over vegetables."

At Burke's voice, Erin simply closed her eyes. When he crossed over and put a hand on her shoulder, she began to scrub with a vengeance.

"What are you doing?"

"I'd think you'd have eyes to see that." She set one plate to drain and attacked another. "If you'll excuse me, I'm behind."

Saying nothing, he walked over to the stove and poured the coffee that was always kept warm there. She was wearing overalls, baggy ones that might have belonged to one of her brothers. Her hair was down, and longer than he'd imagined it. She'd pulled it back with a band to keep it out of her face, but it was thick and curly beyond her shoulders. He sipped, watching her. He didn't quite know what his own feelings were at finding her at the sink, but he was well aware of hers. Embarrassment.

"You didn't mention you worked here."

"No, I didn't." Erin slammed another plate onto the drainboard. "And I'd be obliged if you didn't, either."

"Why? It's honest work, isn't it?"

"I'd prefer it if Dee didn't know I was washing up after her."

Pride was another emotion he understood well. "All right."

She sent him a cautious look over her shoulder. "You won't tell her?"

"I said I wouldn't." He could smell the detergent in the hot water. Despite the years that had passed, it was still a scent that annoyed him.

Erin's shoulders relaxed a bit. "Thank you."

"Want some coffee?"

She hadn't expected him to make it easy for her. Still cautious, but less reserved, she smiled. "No, I haven't the time." She turned away again because he was much easier to look at than she wanted him to be. "I, ah, thought you'd be out by now."

"I'm back," he said simply. He'd intended to grab a quick cup and leave, take a leisurely walk around town or duck into the local pub for conversation. He studied her, her back straight at the sink, her arms plunged deep into the soapy water. "Want a hand?"

She stared at him this time, caught between astonishment and horror. "No, no, drink your coffee. I'm sure there're muffins in the pantry if you like, or you might want to go out and walk. It's a fine day."

"Trying to get rid of me again?" He strolled over and picked up a dishcloth.

"Please, Mrs. Malloy—"

"Is at the market." He picked up a dish and began to polish it dry.

He was standing close now, nearly hip-to-hip with her. Erin resisted the urge to shift away, or was it to shift closer? She plunged her hands into the water again. "I don't need any help."

He set down the first dish and picked up another. "I've got nothing else to do."

Frowning, she lifted out a plate. "I don't like it when you're nice."

"Don't worry, I'm not often. So what else do you do except wash dishes and dance?"

It was a matter of pride, she knew, but she turned to him with her eyes blazing. "I keep books, if you want to know. I keep them for the inn and for the dry goods and for the farm."

"Sounds like you're busy," he murmured, and began to consider. "Are you any good?"

"I've heard no complaints. I'm going to get a job in Dublin next year. In an office."

"I can't see it."

She had a cast-iron skillet in her hand now and was tempted. "I didn't ask you to."

"Too many walls in an office," he explained, and lowered the pan into the water himself. "You'd go crazy."

"That's for me to worry about." She gripped the scouring pad like a weapon. "I was wrong when I said I didn't like you when you were nice. I don't like you at all."

"You know, you've only to ask and Dee would take you to America."

She tossed the pad into the water, and suds lapped up over the rim of the sink. "And what? Live off her charity?

Is that what you think I want? To take what someone is kind enough to give me?"

"No." He stacked the next plate. "I just wanted to see you flare up again."

"You're a bastard, Mr. Logan."

"True enough. And now that we're on intimate terms, you ought to call me Burke."

"There's plenty I'd like to be calling you. Why don't you be on your way and let me finish here? I've got no time for the likes of you."

"Then you'll have to make some."

He caught her off guard, though she told herself later she should have been expecting it. With her arms still elbow deep in water, he curled a hand around her neck and kissed her. It was quick, but a great deal more of a threat than a promise. His lips were hard and firm and surprisingly warm as he pressed them against hers. For a second, for two. She didn't have time to react, and certainly no time to think before he'd released her again and picked up another dish.

She swallowed, and beneath the soapy water her hands were fists. "You've a nerve, you do."

"A man doesn't get very far without any—or a woman."

"Just remember this. If I want you touching me, I'll let you know."

"Your eyes say plenty, Irish. It's a pleasure to watch them."

She wouldn't argue. She wouldn't demean herself by making an issue of it. Instead, she pulled the plug on the sink. "I've the floor to do. You'll have to get your feet off it."

"Then I guess I'd better take that walk." He laid the cloth down, spread open so it would dry. Without another word or another glance, he strolled out the back door. Erin waited a full ten seconds, then gave herself the satisfaction of heaving a wet rag after him.

Two hours later, after a quick change into a skirt and sweater, Erin met the Grants in the public room of the inn. Joe's overalls were bundled into a sack tied on the back of her bike, and she'd used some of Mrs. Malloy's precious cream to offset the daily damage she did to her hands. Burke was there. Of course he was, she thought, and deliberately ignored him as he bounced young Brady on his knee.

"Ma sent this." Erin handed Dee a plate wrapped tightly in a cloth. "It's her raisin cake. She didn't want you to think Mrs. Malloy could outcook her."

"I remember your mother's raisin cake." Dee lifted the corner of the cloth to sniff. "Now and then she'd bake an extra and have one of you bring it by the farm." The scent brought back memories—some sweet, some painful. She covered the cake again. "I'm glad you could come with us today."

"You remember it's only on the condition that you come by and visit. Ma's counting on it."

"Then we'd best be rounding up the brood. Burke, if you give the lad chocolate you deserve to have him smear it on you. Brendon, Keeley, into the van now. We're going for a ride."

They didn't have to be told twice.

First they went to the cemetery, where the grass was high and green and the stones weathered and gray. Flowers grew wild, adding the promise of life. Some of Erin's family were buried there; most she barely remembered. She'd never lost anyone close or grieved deeply. But she loved deeply when it came to her family, and thought she could understand how wrenching it would be to lose them.

Yet it had been so long ago, Erin thought as she watched her cousin stand between the graves of her parents. Didn't a loss like that begin to fade with time? Adelia had been only a child when they'd died, nine or ten. Wouldn't her memory of them have dimmed? Still, though she could imagine a world away from her family, she couldn't imagine one where they didn't exist.

"It still hurts," Dee murmured as she looked down at the stones that bore her parents' names.

"I know." Travis ran a hand down her hair.

"I remember Father Finnegan telling me after it happened that it was God's will, and thinking to myself that it didn't seem right. It still doesn't." She sighed and looked up at him. "I'll never be able to figure it out, will I?"

"No." He took her hand in his. There was a part of him that wanted to gather her up and take her away from the grief. And a part of him that understood she'd been strong enough to deal with it years before they'd even met. "I wish I'd known them."

"They'd have loved you." She let the tears come, but smiled with them. "And the children. They'd have fussed over the children, spoiled them. More than Hannah does. It comforts me that they're together. I believe that, you know. But it's painful that they missed knowing you and the babies."

"Don't cry, Momma." Keeley slipped a hand into Adelia's. "Look, I made a flower. Burke showed me. He said they'd like it even though they're in heaven."

Dee looked at the little wreath fashioned of twigs and wild grass. "It's lovely. Let's put it right in the middle, like this." Bending, she placed it between the graves. "Aye, I'm sure they'll like this."

What a strange man he was, Erin thought as she sat beside Burke in the van and listened to Brendon's chattering. She'd seen him sit in the grass and twine twigs together for Keeley. Though she'd kept herself distant enough that she hadn't heard what he'd said, she'd been aware that the girl had listened attentively and had looked at him with absolute trust.

He didn't seem to be a man to inspire trust.

She knew the road that led to the farm that had been the Cunnanes'. She remembered Dee's parents only as the vaguest of shadows, but she did remember Lettie Cunnane well, the aunt Dee had lived with when she'd been orphaned. She'd been a tough, stern-faced woman, and because of her Erin had kept her visits to the farm few and far between. That was behind them now, she reminded herself as she gestured toward the window for Brendon. "You see, just over this hill is where your mother grew up."

"On a farm," he said knowledgeably. The patches of green pasture and yellow gorse meant little to him. "We have a farm. The best one in Maryland." He grinned at Burke as if it was an old joke.

"It'll still be the second best when I'm finished," Burke answered, willing to rise to the bait.

"Royal Meadows has been around for gener… gener…"

"Generations," Burke supplied.

"Yeah. And you're still wet behind the ears 'cause Uncle Paddy said so."

"Brendon Patrick Grant." It was all the warning Hannah had to give. She turned her stern eye on Burke. "And you should know better than to encourage him."

Burke merely grinned and tousled the boy's hair. "Doesn't take much."

"Burke won his farm in a poker game," Brendon supplied as the van shuddered to a halt. "He's teaching me to play."

"That's so when Royal Meadows belongs to you, I can win that, too." He pushed open the sliding door, then grabbed the giggling boy around the waist.

"Did he really?" Erin asked in an undertone as Hannah took Keeley's hand. "Win his horse farm gambling?"

"So I'm told." Hannah stepped a bit wearily out of the van. "Rumor is he's lost and won more than that." She glanced over as Burke settled Brendon on his shoulders. "It's hard to hold it against him."

She wouldn't, Erin thought as she joined the others. She was too Irish to turn her nose up at a gambler, especially a successful one. Trailing behind Dee, she looked over the rise to the farm below.

It hadn't changed much, not in her memory. Oh, the milking parlor was new, and a fresh coat of paint had been slapped on the barn a year or so before. It was the only farm in sight. To the east, the hills rose up and blocked the view. The vegetable garden was already tilled and planted, and a smattering of the dairy cows could be seen in the strip of pasture. There was smoke spiraling out of the chimney of the little stone cottage, which was a great deal like her own. The good, rich smell of peat carried on the wind.

"The Sweeneys are a nice family," she said at length because her cousin stared down so long without speaking. "I know they wouldn't mind if you wanted to go down and look about."

"No." She said it too quickly, then softened the refusal with a touch of her hand. "I don't mind looking from here." The truth was she couldn't bear to go any closer to what had been and was no longer her own. "Do you remember, Erin, when Aunt Lettie was so sick and you and your mother came visiting?"

"Yes, you gave Ma one of the roses from the bush there." The bush had been her mother's, Erin remembered, and she linked her fingers briefly with Dee's. "The roses still bloom every summer."

She smiled at that. "Such a little place. Smaller now than even I remember. Look, Keeley, see that window there." She crouched down to show her daughter. "That was my room when I was your age."

Adelia stood again. There was only her and Travis now as the others strolled down the side of the road. "Dee, I've told you before, you can have it back if you want. We can make the Sweeneys a good offer for it."

She continued to look down, remembering. Then, with a little sigh, she slipped an arm around Travis's waist. "You know, when I left here all those years ago, I thought I'd lost everything." She tilted her head back and kissed him. "I was wrong. Let's walk a little ways. It's such a beautiful day."

Erin watched them. There was a small meadow that was green now but would be choked with wildflowers in only a matter of weeks. She heard Burke behind her and spoke without thinking.

"If I were to go, to leave here and find something else, I'd never look back."

"If you don't look over your shoulder once in a while, things catch up with you faster than you think."

"I don't understand you." She turned, and her hair fluttered around her face and shoulders, free of bonds. "One minute you sound like a man without any roots at all, and the next you sound as though you've just transplanted them where it's convenient."

"But not too deep." He caught the ends of her hair in

his fingers. He was becoming more and more fascinated by it. It wasn't silk; it was too wild and untamed for silk. "Maybe that's the trick, Irish, not letting them sink too deep. You can yank yours up because you'll damn well strangle if you don't, but you'll take some of this with you."

He reached down and took up a handful of soil. "Seems like a good enough base."

"And what's yours?"

He looked down at the rich dirt in his hand. "Have you ever seen the sand in the desert, Irish? No, no, you haven't. It's thin. It'll slip right out of your hands, no matter how hard you hold on to it."

"Grains of sand have a habit of clinging to the skin."

"And are easily brushed away." He glanced around as Brady let out a squeal of laughter at a gull that had glided in from the sea.

"Why did you kiss me before?" She hadn't wanted to ask. Rather, she hadn't wanted him to know it mattered. He smiled at her again, slowly, with the amusement only a hint in his eyes.

"A woman should never wonder why a man kisses her."

Annoyed with herself, she shrugged and turned away. "It wasn't a proper one, anyway."

"You want a proper one?"

"No." She continued to walk, but the devil on her shoulder took over. She glanced around, a half smile on her face. "I'll let you know when I do."

Chapter Three

There was a storm coming. Erin could feel it brewing inside her, just as she could see it brewing in the clouds that buried the sun and hung gloomily over the hills. She worked quickly, routinely, pulling the pins off the line and dropping the dry, billowing clothes in the basket at her feet.

She didn't mind this kind of monotonous, mindless work. It left her brain free to think and remember and plan. Just now, with the wind tossing sheets away from her and the sky boiling, she liked the simple outside chore. She wanted to see the storm break, to be a part of it when the wind and rain raised hell. When it was over, things would settle back into the quiet routine she knew was slowly driving her mad.

What was wrong with her? Erin yanked one of her brother's work shirts from the line, and out of ingrained habit folded it to ward off wrinkles. She loved her family, had friends and work to keep the wolf from the door. So why was she so restless, so edgy? She couldn't blame it all on her cousin's visit or on the unexpected appearance of one Burke Logan. She'd been feeling restless before they'd come, but for some reason their presence—his presence—intensified it.

She couldn't talk to her mother about it. Erin stripped down one of her mother's aprons and buried her face in the cool, fresh scent of the material. Her mother simply couldn't understand discontent or yearnings for more, not when there was a sturdy roof over the head and food enough for everyone. Time and again Erin had wished herself as serene a heart as her mother's. But it wasn't meant to be.

She couldn't go to her father, though Erin knew he would understand the storm inside her. He wasn't a calm, easy man. From the stories she'd heard he'd been a hellion in his youth, and it had taken marriage to his Mary and a couple of babies before he'd begun to take hold. But while her father would understand, Erin knew he would also be distressed. If she wanted more, needed more, he would take it to mean he hadn't given her enough.

There was Cullen. She'd always been able to talk to Cullen. But he was so busy just now, and her feelings were so mixed, the longings so indistinct, that she wasn't sure she could articulate them in any case.

So she would wait, let the storm come and the wind blow.

He'd been watching her for some time. Burke never considered that it was rude to stand and observe people without their knowledge. You learned more about people when they thought they were alone.

She moved well. Even doing something so simple there was an innate sensuality in her movements. She had more fire than showed in her hair. Inside her there was a flame smoldering. He recognized it because he'd been born with one himself. That kind of heat, of passion, could and would break free. It only took the right elements falling into place. Time, place, circumstance.

She didn't hum as she worked now, but occasionally looked up at the sky as if daring it to open and pour its fury on her. Her hair blew back from her face, fighting against the band that held it. Just as she fought whatever held her. He'd wondered what the results would be when she finally broke free. He'd already decided he wanted to be around to see for himself.

"I haven't seen a woman do that for a long time."

Erin spun around, her heels digging into the soft ground, a pillowcase clutched in her hand. He looked so at home, she thought, with the collar of his jacket up against the wind, the buttons undone in contradiction. He had his thumbs hooked in his pockets and that damned devil smile on his face. She'd never known a man to look better or more suited to the raw air and the warring skies. She turned away to snatch another clothespin because she knew her reaction to him would bring her nothing but trouble.

"Don't women take down the wash where you come from?"

"Progress often stamps out tradition." He moved to her with the easy strides of a man used to walking toward what he wanted. He unhooked a cotton slip—her cotton slip—folded it and dropped it in the basket. Erin clamped her teeth together and told herself only a foolish chucklehead would be embarrassed.

"There's no need for you to be putting your hands on the wash."

"Don't worry, they're clean enough." As if to prove it,

he held them out. For the first time she noticed a thin, jagged scar across his knuckles.

"What are you doing here?"

"I came to see you."

She said nothing for a moment. He didn't make it easy when he didn't invent comfortable excuses. "Why?"

"Because I wanted to." He took down a pair of serviceable white panties, folded those, too, without a blush, then laid them on top of the slip.

Erin felt a slow, uncomfortable curling in her stomach. "Shouldn't you be with Travis and Dee?"

"I think they'll survive the afternoon without me. I liked your farm when we were here yesterday." He glanced around now at the neat buildings. The cottage was nearly half again as large as the one where Adelia Grant had grown up, but the roof had the same bleached yellow thatching and sturdy stone walls. There were flowers here as well. The Irish seemed happy to let them grow as they chose—gay, untamed and sturdy. A hedge of wild fuchsia was already blooming. It made him think of home and the snow covering the fields.

The roof of the barn showed fresh patching. The paint on the silo was peeling and no longer white, but the chickens in the coop were fat and clucking. He imagined the McKinnons worked seven days a week to maintain the place. Such was the life of a farmer. "This is a fine piece of land. Apparently your father knows what to do with it."

"It's his life," Erin said simply as she took down the last of the wash.

"What about yours?"

"I don't know what you mean."

He lifted the basket before she could. "It's a good farm, a good life for some. You weren't meant for it."

"You don't know me well enough to say what I'm meant for." She took the basket from him and walked toward the kitchen door. "But I've already told you I'm going north to an office job in a year or so." Taking a deep breath, she swung the door open. Her mother would be horrified if she didn't ask the man in and at least offer him a cup of tea. She turned to him, but before she could issue the invitation he was taking the first step.

"Let's take a walk. I have a proposition for you."

Erin leaned back against the door and studied him coolly. "Oh, I'll just bet you do."

He took the basket from her again, set it inside the door and gave it a little shove. "You're getting ahead of yourself, Irish. Let's just say when I want you in bed I won't ask."

And he wouldn't, she thought as they watched each other. He wasn't the type to court a woman with flowers and pretty words, any more than he was the type to coax a woman gently into his arms. Well, she wasn't the type who wanted to be coaxed, but neither would she be steamrollered. "Just what is it you're wanting, Burke?"

"Let's take a walk," he repeated, but this time he closed his hand over hers.

She could have refused, but then she wouldn't know what it was he had to say. Erin decided that if she shook free and shut the door in his face, he'd tuck his hands in his pockets and stroll off, leaving her the one who was fuming.

There was no harm in walking with him, she told herself as she stepped down beside him. Her mother was in the house, and her father, along with a couple of her brothers, was somewhere on the farm. Added to that was the fact that she had every confidence she could take care of herself.

"I don't have much time," she said briskly. "There's a lot more to be done today."

"This won't take long." But he said nothing more as they walked away from the house. He didn't seem to look, but he saw everything—the care, the sweat that went into the farm, the long hours and the hope. He counted thirty cows. A man could make a living off less, he imagined. It hadn't been so many years since he'd worked backbreaking hours. He hadn't forgotten, just as he never forgot that fate could take what he had just as easily as it had given it to him.

"If it was a tour of the farm you were wanting—" Erin began.

"I had one yesterday, remember?" He paused a moment to look out over a field. He knew what it was to haul rocks from them, to ride sweating over them at baling time and to curse the land as much as you worshiped it. "You grow grain here for the stock?"

"Aye. It'll be plowing time soon."

"You work the fields?"

"I've been known to."

Burke turned her hand palm-up and studied it. It wasn't raw and cracked, but toughened with a ridge of callus. The nails were trimmed short and left unpainted. "You haven't pampered them."

"What good would that do me? I'm not ashamed of the work they've done."

"No. You're too practical for that." He turned her hand over again and looked at her face. "You're not the kind of woman who daydreams about white knights."

She could smile at that, though the intensity of his eyes made her uneasy. "I've always thought white knights would be painfully dull, and the last thing I want is to be a lady in distress. I'd rather be slaying my own dragons."

"Good. I don't have much use for a woman who wants to be taken care of." He still had her hand, he still watched the wind whip furiously through her hair. "Why don't you come back to America with me, Erin?"

She stared at him, speechless. The skies opened up. They were both soaked in a matter of seconds. She might have stood there, wide-eyed and openmouthed, but he grabbed her arm and yanked her inside a shed.

Inside it was dim and smelled of soil and damp. Tools for the vegetable garden lined the walls. Her mother's peat pots and seeds were stacked on shelves waiting for planting. Rain beat on the tin roof, and the wind snaked through the cracks in the boards and moaned.

Erin stood shivering just inside the door, her hair plastered to her head, her sweater dripping at the hem. But her senses had come back, full force.

"You're a madman, Burke Logan. By the saints, you're as mad as a hatter. Do you think I'd just bundle up my skirts and cross an ocean with you?" She still shivered, but the more she spoke, the hotter her temper became. "Sure and it's a conceited ox you are to believe all you have to do is crook your finger to have me tagging after you. I don't even know you." She swiped a hand over her face to dry it, then went one better and shoved him hard in the chest. "And it's the God's truth that I have no desire to."

She turned to the shed door and would have yanked it open if he hadn't caught her by the shoulders.

"Take your hands off me, you snake." On impulse, she grabbed a rake and turned on him with it. "Touch me again and I'll slice you into pieces, little ones that won't be put back together easily."

So she'd slay her dragons with a garden rake, he thought, lifting both hands, palms out, in a gesture of peace. "You don't have to defend your honor, Irish. I'm not after it—yet. This is business."

"What business would I be having with you?" When he took a step toward her, she gestured with the rake. "Come closer and I promise you'll be missing an ear at the very least."

"Fine." He made as if to take a step back. Then he moved quickly. Erin cursed him when he wrenched the rake out of her hands. Even as it clattered to the floor, her back was against the wall. "You'll have to learn not to drop your guard." His face was close, so close she could see his eyes, smoky and dark, and little else. She twisted, but his fingers only dug in harder. "Hold still a minute, will you? You're making a fool of yourself."

Nothing he could have said would have struck the light to her temper faster. She all but bared her teeth and snarled. "There'll come a time and there'll come a place when you'll pay for this."

"Everyone pays, Irish. Now take a deep breath, shut your mouth and listen. I'm offering you a job, that's all." She stopped wriggling to stare at him again. "I need someone sharp, someone clever with figures, to run my books."

"Your books?"

"The farm, expenses, payroll. The man I had was a little too creative. Since he's going to be a guest of the state for the next few years, I need someone else. I want someone I know, someone I can see and talk to, handling my money rather than a big shiny company that doesn't give a damn about the farm or me."

Because her head was whirling, she took one long breath before she spoke again. "You want me to come to America and keep your books?"

He smiled because she sounded almost disappointed.

"I'm not offering you a free ride. You're a pleasure to look at, Erin, but at the moment all I intend to pay for is your brain."

"Move back," she ordered in a voice that was suddenly firm. "I can't breathe with you pushing me through the wall."

"No more attacks with garden tools?"

Her chin came up. "All right. Just move aside." When he did, she took a couple of deep breaths. She had to keep a clear head now. She didn't mind taking a new road; in fact, she'd often fretted to do just that. She only wanted to study all the curves and angles of it first. "You want to hire me?"

"That's right."

"Why?"

"I've just told you."

She shook her head, still cautious. "You told me you need a bookkeeper. I imagine there're plenty of them in America."

"Let's just say I like your style." Bending, he picked up the rake and replaced it. He wondered briefly if she would have used it. Yes, indeed, he thought, grinning to himself. Oh, yes, indeed.

"For all you know, I can't add two and two."

"Mrs. Malloy and O'Donnelly at the dry goods say differently." He leaned back against a workbench. Studying her from there, he decided he'd spoken no less than the truth. Even wet and dripping, she was a pleasure to look at.

"Mrs. Malloy. You've spoken to her? You went to Mr. O'Donnelly and asked questions about me?"

"Just checking your references."

"No one told you to go poking about the town asking questions about me."

"Business, Irish. Strictly business. What I found out is that you're neat as a pin and dependable. Your figures tally and your books are clean. That's good enough for me."

"This is crazy." Struggling against a surge of excitement, she dragged a hand through her still-dripping hair. "A body doesn't hire someone they've known only a few days."

"Irish, people are hired after a ten-minute interview."

"That's not what I mean. This isn't a matter of me giving you a résumé, then catching a bus to take a new job across town. You're talking about me coming to America and taking on a job that's bigger than the inn, the farm and the dry goods put together."

He only moved his shoulders. "It's just a matter of more figures, isn't it? You're talking about going north in a year. I'm giving you a chance to go to America now. Make the break."

"It's not so simple." Along with the excitement was a growing panic. Wasn't this what she'd always wanted? Now that it was nearly as close as a handspan, she was terrified.

"It's a gamble." He was watching her again in that quiet, intense way. "Most things worth winning are. I'll pay for your ticket as a sign of good faith. You'll start out at a weekly salary." He considered a moment, then named a figure that had her mouth dropping open. "If it works out, there'll be a ten-percent raise in six months. For that you take care of all the details, all the figures, all the bills. I'll want a weekly report. We'll leave in two days."

"Two days?" She was numb now, so numb she could

only stare at him. "But even if I agreed, I could never be ready to leave by then."

"All you have to do is pack and say your goodbyes. I'll handle the rest."

"But I—"

"You have to make up your mind, Erin. Stay or go." He stepped toward her again. "If you stay, you'll be safe, and you'll always wonder what if."

He was right. The question was already nagging at her. "If I go, where will I live?"

"I've got plenty of room."

"No." On this she would have to be firm, right from the start. "I won't agree to that. I may say I'll work for you, but I won't live with you."

"It's your choice." Again he moved his shoulders as if it didn't matter. He'd already anticipated her balking there. "I don't imagine Adelia would have any problem putting you up. In fact, I think you know she'd love to have you with her. It wouldn't be charity," he said, keeping one step ahead of her. "You'd be bringing in a wage. You could get your own place, for that matter, but I think you'd be more comfortable with your cousin at first. And our farms are close enough to make it convenient."

"I'll talk to her." Sometime during the last two minutes her mind had been made up. She was going. Her bridges might not be burning behind her, but they were certainly smoking. "I'll have to speak to my family, as well, but I'd like to accept your offer."

She held out her hand. Burke took it just as casually, though he wondered about the wild surge of relief that coursed through him. "I expect a day's work for a day's pay. I don't doubt you'll give it to me."

"That I will. I'm grateful for the chance."

"I'll remind you of that after you've spent a few days

sorting through the mess my last bookkeeper left me with."

She stood very still for a moment, letting it all soak in, layer by layer. Then she spun in a quick circle and laughed. "I can't believe it. America! It's like some kind of a mad dream. I've hardly been more than fifty kilometers from Skibbereen, and now I'm going thousands in the blink of an eye."

He liked to see her this way, her face flushed with pleasure, her eyes lit with it. And the rain still drummed on the roof. "It takes a bit longer than that to cross the Atlantic."

"Don't be so literal." But she was too excited to take offense. "In a matter of days I'll be in a new country, a new place, a new job. New money."

He started to reach for a cigar, then thought better of it. "The money puts a gleam in your eye."

"Anyone who's ever been poor gleams a bit when they've got enough money."

He acknowledged this with a nod. He'd been poor, but he doubted Erin would understand that degree of poverty. He appreciated money, though if he lost it, as he had before, he would simply shake the dust off his shoes and make more. "You'll earn it."

"I wouldn't be having it any other way." She stopped as reality began to seep through. "But I need a passport and the green card that allows you to work. There must be a pile of papers that have to be processed."

"I told you I'd see to it." He drew a paper out of his pocket. "Fill this out and drop it off at the inn tonight. It's an application," he explained as she studied it. "I've already arranged to have it processed tomorrow. Your passport and whatever else you need will be in Cork when we get there."

She tapped the paper slowly against her palm. "You were damn sure of yourself, weren't you?"

"It pays to be. You'll need a picture they can use, too. A recent one."

"What if I'd said no?"

He simply smiled. "Then you'd have been a fool and I'd have thrown the application away."

"I can't figure you." She tucked the application in the pocket of her baggy pants, but shook her head at him. "You've made me a very generous offer, you're giving me the opportunity to do something I've wanted to do for as long as I can remember. But even as you're doing it, it doesn't seem to matter to you one way or the other."

He remembered the surge of relief, but chose to ignore it. "Things matter too much to people. That's how they get hurt."

"Are you saying that things don't matter to you? Nothing at all? What about your farm?"

He shifted a bit, surprised that the question, when she asked it, made him uncomfortable. "It's a place. A comfortable and fairly profitable one at the moment. But that's all it is. I don't have the ties to it that you have to the land here, Erin. That's why if I leave it I will leave without a second glance. When you leave Ireland, no matter how much you want to go, you're going to hurt."

"There's nothing wrong in that," she murmured. "It's my home. It's only right to miss your home."

"Some people don't make homes. They just live somewhere and leave it at that."

She saw more clearly now, though the light was still dim. She saw, though she'd told herself she didn't care, that there were places inside him no one, no woman, would ever touch. "That's a cold and sorry way to live."

"It's a choice," he corrected. Then he pushed the subject

aside. "Make sure you get me the application tonight. I'm leaving for Cork first thing in the morning."

"But you said we weren't going for a couple of days."

"I'll meet you there."

"All right, then. I should be getting along. There's a lot to be done."

"There's something else I think we should get out of the way." He rocked back on his heels a moment, then stunned her by grabbing both her arms and dragging her against him. "This has nothing to do with business."

Infuriated, she brought her hands to his chest and gave him one hard shove. It didn't budge him an inch. Then he clamped his mouth down on hers, rough and ready and with no patience at all.

She would have ripped and clawed at him. She would have struggled and bit and cursed. That was what she told herself she would have done if she hadn't been so stunned by the heat. His lips were firm. That she already knew. But she hadn't known they could be so hot, so passionate, so tempting.

Her head filled with sounds—louder, deeper sounds than the rain that drove furiously on the roof above. Her hands were trapped between their bodies so that she could feel the pounding of a heart without knowing which of them it came from.

This is what the apple must have tasted like when Eve took the first forbidden bite, she thought giddily. Succulent, tart, unbearably delicious. Nothing else ever tasted would be as satisfying. Lost in the flavor, she parted her lips and let him take more.

He'd known what he'd wanted but hadn't been sure what to expect. If she'd hissed at him, he would have ignored her and taken his fill. If she'd struck out at him in anger, he would have taken her struggles in stride and enjoyed the fury. He'd fought or gambled for everything he'd wanted all of his life. For days he'd been trying to convince himself that Erin McKinnon was no different. But she was.

She gave. After the first stunned instant she gave passionately, with the kind of desperation that left him shaken and edgy for more. Her mouth was avid and mobile, her body taut and trembling. He could feel the raw, jagged need raging through her, rising, speeding up to meet and match his own.

He wanted to take her there, on the damp floor with the smell of rain and earth everywhere. He wanted her to touch him, to feel those capable hands on his flesh. To hear her say his name. To watch her eyes go dark as midnight as he covered her body with his. It could be now. He could feel it in the press of her body against his, in the give of her mouth.

It could be now. There had been times, and there had been women with whom he wouldn't have hesitated. Why he did so now he couldn't be sure. But he drew her away, though his hands stayed on her shoulders and his eyes stayed on hers as they slowly fluttered open.

She couldn't speak, not for a moment. The feeling was so immense it left no room for words. She'd never known that a body could be filled so quickly with sensations or that a mind could be emptied of them just as swiftly. She knew now. If anyone had told her that the world could change in the single beat of a heart, she would have laughed. Now she understood.

He didn't speak. Erin struggled to find her footing as he kept his silence. She couldn't allow herself that kind of madness, not again. If she were to travel an ocean with him, work for him, understand him just a little, she couldn't let this happen again. Not with a man like him. Taking a deep breath, she steadied herself. No, never with him. If the past few moments had taught her anything, it was that he was a man who knew women and who understood their weaknesses very well.

"You had no right to do that." She didn't unleash her temper, knowing she hadn't the energy left for it.

He was shaken, down to the bone, down to the heart, but it wasn't the time to dwell on it. "It wasn't a matter of right but of want. That was a proper kiss, Irish, and we needed to get it out of our systems whether you were coming with me or not."

She nodded, hoping she sounded as casual as he. She'd rather have died on the spot than have admitted her own inexperience. "Now that our systems are clear, there'll be no need for it to happen again."

"Don't ask me for promises. You'll be disappointed." He strolled to the door, pushing it open so that the wind and rain lashed their way in. It helped cool his head and steady his heart rate. "You can talk to Dee and Travis when you bring the papers in. Give your family my best."

Then he was gone, into the storm. Though Erin dashed to the door, he was only a quickly fading shadow in the gloom.

A shadow, she thought, who she knew nothing about. And she would be going with him to America.

Chapter Four

Americia. Erin wasn't naive enough to believe the streets were paved with gold, but she was determined to make it the land of opportunity. Her opportunity.

It was the speed of things that struck her first, the hurry every living soul seemed to be in. Well, she was in a bit of a hurry herself, she decided as she sat in the back of her cousin's station wagon and tried not to gawk.

The cold had surprised her, too, a numbing, bone-chilling cold she'd never experienced in the mild Irish climate. But the snow was novelty enough to make it a small inconvenience. Piles of it, more than she'd ever seen, rolling over the gentle hills and heaped on the sides of the road. It was a different sky above, different air around her. So what if she gawked, Erin thought to herself, and she smiled as she tried to see everything at once.

Burke had been true to his word. The paperwork had gone so smoothly that in a matter of days after he'd offered her the job she'd been across the Atlantic. He'd left her with her cousin's family at the airport in Virginia, with a casual comment that he'd see her in a couple of days, after she'd settled in. Just like that. Erin was still trying to catch her breath.

She'd hoped he'd say more. She'd hoped—perhaps foolishly—that he would seem more pleased that she was there. She'd even waited to see that half smile, that dark amusement in his eyes, or to feel the flick of his finger down her cheek. But he'd only dismissed her as an employer dismisses an employee. Erin reminded herself that was precisely what they were now. There would be no more waltzes or wild embraces.

Did she wish there would be? The devil of it was she'd done just as much thinking about Burke Logan as she had about coming to America. Something had told her that they were both chances, the man and the country. Sometime, somehow, she'd begun to mix them together and had discovered she wanted both. She knew she was being foolish again and resolved to settle for the land.

It was beautiful. The mountains dark in the distance reminded her just enough of home to make her comfortable, while the whiz of the cars beside them in three lanes were foreign enough to add excitement. Erin found it a palatable combination and was already hoping for more.

Adelia shifted in her seat so that she could smile back at her cousin. "I remember my first day here, when Uncle Paddy picked me up at that same airport. I felt like I'd been plopped down in the middle of a circus."

"I'll get used to it." Erin smiled and took another long look out the window. "I'll get used to it very quickly, as soon as I believe I'm really here."

"I for one am grateful to Burke." Distracted a moment,

Dee murmured to Brady, who was fretting in his car seat, then soothed him with a stuffed dog. "It was never in my mind when we went to Ireland that we'd be bringing family back with us."

The guilt tingled a little, shadowing the pleasure. "I know it was all very sudden, and I'm beholden to you, Dee."

"Oh, what a pack of nonsense. I feel like a girl again, having my best friend come to stay. We'll have a party." The minute the thought struck, Adelia rolled with it. "A proper one, too, don't you think, Travis?"

"I think we could handle it."

"I don't want you to go to any trouble," Erin put in.

"If you don't let Dee go to any trouble, you'll break her heart," Travis said without embellishment. They crossed over the line into Maryland. "Nearly home now, love."

"I'm as excited to be back as I was to leave. Brendon, if you don't stop teasing your sister you'll be seeing nothing but the four walls of your room until morning." Dee sighed a bit and shifted.

"All right?" Travis sent her a quick, concerned glance.

"They're just active." She patted his hand to make light of the discomfort. "Probably squabbling between themselves already."

"I'd like to help with the children." The closer they came, the more Erin's nerves began to jump. "Or however else I can to pay you back for taking me in this way."

"You're family," Adelia said simply. Then she sat up straighter as they drove between the stone pillars that led to home. "Welcome to Royal Meadows, cousin. Be happy."

Erin didn't know what she'd been expecting. Something grand, surely. She wasn't disappointed. The sun shone hard on the February snow, causing the thin crust to glitter and shine. Acres of it, Erin thought. This world was white and gleaming. Even the trees were coated with it, their bare black branches mantled with snow and dripping with cold, clear ice. Like a fairyland, she mused, then called herself foolish.

When the house came into view, she could only stare. She'd never seen anything so big or so lovely. The stone rose up as sturdy as it was majestic from the white base of snow. Charm was added by the wrought-iron-trimmed balconies that graced the windows.

"It's beautiful," Erin murmured. "It's the most beautiful house I've ever seen."

"I've always thought so, too." Dee reached over to unhook Brady as Travis brought the car to a halt. "And it's so good to see it again. Come now, my lad, we're home."

"Uncle Paddy!" From the back seat, both Brendon and Keeley began to shout. Then they were out and kicking through the snow. A short, stocky man with wiry gray hair and a face like an elf spread his arms wide for them.

"Give me the baby, missy," Hannah told Dee. "You're already carrying two. And we'll let the men handle the bags while you come in for a nice cup of tea and put your feet up."

"Stop fussing," Dee said. Then she laughed as her uncle grabbed her in a fierce hug.

"How's my best girl?"

"Fit as a fiddle and glad to be home. Look what we brought back with us from Skibbereen." Still laughing, she held out a hand to Erin. "You remember Erin McKinnon, Uncle Paddy. Mary and Matthew McKinnon's daughter."

"Erin McKinnon?" His face seemed to scrunch together as he thought back. Then, with a hoot, he was beaming. "Erin McKinnon, is it? Faith, lass, the last time I saw you you were no more than a baby. I used to raise a glass with your da now and then, but you wouldn't be remembering that."

"No, but they still speak of Paddy Cunnane in the village."

"Do they now?" He grinned as if he knew exactly what was said. "Well, get inside out of the cold."

"I can help with the bags," Erin began as Adelia started to shoo her children indoors.

"I'd appreciate it if you'd go with Dee, let her show you your room." Travis was already pulling out the first of the luggage. Even as he set them in the drive, his gaze was following his wife. "She doesn't like to admit she gets tired, and having you to fuss over will keep her from overdoing."

Erin stood a moment, torn between carrying her own weight and doing what was asked of her. "All right. If you like."

"It wouldn't hurt if you told her you'd like to sit down with a cup of tea."

Quietly domineering, Erin thought again. On impulse, she leaned over and kissed Travis's cheek. "Your wife's a fortunate woman. I'll see that she rests without knowing she's been maneuvered into it." Still, she picked up one of the cases and took it inside with her.

The warmth struck her immediately, not just the change of temperature but the colors and the feel of the house itself. The children were already racing through the rooms as if they wanted to make sure nothing had changed in their absence.

"You'll want to go up first, see your room." Dee was

already stripping off her gloves and laying them on an ornamental table in the hall. Hooking her arm through Erin's, she started up the stairs. "You'll tell me if it suits you or not, and if there's anything else you want. As soon as you feel settled in, I'll show you the rest."

Erin only nodded. The space alone left her speechless. Adelia opened a door and gestured her inside.

"This is the guest room. I wish we'd had time to have some flowers for you." She glanced around the room, regretting she hadn't been able to add a few more personal touches. "The bath's down the end of the hall, and I'm sorry to say the children are always flinging wet towels around and making a mess of it."

The room was done in gray and rose with a big brass bed and a thick carpet. The furniture was a rich mahogany with gleaming brass pulls and a tall framed mirror over the bureau. There were knickknacks here and there, a little china dog, a rose-colored goblet, more brass in a whimsical study of a lion. The terrace doors showed the white expanse of snow through gauzy curtains, making a dreamlike boundary between warmth and cold. Unable to speak, Erin gripped her case in both hands and just looked.

"Will it suit you? You're free to change anything you like."

"No." Erin managed to get past the block in her throat, but her hands didn't relax on the handle of the case. "It's the most beautiful room I've ever seen. I don't know what to say."

"Say it pleasures you." Gently Dee pried the case from her. "I want you to feel comfortable, Erin, at home. I know what it's like to leave things behind and come to someplace strange."

Erin took a deep breath. She wasn't able to bear it, not for another second. "I don't deserve this."

"What foolishness." Businesslike, Dee set the case on the bed with the intention of helping her cousin unpack.

"No, please." Erin put her hand over Dee's, then sat. She didn't want her cousin to tire herself, and she didn't want her to see what a pitiful amount she'd brought with her. "I have to confess."

Amused, Dee sat beside her. "Do you want a priest?"

With a watery laugh that shamed her, Erin shook her head. "I've been so jealous of you." There, it was out.

Dee considered a minute. "But you're much prettier than I am."

"No, that's not true, and that's not it, in any case." Erin opened her mouth again, then let out a long breath. "Oh, I hate confession."

"Me, too. Sinning just comes natural to some of us."

Erin glanced over, saw both the warmth and humor and relaxed. "It comes natural enough to me. I was jealous of you. Am," she corrected, determined to make a clean breast of it. "I'd think about you here in a big, beautiful house, with pretty things and pretty clothes, your family, all the things that go with it, and I'd just near die with envy. When I met you at the airport that day, I was resentful and nervous."

"Nervous?" She could pass over resentment easily. "About seeing me? Erin, we all but grew up together."

"But you moved here, and you're rich." She closed her eyes. "I've a powerful lust for money."

A smile trembled on Dee's lips, but she managed to control it. "Well, that doesn't seem like a very big sin to me. A couple of days in purgatory, maybe. Erin, I know what is it not to have and to wish for more. I don't think less of you for envying me—in truth, I'm flattered. I suppose that's a sin, too," she added after a moment's thought.

"It's worse because you're so kind to me, all of you, and I feel like I'm using you."

"Maybe you are. But I'm using you as well, to bring Ireland a little closer, to be my friend. I have a sister— Travis's sister. But she moved away about two years ago. I can't tell you how much I miss her. I guess I was hoping you'd fill the hole."

Because her conscience was soothed by the admission, Erin touched a hand to Dee's. "I guess it's not so bad if we use each other."

"Let's just see what happens. Now I'll help you unpack."

"Let's leave it. I'd really like to go down and have a cup of tea."

As Erin rose, Adelia eyed her. "Did Travis tell you to keep me off my feet?"

"I don't know what you're talking about."

"Lying's a sin, too," Dee reminded her, but she smiled as she led her downstairs.

She dreamed of Ireland that night, of the heady green hills and the soft scent of heather. She saw the dark mountains and the clouds that rushed across the sky ahead of the wind. And her farm, with its rich plowed earth and grazing cows. She dreamed of her mother, telling her goodbye with a smile even as a tear slid down her cheek. Of her father, holding her so tight her ribs had ached. She heard each of her brothers teasing her, one by one.

She cried for Ireland that night, slow, quiet tears for a land she'd left behind and carried with her.

But when she woke, her eyes were dry and her mind

clear. She'd made her break, chosen her path, and she'd best be getting on with it.

The plain gray dress she chose was made sturdily and fit well. Her mother's stitches were always true. Erin started to pin her hair up, then changed her mind and tamed it into a braid. She studied herself with what she hoped was a critical and objective eye. Suitable for work, Erin decided, then started downstairs.

She heard the hoopla from the kitchen the moment she'd reached the first floor. At ease with confusion, she headed toward it.

"You'll have plenty to tell your friends at school." Hannah was at the stove, lecturing Brendon as she scooped up scrambled eggs.

"You've missed two weeks, my lad." At the kitchen table, Dee was fussing with a ribbon in Keeley's hair. "There's no reason in the world you shouldn't go back to school today."

"I have jet lag." He made a hideous face at his sister, then attacked the eggs Hannah set in front of him.

"Jet lag, is it?" With an effort, Dee kept a straight face. After kissing the top of Keeley's hair, she nudged her daughter toward her own breakfast. "Well, if that's the truth of it, I suppose we have to forget those flying lessons when you're sixteen. A jet pilot can't be having jet lag."

"Maybe it's not jet lag," Brendon corrected without missing a beat. "It's probably some foreign disease I caught when we were in Ireland."

"Bog fever," Erin said from the doorway. Clucking her tongue, she walked over to rest a hand on Brendon's brow. "Sure and that's the most horrible plague in Ireland."

"Bog fever?" Dee made sure there was a tremor in her voice. "Oh, no, Erin, it couldn't be. Not my baby."

"Young boys are the ones who catch it easiest, I'm afraid. There's only one cure, you know."

Dee shuddered and closed her eyes. "Oh, not that. Poor darling, poor little lad. I don't think I could bear it."

"If the boy has bog fever, it has to be done." Erin put a hand on his shoulder for comfort. "Nothing but raw spinach and turnip greens for ten days. It's the only hope for it."

"Raw spinach?" Brendon felt his little stomach turn over. He wasn't sure precisely what turnip greens were, but they sounded disgusting. "I feel a lot better."

"Are you sure?" Dee leaned over to check his brow herself. "He seems cool enough, but I don't know if we should take any chances."

"I feel fine." To prove his point, he jumped up and grabbed his coat. "Come on, Keeley, we don't want to miss the bus."

"Well, if you're sure..." Dee rose to kiss his cheek, then Keeley's. "Uncle Paddy's going to drive you to the end of the lane. It's cold, so stay in the car until the bus comes."

Dee waited until the door slammed behind them before she lowered herself in the chair again and howled with laughter. "Bog fever? Where in the blue heaven did you dig that up?"

"Ma always used it on Joe. It never failed."

"You've a quick mind." Hannah chuckled as she turned around. "What can I fix you for breakfast?"

"Oh, I don't—"

"If you think Mrs. Malloy can cook, wait until you taste Hannah's muffins." Understanding her cousin's embarrassment, Dee took the cloth off a little wicker basket. "Why don't you have some eggs to go with it? I have the appetite of a hog when I'm carrying, and I hate to eat alone."

"Coffee?" Hannah was by her shoulder with the pot.

"Please. Thank you. Ah, is Travis not up yet?"

"Up and gone," Dee said comfortably. "He's been down at the stables for more than an hour. When he travels on business, I'm never sure if he misses me or the horses more." She glanced at the muffins, lectured herself, then took another anyway. After all, she was eating for three. "Brendon's in the first grade now, and Keeley goes mornings to kindergarten. So there's only Brady." She gestured to the high chair where he sat, his face covered with oatmeal as he sang to his fingers. "He's the best-tempered child in the world, if I do say so myself. Now what would you like to do today?"

"Actually, I thought I'd go over to Mr. Logan's and begin work."

"Already?" Dee smiled her thanks at Hannah as the breakfast plates were set in front of them. "You've only just got here. Surely Burke's willing to give you a day or two to get your bearings."

"I know, but I'm anxious to get started, to see what there is to be done. And to make certain I can do it."

"I can't imagine Burke Logan putting anyone on his payroll who didn't know their business."

"It's different for me. Even thinking in dollars instead of pounds is different. If I'm in the middle of it working my way out, I won't worry so much about making a mess."

Dee remembered how anxious she herself had been to begin work when she'd come to America, to prove to herself she was still competent and able to make her own way. "All right, then, I'll drive you over myself after breakfast."

"Not on your life, missy," Hannah said from the stove.

"Oh, for pity sakes, I can still fit behind the wheel of a car."

"You're not driving anywhere until you have your next checkup and the doctor clears it. Paddy can take Miss McKinnon."

Dee wrinkled her nose at Hannah's back, but subsided. "I'm a prisoner in my own house. If I go down to the stables, Travis has every hand on the place watching me like a hawk. You'd think I never had a baby before."

"Twins come early, as you know very well."

"The sooner the better." Then she smiled. "Well, I'll just stay in and plan the party. And Brady and I can build block houses, can't we, love?"

In answer, he squealed and slapped his hand into his oatmeal.

"After he has a bath."

"Why don't I take care of that?" Rising, Erin moved over to free Brady from his high chair.

"You're not going to start pampering me, too. I'll go mad."

"Nothing of the kind. I just think it's time this hand-some young man and I got better acquainted."

By the time she was finished, Erin had to clean the oatmeal off herself as well. Bundled inside a cardigan and a coat, she drove with Paddy Cunnane to Burke's neighboring horse farm. The nerves were back. She could feel them tense in her fingers as she curled them together.

It was a waste of time to be nervous about the likes of him, she told herself. What had happened on that stormy morning in the shed was over and done with. Now they were nothing more than boss and employee. He'd said he expected a day's work for a day's pay, and she intended to give it to him.

Whatever other feelings she'd had had been born of the moment. Lust, she said firmly, telling herself she was mature enough to face that as a fact of life. Just as she would be strong enough to resist it.

She was a bookkeeper now. Her nerves were suddenly tinged with excitement. A bookkeeper, she repeated silently, with a good job and a good wage. Within the month she could start sending money home, with enough left over to buy... Lord, she couldn't begin to think what would be first.

Paddy turned the Jeep under an arch. The sign was large, wrought iron, strong rather than fancy with its block letters. Three Aces. Erin caught her lip between her teeth. Was that the hand he'd won it with, or the hand the former owner had lost it with?

The snow lay here as well, but the rise of hill wasn't as gentle. She saw a willow, old and gnarled, with its leaves dulled and yellow from winter. Perhaps in the summer it would look peaceful and lovely, but for now it looked fierce. Then she saw the house. She'd thought nothing could surprise her after the Grants'. She'd been wrong.

It had cupolas, like a castle, and the stone was dull and gray. The windows were arched, some of them with little parapets. Across from the steps and circled by the drive was an oval island that was now covered with untrampled snow.

"Do people really live in places like this?" she said half to herself.

"Cunningham, he'd be the owner before Logan, liked to think of himself as royalty." Paddy sniffed, but Erin wasn't entirely sure if the sound was directed at the present or the former owner. "Put more money into fancying up this place than into the stables and the stock. Got a pool right inside the house."

"You're joking."

"Indeed not. Right inside the house. Now you've only to call when you've finished here. I'll come fetch you, or one of the boys will."

"I'm obliged to you." But her fingers seemed frozen on the handle.

"Good luck to you, lass."

"Thanks." Screwing up her courage, she pushed out of the Jeep. She was grateful it stayed parked where it was as she climbed the stone steps to the front door.

And what a door, she thought. As big as a barn and all carved. She ran a hand over it before she pulled back the knocker. Erin counted slowly under her breath and waited. It was opened by a dark-haired woman with big eyes and a small, erect figure. Erin swallowed and kept her chin up.

"I'm Erin McKinnon, Mr. Logan's bookkeeper."

The woman eyed her silently, then stepped back. Erin managed to throw a smile to Paddy over her shoulder before she stepped inside.

By the saints, she thought, tongue-tied again as she stood in the atrium. She'd never seen anything to match it, with its high ceilings and lofty windows. It seemed the sun shone in from all directions and slanted over the leaves of thick green plants. A balcony ran all the way around in one huge circle, the rail gleaming and carved as the door had been. The heels of her sensible shoes clicked on the tile floor, then stopped as she stood, uncertain what to do next.

"I'll tell Mr. Logan you're here."

Erin only nodded. The accent sounded Spanish, making her feel more out of place than ever. Erin wiped her hands on her skirt and thought she knew what Alice had felt like when she'd stepped through the looking glass.

"Are you eager to work, or did you just miss me?"

She turned, knowing she'd been caught gaping. He was in jeans and boots, and the smile was the same. The confidence she'd lost when she'd stepped inside came flooding back. It was the best defense.

"Eager to work and earn a wage."

The cold and excitement had heightened the color in her cheeks and darkened her eyes. As she stood in the center of the big open room, Burke thought she looked ready and able to take on the world.

"You could have had a day or two to settle in."

"I could, but I didn't want it. I'm used to earning my way."

"Fine. You'll certainly earn it here." He lifted a hand and gestured her to follow. "Morita, my last bookkeeper, managed to embezzle thirty thousand before the cage shut on him. In the process, he made a mess of the records. Your first priority is to straighten them out again. While you're doing that, you're to keep up the payroll and the current invoices."

"Of course." Of course, a little voice inside her said mockingly.

Burke pushed a door open and led her inside. "You'll work here. Hopefully you won't have to ask me a bunch of annoying questions, but if something comes up, you can call Rosa on the intercom and she'll pass it on to me. Make a list of whatever supplies you think you'll need, and you'll have them."

She cleared her throat and nodded. Her office was every bit as large as O'Donnelly's entire storeroom. The furniture was old and glossy, the carpet like something out of a palace. Determined not to stare again, Erin walked over to the desk. He had been right about one thing. It was a mess. For the first time since she'd approached the big stone house, she felt relief. Here was something familiar.

Ledgers and books and papers were piled together in one heap. There was an adding machine, but it was nothing like the clunky manual one she'd used before. Besides the clutter, there was a phone, a china holder stuffed with pencils and a basket clearly marked In and Out.

Burke moved behind the desk and began opening and closing drawers. "You've got stamps, stationery, extra work sheets, checkbooks. Since Morita, nothing goes out without my signature."

"If you'd taken that precaution before, you'd be thirty thousand dollars richer."

"Point taken." He didn't add that Morita had worked for him for ten years, during lean times and better. "Set your own pace, as long as it's not sluggish. Rosa will fix you lunch. You can take it in here or in the dining room. There may be times I'll join you."

"Are you here most of the day?"

"I'm around." He settled a hip on the corner of the desk. "You didn't sleep well."

"No, I…" But her fingers had automatically lifted to the slight smudges under her eyes. "The time change, I guess."

"Are you comfortable at the Grants'?"

"Aye, they're wonderful to me. All of them."

"They're extraordinary people. You won't find many like them."

"You're not." She hadn't meant to say it, but told herself it was too late to be sorry she had. "You've an edge to you."

"Then be careful you don't get too close. Edges can be sharp."

"I've already seen that for myself." She said it lightly as she reached for the first stack of papers. He closed his hand slowly and firmly around her wrist.

"Are you trying to provoke me, Irish?"

"No, but I don't imagine it takes much."

"You're right there. It might be fair to tell you that I have a short fuse, and a dangerous one."

"I'm so warned." She looked amused, but when she tried to free her hand, his fingers only tightened.

"One more warning, then. Since you've moved into our little community, you'll hear it from others soon enough. When I find a woman who attracts me, I find a way to have her. Fair means or foul, it doesn't mean a damn to me."

It wasn't a warning, Erin realized. It was a threat. Beneath his fingers, her pulse was beating hard and fast, but she kept her eyes even with his. "I didn't have to be told to know that, nor have I any intention of attracting you."

"Too late." He grinned but released her hand. "I find you intriguing enough to dance in the moonlight with, desirable enough to kiss in a garden shed, and passionate enough to imagine making love to."

Her stomach knotted with fear, with longing. "Well, a woman's head could be turned clear around with such flattery, Mr. Logan. Tell me, did you bring me to America to sleep with you or to fix your books?"

"Both," he said simply, "but we'll deal with business first."

"Business is all we'll deal with. Now I'd like to begin."

"Fine." But instead of leaving, he ran his hands up her

arms. Erin stiffened, but didn't back away. She wouldn't play the fool and struggle. Though she braced herself for the hot passion she'd experienced before, he only brushed a kiss over her cheek.

He'd thought of her and little else since he'd come home again. He'd thought of how she'd felt in his arms, of how his system reacted when she smiled, of how her voice flowed, warm and sweet, so that a man didn't care what the words were as long as she spoke again.

He knew he could have her. Her response had been too quick and too encompassing before for either of them to pretend otherwise. He knew she wanted him, though it didn't sit well with her. Even now, as he kissed her lightly, avoiding her lips, her breath was beginning to tremble. He'd never known a woman whose passion was so close to the surface. Now that she was here, in his home, he knew he wouldn't rest until he had all of it.

But she would come to him. His pride demanded it. So he teased her with his lips, knowing he stirred her. He teased her with his lips, knowing he was slowly killing himself.

"Fair means or foul," he murmured, nipping gently at her earlobe. "I want you."

Her eyes were closed. How was it possible to be swept away so quickly, to want so desperately what you knew you shouldn't have? She put a hand to his chest, willing it to be steady. "And you're used to taking what you want. I understand that. I won't deny you move something in me, but I'm not here for the taking, Burke."

"Maybe not," he murmured. Some women were only there for the earning. "I can be patient, Irish. When a man's got the cards, he's got to know when to hold and when to lay them on the table." Thoughtfully he ran a finger down her braid. "We'll play out this hand sooner or later. I'll let you get started."

Erin waited until he'd left before she let out a long breath. How was it he could be that arrogant and still make her want to smile? With a shake of her head, she sat behind the desk in a plush leather chair that made her sigh.

Burke was right about one thing, she mused. They would play out the hand sooner or later. The problem was, Erin was afraid that even if she won, she'd lose.

Chapter Five

Within a week, Erin had developed a routine that pleased
her. In the mornings she rose early enough to help Dee
ready the children for school, then drove a borrowed car
to the Three Aces to report to work by nine.

The mess of Burke's bookkeeping had been an enormous understatement. So had her estimate of his wealth.
As she tallied figures and pored over ledgers, she tried
to think of it in simple, practical terms. Numbers, after
all, were just numbers.

She was rarely interrupted, and took her lunch from
the silent Rosa at her desk. By the end of the first week,
she'd made enough headway to feel pleased with herself.
Only once or twice had she been made to feel foolish.
She'd had to ask Burke for the instruction book on the
adding machine. Then she'd asked him to supply her with
a pencil sharpener. He'd simply picked up a cylinder with
a hole in it and handed it to her.

"And what good is this?" she'd demanded. "It doesn't even have a crank."

He'd picked up a pencil and shoved it in the hole; then, damn him, had laughed when she'd jumped at the grinding. "Batteries," he'd said, "not magic."

She'd gotten over that small humiliation by burying her face in the account books. Maybe she wasn't used to gadgets, but by the saints, she'd balanced his books. Now she sat at the little electric typewriter and wrote up her weekly report. After tidying her desk, Erin picked up her report and went to find Burke.

His house was still almost completely uncharted territory to her. In the atrium, Erin hesitated. She could have called for Rosa on the intercom, but talking into the blasted thing always made her feel foolish. Instead, Erin set off in what she hoped was the general direction of the kitchen.

The place went on forever, she thought, and found it increasingly difficult not to open doors and peek inside as she went. Hearing a hum, she turned in that direction. Dishwasher, she thought, or a washing machine. With a shrug, she decided she'd find Rosa at the end of it.

The woman was a mystery, Erin thought as she walked. Rosa rarely spoke and always seemed to know precisely where to find Burke. Though the housekeeper referred to Burke as Mr. Logan, Erin sensed something less formal between them. She'd wondered, though it hadn't brought her any pleasure, if they were or had been lovers. Pushing the thought aside, she moved to the south end of the house.

But it wasn't the kitchen she found, or the laundry room. As she pushed open one of a pair of double doors, Erin entered the tropics. The pool was an inviting blue, sparkling under the sun that poured through the glass roof

and walls. There were trees here the likes of which she'd
never seen, planted in huge pottery urns. And flowers.
She stepped in farther, overwhelmed by the heady scent
when she could still see the snow through the glass. There
were rich red petals, brilliant orange and yellow, exotic
blues. If she closed her eyes, she imagined, she'd hear the
chatter of parrots. Paradise, she thought, smiling as she
walked farther.

With his eyes half-closed and his body just beginning
to relax, Burke watched her. She didn't look sultry like
the room, but fresh, untouched. The sun was all over her
hair, drawing out the fire, licking at the layers of light.
She'd pulled it back in a band as he'd seen her wear it in
Ireland. And he could remember very well, too well, what
it felt like to run his fingers through its mass.

He saw her reach for a flower as if her fingers itched
to pick it, then draw back her hand and bury her face in
the blooms instead. Her laugh was quiet, delighted, and
he knew she thought herself alone.

So the Irish rose had a weakness for flowers, he
thought, then watched her shake her head and look wonderingly, longingly around. And for money. At the latter,
he shrugged his shoulders. It was difficult for someone
in his position to blame her.

He could blame her, however, for the fact that his body
was no longer even close to relaxing.

"Want a swim, Irish?"

At the sound of his voice, she whirled around. She'd
forgotten about the hum. She saw its source now, and
Burke in the middle of it. Another pool—no, not a pool,
she corrected. She wasn't a complete dunderhead. She'd
seen pictures of spas with their jets and bubbles and
steamy water. And she couldn't help, for just a moment,
wondering what it felt like to lower one's body into it.

"Want to join me?"

Because he grinned when he said it, Erin merely shrugged. "Thank you, but I'll be leaving for home in a few minutes. I've finished for the day and brought you your first report."

He nodded, but merely gestured to a white wicker chair beside the spa. "Have a seat."

Biting off a sigh, Erin did as he asked. "You may be a man of leisure yourself, but I've things to do."

Burke stretched his arms along the edge of the spa. He didn't mention that he'd been up and at the stables since dawn, or that he'd strained every muscle in his body overseeing the mating between a stud and a particularly high-strung mare. "You've still got a few minutes on the clock, Irish. So how are my finances?"

"You're a rich man, Mr. Logan, though how that might be with the mess your books were in amazes me. I've done a bit of studying and come up with a new system." The truth was she'd spent two nights burning the midnight oil with books on accounting. "If you like, I'll wait until you've finished and go over it with you."

"It'll keep."

"Suit yourself. By the end of next week I should have everything running smoothly enough."

"That's good to know. Why don't you tell me how?"

He stretched his shoulders. Erin watched the muscles ripple along the damp skin, then deliberately shifted her gaze above his head. This was no place for her to be, she told herself. Especially when her mind was wandering away from accounting. "It's all in this report, if you'd care to pull yourself out of the tub there and have a look at it."

"Have it your way." Burke pushed the button that shut off the jets, then stood. Erin's limbs went weak as she saw he wore no more than he'd been born with. She was grateful color didn't rise to her cheeks, though she couldn't prevent some from leaving.

Burke took a towel and swung it easily over his hips as he stepped from the spa.

"You've no shame, Burke Logan."

"None at all."

"Well, if you'd meant to shock me, I'll have to disappoint you. I've four brothers, if you'll remember, and…" She glanced over again, prepared to look at him without interest. It was then she noticed the darkening bruise just under his left ribs. "You've hurt yourself." She was up immediately and laying gentle fingers on it. "Oh, it's a nasty one." Without thinking, she took her fingers up over his ribs, carefully checking. "You didn't break anything."

"Not so far," he murmured. He was standing very still, the amusement he'd felt completely wiped out. Her fingers felt so cool, so tender on his skin. She touched him as if she cared. That was something he'd learned to live a long time without.

"It'll look worse yet tomorrow," she said with a cluck of her tongue. "You should put some liniment on it." Then she realized her fingers were spread over his chest, and his chest was hard and smooth and wet. Erin snatched her hand away and stuck it behind her back. "How'd you come by it?"

"The new colt I picked up in Ireland."

She closed her hand into a fist. It was damp from his skin. "You'll have to give him more room next time." The shudder inside her came as no surprise and was quickly controlled.

"I intend to. I have the highest respect for the Irish temper."

"And so you should. If you'd look over the report now,

I could answer any questions you might have before I leave."

Burke picked up the neatly typed sheets. Erin found it necessary to clear her throat as she turned to look out through the glass, now lightly fogged from the steam of the spa. But she didn't see the snow. She could still see him—the long arms roped with muscle, the hard chest glistening with water, the narrow hips leading to taut thighs.

A fine specimen, some would have said, herself included. And she could have murdered him for making her want.

"It seems clear enough." She jolted a bit, then cursed herself. "You know your business, Erin, but then I wouldn't have hired you if I hadn't believed that." No, he wouldn't have, but he'd have found some other way to bring her back with him. "Got anything in mind for your first paycheck?"

"A thing or two." She relaxed enough to smile at him, schooling her gaze to go no lower than his neck. Half the money would be on its way to Ireland in the morning. And the rest… She couldn't begin to think of it. "If you're satisfied, I'll be going home now."

"I'm a long way from satisfied," Burke said under his breath. "Listen, did you ever think the bookkeeping would be more interesting if you knew more about the stables, the racing?"

"No." Then she moved her shoulders as the thought he'd planted took root. "I suppose it might, though."

"I've got a horse running tomorrow. Why don't you come along, see where the money comes from and where it goes?"

"Go to the races?" She caught her lip between her teeth as she thought of it. "Could I bet?"

"There's a woman after my heart. Be ready at eight. I'll take you around the stables and paddock first."

"All right. Good day to you." She started out, then glanced over her shoulder. "I'd put some witch hazel on that bruise."

Erin paced the living room. It was her first day off, and she was going to spend it at the races. There would be mobs of people she'd never met; she'd hear dozens of voices for the first time. She ran a hand down her hair and hoped she looked all right. Not for Burke, she thought quickly. For herself, that was all. She wanted to look nice, to feel she looked nice when she stood in the midst of all those people.

The minute she heard Burke's car, she was racing out of the house. She hesitated on the steps, staring down at the fire-red sports car with its long, sleek hood. She made a mental note of the make so she could write home and tell Brian.

"You're prompt," Burke commented as she climbed in beside him.

"I'm excited." It didn't seem foolish to admit it now. "I've never been to the races before. Cullen has, and he told me the horses are beautiful and the people fascinating. Faith, look at all these dials." She studied the dash. "You'd have to be an engineer to drive it."

"Want to try?"

When she glanced at him and saw he was serious, she was sorely tempted. But she remembered all the cars that had been on the highway when they'd driven from the airport. "I'll just watch for now. When does the racing start?"

"We've got plenty of time. How's Dee?"

"She's fine. The doctor gave her a clean checkup but

told her she had to stay off her feet a bit. She grumbles because she can't spend as much time down at the stables, but we're keeping her busy. The snow's melting."

"A few more days like we've been having and it'll be gone."

"I hope not. I like to look at it." She settled back, deciding that riding in the sports car was like riding on the wind. "Are you going to be warm enough?" she asked, looking at his light jacket and jeans. "There's still a bite in the air."

"Don't worry. So what do you like best about America so far, besides the snow?"

"The way you talk," she said instantly.

"Talk?"

"You know, the accent. It's charming."

"Charming." He glanced over at her, then laughed until the bruise began to throb. Still chuckling, he rubbed a hand over it absently.

"Is that troubling you?"

"What, this? No."

"Did you use witch hazel?"

He knew better than to laugh again. "I couldn't put my hands on any."

"I'd imagine you'd have a case or two of horse liniment down in the stables. Oh, look at the little planes." When he turned into the airport, she looked over at him. "What are we doing here?"

"Taking a ride on one of the little planes."

Her stomach did a quick flip-flop. "But I thought we were going to the races."

"We are. My horse is racing at Hialeah. That's in Florida."

"What's Florida?"

Burke paused in the act of swinging his door closed.

On the other side of the car, Erin stared at him. "South," he told her, and held out a hand.

Too excited to think, too terrified to object, Erin found herself bundled onto a plane. The cabin was so small that even she had to stoop a bit, but when she sat the chair was soft and roomy. Burke sat across from her and indicated the seat belt. Once hers was secured, he flipped the switch on an intercom. "We're set here, Tom."

"Okay, Mr. Logan. Looks like smooth sailing. Skies are clear except for a little patch in the Carolinas. We ought to be able to avoid most of them."

When she heard and felt the engines start, Erin gripped the arms of the chair. "Are you sure this thing's safe?"

"Life's a gamble, Irish."

She nearly babbled before she caught the amusement in his eyes. Deliberately she made her hands relax. "So it is." As the plane started to roll, she looked out the window. Within minutes the ground was tilting away under them. "It's quite a sight, isn't it?" She smiled, leaning a little closer to the window. "When all of you landed in Cork, I looked at the plane and wondered what it would be like to sit inside. Now I know."

"How is it?"

She gave him a sideways smile. "Well, there's no champagne."

"There can be."

"At half past eight in the morning?" With a laugh, she sat back again. "I think not. I should have thanked you for asking me to go today. The Grants have been nothing but kind to me, so I'm really grateful to give them a day to themselves."

"Is that the only reason you should have thanked me?" He stood and went into a little alcove.

"No. I appreciate the chance to go."

"You want cream in this coffee?"

"Aye." He could have said you're welcome, she thought, then let it pass. Nothing was going to spoil her mood. When he sat, she took the cup but was too wound up to drink. "Will you give me an answer if I ask a question that's none of my business?"

Burke drew out a cigar, then lit it. "I'll give you an answer, but not necessarily the truth." He kicked out his legs, then rested his ankles on the seat beside her.

"Did you really win Three Aces in a poker game?"

He blew out smoke. "Yes and no."

"That's not an answer at all."

"Yes, I played poker with Cunningham—quite a bit of poker with Cunningham—and he lost heavily. When you gamble you have to know when to stick and when to walk away. He didn't."

"So you won the farm from him."

She'd like that, he thought, watching her eyes. He imagined she saw a smoky, liquor-scented room with two men bent over five cards each and the deed to the farm between them. "In a manner of speaking. I won money from him, more money than he had to lose. He didn't have enough cash to pay me, or for that matter to pay certain other parties who were growing tired of holding IOUs. In the end, I bought the farm from him, dirt cheap."

"Oh." It wasn't quite as romantic. "You must have been rich before then."

"You could say my luck was on an upswing at the time."

"Gambling's no way to make a living."

"It beats sweeping floors."

Since she could only agree, Erin fell silent a moment. "Did you know about horses before?"

"I knew they had four legs, but when you've got your

money riding on a game, you learn fast. Where did you learn to keep books?"

"Arithmetic came easily to me. When I could I took courses in school, then I started to run the books at the farm. It was more satisfying than morning milking. Then, because everyone knows what everyone else is up to back home, I found myself working for Mrs. Malloy, then Mr. O'Donnelly. I worked for Francis Duggan at the market for a time, too, but his son Donald thought I should marry him and have ten children, so I had to let that job go."

"You didn't want to marry Donald Duggan?"

"And spend my life counting potatoes and turnips? No, thank you. It came to the point where I knew I had to either black both his eyes or give up the job. It seemed easier to give up the job. What are you smiling at?"

"I was just thinking that Donald Duggan was lucky you didn't carry a rake."

Erin tilted her head as she studied him. "It's you who're lucky I held myself back." Comfortable now, she tucked her legs under her and sipped her cooling coffee. "Tell me about the horse you're racing today."

"Double Bluff, he's a two-year-old. Temperamental and nervy unless he's running. He's proved himself from his first race, took the Florida Derby last weekend. That's the biggest purse in the state."

"Aye, I heard Travis mention it. He seems to think this horse is the best he's seen in a decade. Is it?"

"Might be. In any case, he'll be my Derby entry this year. His sire won over a million dollars in purses in his career, and his dam was the offspring of a Triple Crown winner. Likes to come from behind, on the outside." He took another puff, and again Erin noticed the scar along his knuckles.

"You sound as though you're fond of him."

He was, and that fact was a constant surprise. Burke only shrugged. "He's a winner."

"What about the one you bought in Ireland, the one who kicked you?"

"I'm going to start him off locally—Charles Town, Laurel, Pimlico, so I can keep an eye on him. If my hunch is right, he'll double what I paid for him in a year."

"And if your hunch was wrong?"

"They aren't often. In any case, I'd still consider my trip to Ireland paid off."

She wasn't completely comfortable with the way he looked at her. "Being a gambler," she said evenly, "you'd know how to lose."

"I know how to win better."

She set her coffee down. "How did you get the scar on your hand?"

He didn't glance at it as most people would, but tapped out his cigar as he watched her. "Broken bottle of Texas Star in a bar fight outside of El Paso. There was a disagreement over a hand of seven-card stud and a pretty blonde."

"Did you win?"

"The hand. The woman wasn't worth it."

"I suppose it makes more sense to gash your hand open over a game of cards than it does for a woman."

"Depends."

"On what? The woman?"

"On the game, Irish. It always depends on the game."

When they arrived, Erin stepped off the plane into another new world. Burke had told her to leave her coat on the plane, but even so she hadn't been expecting the warmth or the glare of the sun.

"Palm trees," she managed, then laughed and grabbed Burke's hands. "Those are palm trees."

"No fooling?" Before she had a chance to be annoyed, he swung an arm over her shoulders and swept her away. There was a car waiting for them. Erin slipped inside, wanting to pretend she did such things every day. "There's no handle for the window," she began. Burke leaned over and pressed the button to lower it. "Oh." After ten seconds, she gave up trying to be poised. "I can't believe it. It's so warm, and the flowers. Oh, my mother would die for the flowers. It's like that room in your house with all the glass. Two weeks ago I was scrubbing Mrs. Malloy's floor, and now I'm looking at palm trees."

He drove competently, without asking directions or checking a map. Erin realized this life wasn't new to him. Here she was babbling and sounding like a fool. She made one attempt to restrain herself, then gave it up. It didn't matter how she sounded.

He hadn't realized he'd get such enjoyment out of seeing someone take little things and make them special. For a moment he wished they could just keep driving so that she would go on talking, laughing, asking questions. He'd nearly forgotten there were people who could still find things fresh and new no matter how often they'd been used.

Traveling was a profession to him, and like most professional travelers he'd long ago stopped looking at what was around him. Now, with Erin pointing out white sand, young skateboarders and towering hotels, he began to remember what it was like to see something for the first time.

They knew him at the track. Erin noticed as they walked over the green lawn toward the spread of stables that people nodded in his direction or greeted him as

Mr. Logan. There were jockeys and trainers and grooms already preparing for the afternoon races.

"Logan."

Erin glanced over and saw a big, potbellied man in a straw hat. She saw the flash of a diamond on his finger and the light film of sweat the heat had already drawn on his face. "Durnam."

"Didn't know you were coming down for a look-see."

"I like to keep an eye on things. Your horse ran well last week."

"At Charles Town. I didn't know you were there."

"I wasn't. Erin McKinnon, Charlie Durnam. He owns Durnam Stables in Lexington."

"Real horse country, ma'am." He took her hand and flashed her a smile. "A pleasure, a real pleasure. Nobody picks the fillies like Logan."

"I won't be running any races, Mr. Durnam," she told him, but she smiled, judging him harmless.

"From Ireland, are you?"

"She's Adelia Grant's cousin." Burke spoke mildly, giving Durnam a straight look until he released Erin's hand.

"Well, ain't that something? I tell you, ma'am, any friend of the Grants is a friend of Charlie Durnam's. Fine people."

"Thank you, Mr. Durnam."

"I'm going to go check on my horse, Charlie. See you around."

"Take a look at Charlie's Pride while you're at it," he called after them. "That's a real piece of horseflesh."

"What a funny man," Erin murmured.

"That funny man has one of the best stables in the country and a roving eye."

She glanced back over her shoulder and chuckled. "His eye can rove all it pleases. I can't imagine he has much luck on a landing."

"You'd be surprised the kind of luck ten or fifteen million can buy." Burke nodded to a groom. "I'm running against him today."

"Is that so?" Erin tossed her hair back and was sure the sun had never shone brighter. "Then you'll just have to beat him, won't you?"

With a grin, Burke put his arm around her shoulders again. "I intend to." He walked by a few stalls. Erin cautiously kept on the far side of him. The smell of horse and hay was familiar, and so was the little knot in her stomach. Ignore it, she told herself, stepping up beside Burke as he stopped at a stall.

"This is Double Bluff."

She judged the dark bay to be about fifteen hands, broad at the chest and streamlined for speed. The beauty of him struck her first; then she froze when he tossed his head. "He's a big one." Her throat had gone bone-dry, but she forced herself to take one step closer.

"Ready to win?" With a laugh, Burke reached up to stroke his nose. The colt's ears came forward in acknowledgment, but he continued to prance. "Impatient. This one hates to wait. He's an arrogant devil, and I think he might just win Three Aces its first Triple Crown. What do you think of him?"

"He's lovely." Erin had taken a step backward the first time the colt had looked in her direction. "I'm sure he'll do you proud."

"Let's have a closer look, make sure the groom's done his job." Burke opened the stall door and stepped in. Erin steeled herself, and with her heart pounding walked to the opening. "You look good, fella." Burke ran his hands over the colt's flank, then dipped under him to check the other side. He lifted each hoof, then nodded in approval. "Clean as a whistle. Wait until they put a saddle on him. The minute they do, he's ready. You have to hold him back from the starting gate."

As if he understood, Double Bluff pawed the ground. He tossed up his head and whinnied as Burke laughed. Erin fainted dead away.

When she surfaced, there was an arm supporting her. Something cool and wet was being urged through her lips. She swallowed reflexively, then opened her eyes. "What happened?"

"You tell me." Burke's voice was rough, but the hand that stroked her cheek was gentle.

"Probably too much sun." Erin heard the drawled pronouncement and shifted her gaze beyond Burke's shoulder. She saw a young face and a thatch of sandy hair.

"That's right," she said, grabbing the excuse. "I'm fine now."

"Just sit still." Burke held her down as she tried to get up. "It's okay, Bobby, I'll handle it from here."

"Yes, sir, Mr. Logan. You take it easy now, miss, stay in the shade."

"Thank you. Oh…" Erin closed her eyes and cursed herself for seven kinds of a fool. "I'm sorry I caused a scene. I don't know what could have happened."

"You were fine one minute and in a heap the next." And nothing, absolutely nothing in his life, had ever scared him so badly. "You're still pale. Why don't we take Bobby's advice and get you up and into some shade?"

"Aye." She let out a breath of relief. Just as Burke started to help her up, Double Bluff stuck his head out again and shook the stall door. With a muffled cry, Erin threw her arms around Burke's neck and clung.

It took him only a moment to put one and one together. "For God's sake, Erin, why didn't you tell me you were afraid of horses?"

"I'm not."

"Nitwit," he muttered, hauling her unceremoniously into his arms.

"Don't carry me. I've had enough humiliation already."

"Shut up." When he judged they were far enough away from the stables, he set her down under a palm. "If you'd had the brains to tell me, you wouldn't have shaved ten years off my life." With another oath, he dropped down beside her. His heart had yet to resume its normal rhythm.

"The last thing I'm wanting from you is a lecture." She would have stood and stormed away, but she knew her legs weren't ready to carry her. "Besides, there was nothing to tell. I thought I was over it."

"You thought wrong." Then, because she was still pale, he relented and took her hand. "Why don't you tell me about it?"

"It's childish."

"Tell me anyway."

"We had some field horses, two good ones." She let out a long breath. He could hardly think her any more of a fool than he did now. "We had them out, and a storm was coming up. Brian unhooked the one to take him back to the barn. There was a lot of thunder and lightning, so the horses were nervous. Joe was unhooking the second, and I was at the head trying to calm him. I don't know, it happened fast, lightning spooked him and he reared. God, those hooves are big when they're over your head." She shuddered once. "I fell, and he ran right over me."

"Oh, God." Burke tightened his fingers on her hand.

"I was lucky, it wasn't that bad. A couple of broken

ribs only, bruises, but I've just never been able to get too close to one without panicking."

"If you'd told me I never would have brought you."

"I thought I'd beaten it by now. It was more than five years ago. Stupid." She ran a hand over her face, then tucked back her hair. "I've been making excuses all week to Dee and Travis why I don't go down to the stables."

"Why don't you just tell them?" When she only shrugged, he shifted closer. "It's not half as stupid to be afraid as it is to be ashamed of it."

Her chin came up; then she sighed. "Maybe." Avoiding his eyes, she plucked a blade of grass. "Don't tell them."

"More secrets?" Patiently he caught her chin in his hand and turned her face to his. It was far more difficult to resist her now when her cheeks were pale, her eyes a little damp and the vulnerability like a sheen on her skin. "You shouldn't worry so much about what people think of you. I know you wash dishes and faint at the sight of horses, but I still like you."

"Do you?" A reluctant smile tugged at her mouth. "Really?"

"Well enough." Unaccustomed to resisting any desire for long, he lowered his mouth to hers, to taste, to nibble, to explore. She lifted a hand to his chest as if to hold him off, but then her fingers simply curled into his shirt and held him there.

His other kisses hadn't made her feel peaceful or secure. Anything but. Yet this one was different. Even as excitement shimmered warm in her stomach, she felt safe. Maybe it was the way his hand curved around her neck, with his fingers gentle and soothing. Or maybe it was the way his lips made hers feel soft and tingly.

He wanted to draw her close, to cuddle her, to rock

her on his lap and murmur foolish things. He'd never had that urge with a woman before. It was an odd and uneasy sensation, and at the same time…comforting.

He drew away slightly, but kept her close. "I'll take you home."

"Home? But I want to see the races." For some reason she felt as though she could face anything at that moment. "I'm fine, I promise you. Besides, maybe if I can learn to watch them from a distance I won't freeze up when I'm near one." She stood, grateful that her legs were sturdy again. "Come now, Burke, we didn't fly all the way to— where are we?"

"Florida," he told her, and rose.

"Aye, Florida to turn right around and go home again. That great beast in there is going to win, isn't he?"

"I've got my money on him."

"And I've got ten more on the nose."

With a laugh, he accepted the hand she held out. "Let's go get a seat."

The stands were already filling up. In them, Erin indeed saw many faces, tanned and sunburned ones, faces with lines spreading out from the eyes and more with skin as smooth as new cream. Some people pored over racing forms, others smoked fat cigars or sipped from plastic cups.

But in the boxes was elegance, the kind that spoke of confidence and poise. Sheer summer dresses in pastels mixed well with light cotton suits and straw hats. She saw more than one tanned, slender woman tilt a head in Burke's direction. Now and then he lifted a hand, but he made no effort to mix with them.

From Burke's box in the front, she could see the wide brown oval where the horses would run and the lush green infield filled with tropical flowers and pink flamingos.

Still farther away were more stands with more people. Every minute, more were filing in.

"I've never seen so many people in one place at one time. And they're all here to watch the race."

"Want a beer?"

Erin nodded absently and continued to take in everything as Burke left her. She spotted Durnam not far away, talking to a woman in the tiniest pair of shorts Erin had ever seen. Erin passed over him and looked at the electronic board that was beginning to flash with numbers and odds for the first race.

"I want you to explain to me what it all means up there," Erin began before Burke had a chance to sit down again. "So I'll know best how to bet."

"If you want a tip, you'll wait for the third race, bet on number five."

"Why?"

"The horse is out of Royal Meadows. Sentiment aside, he's a strong runner. Record's a little shaky, but he looks good today. First race is anybody's game. So far the odds aren't spectacular."

"Are you betting on it?"

"No."

"I thought you were a gambler."

"I like to pick my own game."

Erin sat back and listened to the announcements for the first race. "Crystal Maiden sounds pretty."

"Pretty names don't win races. Hold on to your money, Irish."

She settled back and contented herself with absorbing the sounds and sights around her. By the time the horses were brought to the starting gate, she was leaning forward in her chair. "They *are* beautiful," she said, but she felt a great deal better when Burke's hand rested lightly on hers.

Her pulse was hammering. He gauged it to be almost as much from excitement as nerves. He'd been right about the contradictions in her. As the gates opened, her fingers linked hard with his, but she didn't cringe.

"What a noise," she murmured, while her heart beat almost as loudly as hooves on turf. As they rounded the first turn, she strained to keep following them. That was power, she thought, both raw and controlled. They might well have made it a business, but she could see why it had been and was still the sport of kings.

When it was over, she laid a hand on her breast. "My heart's still pounding. Don't smile at me like that," she warned, but laughed with it. "It's the most wonderful thing I've ever seen. All those colors, all that energy. Can you imagine doing this every day?"

"There are plenty who do."

But she only shook her head. Today was special, a once-in-a-lifetime day. "I want to bet on the next one."

"Third race," Burke repeated, and sipped his beer.

When her time came, she insisted on betting herself. Erin put the stub in the pocket of her shirt, then changed her mind and tucked it carefully in her billfold. Seated beside Burke again, she fretted until the horses were brought to the gate.

"I don't mind losing," she said with a quick grin, "but I'd sure as hell like to win better."

When they were off, she stood and leaned against the rail. "Which one is he?" she demanded, grabbing Burke's hand to drag him forward with her.

"Fourth back on the inside. Red-and-gold silks."

"Aye." She watched, urging him on. "He runs well, doesn't he?"

"Yes."

"Oh, look, he's moving up."

"Better hang on, Irish. They've got half a mile to go."

"But he's moving up." She gave a hoot of laughter as she pointed. "He's in second now."

There was shouting all around her, competing with the announcer and the thundering of hooves. Erin strained to hear all three as she grabbed Burke's shirt and tugged.

"He's taken the lead. Look at him!" She spun away from the rail and into Burke's arms as he finished half a length ahead. "He won! *I* won!" Laughing, she kissed Burke hard. "How much?"

"Mercenary little witch."

"It's nothing to do with mercenary and everything to do with winning. I'm going home and tell Dee I bet on her horse and won. How much?"

"The odds were five to one."

"Fifty dollars?" She gave another peal of laughter. "I'll buy the next beer." She took him by the hand. "When does your horse race?"

"In the fifth."

"Thank goodness. It'll give me time to recover."

She bought him a beer, then went one better and bought them both hot dogs. The only time she could remember spending such a frivolous day was at a fair. This seemed like one to her, with the noise and smells and colors. She had another ticket in her pocket and Burke's sunglasses on by the time the fifth race was announced.

"I really hope he wins," she told him with her mouth full. "Not just because I bet on him, either."

"That makes two of us."

"How does it feel to own one?" she wondered. "Not just a horse, but a horse from a great line."

"Most of the time it's like having an expensive lover, one you have to keep happy and lavish money on for moments of intense gratification."

Erin turned and, tipping the glasses down, looked at him over them. "You're full of blarney."

"At the very least."

He turned and watched his horse charge through the gate. How did it feel? Burke asked himself. How did it feel for a dirt-poor bastard from New Mexico to sit and watch his six-figure horse come flying by? Incredible. So incredible he couldn't begin to describe it and wasn't sure he wanted to. It could all be gone tomorrow.

And what of it?

He'd taught himself long ago that when you held on to something too tightly it squeezed through your fingers. He was giving Three Aces the best he had, though he'd never intended to get involved with the running of it. He'd certainly never intended to get attached to it. He worked better on the move. Yet he'd been in one place for four years.

Just recently he'd been telling himself that maybe it was time for him to get a manager for the place and take an extended vacation. Monte Carlo, San Juan, Tahoe. If a man stuck with one game too long, didn't he get stale? But then he'd gone to Ireland. And had come back with Erin.

The damnedest thing was, he wasn't thinking about Monte Carlo or playing the wheel anymore. It was becoming easier and easier to stay in one place. And think about one woman.

"You won!" Suddenly she was laughing and her arms were around his neck. "You won by two lengths, maybe three, I couldn't tell. Oh, Burke, I'm so pleased for you."

"Are you?" He'd forgotten the race, the horse and the bet.

"Of course I am. It's wonderful that your horse won, and he looked so beautiful doing it. And I'm happy for me, too." She grinned. "The odds were eight to five."

Then he stunned her by dragging her closer and kissing her with a power and passion that left her limp. She didn't protest but, held trapped in his arms, allowed herself to be buffeted by the storm.

"The hell with the odds," Burke muttered, and kissed her again.

Chapter Six

She didn't know what to think. No one could have been kinder than Burke the day Erin had spent with him. She'd watched the races, the strong, beautiful horses striving for speed. She'd seen women dressed in elegant clothes and jockeys in brilliant silks. She'd heard the noises that came from thousands of people in the same place. She'd seen exotic birds and flowers, had sipped champagne in a private plane. But her clearest memory of the day was of sitting on the grass in Burke's arms.

She didn't know what to think.

Since then, the days had passed routinely. Erin had to remind herself she was doing exactly what she'd set out to do—making a wage, starting a life, seeing new things. But Burke's visits to her office had become few and far between. She began to catch herself watching the door and wishing it would open.

She told herself that her feelings for him were surface

ones. He made her laugh, showed her exciting things and could be kind enough when it suited him. He was just arrogant enough to keep an edge on without alienating her. A woman could like a man like that without putting her heart at risk. Couldn't she? A woman could even kiss a man like that without falling too deep. Wasn't that right?

And yet she knew she'd come to the point where she thought of him a bit too easily and watched for him far too often.

He'd stayed away from her long enough. That was what Burke told himself as he came in through the back of the house from the stables. He'd stayed away from her since their quick trip to Florida because his feelings were mixed. He was used to clear thinking and well-defined emotions, not this jumbled mess of needs and restraint.

He couldn't stop thinking about the way she'd looked at the track, watching the horses race by. She'd been vivid, excited, exciting. The kind of woman he could handle. Yet he couldn't stop thinking about the way she'd looked when she'd fainted all but at his feet. She'd been pale and helpless, frightened. He'd needed to protect and soothe.

He'd never wanted the responsibility of a woman who needed protection or care. Yet he wanted Erin. She wasn't the kind of woman you took to bed for a night of mutual enjoyment, then strolled away from. Yet he wanted her. For all her strong talk, she was a woman who would put down roots and sink them deep. He'd never wanted the restriction or the responsibility of a home in the true sense. Yet he still wanted Erin McKinnon.

And he'd stayed away from her long enough.

When he walked into the office, she was marking in

the ledger in her clear, careful hand. She knew it was him—even without looking she knew—but made herself finish before she glanced up.

"Hello. I haven't seen much of you lately."

"I've been busy."

"That's clear from the papers on my desk. I've just paid your vet bill. Dr. Harrigan back home could live a year off what you pay a month. Are the new foals well?"

"They'll do."

"I see you've hired a new stable boy."

"My trainer sees to the hiring."

Erin lifted a brow. So he was going to play master of the estate, was he? "I see your Ante Up ran well at Santa Anita."

"Reading the sports page these days?"

"I figure living with the Grants and working for you I should keep up." Erin picked up her pencil again. "Now that we've had such a pleasant little talk I'll get back to work, unless there's something you're wanting."

"Come with me."

"What?"

"I said come with me." Before either of them had a chance to think it through, he took her arm and hauled her to her feet. "Where's your coat?"

"Why? Where are we going?"

Instead of answering, he glanced around and spotted it folded on a chair. "Put this on," he told her. Then, even as he thrust it at her, he began to walk.

"A fine thing," Erin began breathlessly as he pulled her down the hall. "Interrupting my work in the middle of the day, dragging me off without any explanation. Just because you pay me, Burke Logan, doesn't mean I have to jump at your bidding. An employee has rights in this country. Which reminds me, I've been meaning to ask you about my paid holidays."

"You learn fast," he muttered as he pushed the door open.

"If you don't let go of my arm, I won't be able to put it in my coat." When he did, Erin rammed her arm in the sleeve but left the coat unbuttoned. "Sure and it's a fine day. The ground's a bit of a mess with the snow melting, but that's all the better for spring growing. If that was all you wanted to show me, I'll go back to work."

She managed to hiss out a protest when he grabbed her arm and began walking again.

"Burke, what the devil's got into you? If there's something you want me to do or see, fine, but there's no need to strong-arm me."

"How long have you been working for me?"

"Three weeks." Giving up, Erin matched her stride to his.

"And in three weeks you've barely poked your head out of the office."

"I work in the office," she reminded him.

"Did it ever occur to you that you can't understand the work if you've never looked at where the money comes from or where it goes?"

"I thought that's why we went to the races."

"There's more to this place than one race."

"Why do I have to understand as long as the figures tally?"

He wasn't sure of the answer himself, but he knew he wanted her to see what was his, to understand it, to move closer to it.

Pushing the hair out of her eyes, she glanced up at him. His profile was set, and she thought she detected a shadow in his eyes. "Is there something troubling you?"

"No." He said it sharply, almost defensively, then made himself relax. "No, nothing." Except the need tethered tight inside him that strained hard at the scent of her. What the hell was happening to a man who could only think of one woman, of one voice, of one taste?

She continued to walk beside him in silence, but she noticed the crocuses—big fat purple ones that pushed their way up through the soggy ground, unmindful of the patches of snow. She saw the way the land sloped, the way the sun slanted over it. And she saw the stables, with their white wood gleaming in the sunlight. She saw the checkerboard of paddocks and the long oval track where even now a horse was being ridden.

"Why, it's lovely," she murmured. "Like something out of a book. You must be proud that it's yours."

He wasn't sure he had been, but he stopped and looked out as she did. He'd won it fairly, but then he'd won and lost a great deal in his life. It had never been his intention to stay, but rather reorganize so that the gamble paid off. He'd come into this knowing little about horses and nothing about racing or breeding, and had told himself he'd better learn in order to turn a true profit.

That had been four years ago, and he was still here. Looking out with Erin beside him, he began to understand why. It was lovely, it was his, and it was and would always be a gamble.

Keeping Erin's hand in his, he began to walk again. "We've got thirty horses, two of which are studs that do nothing but please the ladies."

"And themselves," Erin added.

"Two of the mares just foaled, and we've two more that are due any day. Nearly half of what's left are being trained for next year. At the moment I've got five prime two-year-olds and a few veterans that have another season or two in them before they go out to stud or retirement. There, you see the horse being exercised now? That's one of the pair I picked up in Ireland."

Erin looked back at the track. The rider was up in the stirrups and bent low, but he earned no more than a glance. The horse was magnificent, a chestnut with a slash down his face like white lightning. Already his legs were spreading out in a rhythm that picked up speed and pounded on the soggy track.

"He's fast."

"And mean as hell."

"That would be the one that kicked you." Erin looked back again. Beautiful he might be, but she'd keep her distance. "If he's bad-tempered, why did you buy him?"

"I liked his style." As he started to walk again, Erin held back.

"I'd just as soon not be on closer acquaintance."

"I want to show you something else."

Erin told herself to relax as she walked with him. "If you'd told me we were going tramping around the yard, I'd have worn boots."

He glanced down but kept walking. "You could use some new shoes anyway."

"Thank you very much."

"I'd have thought you'd have gone shopping by now with a couple of paychecks under your belt."

"I'm thinking about it." They passed the stables, where the scent of horses and wet grass was strong. She could hear men talking inside. Erin braced herself, but he continued to walk. Then she saw the paddock where the mare was standing nursing a fawn-colored foal.

"That's one of the newest residents of Three Aces."

Cautiously Erin approached the fence. "They're sweet when they're little, aren't they?" She relaxed enough to curl her hands over the top rail and lean a little closer. The air was mild, with just a hint of spring. It wasn't the green or the scent of Ireland, but she found herself suddenly content. "We never had much time to think of an animal as any more than a means to an end." She smiled as the foal burrowed deeper and sucked. "Joe was always the one for animals, cooing at them and stroking. He'd love to see this."

"You miss your family."

"It's strange not seeing them every day. I hadn't realized…" She let the words trail off. "Word from home is everyone's fine. Cullen's back in Dublin playing at one of the clubs, and Brian's taken a fancy to Mary Margaret Shannesy. Ma says he's making a fool of himself, but that's to be expected."

The foal, having had his fill, began to scamper around the paddock. Erin watched him absently, thinking of home. "Frank's wife's nearly ready to have the baby. I could be an aunt already. It's funny, most mornings when I wake up I think it's time to go down to the henhouse. But there's no henhouse here."

The foal came over to the fence to sniff at her. Without thinking, Erin reached out a hand and rubbed between his ears.

"Do you wish there were?"

"I suppose I could live my life happily enough without gathering eggs again." She glanced down and, focusing on the foal, started to draw her hand back automatically. Burke set his on top of hers and rested it on the foal's head.

"Trusting little soul, isn't he?"

"Aye, but his mother—"

"Is probably relieved that he's distracted for a few minutes. Sometimes if you're afraid it's best to face it in small doses."

"I suppose." The foal was soft as butter and nuzzled its nose between the rails to nip at her coat. "Find something else to chew on," she said laughing. "It's all I brought with me." Finding nothing of interest, the foal scampered away to race around his mother. "Will he be a champion?"

"If it's in the cards."

Erin stepped away from the fence and, dipping her hands in her coat pockets, looked at him. "Why did you bring me out here?"

"I don't know." He didn't think about the men walking around the yard and going in and out of the stables. He thought only of her as he lifted a hand to her cheek. "Why should it matter?"

Had it come so far, so fast, that it only took the touch of his fingers on her skin to send her heart racing? Inside her pockets, the palms of her hands grew damp. "I think it does, and I think I should go back in."

"You've faced one fear today, why not face another?"

"I'm not afraid of you." That was true, and she felt a surge of relief that it was. Her heart might not be steady, but it wasn't in fear that it raced.

"Maybe not." He slid his hand from her cheek to the back of her neck as he drew her closer. He was afraid, afraid of what she was doing to him without his planning, without his calculations.

She yearned toward him. She strained away. "I don't think it's wise for you to kiss me that way again."

"All right. We'll try another way."

So he nibbled, teasing, tempting, tormenting. She felt the scrape of his teeth, then the moist trace of his tongue. Her hand went to his cheek and rested there as she opened herself for an emotional assault like nothing she'd ever experienced.

So he could be sweet and patient and alluring. She hadn't known. Her fingers crept into his hair as her lips parted and invited. No, she wasn't afraid, not of him. If what he brought to her was more than she'd ever imagined, then she was willing, even eager to accept it. With a sigh she tilted her head back and let him take.

He held himself back. The more generosity she showed him, the more wary he became of accepting. Burning inside him was a desire to sweep her away to some dim, private place where they could both take their fill. To touch her. He pressed his lips over hers and imagined how it would be to fill his hands with her. No barriers. While her teeth nipped gently, he imagined what it would feel like to have her flesh slide warm over his.

There was such a flavor here, warm and wild and willing. But he wanted more than her mouth. As her sigh whispered into him, he knew he needed more.

He took his hand to her hair and held her close against him. "I want you to stay with me tonight."

"Stay?" She floated up out of the dream and was stunned by the heat and passion that had turned his eyes to smoke.

"Stay," he repeated. "Tonight. Damn it, more than tonight. Get your things and bring them here."

The thrill moved through her. There was something in the command, in the look in his eyes as he gave it, that called to her even as it raised her hackles. "Move in with you?" She lifted her hands to his chest and struggled to keep her voice calm. "You want me to live under your roof, eat your food, sleep in your bed?"

"I want you with me. You know damn well I've wanted that since the first time I put my hands on you."

"Aye, maybe I did. But what I agreed to do was work for you." She tilted her head back again, but not in surrender this time. Yes, she'd been willing to accept the feelings he stirred in her, but not to compromise her principles for them. "Do you think I'd be your mistress? Do you think I'd let you keep me in your fine house?"

"No one's talking about keeping."

"No, you're not a man for keeping, are you, but for taking, enjoying and moving on. I'll tell you now, no matter how you make me feel, how you make me want, I'll not be any man's mistress."

It was foolish to be hurt, ridiculous to be insulted, but she was both. Erin jerked out of his hold and stood with her feet planted. "If I kiss you, it's because it pleasures me to do so, and nothing more. I'll not live in your house, shaming my family, until you're tired of me." She tossed back her hair and crossed her arms. "I'll be going back to work now, and you'd best keep out of my way unless you want to explain to your men why the payroll isn't done."

She turned on her heel and strode away. Burke leaned back against the paddock fence. A smart man would have folded his cards and pushed away from the table. He figured he'd stay for the next hand and see where the chips fell.

Whether she was feeling festive or not, Erin was swept along in her cousin's plans for the party. And what better day to celebrate than St. Patrick's Day? Erin decided if there'd been a dog around, she'd surely have kicked it.

No "come live with me and be my love" from the likes of Burke Logan, she thought. She attacked a silver platter with a polishing cloth as though she could have rubbed through the metal. Oh, no, with him it was just "pack your things and be quick about it." Hah!

As if she'd want pretty words from that swine of a man. The truth of it was Erin McKinnon didn't want pretty words from anyone. What she wanted was to be left alone to pursue her new career. In six months she'd have a place of her own and a new job altogether, she decided. She'd find a job where she didn't have to put up with a man who made her laugh one minute and steam the next. And steam in more ways than one, she added as she tossed the polishing cloth aside.

Turning the platter over, she studied her own reflection. He was toying with her, he was. Hadn't she known that right from the beginning? Well, what was fine for him was fine for her. She could do some toying herself, and tonight was as good a time as any to start it. From what Dee had told her, there would be plenty of men at the party tonight. Including a certain snake in the grass.

"Have you finished scowling at yourself?" From the other side of the table, Dee set aside another tray.

"Almost."

"That's good, then, because we've only a couple more hours." Rising, she stacked the bowls and platters beside the crystal. Between Hannah and the caterers, the rest could be easily handled. "Is there anything you'd like to talk to me about?"

"No."

"Nothing that might have to do with why you've been muttering to yourself for the past week or so?"

Erin set her teeth, then dropped her chin on her hand. "I think American men are even more rude and arrogant than Irish men."

"I've always thought it was a draw." Adelia came over

to lay a hand on her shoulder. "Has Burke been troubling you?"

"To say the least."

Something in the way Erin said it caused Dee to smile. "He has a way with him."

"Not my way."

"Well, then, we won't be worrying about him anymore. We've a party to get ready for."

Erin nodded as she rose. She'd known she was in trouble as soon as she'd seen the silver and crystal. Things had only gotten worse when she'd watched the team of caterers descend to fuss over things like salmon mousse and gooseliver pâté. She'd seen the cases of champagne delivered. Cases, by God. Then there was the black caviar she'd managed to sample while no one was looking. And there were the flowers, tubs of them, that were being arranged even as she walked with Dee down the hall.

"A madhouse, isn't it?" Dee began when they started up the stairs. "Later, if you've had your fill of hearing about horses and tracks and stud fees, just send me a sign."

"I like listening. It's a bit like learning a new language."

"It's all of that." Dee moved into her room and took a large box off the bed. "Happy St. Patrick's Day."

Automatically Erin put her hands behind her back. "What is it?"

"It's a present, of course. Aren't you going to take it?"

"There's no need for you to give me presents."

"No, but I didn't think of it as a need." Pride was something Adelia understood too well. Her own had been bruised repeatedly. "I'd like you to have it, Erin, from all of us as a kind of welcome to a new place. When I came here I had only Uncle Paddy. I think I understand now how happy it made him to share with me. Please."

"I don't mean to seem ungrateful."

"Good, then you'll pretend to like it even if you don't." Dee sat on the bed and gestured with both hands. "Open it. I've never been long on patience."

Erin hesitated only another moment, then laid the box on the bed to draw off the top. Under a cushion of tissue paper was dark green silk. "Oh. What a color."

"It's expected today. Well, take it out," she demanded. "I'm dying to see if it's right on you."

Cautiously Erin touched the silk with her fingertips, then lifted the dress from the box. The material draped softly in the front and simply fell away altogether in the back to a slim skirt. Dee rose to hold the dress in front of her cousin.

"I knew it!" she said, and her face lit up. "I was sure it was right. Oh, Erin, you'll be dazzling."

"It's the most beautiful thing I've ever seen." Almost reverently she brushed her fingers over the skirt. "It feels like sin."

"Aye." Then, with a laugh, Dee stepped back for a better viewpoint. "It'll look like it, too. There won't be a man able to keep his eyes in his head."

"You're kinder to me than I deserve."

"Probably." Gathering up the box, she handed it to Erin. "Go put it on, fuss with yourself awhile."

Erin kissed her cheek. Then, letting her feelings spread, she gave her cousin a hard, laughing hug. "Thank you. I'll be ready in ten minutes."

"Take your time."

Erin paused at the door. "No, the sooner I have it on, the longer I can wear it."

* * *

The party was already underway when Burke drove up. He'd nearly bypassed it altogether. Restless and edgy, he'd thought about driving up to Atlantic City, placing a few bets, spinning a few wheels. That was his milieu, he told himself, casinos with bright lights, back rooms with dim ones. A party with the racing class, with their old money and closed circles, wasn't his style.

He told himself he was here because of the Grants. The fact that Erin would be there hadn't swayed him. So he told himself. Since their last encounter he'd nearly talked himself out of believing there was something between them. Oh, a spark, certainly, a frisson, a lick or two of flame, but that was all. That overwhelming and undesirable feeling that there was something deeper, something truer, had only been his imagination.

He hadn't come tonight to prove that, either. So he told himself.

It was Travis who let him in. Burke could hear voices raised in the living and dining rooms along with the piping Irish music that set the tone.

"Dee was worried about you." Travis closed the door on the nippy mid-March air outside.

"I had a few things to see to."

"No problems?"

"No problems," Burke assured him. But if that was true, he wondered why his shoulders were tensed, why he felt ready to jump in any direction.

"You'll know just about everyone here," Travis was saying as he led him into the living room.

"You've got quite a crowd," Burke murmured, and was already searching through it, though he didn't move beyond the doorway.

"I think you'll see that Dee's outdone herself in more

ways than one." With the slightest gesture, Travis had
Burke's gaze traveling to the far end of the room and
Erin.

He hadn't known she could look like that, coolly sexy,
polished. She was sipping champagne and laughing over
the rim of her glass at Lloyd Pentel, heir to one of the
oldest and most prestigious farms in Virginia. Flanking
her were two more men he recognized. Third- and fourth-
generation racing barons, with Ivy League educations
and practiced moves. Burke felt his blood heat as one of
them leaned close to murmur something in her ear.

Both amused and sympathetic, Travis laid a hand on
Burke's shoulder. "Beer?"

"Whiskey."

He downed the first one easily, appreciating its bite.
But it did nothing to relax his muscles. He took a second
and sipped it more slowly.

Erin was perfectly aware that he was there. She doubted
he'd been in the room ten seconds before she'd felt his
presence. She smiled and flirted with Lloyd and the others
who wandered her way, and told herself she was having
a wonderful time. But she never stopped watching Burke
and the women who gravitated to him.

Adelia had been right—the talk was horses. Purses, the
size of which made the head reel, were discussed and the
politics of racing dissected. Erin took it in, determined to
hold her own, but as she nursed her single glass of champagne her gaze kept roaming.

The man didn't even have the courtesy to say "how
do you do," she decided. But then he seemed more interested in the leggy blonde than in manners. Erin accepted
a dance with Lloyd, and if he held her a bit too close she
ignored it. And watched Burke.

It didn't appear to bother her to have the young Pentel

stud pawing her, Burke noted as he swirled his whiskey. And where in the hell had she gotten that dress? Setting down his whiskey, he lit a cigar. She was nothing to get worked up over, he reminded himself. If she wanted to wear a dress that was cut past discretion and bat her baby blues at Pentel, that was her business.

The hell it was. Burke crushed out his cigar and, leaving the blonde who had snuggled up beside him staring, walked over to Erin.

"Pentel."

Annoyed, but as well-bred as his father's prize colt, Lloyd nodded. "Logan."

"I have to borrow Erin a minute. Business."

Before either of them could object, Burke had maneuvered his way between and had Erin in his arms.

"You're a rude, shameless man, Burke Logan." She was delighted.

"I wouldn't talk about shameless while you're wearing that dress."

"Do you like it?"

"I'd be interested to hear what your father would say about it."

"You're not my father." Though she smiled, there was more challenge than humor in the curve of lips. "Doesn't a man like you worry about luck, Burke? No wearing of the green on St. Patrick's Day?"

"Who says I'm not?" His eyes tossed the challenge right back.

"Money doesn't count."

"I was talking about something more personal than money. If you want to go somewhere private, I'll be happy to show you where I'm wearing my green."

"I'm sure you would," she murmured, and tried not to be amused. "Now, what business do we have?" He wasn't holding her as close, not nearly as close as Lloyd had been, but she felt the pull of him.

"You've come a long way from dancing in moonlit fields, Irish."

"Aye." Some of the pleasure went out of her as she studied him. "What does that mean?"

"You're an ambitious woman, one who wants things, big things." God, it was driving him mad to be this close, to smell her as he had once before in a dim garden shed with rain pelting the roof.

"And what of it?"

"Lloyd Pentel's not a bad choice to give it to you. He's young, rich, not nearly as shrewd as his old man. The kind of man a smart woman could twist easily around her finger."

"It's kind of you to point that out," she said in a voice that was very low and very cold. She didn't know what possessed her to go on, but whatever it was, she swore she wouldn't regret it. "But why should I settle for the colt when I can have the stallion? The old man's a widower."

Burke's mouth thinned as he smiled. "You work fast."

"And you. The skinny blonde's still pouting after you. It must be rewarding to walk into a room and have six females trip over themselves to get to you."

"It has its compensations."

"Well, why don't you get back to them?" She started to pull away, but his hand pressed into her back so that their bodies bumped. The flame that was never quite controlled flared at the contact. "Damn you," she said from the heart as he tightened his fingers on hers.

"I'm tired of playing games." He had her across the

room and into the hall before she found the breath to speak.

"What are you doing?"

"We're leaving. Where's your coat?"

"I'm not going anywhere, and I—"

He merely stripped off his jacket and tossed it over her shoulders before he yanked her outside. "Get in the car."

"Go to hell."

He grabbed her then, hard and fast. "There'll be little doubt of that after tonight." When his mouth came down on hers, her first reaction was to fight free, for this was a man to fear. But that reaction was so quickly buried under desire that she moved to him.

"Get in the car, Erin."

She stood at the base of the steps a moment, knowing no matter how strong, how determined he was, the choice would be hers. She opened the door herself and got in without looking back.

Chapter Seven

Had she lost her mind? Erin sat in Burke's car, watching his headlights cut through the night, and heard nothing but the sound of her own heart pounding in her ears. She must be mad to have thrown all caution, all sense, all pretense of propriety to the winds. Why had no one ever told her that madness felt like freedom?

She'd never been self-destructive. Or had she? she asked herself, almost giddy from the speed and the night and the man beside her. Perhaps that was one more thing he'd recognized in her. A need to take risks and damn the consequences. If that wasn't true, why didn't she tell him to stop, to turn back?

Erin gripped her fingers together until the knuckles turned white. She wasn't at all sure he'd listen, but that wasn't the reason she didn't speak. No, the reason she didn't speak was that she'd lost more than her mind. Her heart was lost as well.

Perhaps one was the same as the other, Erin thought. Surely it was a kind of madness to love him. But love him she did, in a way she'd never imagined she could love anyone. There was a ferocity to it, an edgy sort of desperation that didn't swell the heart so much as tighten it. Indeed, it felt like a hard, hot lump beneath her breast even now.

Was this the way love should feel? Shouldn't she know? There should be a warmth, a comfort, a sweetness—not this wild combination of power and terror. Though she searched, she could find no tenderness in her feelings. Perhaps they were a reflection of his. At a glance she could see no gentleness in the man beside her. His hands gripped the wheel tightly and he looked nowhere but straight ahead.

Erin pressed her lips together and told herself not to be a romantic fool. Love didn't have to be gentle to be real. Hadn't she known all along that her emotions when it came to Burke would never be ordinary or simple? She didn't want them to be. Still, she would have liked to have laid a hand over his, to have offered some word to show him how deep her feelings went and how much she was willing to give. But more than her heart was involved. There was pride and spirit as well. She had to be realistic enough to understand that just because she loved didn't mean he loved in return.

So she said nothing as they drove under the sign and onto his land.

Why did he feel as though his life had just changed irrevocably? Burke saw the lights of his house in the distance and tensed as though readying for a blow. He wanted her, and if the need was stronger than he wanted to admit, at least tonight it would be assuaged. She hadn't said a word. His nerves neared the breaking point as he rounded the first curve in the drive. Did it mean so little to her, could she take what was happening between them so casually that she sat in silence?

He didn't want this. He wanted it more than he'd ever wanted anything in his life.

What was she feeling? Damn it, what was going on inside her? Couldn't she see that every day, every hour he'd spent with her had driven him closer and closer to the brink? Of what? Burke demanded of himself. What line was he teetering on that he'd never crossed before? What would his life and hers be like once he'd stepped over it?

The hell with it. Burke braked at the base of the steps and without sparing her a glance, slammed the door and got out of the car.

Legs trembling, Erin got out and started up the steps. The door looked bigger somehow, like a portal to another world. With one long breath, she passed through.

Was it always so silent and angry when lovers came together? she wondered as she started up the staircase. Her hand on the banister was dry—dry and cold. She wished he'd reached for it, held it, warmed it in his own. That was nonsense, she told herself. She wasn't a child to be coddled and soothed, but a woman.

He walked into the bedroom ahead of her, waiting for her to smile, to offer her hand, to give him some sign that she was happy to be with him. But when the door closed at her back she simply stood, chin up, eyes defiant.

The hell with it, he thought again. She didn't need sweetness and neither did he. They were both adults, both aware and willing. He should have been glad she didn't want coaxing and candlelight and the promises that were so rarely kept.

So he pulled her against him. Their eyes met once, acknowledging. Then his mouth was on hers and the chance for quiet words and gentle caresses was past.

This was enough, Erin told herself as the heat rose like glory. This had to be enough, because she would never have more from him. Accepting, she pressed against him, offering her mind and body along with her heart he didn't know was already his. There was no hesitation now as her lips parted, as their tongues met in a hot, greedy kiss. When his hands roamed over her back, pressed into her hips, she only strained closer. She was prepared to trust him to show her the art of intimacy. She was prepared to risk self-destruction as long as he was part of the gamble.

Her fingers trembled only slightly as they dug into his arms. The strength was there, an almost brutal kind of strength that had her heart racing and her body yearning.

Good God, no woman had ever taken him so close to desperation so quickly. It only took a touch, a taste. When she kissed him avidly for one sweet moment he could almost believe he was the only one. That was its own kind of madness. A sane man would think of just this one night, but like a drug she was seeping into his system, making his heart race and his mind swirl.

He tugged on her dress and she moved against him, murmuring. He recognized the excitement, the tremble of anticipation, but not the modesty. When her flesh was freed for him he took, with rough hands that incited both desire and panic. No one had ever touched her like this, as if he had a right to every part of her. No one had ever caused this hard fist of need to clench inside her so that she was willing to cede to him that right.

Then she was naked, tumbling to the bed so that his body covered hers. His hands found her, sent her spiral-

ing so that she arched against him even as the fear of the
unknown began to brew. Her breath caught with the sensation of being pressed under him, vulnerable, dizzy with
desire. Her own body seemed like a stranger's, filled with
towering emotions and terrifying pleasures. She wanted a
moment, just one moment of reassurance, one soft word,
one tender touch. But she was beyond asking, and he
beyond listening.

Greedy, impatient, he took his lips over her as he
wrestled out of his shirt. He wanted the feel of her flesh
against his. How many times had he imagined them
coming together this way, urgently, without questions?
She was murmuring his name in a breathy, desperate
whisper that had his passion snowballing out of control.
He dragged at his clothes, swearing, hardly able to breathe
himself and far beyond the capacity to think.

Her body was like a furnace beneath his, and with each
movement she stoked the flames higher. She dug her nails
into his shoulders; he fused his mouth with hers. Past all
reason, he plunged into her.

She was curled away from him, trembling. Burke lay in
the dark and tried to clear his head. Innocent. Dear God,
he'd taken her with all passion and no care. And he was
the first. He should have known. Yet from the first time
he'd held her she'd been so ripe, so ready. There had been
the strength, the hotheaded passion, the unquestioning
response. It had never crossed his mind that she hadn't
been with anyone else.

He ran his hands over his face, rubbing hard. He hadn't
seen because he was a fool. The innocence had been there
in her eyes for any man to see who'd had the brains to
look. He hadn't looked, perhaps because he hadn't wanted
to see. Now he'd hurt her. However careless, however

callous he had been with women in the past, he'd never hurt one. Because the women he'd chosen before had known the rules, Burke reminded himself. Not Erin. No one had ever taught them to her.

Searching for a way to apologize, he touched her hair. Erin only drew herself closer together.

She wouldn't cry. She squeezed her eyes tight and swore it. She was humiliated enough without tears. What a fool he must think her, sniffling like a baby. But how could she have known loving would be all heat and no heart?

The hell of it was, he was lousy at words. Burke reached down to the foot of the bed and drew a cover over her. As he tried to sort through and pick the best ones, he continued to stroke her hair.

"Erin, I'm sorry." By God, he *was* lousy with words if those were the pick of the litter.

"Don't apologize. I can't bear it." She turned her face into the pillow and prayed he wouldn't do so again.

"All right. I only want to say that I shouldn't have..." What? Wanted her? Taken her? "I shouldn't have been careless with you." That was beautiful, he thought, detesting himself. "I hadn't realized that you hadn't—that tonight was your first time. If I'd known, I would have..."

"Run for cover?" she suggested, pushing herself up. Before she could climb out of the bed, he had her arm. He felt her withdrawal like a blade in the gut.

"You've every right to be angry with me."

"With you?" She turned her head and made herself look at him. He was hardly more than a silhouette in the dark. They had loved in the dark, she thought, unable to see, unable to share. Perhaps it was best it was dark still so that he couldn't see the devastation. "Why should I be angry with you? It's myself I'm angry with."

"If you'd told me—"

"Told you?" She sniffed again, but this time there was more than a little derision in it. "Of course. I should have told you, while we were rolling around on the bed naked as the day we were born, I might have said, *'Oh, by the way, Burke, you might be interested in knowing I've never done this before.'* That would have put a cap on it."

He was amazed to find himself smiling even as he reached for her hair again and she jerked her head away. "Maybe the timing could have been a bit better than that."

"It's done, so there's no sense pining over it. I want to go home now before I humiliate myself again."

"Don't."

"Don't what?"

"Don't go." That was a tough one. He hadn't known he'd had it in him to ask. "What happened wasn't wrong, it was just done badly. And that's my fault." He caught her chin in his hand as she started to turn away. "Look, I'm not good at asking, but I'd like you to let me make it up to you."

"There's no need." She wasn't aware that it was the gentleness in his voice that was calming her. "I told you I'm not angry with you. It's true it was my first time, but I'm not a child. I came here of my own free will."

"Now I'm asking you to stay." He took her hand and, turning it palm up, pressed his lips to the center. When he looked up at her again she was staring, her lips parted in surprise. He cursed himself again. "I'll draw you a bath."

"You'll what?"

"Draw you a bath," he said, snapping off the words. "You'll feel better."

When he disappeared into the adjoining room, Erin

simply continued to stare after him. What in the world had gotten into him? she wondered. She gathered the blanket around her and stood as Burke came back in. He was wearing a robe tied loosely at the waist. The light from the bath angled out onto the floor. She could hear the sound of water running and sensed—but surely she was mistaken—a hesitation in him.

"Go ahead in and relax. Do you want something. Tea?"

Mutely she shook her head.

"Take your time, then. I'll be back in a few minutes."

Not a little baffled, Erin walked in and lowered herself into the tub. The water was steaming so that she felt the tension and the ache begin to diminish almost immediately. Sinking down, she closed her eyes.

She wished she had another woman to talk to, another woman to ask if this was all there was to lovemaking. She wished there was someone she could talk to about her feelings. She loved Burke, yet she felt no fulfillment after being with him. It had been exciting. The way he had touched her, the way his body had felt against hers, made her tremble and ache. But there had been no glorious glow, no beautiful colors, no feeling of rightness and contentment.

She was probably a fool for imagining there would be. After all, it was the poets and dreamers who promised more. Pretty words, pretty images. She was a practical woman, after all.

But Burke had been right. The bath had made her feel better. There was no reason for humiliation or for regret. If she was no longer innocent, she had brought about the change herself, willingly. One thing her parents had always told her was to follow what was in your heart and to blame no one.

Steadier, she stepped from the bath. She would face Burke now. No tears, no blushes, no recriminations.

Seeing no other cover, she wrapped the towel securely around her and stepped into the bedroom.

He'd lighted candles. Dozens of them. Erin stood in the doorway, staring at the soft light. There was music, too, something quiet and romantic that seemed to heighten the scent of wax and flowers. The sheets on the bed were fresh and neatly turned down. Erin stared at them as all the confidence she'd newly built up began to crumble.

He saw her glance at the bed and saw the quick, unmistakable flash of panic that went with the look. It brought him guilt and a determination to erase it. There were other ways, better ways. Tonight he would show both of them. Rising, he went to her and offered a rose he'd just picked in the solarium.

"Feel better?"

"Aye." Erin took the rose, but her fingers nearly bit through the stem.

"You said you didn't want tea, so I brought up some wine."

"That's nice, but I—" The words jammed in her throat as he lifted her into his arms. "Burke."

"Relax." He pressed a kiss to her temple. "I won't hurt you." He carried her to the bed and laid her against the pillows. Taking two glasses already filled with pale wine, he offered her one. "Happy St. Patrick's Day." With a half smile, he touched his glass to hers. Erin managed a nod before she sipped.

"This is a fine room…" she began lamely. "I didn't notice…before."

"It was dark." He slipped an arm around her shoulders and settled back even as she tensed.

"Aye. I've, ah, wondered what the other rooms were like."

"You could have looked."

"I didn't want to pry." She sipped a little more wine and unconsciously brushed the rose over her cheek. Its petals were soft and just on the verge of opening. "It seems like a big place for one man."

"I only use one room at a time."

She moistened her lips. What was this music? she wondered. Cullen would know. It was so lovely and romantic. "I heard Double Bluff won his last race. Travis said he beat Durnam's colt by a length. Everybody's talking about the Kentucky Derby already and how your horse is favored." When she realized her head was resting against his shoulder, she cleared her throat. She would have shifted away, but he was stroking her hair. "You must be pleased."

"It's hard not to be pleased when you're winning."

"And tonight at the party, Lloyd told me that Bluff was the horse to beat."

"I didn't tell you how wonderful you looked tonight."

"The dress. Dee gave it to me."

"It made my heart stop."

She was able to chuckle at that. "What blarney."

"Then again, you managed to stop it wearing overalls."

She slanted a look up at him. "Aye, now I'm sure there's some Irish in you."

"I discovered I had a weakness for women taking in the wash."

"I'd say it's more a matter of a weakness for women in general."

"Has been. But just lately I've preferred them with freckles."

Erin rubbed rueful fingers over her nose. "If you're trying to flirt with me, you ought to be able to do better."

"Works both ways." Lifting the hand that still held the rose, he kissed her fingers. "You could say something nice about me."

Erin caught her lip between her teeth and waited until he glanced up. "I'm thinking," she said, then laughed when his teeth nipped her knuckle. "Well, I suppose I like your face well enough."

"I'm overwhelmed."

"Oh, I'm picky, I am, so you should be flattered. And though you haven't Travis's build, I'm partial to the wiry type."

"Does Dee know you've had your eye on her husband?"

Erin laughed into her glass. "Surely there's no harm in looking."

"Then look here." Tilting her face up to his, he kissed her. His lips lingered softly, more a whisper than a shout.

"There's the way you do that, too," she murmured.

"Do what?"

"Make my insides curl all up."

With his lips still hovering over hers, he took the glass from her and set it aside. "Is that good?"

"I don't know. But I'd like you to do it again."

With a hand to her cheek, he nuzzled. Drawing on a tenderness he hadn't known he possessed, waiting for her lips to warm and soften beneath his. She hesitantly touched a hand to his shoulder. She knew his strength now, what it was capable of, and yet…and yet his mouth was so patient, so sweet, so beautifully gentle. When he increased the pressure, her fingers tensed. Immediately he drew back to nibble again until he felt her begin to relax.

He wanted to take care, and not just for her, he realized, but for himself. He wanted to savor, to explore, to open doors for both of them. He'd never been a man to bother with candlelight and music, had never looked for the romance of it. Now he found himself as soothed and seduced by it as she was.

The scent of her bath was on her skin, fresh, clean. On her his soap seemed feminine, somehow mysterious. Her skin was smooth but not frail. Beneath it were firm muscles, honed by an unpampered life. He would never have found frailty as appealing. Still, he could feel the nerves jangle inside her. Now he would treat her as though she'd never been touched. Where there was innocence there should be compassion. Where there was trust there should be respect.

And somehow, wonderingly, he felt as though it was his own initiation.

She heard the rustle of the sheets as he shifted. Her body hammered with need even while her fears held her back. It was natural, she reminded herself. And now that she wasn't expecting, she wouldn't be disappointed. Then her breath caught as a new thrill coursed over her skin. Confused, she brought a hand to his chest.

"I won't hurt you again." He drew away from her to brush the hair from her face. His fingers weren't steady. God, he had to be steady now, he warned himself. He couldn't afford to lose control, to lose himself a second time. "I promise I won't hurt you."

She didn't believe him. Even as she opened her arms in acceptance, he saw she didn't believe him. So he lowered his mouth to hers again and thought only of Erin.

He'd never been a selfish lover, but he'd never been a selfless one, either. Now he found himself ignoring his own needs for hers. When he touched her, it wasn't to fulfill his own desire but to bring her whatever passion he was able. He felt the change in her start slowly, a gradual relaxation of the limbs, a dreamy murmuring of his name.

She'd waited, braced, for the speed, the pressure, the pain. Instead he gave her languidness, indulgence and pure pleasure. He moved his hands over her freely, as he had before, but this time there was a difference. He stroked, caressed, lingered until she felt as though she was floating. The sensation of vulnerability returned, but without the panic. Light and sweet, he brought his mouth to her breast to nibble and suckle so that she felt the response deep inside, a pull, a tug, a warmth that spread to her fingertips.

With a moan she wrapped her arms around him, no longer simply accepting but welcoming.

My God, she was sweet. With his lips rubbing over her skin he discovered she had a taste like no other, a taste he would never be able to do without again. Her body was so completely responsive under his that he knew he could have her now and satisfy them both. But he was greedy in a different way this time. Greedy to give.

Reaching for her hand, he linked his fingers with hers. Even that, just that, was the most intimate gesture he'd ever made. In the candlelight he saw her face glow with pleasure, the soft, silky kind that could last for hours.

So he came back to her mouth to give them both time.

She tasted the wine, just a hint of it, on his tongue. Then she felt his lips move against hers with words she heard only in her heart.

Here was the glow she'd once imagined, and all the bright, beautiful colors the poets had promised. Here was music flowing gently and light soft as heaven. Here was everything a woman who'd given her heart could ask in return.

She'd loved him before. But now, experiencing the compassion, the completeness, she fell deeper.

Slowly, carefully, he began to show her more, finding all the pleasure he could want from her response. Her body shuddered and strained toward him without hesitation, without restrictions. When he nudged her over the first peak, he saw her eyes fly open with shock and dark delight.

Breathless, she clung to him. It felt as though her mind was racing to keep pace with her body. And still he urged her on in ways she'd never dreamed existed. The next wave struck with a force that had her rearing up. There couldn't be more. The colors were almost too bright to bear now, and need and pleasure had mixed to a point that was both sharp and sweet.

She held him, moaning out his name. There couldn't be more.

But he filled her and showed her there was.

She was trembling again, but she wasn't curled away from him. This time she was turned to him, her face pressed against his shoulder, her arms holding tight. Because he was more than a little dazed himself, he kept her close and said nothing.

He was no novice at this game, Burke reminded himself. So why did he feel as though someone had just changed the rules? The candlelight flickered its shadows around the room so that he shook his head. It looked as if he'd changed them himself. Soft light, soft music, soft words. That wasn't his style. But it felt so damn right.

He was used to living hard, loving hard and moving on. Win, lose or draw. Now he felt as though he could go happily to the grave if he never moved beyond this spot. As long as Erin stayed with him.

That thought had several small shock waves moving through him. Stayed with him? Since when had he started thinking along those lines? Since he'd laid eyes on her, he realized, and let out a long, none-too-steady breath. Good God, he was in love with her. He'd gone through his life without taking more than a passing interest in any woman. Then someone had opened the chute, and he'd fallen face first in love with a woman who hadn't had time to test the waters.

He didn't have time for this. His life was unsettled, the way he wanted it. His days, his decisions, his moves were his own. He had plans, places to go. He had…nothing, he thought. Absolutely nothing without her.

Closing his eyes, he tried to talk himself out of it. It was crazy, he was crazy. How did he know what it meant to love someone? There had only been one person he'd loved in his life, and that was long ago. He was a drifter, a hustler. If he'd stayed in one place a little too long, it was only because…because there hadn't been a better game, that was all. But he knew it was a lie.

He should do them both a favor and take that trip to Monte Carlo. He should leave first thing in the morning. The hell with the farm, the responsibilities. He'd just pick up and go, the way he always had. Nothing was keeping him.

But her hand was resting on his heart.

He wasn't going anywhere. But maybe it was time he upped the stakes and played out his hand.

"You okay?" he asked her.

Erin nodded, then lifted her face to look into his. "I feel... You'll think I'm foolish."

"Probably. How do you feel?"

"Beautiful." Then she laughed and threw her arms around his neck. "I feel like the most beautiful woman in the world."

"You'll do," he murmured, and knew in that moment that no matter how hard he struggled he was already caught.

"I never want to feel any different than this." She drew him closer to press kisses along his jawline and throat.

"You will, but there's no reason you can't feel like this as often as possible. We'll bring your things over tomorrow."

"What things?" Still smiling, her arms still around his neck, she drew back.

"Whatever things you have. There's no reason to bother moving tonight. Tomorrow's soon enough."

"Moving?" Slowly she unwound her arms. "Burke, I told you once before I won't live here with you."

"Things have changed," he said simply, reaching for the wine. He wished it was whiskey.

"Aye, but that hasn't. What happened tonight..." Had been beautiful, the most beautiful experience of her life, and she didn't want it spoiled by talk of sharing a life with him that wouldn't be a true one. "I want to remember it. I'd like to think that there may be a time when we might—when we might love each other this way again, but that doesn't mean I'll toss my beliefs aside and move in as your mistress."

"Lover."

"The label doesn't really matter." She started to move away, but he grabbed her shoulders. The glass tilted to the floor and shattered.

"I want you, damn it, don't you understand? Not just once. I don't want to have to drag you away from the Grants every time I want an hour with you."

"You'll drag me nowhere." The afterglow of love was replaced by angry pride. "Do you think I'll move in here so it'll be convenient for you when you have an urge to wrestle in bed? Well, I won't be a convenience to you or any man. The hell with you, Burke Logan."

She pushed away and had swung her legs off the bed when she went tumbling backward to find herself pinned under him. "I'm getting tired of you wishing me to hell."

"Well, get used to it. Now take your hands off me. I'm going home."

"No, you're not."

Her eyes narrowed. "You'll not keep me here."

"Whatever it takes." Then she twisted under him. Before he realized her intent, her teeth were sunk into his hand. He swore, and they rolled from one end of the bed to the other before he managed to pin her again.

"I'll draw blood next time, I swear it. Now let me go."

"Shut up, you crazy Irish hothead."

"Name-calling, is it?" Erin sucked the breath between her teeth. The words she uttered now were Gaelic.

This was hardly the time to be amused, he reminded himself. But there was no help for it. "What was that?"

"A curse. Some say my granny was a witch. If you're lucky, you'll die fast."

"And leave you a widow? Not a chance."

"Maybe you'll live, but in such pain you'll wish… What did you say?"

"We're getting married."

Because her mouth went slack and her bones limp, he released her to suck on his wounded hand.

"It's a relief to know you've got good teeth." He reached to the bedside table for a cigar. "Nothing to say, Irish?"

"Getting married?"

"That's right. We could fly to Vegas tomorrow, but then Dee would give me grief. I figure we can get a license and do it here in a few days."

"A few days." She shook her head to clear it, then sat up. "I think the wine's gone to my head." Or he had, she thought. "I don't understand."

"I want you." He lit the cigar, then spoke practically, deciding it was the style she'd relate to best. "You want me, but you won't live with me. It seems like the logical solution."

"Solution?"

Calmly, as if his life wasn't on the line, he blew out smoke. "Are you going to spend the rest of the night repeating everything I say?"

Again she shook her head. Trying to keep calm, she watched him, looking for any sign. But his eyes were shuttered and his face was closed. He'd played too many hands to give away the most important cards he'd ever held.

"Why do you want marriage?"

"I don't know. I've never been married before." He blew out another stream of smoke. "And I don't intend to make a habit of it. I figure once should do me."

"I don't think this is something you can take lightly."

"I'm not taking it lightly." Burke studied the end of his cigar, then leaned over to tap it out. "I've never asked another woman to marry me, never wanted one to. I'm asking you."

"Do you…" Love me? she wanted to ask. But she couldn't. Whatever answer he gave wouldn't be the right one, because she'd posed the question. "Do you really think that what we had here is enough for marriage?"

"No, but we're good together. We understand each other. You'll make me laugh, keep me on my toes, and you'll be faithful. I can't ask for more than that." And didn't dare. "I'll give you what you've always wanted. A nice home, a comfortable living, and you'll be the most important person in my life."

She lifted her head at that. It could be enough. If she was indeed important to him. "Do you mean that?"

"I rarely say what I don't mean." Because he needed to, he reached for her hand. "Life's a gamble, Irish, remember?"

"I remember."

"Most marriages don't make it because people go into them thinking that in time they'll change the other person. I don't want to change you. I like you the way you are."

He took her fingers to his lips, and her heart simply spoke louder than her head. "Then I guess I'll have to take you the way you are as well."

Chapter Eight

"This is all happening so fast." Dee sat in Erin's bedroom, where even now a dressmaker was pinning and tucking a white satin gown on her cousin. "Are you sure you don't want a little more time?"

"For what?" Erin stared out the window, wondering whether if one of the dressmaker's pins slipped and pierced her skin she would discover it was all a dream.

"To catch your breath, think things through."

"I could have another six months and still not catch my breath." She lifted a hand to her bodice and felt the symphony of tiny freshwater pearls. Who would have thought she'd ever have such a dress? In another two days she would put it on to become Burke's wife. Wife. A chill ran up her spine, and at her quick shudder the dressmaker murmured an apology.

"Have a look, Miss McKinnon. I think you'll be pleased with the length. If I do say so myself, the dress is perfect for you. Not every woman can wear this line."

Holding her breath, Erin turned to the cheval mirror. The dress was the real dream, she thought. Thousands of pearls glimmered against the satin, making it shimmer in the late-afternoon light. She thought it was something a medieval princess would wear, with its snug sleeves coming to points over her hands and its miles of snowy skirts.

"It's beautiful, Mrs. Viceroy," Adelia put in when her cousin only continued to stare. "And it's a miracle indeed that you could have it ready for us in such a short time. We're beholden to you."

"You know you've only to ask, Mrs. Grant." She eyed Erin as she continued to stare into the glass. "Is there something you'd like altered, Miss McKinnon?"

"No. No, not a stitch." She touched the skirt gingerly, just a fingertip, as if she was afraid it would dissolve under her hand. "I'm sorry, Mrs. Viceroy, it's only that it's the most beautiful thing I've ever seen."

More than placated, Mrs. Viceroy began to fuss with the hem. "I think your new husband will be pleased. Now let me help you out of it."

Erin surrendered the dress and stood in the plain cotton slip Burke had once unhooked from the clothesline. As the wedding gown was packed away, she slipped into her shirtwaist and thought she understood what Cinderella must have felt like at midnight.

"If I might suggest," the dressmaker continued, "the dress and veil would be most effective with the hair swept up, something very simple and old-fashioned."

"I'm sure you're right," Dee murmured as she continued to watch her cousin. Erin was staring out the window as if she was looking at a blank wall.

"And, naturally, jewelry should be kept to the bare minimum."

"She'll have my pearl earrings for something borrowed."

"What a sweet thought."

"Thank you again, Mrs. Viceroy," Dee said, rising. "I'll show you out."

"No need for you to go up and down those stairs in your condition. I know the way. The dress will be delivered by ten, day after tomorrow."

Day after tomorrow, Erin thought, and felt the chill come back to her skin. Would it always be now or never when it came to Burke?

"A lovely lady," Dee said after she closed the bedroom door.

"It was kind of her to come here."

"Kind is one thing, business another." Since the weight of the twins seemed to grow heavier every day, she sat again. "She would hardly pass up the opportunity to please the future Mrs. Burke Logan. Erin…I'm happy for you, of course. Oh, I feel like a mother hen. Are you sure this is what you want?"

"I'm not sure of anything," Erin blurted out, then sank onto the bed. "I'm scared witless, and I keep thinking I'll wake up and find myself back on the farm and this all something I dreamed up."

"It's real." Dee squeezed her hand. "You have to understand that everything happening now is as real as anything can be."

"I do, and that only scares me more. But I love him. I wish I knew him better. I wish he'd talk to me about his family, about himself. I wish Ma was here and my father and the rest of them. But…"

"But," Dee coaxed as she moved over to sit beside her.

"But I love him. It's enough, isn't it?"

"Enough to start." She remembered that in the beginning all she'd had was a blind, desperate love for Travis. Time had given her the rest. "He's not an easy man to know."

"But you like him?"

"I've always had a soft spot for Burke. He's got a kind heart, though he'd rather no one noticed. He's a tough one, but I believe he'd do his best not to hurt someone he loved."

"I don't know if he loves me."

"What's this?"

"It doesn't matter," Erin said quickly, and rose to pace. "Because I love him enough for the two of us."

"Why would he want to marry you if he didn't love you?"

"He wants me." Better to face it now, head-on, she told herself as she turned back to Dee.

"I see." And because she did, she chose her words with care. "Marriage is a mighty big step for a man to take only for a want, a bigger step yet for a man like Burke. If the words are hard to come by, it might be that he hasn't learned how to say them."

"It doesn't matter. I don't need words."

"Of course you do."

"Aye, you're right." She turned back with a sigh. "But they can wait."

"Sometimes a person needs to feel safe before he can speak what's in his heart."

"You're good for me." Erin reached out both hands and grasped Dee's. "I'm happy, and despite the both of us I'm going to make him happy."

Brave words aside, when she stood at the top of the staircase two days later, clinging to Paddy's arm, Erin wasn't sure she could walk as far as the atrium, where the ceremony would take place. The music had begun. In truth, she could hear nothing else. She took one step and stopped. Then she felt Paddy's comforting pat on her hand.

"Come now, lass, you look beautiful. Your father would be proud of you today."

She nodded, took two slow, easy breaths, then descended.

Burke thought the tux would strangle him. If he'd had his way, they would have walked into the courthouse, said a few words and walked out again. Mission accomplished. It had been Dee who had browbeaten him into a wedding. Just a simple one, she'd said, Burke thought with a grimace. A woman was entitled to white lace and flowers once in her life. She herself hadn't been given the choice, but she wanted it for Erin. He'd relented because he'd been certain she couldn't pull it off in the two weeks he'd given her. Of course, she had.

The simple wedding she'd promised had swelled into what he considered a sideshow, with two hundred people eager to watch him juggle. The house was full of white and pink roses, and he'd been forced to pull himself into a tux. She'd ordered a five-tiered wedding cake and enough champagne to fill his pool. Wasn't it enough that he was about to make a lifetime commitment without having a trio of violins behind him?

Burke stood with his hands at his side and his face carefully blank and wondered what in the hell he was doing.

Then he saw her.

Her hair was glowing, warm and vibrant under layers of white tulle. She seemed pale, but her eyes met his without hesitation. How was it he'd never noticed how small she was, how delicate, until now, when she was about to become a permanent part of his life? Permanent. He felt the quick sliver of panic. Then she smiled, slowly, almost questioningly. He held out a hand.

Her fingers were icy. It was a relief to find his equally cold. She held tight and turned to face the priest.

It didn't take long to change lives. A few moments, a few words. She felt the ring slip onto her finger, but she was looking at him. Her hand was steady when she took the gold band from Dee and placed it on Burke's finger.

And it was done. He lifted the veil and touched the warm skin beneath. He brought his lips to hers, lightly, then more strongly. With a laugh, Erin threw her arms around his neck and held him. And it was sealed.

Then, almost from the moment she became his wife, she was spun away to be congratulated, complimented and envied.

It became like a dream, full of music and strangers and frothy wine. She was toasted and fussed over. Cameras flashed. There was caviar and elegant little hors d'oeuvres and sugared fruit that sparkled like diamonds under the lights. Erin found herself answering questions, smiling and wishing herself a hundred miles away.

Then she was dancing with Burke, and the world snapped back into focus.

"This didn't seem real. Until now." She rested her cheek against his and sighed. "I always dreamed of a day like this. Are we really married, or am I still imagining?"

He lifted her hand, running a finger over her ring. "Looks real to me."

Smiling, she looked down, then caught her breath. "Oh, Burke, it's beautiful." Stunned, she turned her hand so that the layers of diamonds and sapphires glittered. "I never expected anything like this."

"You've had it on for an hour. Haven't you looked?"

"No." It was foolish to cry now, but she felt the tears sting her eyes. "Thank you." She was grateful the music stopped while she still had control. "I'll be back in just a minute."

"You'd better be. I'll be damned if I'll deal with this crowd alone."

She tucked her thumb into her fist so that she could run it along the ring as she hurried upstairs. She just needed a minute, Erin told herself. To compose, to adjust, to believe.

Stepping inside the bedroom, she leaned back against the door and caught her breath. Tonight, she thought, this would be her room, just as Burke would be—was—her husband. She would sleep in this bed, wake in it, tidy the sheets, fuss with the curtains. And one day it would become usual.

No, she thought with a laugh, and hugged herself. It would never become usual. She wouldn't let it. From this day on her life would be special. Because she loved and belonged.

Touching her cheeks to be certain they were cool and dry, she started to open the door. A trio of women were passing on their way downstairs.

"Why, for his money, of course." This from a woman Erin recognized from Adelia's party, one with beautiful white hair and a watered-silk suit. "After all, she hardly knew the man. Why else would she marry him? You don't think she came all the way from Ireland to settle for keeping his books."

"It seems strange that Burke would marry her, a nobody, when he could have had his pick of some of the most acceptable women in the area." The leggy blonde from the party fussed with the snap of her purse.

"I thought they made a lovely couple." The third woman merely shrugged as the white-haired matron looked down her nose. "Really, Dorothy, a man hardly marries without reason."

"No doubt she's got a few tricks up her sleeve. It's one thing to get a man into bed, after all, and another to get him to the altar. Men are charmed easily enough, and bore just as easily. I imagine he'll be finished with her in a year. If she's as smart as I think she is, she'll tuck away a nice settlement—starting with that ring he gave her. Ordered it from Cartier's, you know. Ten thousand. Not a bad start for a little farm girl from nowhere."

The blonde fussed with her hair as they approached the head of the stairs. "It should be interesting to see her struggle to climb the social ladder in the next few months."

"She's not one of us," the white-haired woman announced with a flick of the wrist.

Erin stood with her hand on the knob and watched them descend the stairs. Not one of them? Through the first shock came the tremble of anger. Well, damned if she wanted to be. They were nothing but a bunch of gossiping old broody hens with nothing better to do than make cruel remarks and speculate on the feelings of others.

For his money? Did everyone really believe she'd married Burke for his money? Did he? she wondered with a sudden and very new shock. Anger drained as she let her hand slip off the knob. Oh, sweet God, did he? Was that what he'd meant when he'd said he could give her what she wanted?

She put her hands to her cheeks again, but they were no longer cool. Could he believe that her feelings were tied up in what he had instead of what he was? She hadn't done anything to show him otherwise, Erin realized with a sinking heart.

But she would. Lifting her head, she started out of the room. She would show him, she would prove to him that it was the man she had married, not his fine house or his rich farm. And to hell with the rest of them.

When she descended the steps this time, she didn't look like the pale, innocent bride. Her color was high, her eyes dark. She might not be one of them, she thought, but she would find a way to fit in. She would make Burke proud of her. Forcing a smile, she walked directly to the woman in watered silk.

"I'm so glad you could come today."

The woman gave Erin a gracious nod as she sipped champagne. "Wouldn't have missed it, my dear. You do make a lovely bride."

"Thank you. But a woman's only a bride for a day, and a wife for a lifetime. If you'll excuse me." She crossed the room, her dress billowing magnificently. Though Burke was surrounded, she moved directly to him and, putting her arms around him, kissed him until the people around them began to murmur and chuckle. "I love you, Burke," she said simply, "and I always will."

He hadn't known he could be moved by words, at least not such well-used ones. But he felt something shift inside him as she smiled. "Is that a conclusion you just came to?"

"No, but I thought it past time I told you."

He thought he'd never nudge the last guest out the door. No one loved a party and free champagne like the privileged class.

Erin stood in the center of the atrium with her hands

clasped together. "It's going to take an army to put this place to rights."

"No one's walking through that door for twenty-four hours."

She smiled, but the fatigue and nerves were beginning to show. "I should go up and change."

"In a minute." Before she could move, he took both her hands. "I should have told you how beautiful you are. I can't remember ever being as nervous as I was when I stood down here waiting for you."

"Were you?" Her smile came fully now as she pressed against him. "Oh, I was scared to death. I nearly picked up my skirts and bolted."

"I'd have caught you."

"I hope so, because there's no place I want to be but here with you."

He framed her face with his hands. "You haven't had much chance to compare."

"It doesn't matter."

But he wondered. He was the only man she'd ever known. Now he'd done his best to be certain he was the only one she ever would. Selfish, yes, but a desperate man takes desperate measures. He kissed her again and then, while his lips were on hers, lifted her into his arms. "There's no threshold to carry you over."

Her eyes laughed at him. "There's one in the bedroom."

"I told you that you were a woman after my heart," he said, and carried her up the stairs. Rosa had champagne chilling in a bucket and two glasses waiting.

"Burke, I wonder, would you mind giving me ten minutes?"

"Who's going to help you out of that dress?"

"I can manage. I'm sure it's bad luck for the bridegroom to do so. Just ten," she repeated when he set her down. "I'll be quick."

With a shrug, he pulled a robe out of his closet. "I suppose I can get out of this straitjacket somewhere else."

"Thank you."

He didn't give her a minute more than that, but she was ready. She was still in white, but this gown was like a cloud, wisping down, shifting with each breath she took. Her hair was loose over the shoulders, fire against snow. He closed the door quietly behind him and looked his fill.

"I didn't think you could be more beautiful than you were this afternoon."

"I wanted tonight to be special. I know we've already… we've already been together, but—"

"This is the first time I'll make love to my wife."

"Aye." She held out her hands. "And I want you to love me. I want you more now than I did before. If you could—" It was foolish to blush now. She was a married woman. "If you could teach me what to do."

"Erin." He didn't know what to say. He simply didn't have the words. But he took her hand and pressed a kiss to her brow. "I have something for you."

When he took a box out of his pocket and handed it to her, she moistened her lips. "Burke, I don't want you to feel obliged to buy me things."

"If I don't, how am I going to please myself by looking at you wear them?" So he opened the box himself. Inside was a rope of diamonds holding one perfect sapphire.

"Oh, Burke." She wanted to cry because it was so lovely. She wanted to cry because she was afraid he thought she required it. "It matches my ring," she managed.

"That was the idea." But he was watching her, frowning at the look in her eyes. "Don't you like it?"

"Of course I do, it's like something out of a palace. I think I'm afraid to wear it."

He laughed at that and turned her toward the mirror. "Don't be silly. It's made to be worn. See?" He held it up around her throat. The sapphire gleamed dark against her skin and the wink of diamonds. "What good are pretty stones if a woman doesn't wear them? You'll need more than this before it's done. We can pick up some things on our honeymoon." He kissed the curve of her throat. "Where do you want to go? Paris? Aruba?"

Ireland, she thought, but was afraid he'd laugh at her. "I was thinking maybe we should wait awhile for that. After all, this is one of the busiest times of year for you, with the Derby coming up. Could we wait a few months before we go away?"

"If you like." He placed the necklace back in the box before turning her to face him. "Erin, what's wrong?"

"Nothing. It's just all so new and… Burke, I swear to you I won't do anything to cause you shame."

"What the hell is this?" Patience gone, he took her by the arm and set her on the bed. "I want to know what you've got into your head and how it got there."

"It's nothing," she said, furious with herself that she was always an open book to him while she could never dig beneath the top layer. "It's just that I realized today that I don't really fit in with your people and life-style."

"My people?" His laugh wasn't amused and had her tensing. "You don't know anything about my people, Irish, and you can consider yourself fortunate. If you mean the people who were here today, two-thirds of them aren't worth the snap of your fingers."

"But I thought you liked them. You've friends among them, and associates."

"Associates, for the most part. And that can change

at any time. We can go to parties, and you can join any clubs or committees you like. But if you want to thumb your nose at the lot of them, it wouldn't matter to me."

"You're part of the racing world," she insisted. "And married to you, so am I. I won't have anyone saying you married some little nobody who can't fit in."

"And someone did," he murmured. She didn't have to confirm with words what he could see so clearly in her eyes. "You listen to me. It only matters what we think. I married you because you were what I wanted."

"I'm going to be." She lifted her hands to his face. "I swear to you." She brought her mouth to his with all the passion, love and longing she had.

She wanted the night to be special, but that meant more than champagne and white lace. It meant showing him what was in her heart, what she was just beginning to understand for herself. That she loved him unrestrictedly. With her arms around him, her mouth on his, she lowered onto the bed. Their marriage bed.

He had shown her what loving could be. Now she hoped she could give some of that beauty back to him. Since experience wasn't hers, she could only act on what was in her heart. She had no idea if a man could feel more than need and satisfaction, but she wanted to try to give him some of the sweetness, some of the comfort he had given to her.

Hesitant, unsure, she pressed her lips to his throat. His taste was darker there, potent, and she could feel the beat of his pulse beneath her mouth. Its rhythm quickened. She smiled against his skin. Yes, she could give him something.

She liked the way he felt under her hands, the muscles that bunched and flowed as she moved her fingers over them. Tentatively she parted his robe. When she felt him tense, she retreated immediately, an apology forming on her lips.

"No." With a half laugh, he took her hand and brought it back to him. "I want you to touch me."

He kept his own hands gentle, though each hesitant stroke of her fingertips drove him mad. He was already caught in the innocence and passion of her, in her willingness to be taught, her eagerness to please and be pleased.

So they loved slowly, taking time to teach, to learn. There was no shyness on her part when he drew the lace from her shoulders, but rather a wonder that he found her so desirable. In answer, she slipped his robe away and let herself marvel at the strength and beauty that was her husband.

Perhaps it didn't make sense, but it was more exciting now that he belonged to her. The hard fist of need hadn't lessened, the trembles of anticipation and anxiety were just as sharp. But now, along with desire, was the simple joy that the man who held her was the man who would hold her night after night. This was only the beginning, she thought. Laughing, she rolled over him.

"Something funny?" he managed. He felt as though his body was stretched beyond the breaking point.

"I'm happy." She brought her mouth down hard on his, then, incredibly, felt her bones liquify. With a soft moan, she took him into her. When the whirlwind started, she could only hold her breath and grip his hands tight. Her body took control now, moving with his instinctively as pleasure built and crested and built again.

Her head was thrown back. He thought she looked like a goddess, red hair streaming over white shoulders, her slender body strong and agile as it merged with his. He wanted to hold her like this, to see her like this again and again in his mind's eye. Then the pleasure was so complete that it blinded him.

Erin woke on her first day as Mrs. Logan to a gray morning lashed by spring rain. She thought it was beautiful. Smiling, she shifted over to reach for Burke. And found him gone. Terrified she'd dreamed it all, she sat straight up.

"Do you always wake up like that?" Across the room, Burke hooked his belt and watched her.

"No, I thought…" It wasn't a dream. Of course, it wasn't. She laughed at herself and shook her head. "Never mind. Where are you going?"

"Down to the stables."

"So early?"

"It's seven."

"Seven." She rubbed her hands over her eyes as she struggled up. "I'll fix your breakfast."

"Rosa'll see to it. You should get some more sleep."

"But I—" She wanted to fix his breakfast. It was one of the small and very vital things a wife could do for her husband. She wanted to sit in the kitchen with him, talking of the day to come and remembering the night that had passed. But he was already pulling on his boots. "I'm not tired. I could go down and start on the books."

"You've gotten them in good enough shape to take a couple of days off. In fact, we haven't talked about it, but you don't have to continue with that if you don't like."

"Well, of course I'll continue with it. That's why I came here."

He lifted a brow as she tugged on a robe. "Things have changed. I don't want my wife to have to close herself up in an office all day."

"If it's all the same to you, I'd like to work." Uncomfortable, she began to tug on the sheets. "If you don't want me to be doing your books anymore, I'll find another job."

"I don't care if you work on them or not, I just want you to know you have a choice. What are you doing?"

"I'm making the bed, of course."

Crossing over, he caught her hand in his. "Rosa takes care of the bed-making, as well."

"There's certainly no need for her to make mine— ours."

"That's her job."

He kissed her brow, then changed his mind and drew her close against him. "Good morning," he murmured against her lips.

Hers curved just slightly. "Good morning."

"I'll be back in a few hours. Why don't you take a swim?"

When the door closed behind him, Erin crossed her arms. Take a swim? On her first day as a wife, she wasn't supposed to cook breakfast or make a bed but to take a swim? Walking over to the mirror, she stared at herself. She didn't look so very different. But feelings didn't always show. Wasn't it odd that she'd refused to be Burke's mistress, but now she was feeling more like that than a wife?

Married him for his money.

Erin pushed away from the mirror. The hell with that. It was past seven and she had work to do.

Rosa wasn't any more cooperative than Burke. There was no reason for the *señora* to do that. There was no reason for the *señora* to do this. Perhaps the *señora* would like to take a book into the solarium. In other words, Erin thought, you're of no use here. That was going to change, she decided.

She threw herself into her paperwork. When Burke didn't return for lunch, Erin took matters into her own hands. Filling a pail with hot water and detergent, she took it and a mop to the atrium. Glasses and plates had already been cleared away, but Rosa hadn't yet gotten to the tiles. Erin felt a stab of satisfaction at having beaten her to it.

This is my house, she told herself as she sloshed out soapy water. My floor, and I'll damn well wash it if I like.

Burke strode through the streaming rain, thinking that the horse he had entered at Charles Town that night would have an edge on the muddy track. His second thought was that Erin might get a kick out of taking the trip to West Virginia to see the run. It would give him a chance to show her off a bit.

God, she'd looked beautiful that morning, all heavy-eyed and dewy-skinned. He was far from certain he'd done the right thing for her by rushing her into marriage, but he was more certain than ever that he'd done the right thing for himself. He couldn't remember ever being at peace before or ever feeling as though each day had a solid purpose to it.

He could give her the things in life she'd always wanted. The money didn't matter to him, so he didn't give a hang how she spent it. In turn she was giving him a solid base, something he hadn't known he'd wanted.

Inside, he shook the rain out of his hair and went to look for her. When he entered the atrium, he stopped. She was on her hands and knees, scrubbing. Even as she heard his steps and glanced up, he was dragging her to her feet.

"What in hell are you doing?"

"Why, I'm washing the floor. It took a beating yesterday. You'd be amazed what people can drop and what they don't bother to pick up again. Burke, you're hurting my arm."

"I don't ever want to see you down on your knees again. Understand?"

"No." Studying him, she rubbed her arm. She knew real anger when she looked it in the face. "No, I don't."

"My wife doesn't scrub floors."

"Now wait a minute." As he turned on his heel, she caught him. "She'll scrub them if she pleases, and she won't be called *my wife* as though she were something shiny to be kept in a box. What's the matter with you?"

"I didn't marry you so you could scrub floors."

"No, nor that I could cook your breakfast or make the bed, that's plain. Just why did you marry me, then?"

"I thought I'd made that clear."

"Aye." She dropped her hand from his arm. "I suppose you did. So I'm to be your mistress after all, it's just a matter of being a legal one."

He made an effort, an enormous one, to block off the anger. It didn't work. "Don't be a fool. And leave that damn bucket where it is."

"You'll remember the word in the ceremony was changed from obey to cherish." Scowling at him, she gave the bucket a kick and sent soapy water pouring over the tiles. "But I'll be happy to leave it just where it is."

"Where the hell are you going?"

"I don't know," she said over her shoulder. "Surely I can walk through the house even though I'm not allowed to touch anything in it."

"Stop it." He caught her as she stormed down the hall, but she only shook him off and kept going. "Damn it, Erin, you can touch whatever you like, just don't clean it."

"I can see it's time we had the rules straight." She pushed through the doors into the solarium. The heat was like a wall and suited her mood perfectly. "Touching and looking are allowed."

"Stop acting like an idiot."

"Me?" She turned on him and nearly upset a pot of geraniums. "It's me who's an idiot, is it? Out there it's a fool I am and in here an idiot. Well, it wasn't me who went into a rage because the floor was getting washed."

"I thought you came here to get away from that, because you wanted more out of life than washing dishes."

Slowly she nodded. "Aye, I came to America for that, but it's not why I married you. Maybe I can handle others thinking I married you because of your money and your fine house, but not you. I told you yesterday that I loved you. Don't you believe me?"

"I don't know." He ran a hand over his face and struggled for calm, for clear thinking, for the kind of controlled logic that had always brought him out on top of any game he chose. "Why does it matter?"

She had to turn away because it hurt too much to face him. "I didn't lie when I said it, but you can think whatever you like. It doesn't matter at all." Very deliberately she picked up a pottery bowl and sent it crashing to the tiles. "You needn't worry, I won't clean it up."

"Are you finished?"

"I haven't decided." Crossing her arms, she stared at the clear water of the pool.

He put his hand on her shoulder. Perhaps she did love him a little. It would take a bigger fool than he to push her away. "My mother spent more than half of her life on her knees scrubbing other people's floors. She was barely forty when she died. I don't want you on your knees for anyone, Erin."

When he started to draw his hand away, she clasped it in her own. "That's the first thing you've trusted me with." She turned to put her arms around him. "Don't you see you'll drive me mad if you shut me out?"

"You agreed to take me for what I am."

"I have. I will. I do love you, Burke."

"Then let me see you enjoy yourself."

"But I am." Tilting her head back, she grinned at him. "I like to fight."

He ran a finger down her nose. "Then I'm glad to oblige you. Did you take that swim?"

"No, I had the books, and then I argued with Rosa for a while."

"Busy day. Let's take one now."

"I can't."

"More arguing to do?"

"No, I've done with that, but I don't want to swim."

"Can't you?"

Her chin angled as he'd expected. "Of course I can, but I don't have a suit."

"That's okay." Lifting her up, he walked to the edge as she giggled and shoved against him.

"You wouldn't, and if you try, by God, you'll go in with me."

"I never intended it any other way." They went in together, fully dressed.

Chapter Nine

Before she had been married a full month, Erin had taken trips to New York and Kentucky and back to Florida. She grew used to the look and feel of the racetracks, whether they were earthy or glamorous. She grew used to, but never less fascinated by, the people who inhabited them, from the young grooms still shiny with ambition to the older hands who lived from race to race and bet to bet.

The contrasts were a constant curiosity. From her box she could watch the other owners, their families and friends. Seersucker suits and picture hats. While against the rail, elbow to elbow, were the masses who came for the fun or the money. She learned that wagering had its own scent, often a desperate one, always a little sweaty. Away from the stands were the horses, the scales, the tack and the riders. Only a few who watched knew the thrill and the anxiety of ownership.

In Lexington she visited horse farms with Burke and saw stables grander than she had ever thought any house could be. She saw the races of the Thoroughbred world, grew to know the people whose lives were tied to them, and she learned.

At cocktail parties, dinner parties and small celebrations she listened to discussions on breeding, on training, on strategy. She grew to understand that owners often thought of their horses as possessions, while trainers more often than not thought of a horse in their care as an athlete to be disciplined and pampered in the peculiar way of the sportsman. But above all the horse was the focus, for envy or for pride.

After a time she drew together the courage to go as far as the paddocks, where she could watch the horses being examined and saddled for the races. Though the scent and sounds of horses still disturbed her, she was determined that Burke's associates would never twitter about his wife being afraid.

She grew more accustomed to the parties, the lavish ones, that only the successful and the privileged could attend. The talk there was of horses and the people who owned them. Not so different from Skibbereen, she began to think. Certainly this life was more glamorous, but at home the talk had often been just as narrow.

She studied, poring over books on Thoroughbreds, racing and the history of both. She learned that every Thoroughbred descended from three Arabian studs and that the most expensive horseflesh in the world was to be found in Ireland at the Irish National Stud. She'd had to smile at that, not only from home pride but because two such horses were in Burke's stables.

She learned to wager wisely and to win, a skill that never failed to amuse her husband. He'd been right when he'd said she would make him laugh. Erin found more pleasure in that than in all the pretty stones he bought her or the new clothes that hung in her closet. She'd discovered something in a month of marriage. The things she'd thought she'd always wanted weren't important after all.

And she was pregnant.

The knowledge both thrilled and terrified her. She was carrying a child, Burke's child, one that had been conceived on their first night together. In a matter of months they would no longer be just husband and wife but a family. She couldn't wait to tell him. She was afraid of what he would say.

They'd never discussed children. But then, there had been time to discuss little. She hardly knew more of him now than she had when she'd married him. True, she had come to understand that unlike many of his associates his horses were neither possessions nor pets. Nor were they the game of chance he claimed them to be. They had his pride and his affection, and Erin came to see that they had his admiration for simply being what they were. It wasn't just the winning but the heart that made champions.

There was this and little more she had learned of him. He'd never spoken of his mother or his family again. Though she'd tried to question him gently, he'd simply ignored her. Not evaded, Erin thought now, just ignored.

It didn't matter, she told herself as she went to find him. She'd seen him with Dee's children, and he'd been gentle and kind and caring. Surely he would be only more so with a child of his own. She would tell him and he would hold her tight and tell her how happy he was. They would laugh and she would show him all the pamphlets the doctor had given her on childbearing classes and diet.

Then they would plan the nursery, all pinks and blues like a sunrise.

She found him in the library and had to bite back an impatient oath when she saw he was on the phone.

"I'm not interested in selling," he said as he gestured her in. "No, not at that price, not at any. If you want to get back to me in a few years and talk stud fees… Yes, that's a firm no. Tell Durnam none of my stock's for sale at the moment. Yeah, you'll be the first to know." He hung up and pulled a hand through his hair.

"Problems?" Erin crossed over to kiss his cheek.

"No. Charlie Durnam's interested in buying one of the new foals. Makes me think he's the one with problems. So what did you buy?"

"Buy?"

"You said you were going shopping."

"Oh, yes. I didn't buy anything." She rested her cheek against his hair a moment. "Burke, I've something I want to tell you."

"In a minute. Sit down, Erin."

It was the tone that had her retreating. He used that odd flat voice when she'd annoyed him. "What's wrong?"

"I've had a letter from your father."

"From Da?" She was up again almost before she sat. "Is something wrong? Is someone sick?"

"No, nothing's wrong. Sit down." He swiveled in his chair, and for the first time in a month she felt as though they were back on terms of business. "He wrote to welcome me into the family and to express what I suppose is fatherly concern that I take good care of you."

"What nonsense. He knows very well I can take care of myself." She relaxed again, unconsciously resting a hand low on her stomach. "Was that all?"

"He also thanked me for the money you've been

sending over. He says it's been a great help." Burke paused a moment as he flipped through the papers on his desk. "Why didn't you tell me you've been sending more than half your money over to Ireland?"

"I never thought of it," she began. Then she stopped. "How do you know how much I'm sending?"

"You keep excellent and very clear books, Erin." He pushed away from the desk to pace to the window.

"I don't understand why you're angry. The money's mine, after all."

"It's yours," he murmured. "Damn it, Erin, there's a checkbook in the office. If you'd felt the need to send money home, why didn't you just take what you wanted and be done with it?"

"There's more than enough out of my wages."

"You're my wife, damn it, and that entitles you to whatever you want. You're past the point where you have to draw wages."

She was silent a moment, and when she spoke, she spoke carefully. "That's it, isn't it? You still believe that I'm here because of your fat checkbook."

He didn't know what he thought, Burke admitted as he stared out of the window. She was perfect, warm, loving. And the longer she was with him, the more he was certain there had to be a catch. No one gave unconditionally. No one gave without wanting something back. "Not entirely," he said after a moment. "But I don't believe you'd have married me if I didn't have one. I told you before it doesn't matter. We suit well enough."

"Do we?"

"The point is the money's there and you may as well make use of it. You never know how long it'll last." With a half smile, he lit a cigar. "That's a bridge we'll cross when we come to it. Enjoy it, Irish, it's all part of the bargain."

She thought of the child inside her and could have wept. Instead she stood. "Is there anything else?"

"I want you to go write out a check for whatever your family needs."

"All right. Thank you."

"We'll be leaving for Kentucky in a few days. The Bluegrass Stakes and the Derby." He turned and leaned back against the sill. "You should enjoy it. It's quite a show."

"I'm sure it's wonderful." She took a long breath and watched him carefully. "It's a pity Dee's too far along to travel so she and Travis won't be there."

"That's the price you pay for having a family." He shrugged and moved back to his desk.

"Aye," she said quietly, but the light had gone out of her eyes. "I'll let you get back to work."

"Wasn't there something you wanted to tell me?"

"No. It was nothing." Erin closed the door behind her, then covered her face with her hands. Hadn't she told him she loved him? Hadn't she showed him in every way she knew? And now she was carrying physical proof of her feelings, but none of it mattered to him.

Then it would have to matter to her even more. Erin straightened her shoulders and walked away from the door, unaware that Burke stood on the other side, hesitating, his hand on the knob.

He hadn't meant to be angry. She'd looked so happy when she'd come into the room. She'd smiled at him as though...as though she loved him. Why couldn't he get past the block and just accept? Because he didn't believe in that kind of love, not even when he felt it himself.

He did believe that she would stay with him, happily

enough, as long as he continued to provide her with what she needed. When he'd met her, he'd recognized the hunger for more he himself had always felt. He'd recognized the need to see new things, climb new mountains and win. It was just fortunate for both of them that he was in a position to show her those things, to provide her with the means to taste and hear and see the fantasies she'd had.

She could love him for that, and that he could understand.

But what about the man who had come from nothing? What about the man who could be back to nothing at the toss of the dice? What would her feelings be for him? He couldn't afford to find out, because the man who thought love only existed for convenience was desperately in love with his wife.

She was far from aware of it. As Erin walked into the kitchen, she was certain Burke only wanted her as long as she did nothing to upset the balance of his life-style. Sooner or later, he would be aware that together they already had.

Rosa was washing crystal in the sink but stopped the moment Erin walked in the room.

"Is there something you want, *señora*?"

"I'm just going to fix some tea."

"I'll heat the water."

"I can do it myself," Erin snapped as she slammed the kettle onto the stove.

"As you like, *señora*."

Erin leaned her palms against the stove. "I'm sorry, Rosa."

"De nada."

As Rosa went back to her crystal, Erin found a cup and saucer. What kind of wife was it, she wondered, who didn't even know which cupboard held her dishes? How could she be so happy and so unhappy at the same time?

"Rosa, how long have you worked for Mr. Logan?"

"Many years, *señora*."

"Before he came here to this house?"

"Before that."

Like pulling teeth, she thought, determined to pull harder. "Where did you work with him before that?"

"In another house."

Erin turned from the stove. "Where, Rosa?"

She saw the housekeeper's lips tighten. "In Nevada. In the West."

"What did he do there?"

"He had much business. You should ask Mr. Logan yourself."

"It's you I'm asking. Rosa, don't you think I have a right to know who my husband is?"

She saw the brief hesitation before Rosa began to polish glasses. "It's not my place, *señora*."

"I need something." With an angry flick of her wrist, she shut off the flame. "I don't care what he did, what he was. If he's done something wrong it doesn't matter. How can I get through to him if I don't understand him?"

"*Señora*." Carefully Rosa set down the first glass and picked up another. "I'm not sure you would understand even if you knew."

"Tell me, and let me try."

"Some things are better left alone."

"No!" She wanted to throw something, anything, but managed to hold the need back. "Rosa, look at me. I love him." When the housekeeper turned, Erin spoke again. "I love him and I can't stand being kept apart from who he is. I want to make him happy."

Rosa stood silently a moment. Her eyes were very dark and very clear. For a moment Erin felt a stab of recognition. Then it passed. "I believe you."

"It's Burke who needs to believe."

"For some, believing such things doesn't come easily."

"Why? Why for Burke?"

"Do you know what it's like to be hungry? Truly hungry? For food, for knowledge, for love?"

"No."

"He grew up with nothing, less than nothing. When there was work, he worked. When there was not, he stole." She moved her shoulders and picked up the next glass. "Not such a bad life for some. Hell for others. He never knew his father. His mother was not married, you understand?"

"Yes." Erin sat and made no objection when Rosa moved over to the stove to fix her tea.

"His mother worked very hard, though she was never well. But in such places a person always owes much more than they could ever have. At times he went to school, but more often he worked in the fields."

"On a farm?" she asked, remembering the way Burke had looked over hers.

"*Sí.* He lived on one for a while so that he could give his mother his pay."

"I see." And she was beginning to.

"He hated the life, the dirt and the stench of it."

"Rosa, how did you know him when he was a child?"

She set the tea down in front of Erin. "We had the same father."

Erin stared. Then, when Rosa would have walked away, she grabbed her arm. "You're Burke's sister?"

"Half sister. My father took me to New Mexico when I was six. He met Burke's mother. She was pretty, frail and very innocent. After Burke was born he left me with her, promising to send for us all when he had a job. He never did."

"Something might have happened to him. He might—" She stopped when she saw the look in Rosa's eyes.

"Burke's mother discovered he'd met another woman in Utah. That was his way. So she worked, washing up other people's dirt, for twenty years. Then she died. She had done her best for him, but Burke was always wild and restless. The day she was buried, he left. It was five years before I saw him again."

"He found you?"

"No, I found him." Rosa went back to her glasses. "Burke is not a man who looks for anyone. He owned part of a casino in Reno. Because I wouldn't take the money he offered, I went to work for him. He's never been comfortable with it, but he doesn't send me away."

"He couldn't. You're his sister."

"Not to him. Because to him our father never existed. There is no family in Burke's life, no roots, no home."

"That can change."

"Only Burke can change it."

"Aye." Nodding, she stood. "Thank you, Rosa."

She didn't tell him about the baby. Over the next few days she fretted over the secret but didn't speak it. There were races to prepare for. Important ones. Now, as she watched Burke handle his business and deal with his horses, she watched from a different perspective.

How had his early life shaped him? She took note of the way he treated those who worked for him. He was firm and demanding but never unreasonable. Not once had she heard him raise his voice to any of his men.

Because he knew what it was like to be abused by an employer? she wondered. Because he understood how it felt to be dependent for your existence on another?

He loved the horses. She wasn't sure he was aware of it himself, but she could see it in the way he watched them take to the track, the way he supervised their grooming. Perhaps it was true that when he'd won the farm it had been only another game, but he'd made a life out of it whether he realized it or not. That alone gave Erin hope.

The time came for them to fly to Kentucky. Erin vowed she would tell him about the baby when they returned.

There was something different about her, Burke thought as he fixed himself a drink in the parlor of their hotel suite. He just couldn't quite put his finger on it. Her moods were like a roller coaster—up, down and sideways as quick as a wink. Not that he didn't find them interesting. He'd never been one who wanted to settle in too comfortably, and a man would hardly do that with a wife who was raging one minute and smiling sweetly the next. She was always doing the unexpected these days, cuddling up against him and falling into long, thoughtful silences or racing down to the stables to drag him back for a picnic under the willow.

She was the same in public, playing the dignified wife one moment and a flirtatious woman the next. And she didn't always flirt with only him. He couldn't deny it made him jealous, but he was fully aware that was her intent.

He found her daydreaming one minute and rushing around talking about redecorating the next. At times he worried that she was becoming restless again, but then she would reach for him at night, and no one had ever seemed so content.

He'd noticed she seemed to have lost her taste for

champagne, though they attended the spring parties with
regularity. She'd taken to sipping plain juice and discussing bloodlines and the pros and cons of certain tracks.

Then there had been the day he'd given her the earrings, sapphires to match her necklace. She had opened
the box, burst into tears and fled, only to come back an
hour later to gather him close and thank him.

The woman was driving him crazy, and he was enjoying every minute of it.

"Are you almost ready, or do you want to be fashionably
late?" he asked as he strolled toward the bedroom.

"Almost ready. Since we're going to win the race tomorrow, I thought I should look my best for the pictures
they'll be taking tonight. I've never known people with
such love for taking pictures at parties."

"You didn't complain about having yours in the paper,"
he began, then stopped to stand in the doorway. She
smiled when she saw him and turned a slow circle.

She'd chosen the dress carefully, knowing that before
too many more weeks she would be showing and wouldn't
feel proper wearing something daring. The midnight blue
was shot through with silver threads so that she shimmered even standing still. It left her shoulders bare, then
slithered down her body without drape or fold. Without
the slit up the skirt, she wasn't sure she could have moved
in it.

"Well, do you like it? Mrs. Viceroy said I should have
something to show off my necklace."

"Who's going to notice the necklace?" He came to her
and, in the way he had of making her heart stop, took both
her hands to kiss them. "Irish, you're gorgeous."

"It's sinful for me to want the other women to be jealous, isn't it?"

"Probably."

"But I do. I want them to look at you and think he's the most wonderful man here. And she has him." Laughing, she spun another circle. "Then I can just look at them and smile, sort of pitying."

"It's a shame I won't be able to notice, because I won't be able to take my eyes off you."

She turned back to touch his cheek. "You know, when you say things like that, it still makes my insides curl up. Burke…" She wanted to tell him she loved him, but she knew he would only smile and kiss her forehead. Then her heart would break a little because he wasn't able to give the words back to her. "Did you ever think these parties are a little—slow?"

"I thought you liked them."

"Well, I do." She moved closer to run a finger down his lapel. "But sometimes, sometimes I find myself in the mood for something that takes a little more energy." She smiled as she looked up at him under her lashes. "A lot more energy. You smell very nice."

"Thanks." He lifted a brow as she loosened his tie. "Are you trying to start something?"

"And what if I am?" She pushed his jacket off his shoulders.

"Just checking," he murmured while she unbuttoned his shirt. "This isn't going to make all those women jealous."

With a laugh she ran her hands up his chest. "That's what you think." Grinning, she shoved him onto the bed and jumped in after him.

For the first time since she'd fainted, Erin insisted on going down to the stables with Burke. She told him it was a matter of pride, and it was. Pride in him.

She wasn't able to bring herself to go in, but urged him to as she stood in the sun and watched the people.

A long way from Skibbereen indeed, she thought. The air was warm with springtime, and flowers were already in bloom. Trainers and exercise boys she'd come to know by sight nodded or tipped their hats as they passed her and greeted her as Mrs. Logan.

There was excitement in the air as well, the kind that hummed before an important race. Before long, it would be *the* race. The Derby. But for now everyone's attention was on today and the Bluegrass Stakes. A win here added to Double Bluff's record would make him the favorite. Erin smiled as she thought that would lower the odds, but odds didn't matter. She wanted Burke to win, today and at Churchill Downs. She could almost taste the satisfaction of having Double Bluff named Horse of the Year. More than she'd wanted anything, she wanted that for Burke, for him to know he'd done something special, something only the best could accomplish.

"Good day to you, Mrs. Logan."

"Paddy." Pleased to see him, Erin opened her arms for a hug. "Oh, it's a fine day, isn't it? How's Dee?"

"Right as right and mean as a bear. She told me to tell you if Travis's Apollo doesn't win, Burke's Double Bluff better."

"And who are you betting on?"

"Now who do you think? I trained Apollo myself. But if I was hedging my bets, I'd lay some money on the colt out of Three Aces."

"A smart man would put his money down on Charlie's Pride." Durnam came up behind them and slapped Paddy on the shoulder.

"Well, now, it's a fine colt you have there, Mr. Durnam, and that's the truth. But I think I'll stick with my own."

"That's your choice. Hello there, Mrs. Logan. You're looking as pretty as ever."

"Thank you. Good luck to you today."

"You don't need luck when you've got the best." He pulled at the brim of his straw hat and moved on.

"We'll see who's the best," Erin said under her breath.

"Got the fever, do you?" Chuckling, Paddy slipped an arm around her shoulders. "There's a powerful competition in this business. Can't be otherwise when money and prestige change hands in a matter of minutes."

"How do you know when you've got a winner?"

"Well, now, there's breeding and training and a matter of attitude. There's feed and grooming. There's the jockey that sits on top and finding the right man for the right mount. But what it comes down to, darling, is blood. It's in the blood or it isn't, just like with people."

"Aye, the blood." She looked toward the stables and thought of Burke. "So you think that someone could be denied the proper care and feeding, the training, and still be a winner?"

"We talking horses or people?"

"Does it matter?"

"Not much." He gave her shoulder a quick squeeze. "It's in the blood and it's in the heart. I've got to tend to my boy now."

"I'll wave to you from the winner's circle, Paddy Cunnane," she called after him.

"You sound sure of yourself," Burke commented as he crossed to her.

"Sure of you." She gripped his hands as they headed for the stands. "You don't have to walk me up. I know you want to stay to see your jockey weighed in and watch Double Bluff saddled."

"The last time I didn't go with you I found you surrounded by reporters."

"I know how to handle them now. Besides, I did like seeing my picture in the paper."

"You're a vain woman, Irish."

"Aye, and why not?" She brushed a finger over his cream-colored shirt and found herself pleased he didn't go in for the seersucker of his associates. "Whether it's pride or vanity, I find it exciting to see my picture on the society page. Did you know, Mr. Logan, you're a very important man?"

"Is that so?"

"Aye, 'tis so, and so I'm told often enough. Then, by rights, I have to be an important woman."

"You could pass for one today," he decided, taking a quick study of her pale blue suit and pearls. She'd added a plain wide-brimmed straw hat, then had tilted it at an angle so it could no longer be called demure.

"I decided the day called for dignified." Then she laughed and touched the brim of her hat. "Sort of. Burke, I'll be fine, really. I know you want to stay close to the horse."

"I'd rather stay close to you. Mind?"

"No." She hooked her arm through his and grinned. "Why don't I buy you a beer?"

She thought it was a perfect day. The most perfect day of her life. The sky was cloudless, a soft spring blue that made her smile just to look at it. She noticed the woman from her wedding as she stepped into the box, and made sure she tilted her head and smiled coolly in greeting.

"Why do I feel you're always sticking pins in Dorothy Gainsfield?"

"Because I am, darling." She stood on tiptoe and kissed him. "Long, sharp ones. I didn't know until the other day that the skinny blonde who was hanging all over you on St. Patrick's Day was Mrs. Gainsfield's favorite niece." She laughed again, figuring it meant another day in purgatory. "Life can be sweet."

"You'll have to fill me in on all this later."

"In ten or twenty years, perhaps. Look, Burke, television cameras. Can you imagine?"

Delighted with the world in general, she took her seat. Now and then she spotted someone she knew and waved, to Lloyd Pentel, to Honoria Louis, to the elderly Mrs. Bingham.

"Do you know, I've met as many people in a month's time as I've known all of my life. It's an odd and wonderful feeling." She turned to see he was smiling at her. "Why do you look at me like that?"

"It's an education to watch you in a place like this, soaking it all up, storing it away. I wonder what you'll look like when we go to Paris or Rio."

"Probably stand around with my mouth hanging open the whole time and humiliate you."

"There's that." He only laughed when she jabbed him with her elbow. "Try to behave yourself. It's almost post time."

"Oh, Lord save us, so it is, and I haven't bet."

"I bet for you while you were buying my beer and trying to decide if you were going to eat a cheeseburger or two hot dogs. Living in America's improved your appetite."

It wasn't only that that was increasing her appetite, she thought, and wondered when she would work up the nerve to tell him. "It wasn't my fault we missed breakfast," she reminded him. "Where's my ticket?"

Watching the horses being led to the starting gate, he

reached in his pocket. Erin took the stub and was about to tuck it away when she noticed the amount.

"A thousand dollars?" Her voice squeaked so that a few interested heads turned. "Burke, where would I be getting a thousand dollars to bet on a horse?"

"Don't be ridiculous." He didn't spare her a glance. His trainer had moved to Double Bluff's head as the colt reared and danced. "Seems a little more wired than usual," he murmured as two grooms stepped up to help.

"But, Burke, a thousand dollars."

"Afraid you'll lose?"

"No." She stopped. Then, closing the ticket tight in her hand, she said a quick prayer. "No, of course not."

The bell sounded. The gate was released. The horses plunged forward.

She recognized the Pentel colt in the lead. He was a fast starter, she remembered, but he didn't have stamina. With the ticket still clutched in her hand, she put a fist to her breast. The pack was hardly more than a blur, but she could see the green-and-white silks of Burke's jockey. Rounding the first turn he was in fourth, with Travis's colt on his left. The crowd was already shouting so that she could no longer hear the announcer. It didn't matter. With her free hand she gripped the sleeve of Burke's linen shirt and held on.

"He's making his move," Burke murmured.

She saw the whiz of crops, the strain of speed as the jockeys leaned low. Double Bluff moved to the outside. His stride lengthened, eating up distance. It seemed that before her eyes he grew bigger, his coat glossier, his legs longer.

A champion, she thought again, was in the heart. Hers was with the colt. It was more than a race, she knew, more than prestige and certainly more than money. It was

Burke's pride. She understood what it was like to come from little, then to have a chance for everything.

The Pentel colt began to lag. As they came down the stretch it was a race between three, leaving the pack behind. Charlie's Pride held first, with Travis's colt and Double Bluff vying for second. She could see the dirt flying and the sweat. All around her there was one huge, bellowing roar.

"He's going to do it!" She didn't even realize she was shouting as she watched Double Bluff gain on Charlie's Pride. They were nose to nose for what seemed forever. And then he was ahead, by a neck, by half a length, by a length, with his speed only increasing. He was two lengths ahead at the wire.

"Oh, Burke, he did it. You did it!" She hadn't been aware of standing, but found herself on her feet as she turned to throw her arms around him. "Sure and he's the most beautiful horse ever born. I'm so proud of you."

"I wasn't racing."

She drew back to caress his cheek. "Yes, you were."

"Maybe I was," he murmured as he kissed the tip of her nose. He continued to watch as his jockey took the horse around for the victory lap. "Can you manage to stand in the winner's circle with me?"

"I think so." People were congratulating them, and though Erin acknowledged them, her thoughts were already moving forward to standing beside Burke as he accepted the win.

Her arms were still around him when the official winner was declared. Charlie's Pride. Double Bluff had been disqualified.

"Disqualified? What do they mean?"

"We'll find out." Taking her hand, Burke moved out of the stands. The murmurs had already started.

"Burke, they can't say he didn't win. For heaven's sake, I saw it with my own eyes. He was well in the lead. There's a mistake."

"Wait here." Leaving her, he walked over to the paddock area where Double Bluff was being held. She saw a bald man in a suit approach Burke, then two other men join them. It looked so official, she thought. The bald man was talking calmly, pointing to the horse, then to a piece of paper. As he spoke, both the jockey and the trainer began to argue furiously, but Burke simply stood, listening.

She began to feel the heat as she stood there, so she moved over into the shade. It was a mistake, of course, she told herself as she removed her hat to stir air into her face. No one would take away what Burke had earned, what he needed, what she needed for him.

"What is it?" she demanded as Burke strode back.

"Amphetamines. Someone gave the horse amphetamines."

"Drugs? But that's ridiculous."

"Apparently not." His eyes were narrowed as he looked over at the paddock. "Someone wanted him to win very badly. Or to lose."

Chapter Ten

"**W**hat do you mean you're sending me home? I'm not a package to be wrapped and stamped." Erin rushed after Burke as he strode from the parlor to the bedroom of the suite. "You've barely said a word to me since we left the track, and now all you can say is you're sending me home."

"There's nothing else to say, not at the moment."

"Nothing to say?" Because she was breathless after struggling to keep pace with him, she sat. "Double Bluff was just disqualified from one of the most important races of the year because someone gave him drugs. That's plenty to talk about to start."

"It's not your concern." He pulled a suitcase out of the closet, then set it open on the bed. "Pack."

She kept her seat and, just barely, her temper, but her eyes narrowed. "Oh, I see. So this is one more thing I'm not to touch."

Pausing only a moment, Burke studied her. He could see the temper beginning to brew. As far as he was concerned, she was better off angry than dealing with the tempest of the next few days. He'd never considered himself a man of great virtues, but he'd protect his wife.

"You can look at it that way or any other way you like. I've got some calls to make. Pack your things, I'll see that your flight's changed."

"Just one bloody minute." She was up and after him again as he walked into the next room. "I'm sick to death of orders from you. Almost as sick as I am of talking to your back. If you don't put down that phone, Burke Logan, it'll pleasure me to wrap the cord around your neck."

"Erin, I've got enough to deal with at the moment without you adding one of your tantrums."

"Tantrums." Her hands clenched into fists as she walked toward him. "Oh, I've a flash for you, I do. You haven't seen a tantrum yet. Now sit." Taking both hands, she shoved him into a chair. "And it's time you unplugged your ears and listened for a change."

He could have risen again and struck back with his own temper. He decided against it, in the same way he might have decided to bluff his way to a pot with a pair of deuces. The quickest way to have her out and on her way was to show disinterest. "Is this going to take long?"

"As long as needs be."

"Then would you mind if I had a drink?"

Seething, she went behind the bar and grabbed a bottle and a glass. She slammed them down on the table beside him. "Go ahead, have the whole bottle. Drown yourself in it."

"Just one'll do." He poured two fingers, then lifted the glass in a half salute. "Say what's your mind, Irish. I have a few things to see to before your flight."

"If I said half what was on it, your ears would be ringing from now till Gabriel blew his horn. Answer me this, are you going to take this business lying down?"

He lifted the glass and sipped, watching her steadily over the rim. "What do you think?"

"I think you're going to fight, and I think you won't be resting until you find out who's behind this. Then I think you're going to carve them up in little pieces."

He toasted her again, then downed the rest of the whiskey. "That about covers it."

"And I'm not going home to twiddle my thumbs while you're about it."

"That's exactly what you're going to do."

"Did it ever occur to you that I could help?"

"I don't want your help or need it, Erin."

"No, you don't need anyone." She swung away to pace the room, wishing she knew a better way than shouting to handle an argument. "All you need are a few paid servants to deal with the little details while you go on your merry way. You certainly don't need a wife, a partner, to tend to your shirts or hold your hand when there's trouble."

The urge to get up, to hold on to her, was so strong he had to press his fingers into the glass until his knuckles whitened. Because she was wrong. She was very, very wrong about what and whom he needed. "I didn't marry you to do my laundry."

"No, you married me to sleep with, and I know it well enough. But you got more than you bargained for, because I'm not running back home like some weakhearted, whiny female who can't face a spot of trouble."

Pride, he thought, and nearly laughed. It always seemed to be his pride or hers on the line. "No one's insulting your valor, Erin. It would simply make things easier if I didn't have you to deal with."

"You won't have to deal with me. In private I'll stay out of your way and you can do your business however you please. But in public I'm going to be there."

"The loyal and trusting wife?"

"What's wrong with that?"

"Nothing." He sat back, determined to study her calmly. She looked like a comet about to go into orbit. "It matters to you what these people think, what they say?"

"And why shouldn't it?"

Why shouldn't it indeed? he thought as he stared into his empty glass. She was worried about her position, and hers walked hand in glove with his own. "Have it your way, then, I can hardly drag you to a plane and tie you on. But I warn you, it won't be pretty."

"You've said you understand me, almost from the first moment we met you said it, and I believed you. Now I see that you really don't understand me at all." There was no more anger. It had been smothered by a rising despair. If they'd really been married, in the true sense, they would have been able to talk about what had happened, they would have been able to fight together, rage together instead of at each other. "You can make your calls, I'm going for a walk."

But he didn't pick up the phone when she left. It was more than being unused to having someone stand beside him, more than his own penchant for handling his own in his own way. He'd wanted her to go, away from the murmurs and sly looks. He didn't want her to be a part of the suspicion that had already fallen over him and his.

She'd never even asked. Burke scrubbed his hands over his face and tried to get beyond his own fury. It wasn't losing the purse or the race so much as knowing that someone had violated what was his. And she'd never asked if he'd arranged it himself. Could she really believe so blindly in him, or was it a matter of her not caring how he won?

However she felt, he couldn't shield her from the gossip. And gossip there would be, he thought grimly. Once she had a taste of it, he figured she'd be happy enough to go back to the quiet of Three Aces. In the meantime, he was going to find out who'd messed with him. Pushing the bottle aside, Burke picked up the phone.

The action moved to Churchill Downs and Derby week. Erin made certain she attended each function and every qualifying race. She held her head up and, when she heard a whisper, only held it higher.

Not everyone seemed inclined to believe that Burke had had a hand in the drugging of his horse. For every snub and murmur there was someone else to offer support. But the only one who mattered had closed himself off from her. She didn't try to break through the barrier. It took all the energy she had to hold up the pretense of a united couple. The strain was taking its toll, all the more because she worked hard to make sure Burke didn't see it.

He rose early, so she rose early. He went to the track to oversee Double Bluff's morning exercise, so she spent her mornings at the track. There were days when by noon she was so weary she wanted to crawl off into a corner and sleep. But there were races and luncheons and functions, often back-to-back. She refused to miss even one.

Erin McKinnon Logan wasn't hiding in some dim corner until the trouble passed. She would face it, shoulders straight, and dare even one person to look her in the eye and make an accusation. It was hard, and grew harder, so that every day she had to force herself to put in an appearance. There were whispers and knowing looks behind smiles. There were eyes that turned away rather than meet hers. And there were a few who preferred to cloak their insults in manners.

She dressed carefully for a formal dinner party near the end of Derby week. Erin had always felt that a strong outer appearance helped tap the inner strength. Attending alone was only more difficult, but Burke had been called to a meeting at the last minute.

She could have stayed at the hotel, just as Burke had asked. The truth was that a quiet evening, a tray in bed and a good book was exactly what she would have preferred. But that would have been cowardly. So she wore her midnight-blue silk and hung her sapphire around her neck like a badge.

While others sipped cocktails, she nursed orange juice and made conversation. More than ever she was grateful for Paddy. He stayed close, keeping her spirits up and her mind busy with stories of Ireland. But he couldn't shield her from everything, nor from everyone.

"My dear, what a pretty dress." Dorothy Gainsfield swept toward her, her eyes as cold as her diamonds.

"Good evening, Mrs. Gainsfield."

"Tell me, are you enjoying your first Derby week? It is your first, isn't it?"

"Aye, it's my first." If Erin had learned one thing, it was how to return a meaningless smile. "I'm sure you've been coming here for many years."

"Indeed," she said repressively, refusing to be insulted by one so beneath her station. "I don't see your husband."

"He couldn't make it."

"That's understandable, isn't it?"

Erin felt Paddy start forward, and laid a hand on his

arm. "With the race only a couple of days away, Burke is busy."

"I'm sure he is." The older woman gave a dry laugh and sipped her champagne. "You know, I'm rather surprised he's being allowed to enter after that…mishap, shall we say, at the Bluegrass Stakes."

"The racing commission feels Double Bluff's record speaks for itself and for Burke. Once the investigation's complete, that, too, will speak for itself."

"Oh, I don't doubt it, my dear, not for a minute. It isn't unusual for someone to get a bit too enthusiastic about winning. This wouldn't be the first time the method's been used to lower the odds."

"Burke doesn't cheat. He doesn't have to."

"I'm sure you're right." Mrs. Gainsfield smiled again. "But then, I wasn't speaking of your husband…Mrs. Logan." Satisfied with the dig, Mrs. Gainsfield moved away.

"That dough-faced old cow," Paddy began as he fired up. "I'll give her a piece of my mind."

"No." Again Erin put a hand on his arm. "She's not worth it." Erin watched her mingle with the crowd. "When Double Bluff wins, it'll be enough."

Erin was determined that by the end of the week they would have discovered who was responsible for Double Bluff's disqualification and the cloud on Burke's reputation would be gone. She was even more determined that on Sunday, when Churchill Downs opened for the Derby, Burke would win what was rightfully his.

Once that was done, she would face the cracks and scars on her marriage. Perhaps Burke had been wrong when he'd said most marriages didn't work because one person tried to change the other. She knew now that if changes weren't made—in both of them—their marriage would never survive.

She watched him now as he stood near the oval with his trainer. It was barely dawn, with a light so sweet and fragile that it turned the white steeples pink. The air was cool, quiet enough to carry voices to her, if not the words. All around her the stands were empty. In twenty-four hours they would be filling, section by section, until they and the infield grass were packed with bodies. The race would last only a matter of minutes, but for those few minutes, every square inch would be crammed with excitement, with pumping hearts and with hope.

"It has its own magic, this time of day."

"Travis." Erin was up and swinging her arms around him. She hadn't realized until that moment how badly she'd needed someone to hold on to. "Oh, it's so glad I am to see you. But you shouldn't be here." She drew away just as quickly. "What about Dee? Is she all right?"

"All right enough to throw me out. She told me she could use a couple of days without my hovering over her."

"That's nonsense and I know it, but I'm grateful to both of you." She looked beyond his shoulder to her husband. "He needs his friends now."

"How about you?"

She gave a quick laugh and a shake of her head. "Oh, he doesn't seem to need me."

"I don't believe that, but it isn't what I meant. How are you holding up?"

"I'm tough enough to get through a few rough spots yet."

"You're a bit pale," he murmured, then took her chin in his hand. "More than a bit."

"I'm fine, really. Could use a bit more sleep, that's

all." Then she swayed against him. Before she could pull herself back, he was settling her into a seat.

"Just sit back. I'll get Burke."

"No." She gripped his hand and held hard. "I'll be all right in a second. I just need to close my eyes."

"Erin, if you're ill—"

"I'm not ill." She laughed and unconsciously laid a hand on the child that was growing inside her. "I promise you."

He lifted his brow as he studied her. "Then congratulations."

Erin opened her eyes slowly. "You're a sharp one."

"I've been through it a few times." He stroked her hand until a hint of color returned to her face. "How does Burke feel about starting a family?"

"He doesn't know." Steadier, she sat up and was relieved to see Burke's back was still to them. "He has enough to worry about right now."

"Don't you think this would more than balance the scales?"

"No." Letting out a sigh, she faced Travis again. "No, I don't, because I'm not sure he wants children at all. And right now he doesn't want anything more than for me to leave him alone."

"You're underestimating him."

"You're his friend."

"And yours."

"Then stand up with him until this is over. Let me tell him about the baby when the time's right."

"All right. If you promise to take better care of yourself."

She smiled and kissed his cheek. "After tomorrow, I'll sleep for a week."

"Travis." Burke slipped under the rail. "I didn't expect to see you down here."

"Hate to miss a Derby. How are things going?"

Burke glanced over his shoulder to where the horse was being walked and cooled. "The colt's in top form. You can say we're both ready to put things right."

"The investigation?"

"Slow." That was true, at least of the official one. His own was moving quite a bit faster. Now that Travis was here, he would have someone he could trust to listen to his theory. Though he wore his tinted glasses, Erin felt his eyes on her. With a nod of acknowledgment, she rose.

"I'll leave you to discuss business."

"She's worried about you," Travis murmured as Erin walked away from the stands.

"I'd prefer she didn't. What I'd prefer is that she went back to the Three Aces until this is cleared up."

"If you'd wanted a quiet, obedient wife, you shouldn't have picked an Irish one."

Burke pulled out a cigar and contemplated it. "How many times have you been tempted to throttle Dee?"

"In the last seven years, or in the last week?"

For the first time in days, Burke smiled and meant it. "Never mind. Do me a favor and keep an eye on her, will you? I don't think she's feeling well."

"You could try talking to her yourself."

"I'm not much good at talk. I'd like you to take her back with you after the race tomorrow."

"Aren't you coming back?"

"I might have to stay in Kentucky a few more days."

"Got a lead?"

"A hunch." He lit the cigar and blew out smoke. "Trouble is, the racing commission likes proof."

"Want to talk about it?"

He hesitated, only because it still seemed unnatural to confide in another. "Yeah. You got a few minutes?"

Erin wasn't sure why she felt the sudden need, but she walked toward the stables. Maybe if she could prove to herself that she was strong and capable, Burke would begin to believe it. She'd faced the gossip, she'd stood tall against the innuendos. She'd held her own. But there was one thing she'd yet to face, one fear she'd yet to vanquish. So she would do it. Then, tomorrow, she would walk easily beside Burke into Double Bluff's stall, and she would stand beside him without a quiver in the winner's circle.

Three yards from the stables, she stopped to give herself another lecture. It was foolish to be afraid after all this time. It was useless to cling to a feeling that had been caused years before by an accident. She'd been around animals all her life. Married to Burke, she would continue to be around them. And the child... She rested a hand on her stomach. Her child would be raised without fear of his inheritance.

She would walk in alone. Then, tomorrow, even if Burke wished her to hell and back, she would walk in beside him.

She went closer. The scents were there—the hay, the sweet smell of grain, the pungent smell of horse and sweat. The sounds, too—hooves scraping over concrete, harness jingling, the sighs and lazy whinnies of horses at rest. She'd be quiet and go carefully, remembering that each step was one step closer.

The light changed almost from the moment she stepped inside. It was dimmer, softer, and now there was the scent of leather as well.

Most of the horses had already been exercised, and the

grooms were indulging in their own breakfasts before it came time to brush and rub and wrap. She'd chosen this time, the least busy time, so that if she bolted no one would see.

But she didn't bolt. One of the horses dipped its head over the gate and she jumped a little, but she stood her ground. She could touch him, Erin told herself. The gate was latched. She could lay her hand on him just as easily as she had with Burke's foal.

Her fingers trembled a little, but she laid them gingerly against the horse's cheek. He eyed her, but when he shifted his weight she jerked back.

"I'll have to do better than that," she muttered, then laid her hand more firmly on his neck. Her palm was damp and she didn't move a muscle, but she felt a little thrill of victory.

He was a fine-looking animal, she told herself as she made her hand move just a little over his neck. It was the Pentel colt, one she'd seen race nearly as often as she'd seen Bluff.

"There, now," she managed with a sigh. "It's not so bad. My heart's thumping, but I'm here." I'm here, she repeated silently, and I'm coming back every day. Each time it would be a little easier. She drew her hand back, then made herself reach out again. And it was easier. Just as it would become easier to face and overcome her insecurities with Burke. She wasn't going to go through life being cowed and miserable because her husband was too stubborn to accept her love and her support. She might have taken him the way he was, but there would be some changes made. And soon.

When she heard voices, she drew her hand back again, embarrassed. She didn't want one of the grooms wandering in to find her. She didn't think she was quite ready to stand in the stables and hold a conversation. Erin wiped her damp palm on her slacks and fixed a casual smile on her face.

She'd started out when the tone of the voices stopped her. There was anger in them and, though they remained quiet, more than a little desperation. Because she hesitated, she had time to recognize one of them.

"If you want your money, you'll find a way."

"I tell you the horse isn't alone for five minutes. Logan's got him locked up like the crown jewels."

Erin's lips parted, then firmed. She took a step back into the shadows and listened.

"You've got a job to do, one you're paid well for. If you can't get to the horse, get to his feed. I want him out of the running for tomorrow."

"I ain't poisoning no horse, and I'm tired of taking all the risks."

"You didn't have any qualms about using a hypodermic or taking ten percent of the purse from the Bluegrass Stakes."

"Amphetamines is one thing, cyanide's another. That horse dies and Logan's not going to rest until somebody hangs for it. It ain't going to be me."

"Then use the drugs." The voice was impatient, dismissive. Erin found her hands balled into fists. "Find a way, or you won't see a penny. If the colt's found drugged in the Derby, he's out for the season. I need this race."

And she needed to get to Burke. Erin stayed still and waited for them to pass on. But luck wasn't with her. As she saw the two figures enter the stables, she straightened her shoulders and moved forward. It was a gamble, but the best she could hope for was a bluff.

"Good day to you, Mr. Durnam." She made her lips curve even when she saw the shock come into his eyes.

She glanced at the groom, too, one of the new ones Burke's trainer had hired.

"Mrs. Logan." Durnam smiled in return but was already calculating. "We didn't see you in the stables."

"Just thought I'd look over the competition. If you'll excuse me, Burke's waiting."

"I think not." He took her arm as she tried to pass. Because she'd been half expecting it, Erin was already primed to scream. With surprising speed, his hand clamped over her mouth.

"Good God almighty, what are you doing?" the groom demanded. "Logan'll have your head."

"He'll have yours as well if she goes to him and blabs. She heard everything, you idiot." Because Erin's struggles were making him pant, Durnam thrust her at the groom. "Hold on to her. Let me think."

"We've got to get the hell out of here. If someone comes in—"

"Shut up. Just shut up." Durnam's face was already sheened with sweat. He took out a white handkerchief and mopped it. He was a desperate man who had already taken desperate measures. Now it was time to take another. "We'll put her in the van until the race is over tomorrow. By then I'll have thought of something." Taking the handkerchief, he pulled it around her mouth. As an extra precaution, he took the groom's grimy bandanna and tied it over her eyes. "Get some rope. Hurry, tie her hands and feet."

Erin choked on the gag and struggled against both of them, but she was already aware she'd lose. On a desperate impulse she worked her wedding ring off her hand and let it fall to the ground. Then ropes bit into her wrist and she was smothered inside a blanket.

She felt herself being lifted but could do no more than

squirm. Even that was futile as the more she resisted, the harder it was to breathe. She heard a door open just before she was lifted up and set inside on a hard floor.

"What the hell are we going to do with her?" the groom demanded as he stared down at the heap inside the blanket. "The minute we let her go, she'll talk."

"Then we won't let her go." Durnam leaned against the side of the van and this time mopped his brow with his sleeve. Everything was going to go his way, he told himself. He'd come too far, risked too much to have one woman destroy it.

"I ain't having no part in murdering a woman."

Durnam dropped his arm and gave the groom a long, narrow look. "You just take care of the horse and leave the woman to me."

They were going to kill her. Erin struggled to work the blanket from her face as she heard them shut the van door and walk away. She'd heard that in his voice. Even if he'd promised the groom that he'd cause her no harm, she would have known. Whatever had pushed Durnam to this point, he wouldn't hesitate to do away with any obstacle.

Her baby. With a half sob, Erin twisted her wrists and fought against the rope. Mother of mercy, she had to protect her baby. And Burke.

The panic welled up, and for a moment she lost herself in it completely. Before she'd regained control, her wrists were raw and her shoulders bruised. Panting, Erin lay quiet in the dark and tried to think. If she could get up somehow and find the door, she might find a way of forcing it open. She inched her way over to the wall; then, using it as a brace, she managed to get to her knees. She was soaked with sweat by the time she'd struggled to her feet. Keeping her back to the wall, she slid along it, groping with her fingers.

She almost wept when she found the knob. She twisted, straining on her toes before she could fit her fingers around it. Locked. She had to shake her head to keep the tears from coming. Of course it was locked. Durnam might be a brute, but he wasn't a fool. She tried thudding against the door, hoping to draw some attention, but trussed up tightly she was unable to get the momentum to make more than a quiet bump. Erin slid to the floor again and, closing her mind to both panic and pain, continued to work at the ropes.

"Have you seen Erin?"

Travis continued to run his hands down his colt's leg as he looked up at Burke. "Not since this morning. I assumed she'd gone back to the hotel."

"Maybe. She could have taken a cab." It was logical, Burke reminded himself. There was no reason for the sick feeling in his stomach. "We came in together this morning. She usually waits."

"She was looking a little tired." Travis straightened. "She could have gone back to get some rest before tonight."

"Yeah." It made sense. She was probably soaking in a hot tub right now, thinking about the party that night. "I think I'll drive back and check on her."

"Ask her if she'll take pity on a lonely man and save a few dances for me."

"Sure."

"Burke?"

"Yeah?"

"Something wrong?"

His hands were cold. Ice-cold. "No, nothing. See you in a couple hours."

They stayed cold as he drove from the track toward the hotel. It wasn't like Erin to simply go off without a word. But then, they hadn't been exchanging a great many words lately. His fault. He accepted that with a shrug. He didn't feel right about her being there. And he hated seeing her brace herself against the gossip that would certainly swell before it diminished.

If she wasn't so damn stubborn about maintaining a social position…but then, that was one of the things he'd promised her when they'd married. He couldn't help but be grateful that she was sticking by him, whatever her reasons, but with gratitude came only more guilt and responsibility.

He was no fonder of responsibility now than he'd ever been. Maybe it would be a relief to head the car west and keep going. To start from scratch as he'd done so many times before. Nothing had ever held him back before. But then, there hadn't been an Erin before.

Once the race and the scandal were behind them, they would talk. The air had to be cleared, the rules had to be reset. Maybe, just maybe, after it was all done, he'd tell her about his past. The way he'd grown up, the things he'd filled his life with. It was better to have it out, to make it clean now and let her walk away, than to continue waiting for her to find out for herself.

He'd never thought of his past as anything to be ashamed of. That was something else she'd done to him. She'd forced him to look back at his past a little too hard. And he didn't like what he saw.

His mood hadn't improved by the time he reached the hotel. He knew it was ridiculous for him to be angry with her for leaving the track when he'd demanded she leave altogether. But, damn it, she'd made him depend on her. The days were easier to get through when he knew he could look around and see her. He didn't care for that, either.

By the time he walked into their suite, he was primed for a fight. It had been too long since they'd developed a polite veneer and no substance. He was going to shout at her and let her shout back. Then they'd both vent the rest of their frustrations in bed.

"Erin?" He slammed the door behind him, but had gone no farther than the center of the parlor before he knew she wasn't there. And his hands were cold again.

Cursing himself, he walked into the bedroom. Had she left him? Had he pushed her away far enough, consistently enough, that she'd decided to take that final step? He didn't want to lose her. That admission left him shaken as he reached for the closet door. No, he didn't want to lose her any more than he wanted to need her.

He had to make himself pull open the door of the closet, and was nearly dizzy with relief when he saw her clothes undisturbed.

She'd gone shopping, he told himself. Or to have her hair done. But those thoughts didn't relieve his mind as he closed the closet door.

He was pacing the suite nearly thirty minutes later when the phone rang. Burke pounced on it, ready to rail at her no matter what her explanation.

"Burke, it's Travis."

"Yeah?"

"Is Erin back at the hotel?"

"No." And now his mouth was dry. "Why?"

"Lloyd Pentel just brought me her wedding ring. He found it on the floor in the stables."

"What? The stables?" He was lowering himself into a

chair, unaware that he'd moved at all. "That's not right. She wouldn't go in the stables. She's afraid of horses."

"Burke." Travis kept his voice calm. "Has she been back to the hotel?"

"No, she hasn't been here. I want to talk to Pentel."

"I already have. He hasn't seen her. Burke, we may be jumping the gun, but I think you should call the police."

She'd lost track of the time. Once she'd thought the ropes had loosened, but had had to accept it as wishful thinking. More than her wrists hurt now. There were bumps and bruises all over from a fall she'd taken while trying to maneuver standing up. Because the fall had scared her badly with the thought of what might have happened to the baby, she no longer tried to stand. For a time she closed herself off and thought of Burke, as if she could will him to find her.

Would he be worried? Had enough time passed that he would begin to wonder where she was? Would he care? She may have prayed, then slept a little while, dreaming first of Ireland and the farm. Why had she wanted to leave so badly what had been safe and secure? Then she dreamed of Burke and knew that part of the answer was that she'd been meant for him.

"Mrs. Logan."

Her body jackknifed as a hand touched her shoulder. The blindfold was loosened, and she had to blink and struggle to focus. In the dim light she made out the face of the groom, and panic flooded back. He'd come to kill her. And her baby.

"I brought you some food. You gotta promise to be quiet. Durnam would have my hide for coming in here like this. If you promise not to scream, I'll take the gag off so you can eat. If you make noise, I put it back and you get nothing."

She nodded, then drew in fresh air when her mouth was free. It wasn't easy to smother the instinct to cry out, but she could still taste the gag he'd pulled from her mouth. "Please, why are you doing this? If it's money you want, you can have it."

"I'm in too deep." He had a sandwich that was rapidly going stale. "Eat some or you'll get sick."

"What difference does it make?" Just the smell of the meat between the bread made her stomach turn. "You're going to kill me anyway."

"Now, I don't have nothing to do with that." She saw the panic in his eyes and the sweat beading on his lip. He was as afraid as she was. If she could use that, she might yet have a chance.

"You know what Durnam's going to do. He can't let me go."

"He just wants to win, that's all. He needs to. Got himself in some financial trouble, and his stable isn't as good as it was. Charlie's Pride is his best shot, but Logan's colt is better. That's why he had me hire on at Three Aces, so I could keep an eye on things and make sure the race went wrong. But that's it," he added, glancing around. He was talking too much. He always talked too much when he got nervous. And he wanted a drink. The saliva in his mouth had dried to nothing. "I just sweetened the horse some. That's what Durnam wanted. He just needs to put him out of the running. You gotta understand, this is business. Just business."

"You're talking about races. I'm talking about murder."

"I don't want to hear about it. I got nothing to do with that. Now you eat."

"Mr....I don't know your name."

"It's Berley, ma'am. Tom Berley." Ridiculous as it was, he lifted his fingers to his cap.

"Mr. Berley, I'm begging you for my life. And not just for mine, but for the baby I'm carrying. You can't let him kill my baby. Now you'll only be in trouble about the horse, but this is murder. An innocent child, Mr. Berley."

"I'm not going to hear no more talk about killing." His voice had roughened, but his hands weren't steady when they pulled the gag up again. He no longer wanted a drink, he needed one desperately. He started to replace the blindfold, but the look in her eyes had him hesitating. There was nothing for her to see anyway, he told himself. The back of the van was windowless, and the cab was blocked off by a wooden partition.

"You don't want to eat, that's your business. I've got my own to see to." He stuffed the sandwich in his pocket. Erin saw him look both ways before he stepped out the door again and left her in the dark.

Chapter Eleven

"I'd prefer if you'd go out and look for my wife, Lieutenant, rather than sitting here asking me questions."

Lieutenant Hallinger was nearly sixty, and after thirty-seven years on the force he figured he'd seen it all and heard twice as much. He'd certainly experienced more than his share of frustrated and angry spouses. It seemed to him that the man in front of him was both.

"Mr. Logan, we have an APB out on your wife right now, and several officers are asking questions at the track." Though he envied Burke his cigar, he didn't mention it. "It would help clear things up, and give us a better chance of locating your wife, if you'd fill me in."

"I've already told you Erin hasn't come back to the hotel. No one's seen her since this morning, and her wedding ring was found at the stables at Churchill Downs."

"Some people are careless with jewelry, Mr. Logan."

Some people. What the hell was this business about some people? They were talking about Erin, his Erin. Where the hell was she? He looked back at Hallinger again and spoke precisely. "Not Erin. And not with her wedding ring."

"Um-hmm." He made a notation in his book. "Mr. Logan, occasionally this sort of thing comes down to a simple misunderstanding." He could have written a book, Hallinger thought. Yeah, he could've written a book on misunderstandings alone. "Did you and your wife quarrel this morning?"

"No."

"It's possible she rented a car and decided to do a little sight-seeing."

"That's ridiculous." He glanced up as Travis handed him a cup of coffee. Burke accepted it but set it aside. "If Erin had wanted to go for a drive, she would have taken the car we've already rented. She would have told me she was leaving and she would have been back two hours ago. We had plans for this evening."

He'd had plans himself, which had included a nice quiet evening with his own wife. And a footbath. Hallinger wriggled his aching toes inside his shoes. "Derby week can be chaotic. It might have slipped her mind."

"Erin's the most responsible person I know. If she's not here, it's because she can't get here." He thought again of the hateful and terrifying calls he'd already made to the hospitals. "Because someone's keeping her from getting here."

"Mr. Logan, kidnapping usually prompts a ransom call. You're a wealthy man, yet you tell me you haven't been contacted."

"No, I haven't been contacted." But he still broke out

in a sweat every time the phone rang. "Look, Lieutenant, I've told you everything I know. And I'm damn sick of going over the same ground when you should be out doing your job. I'd go out and look myself, but I feel it's more important for me to stay here and…" Wait. Endlessly.

Hallinger glanced over his notes. He was a thin man with small, aching feet and a quiet voice. He was a man who took his appearance as seriously as he took his job. It was possible for him to admire Burke's casually expensive shoes while noting his nerves and anxiety.

"Mr. Logan, you had some trouble at the Bluegrass Stakes. How did your wife feel about that?"

"She was upset, naturally." Crushing out his cigar, he rose to pace.

"Upset enough to want to avoid the crowds tonight and tomorrow? Upset enough to want to escape from it, and you?"

There was a flat and dangerous look in Burke's eyes when he turned. "Erin wouldn't run from anything or anyone. The fact is I asked her to go back home until this thing was settled. She wouldn't do it. She insisted on staying and seeing it through."

"You're a fortunate man."

"I'm aware of that. Now why don't you get the hell out of here and find my wife?"

Hallinger simply made a note in his book and turned to Travis. "Mr. Grant, you're the last person we know of who spoke with Mrs. Logan this morning. What was her mood?"

"She was anxious about the race, about Burke. A little tired. She told me she intended to sleep a week when the Derby was over. The last thing on her mind was missing the race or leaving her husband. She's only been married a few weeks, and she's very much in love."

"Um-hmm," the lieutenant said again with maddening calm. "Her ring was found in the stables. You tell me she didn't go in the stables, Mr. Logan, yet she was seen walking toward them early this morning."

"To prove a point to herself, maybe, I can't be sure." His patience was stretching thinner by the second. If she'd waited for him to go with her…if she'd asked him to take her in, stand with her… He'd been the one who'd pulled away, far enough that she'd stopped asking him for anything.

"What sort of point, Mr. Logan?"

"What?"

Patience was an integral part of Hallinger's job. "You said she might have gone inside the stables to prove a point."

"She had an accident a few years ago and was afraid of horses. Over the past few weeks she's been trying to win out over it. Damn it, what difference does it make why she went in? She was there, and now she's missing."

"I work better with details."

When the phone rang, Burke jumped. His face was gray with strain when he lifted the receiver. "Yes?" With a muttered oath, he offered it to Hallinger. "It's for you."

"They're going to find her, Burke." Travis touched a hand to Burke's shoulder as he passed. "You've got to hold on to that."

"It's wrong. It's very wrong, I can feel it." It was welling up inside him; beyond the first panic, beyond the lingering fear, was a dread, a certainty. "If they don't find her soon, it's going to be too late. I've got to get out of here. Will you stay in case a call comes in?"

"Sure."

Hallinger watched Burke walk to the door and simply gestured for one of his men to follow.

* * *

She must have slept. Erin woke from the nightmare soaked with sweat and shivering with cold. She murmured for Burke and tried to reach out, but her arms wouldn't move.

It wasn't just a dream, she realized as she closed her eyes and took deep breaths to stem another wave of panic. How long? Oh, God, how long? Perhaps they were just going to leave her here to go mad or slowly starve to death.

She wouldn't go mad, because she would think of Burke. She would close her eyes and remember how it felt to lie beside him at night with the moonlight coming through the windows and his body warm against hers. She would think about the way he would kiss her in that way he had—that slow, devastating way that made her bones melt and her mind go dim. She could taste him. Even now she could taste him and feel the way his hand felt as he brushed it over her cheek and into her hair.

He had such wonderful hands, so strong and hard. They were always so steady, always so sure. Sometimes at night she'd reach for his hand and hold it against her cheek just to have it there. She didn't think he ever knew.

If she concentrated hard enough, she could almost feel his hand against her cheek now. She could hold it there as long as she wanted.

When her eyes grew accustomed to the dark, she could see his head on the pillow beside hers. His profile was such a handsome one, with its firm jaw and the sharp planes of his cheeks. She liked it when it was shadowed just a bit with beard. Had she ever told him that? He was such a pleasure to look at.

And if she was careful, she could cuddle close, not waking him. The scent of his skin would lull her to sleep.

He always smelled as she'd thought a man should, without the sweetening of colognes. So she could cuddle close, and sometimes he would shift closer, his arm stretching lazily over her waist. Those were the best times, when she could murmur that she loved him. She'd told herself that if he heard it enough times in his sleep he would begin to believe it.

So Erin kept her eyes closed and thought only of Burke. After a time, she slept again.

It was nearly three, but Burke sat in the same chair. He'd gone out for only an hour, driving to the track with some wild hope that he would find Erin waiting for him. He'd prowled the stables and badgered the stable boys and grooms with the same questions the police had already asked.

But there was no Erin, nor any sign of her.

So he'd come back, to pace the parlor, haunt the bedroom and ignore the coffee that Travis poured for him. For the past hour he'd sat unmoving, staring at the phone.

He'd told Travis to go, to get some sleep, and had been ignored. It reminded him that there had only been one other person in his life who had stuck by him. If he lost her... He couldn't think of that. He knew that luck could change, could turn cruel like a change in the wind. But not with Erin.

She hadn't had her chance yet, not a real one, to see everything there was. Maybe he'd been wrong to lock her in so quickly, to bind her to him. But she still had so much life, so much energy. Why was it he couldn't get past that one sick thought that whatever was happening to her now was because of him?

When the phone rang, he grabbed the receiver with both hands. "Logan." The voice in his ear was thick with liquor, but he understood. And his heart began to thud. "Where is she?"

"I don't want no trouble. Spiking the horse was one thing, but I don't want no trouble."

"Fine. Tell me where she is." He glanced up to see Travis beside him, waiting.

"I didn't want no part of it. He'll kill me if he finds out I'm talking to you."

"Just tell me where she is and I'll take care of it."

"Kept her at the track, in the van. I don't know what he's going to do. Kill her, maybe."

"What van? What van, damn it?"

"I ain't having no part in murder."

When the phone went dead, Burke simply dropped it and rose. "She's at the track. They're holding her in a van."

"I'll call the police and be right behind you."

He drove like a maniac, ignoring red lights and speed limits. *Kill her, maybe.* Those three words drummed in his head over and over so that he didn't notice the speed-ometer hovering at a hundred and ten. The streets were deserted. People were asleep, anticipating the race to-morrow. Some would already be camped on the infield grass.

He prayed that Erin was asleep as well. And when she woke he would be there.

Gravel spit from under the tires as he braked behind the stables. Vans were parked there for trainers, for owners who preferred to stay close to their horses, for grooms and hands who could afford a little luxury.

He only needed to find one.

He started across the lot when he heard steps behind him. Fists clenched and murder on his mind, he whirled.

"Easy, lad," Paddy told him. "Travis called me."

He nodded briefly, though in the moonlight he could see that the old man hadn't slept, either. "Durnam's van. Which is it?"

"Durnam? Travis said you didn't know which."

"Call it a hunch. Which one is Durnam's?"

"The big black one there." Paddy turned as he heard the whine of sirens. "The police are coming." But Burke was already racing to the black van.

"Erin!" The door held fast. For a moment he thought he could tear it off with his bare hands.

"Use this." Paddy handed him a crowbar. "When Travis called and filled me in, I thought we'd have use for it."

Without hesitation, Burke began to pry the door open, all the time calling to her. He wanted her to know it was him. He couldn't stand the thought of her having one more instant of fear. The metal groaned, fought back, then gave. Burke gripped the crowbar like a weapon as he jumped inside. He shoved away the plywood partition that separated the back of the van from the cab.

"Erin?" There was no answer, no sound. What if he was too late? Burke turned the crowbar in his hands, wiping sweat on metal. "Erin, it's all right. I've come to take you out of here." He cursed the lack of light and dropped to his hands and knees. He saw her then, curled in a corner in the rear.

He was with her in an instant, but he was almost afraid to touch her. His hand went to her cheek first. So cold, so still. "Erin." In a fit of rage, he tore the gag away. When her eyes fluttered open, he nearly wept with relief. "Erin, it's all right."

But when he reached for her she cringed, making small sounds in her throat.

"It's all right," he murmured. "I'm not going to let anyone hurt you. It's Burke, darling, it's okay now."

"Burke." Her eyes were still glazed with shock, but she said his name.

"That's right, and I'm going to take you out of here." He shifted her, cursing under his breath each time she whimpered. Her trembles became shudders that none of his soothing words could halt.

He found the ropes, but when he started to loosen them she cried out. "I'm sorry. I have to get them off. I don't want to hurt you. Can you stay very still?"

She simply turned her face to the wall.

The van shook as men entered, and she pressed back in the corner. "I need a knife." He looked up and saw Lieutenant Hallinger. "Give me a damn knife, then get out. She's terrified."

Hallinger reached in his pocket with one hand and signaled his men back with the other.

"Just hold on, Irish, it's all over now." He hurt her. He could feel each jerk and tremble inside his own body as he cut through the bonds. Both his skin and hers were damp before he had freed her feet as well. "I'm going to pick you up and carry you out. Just stay still."

"My arms." She bit her lip, as even the gentlest touch sent the pain throbbing.

"I know." As carefully as he could, he lifted her up. She moaned and pressed her face against his shoulder.

When they stepped outside, the lot was bright with lights. Erin squeezed her burning eyes shut. She couldn't think beyond the pain and fear, and concentrated on the sound of Burke's voice.

"You stay the hell away from her," he said very quietly, his eyes on Hallinger.

"I called an ambulance." Travis stepped between Burke

and the police. "It's here now. Paddy and I will follow you."

As if in a dream, Erin felt herself laid down. The light was still too bright, so she kept her eyes closed. There were voices, too many voices, but she focused in on the only one that mattered. She jolted as she felt something cool over the raw skin of her wrist, but Burke stroked her hair and never stopped talking to her.

He didn't know what he said. Promises, vows, nonsense. But he could see the dried blood on her wrists and ankles and the bruises that ran up her arms. Each time she winced, he thought of Durnam. And how he would kill him.

"In the stables," she murmured. "I heard them in the stables, talking about drugging the horse."

"It doesn't matter." Burke kept stroking her hair.

"In the stables," she repeated in a voice that was thin and tended to float. "I couldn't get away. I tried."

"You're safe now. Just lie still."

They wouldn't let him go with her. Erin was wheeled away the moment they reached the hospital, and Burke was left helpless and hurting in the hallway.

"She's going to be all right." Travis laid a hand on his shoulder.

Burke nodded. The ambulance attendants had already assured him of that. Her wrists were the worst of her physical injuries. They would heal, just as the bruises would fade. But no one knew how badly she'd been scarred emotionally.

"Stay with her. There's something I have to do."

"Burke, you'll do her more good here. And yourself."

"Just stay with her," he repeated, then strode out through the wide glass doors.

He kept his mind carefully blank as he drove out to Durnam's farm. The rage was there, but he held it, knowing it would cloud his thinking. So he thought of nothing, and his mind stayed as cool as the early-morning air.

The thirty-minute drive took him fifteen, but still the police were faster. Burke slammed out of his car in front of Durnam's palatial stone house and faced Hallinger once again.

"Thought I'd see you here tonight." Hallinger lit one of the five cigarettes he allowed himself—which was five more than his wife knew about. "Figured a sharp man like you would have already put it together that Durnam was the one who had your horse drugged."

"Yeah, I put that together. Where is he?"

"He's my guest tonight." Hallinger blew out smoke, then leaned against the hood of Burke's car. If the footbath didn't work, he was going to have to go see the damned podiatrist. "You know, sometimes cops have brains, too. We were here questioning Durnam when the call came in that you were on your way to the track to get your wife."

"Why?"

"Well, assuming that your wife's disappearance had something to do with the trouble last week, which was a big assumption, I had to figure out who had the most to gain. That would be Durnam. I take it you'd already worked that out."

"I had everything but proof."

"We've got that now, too. The man was already on the edge. Our call coming in was all it took to push him over. He'd cleaned out his bank account, what was left of it. Knew that, did you?"

"Yeah, I knew that."

"Had his bags packed. But he wasn't going to miss that

race tomorrow. Today," Hallinger corrected with a glance up at the lightening sky. "He wanted that Derby win bad. Funny how people can set their minds on one thing and forget about the consequences. How's your wife?"

"She's hurt. Where are you keeping him?"

"That's police business now, Mr. Logan." He examined his cigarette thoughtfully before taking another drag. "I know how you feel."

Burke cut him off with a look. "You don't know how I feel."

Hallinger nodded slowly. "You're right. And I doubt you're in the mood for advice, but here it is. You haven't been a Boy Scout, Logan." He smiled, a little sourly, when Burke only continued to stare at him. "I make it my business to check details. You've had a few scrapes in your time. Some bad luck and some good. Right now I'd say you've got yourself a good woman and a chance to make things click. Don't blow it on something as pitiful as Charles Durnam. He lost a hell of a lot more than a horse race. Isn't that enough?"

"No." Burke pulled open the door of his car, then paused to turn back. "He gets out in a year, in twenty years—he's dead."

With some regret, Hallinger flipped the butt of his cigarette away. "I'll keep that in mind."

When Erin awoke, she opened her eyes cautiously. The hospital. The wave of relief came as it did every time she awoke to find herself safe. The light beside her bed was still burning. She'd hated to be weak, but had insisted the nurse leave it on even when the sun was coming up.

Burke hadn't been there. She'd fretted and asked for him, but they'd wheeled her to a private room and tucked her into bed, promising he'd be with her soon. She was to sleep, to relax, she wasn't to worry.

But she wanted him.

Listless, she turned her head. There were already flowers in the room. She imagined Travis or Paddy had seen to that. They'd been so kind.

But she wanted Burke.

Shifting in search of comfort, she pushed herself up in bed. And she saw him. He was standing by the window, his back to her. Everything fled but the pleasure of knowing he was there with her.

"Burke."

He turned immediately. His first thought was that she was sitting up and her cheeks were no longer pale. His second thought was that if it hadn't been for him she wouldn't be in a hospital bed with bandages on her wrists. Because she was holding out a hand, he went to her and touched it lightly.

"You're looking better," he said inadequately.

"I'm feeling better. I didn't know you were here."

"I've been around awhile. Do you want anything?"

"I could eat." She smiled and reached for his hand again, but his was in his pocket.

"I'll get the nurse."

"Burke." She stopped him as he reached the door. "It can wait. Look at you, you haven't slept."

"Busy night."

She tried another smile. "Aye, it was all of that. I'm sorry."

His eyes went hard and flat. "Don't. I'll get the nurse."

Alone, Erin lay back on the pillows. Maybe she was still confused and disoriented. He couldn't really be angry with her. With a half sigh, she closed her eyes. Of course he could. There was no telling with men, and with Burke in particular. Whether it was her fault or not, she'd put him through hell. And now she was tying him to a hospital room on the most important day of his life.

When the door opened again she made sure her smile was cheerful, and her voice, though her throat still tended to ache, mirrored it. "You should be at the track. I had no idea it was so late. Did anyone think to bring me a change of clothes? I can be ready in ten minutes."

"You're not going anywhere."

"You don't expect me to miss my first Derby? I know what the doctor said, but—"

"Then you'll know you're not getting up from that bed for twenty-four hours. Don't be stupid."

She opened her mouth, then firmly shut it again. She wouldn't argue with him. She'd been close to death, and that made a person think about how much time was wasted on pettiness. "You're right, of course. I'll just sit here and be pampered while I watch on television." Why didn't he come to her? Why didn't he hold her? Erin kept her lips curved as he turned again to stare out of the window. "You'd better be on your way."

"Where?"

"To the track, of course. It's nearly noon. You've already missed the morning."

"I'm staying here."

Her heart did a quick flip, but she shook her head. "Don't be silly. You can't miss this. If I'm to be shut up here it's bad enough. At least I can have the pleasure of watching you step into the winner's circle. There's nothing for you to do here."

He thought of how helpless he'd felt through the night. Of how helpless he felt now. "No, I suppose there isn't."

"Then off with you," she told him, forcing her voice to be light.

"Yeah." He rubbed his hands over his face.

"And I don't want to see you back here until you've had some rest."

She lifted her face for a kiss, but his lips only brushed over her brow. "See you later."

"Burke." He was already out of reach. "You're going to win."

With a nod, he closed the door behind him. He leaned against the wall, almost too exhausted to stand, far too exhausted to think. He didn't give a damn about the Derby or any other race. All he could see, playing over and over in his mind, was Erin curled in the corner of that van, cringing away from him.

She'd bounced back, smiling and talking as though nothing had happened. But he could still see the white bandages on her wrists.

He was afraid to touch her, afraid she'd cringe away again. Or, if she didn't, that he'd hurt her. He was afraid to look at her too long because he'd see that glazed shock in her eyes again. He was afraid that if he didn't gather her close, keep her close, that she'd slip away from him, that he would lose her as he'd nearly lost her only hours before.

But she was urging him to go, telling him she didn't need him beside her. All she needed was a win, a blanket of red roses and a trophy. He'd damn well give them to her.

She hadn't realized she would be nervous. But even watching the preliminaries, the interviews, the discussions on television, kept her pulse racing. When she saw Burke caught by the cameras as he stepped out of the stables, she laughed and hugged her pillow. Oh, if she could just be there with him, holding on. But he avoided the reporter, leaving Erin disappointed.

She'd wanted to hear him, to see his face on the screen so that they could laugh about it later.

Then it was the reporter facing the camera, recounting the story that had unfolded since the Bluegrass Stakes. It pleased her to hear that Burke's name had been cleared absolutely and that Double Bluff was considered the favorite in the Run for the Roses.

She listened, trying to be dispassionate as he talked about her kidnapping and Durnam's arrest. The groom had been picked up sleeping off a bottle in a stall. Apparently it hadn't taken much encouragement for him to spill the entire story. There were pictures of the van, with its broken door and police barriers, that she had to force herself to look at.

It almost amused her to be told that she was resting comfortably. Somehow the reporter made it all sound like a grand adventure, something out of a mystery novel—the lady in distress, the villain and the hero. She wrinkled her nose. However much she might consider Burke a hero, she didn't care to think of herself as a lady in distress.

She let it pass as she watched the horses being spotlighted as they were led from the paddock. There was Double Bluff, as big and as handsome as ever. Double Bluff, the three-year-old from Three Aces. Owners Burke and Erin Logan. She smiled at that. Though of course it was Burke's horse and the news people had made a mistake, it still gave her a good feeling to see her name flash on the screen with Burke's.

She laughed at herself again because her palms were getting sweaty. The track was just as she'd known it would be, filled to capacity. The camera panned over Dorothy Gainsfield. Erin gave herself the satisfaction of sticking out her tongue.

Then it focused on Burke, and her heart broke a little.

He looked so tired. Worn to the bone. That was why he'd been so distant before. The man was exhausted. When he'd rested and had time to get his bearings, things would be right again.

"I love you, Burke," she told him, rubbing her cheek against the pillow. "Loving you is what got me through."

Then the screen flashed back to the horses. It was nearly post time.

There was the blare of the trumpet and the roar of the crowd. Again Erin found herself tempted to jump out of bed and hurry to the track. If it hadn't been for the baby, she would have ignored the doctor and done just that. Instead she forced herself to be patient.

"We'll go to our first Derby together," she murmured as she placed a hand on her stomach. "Next year, the three of us will go."

The bell sounded, and for the next two minutes she didn't take her eyes off the screen. It seemed to her that Double Bluff was running with a vengeance. And perhaps he was. Perhaps Burke had transformed some of his emotions to the horse, for the colt ran like fury.

When he broke from the pack early, Erin held her breath. It was too soon. She knew the jockey had been instructed to hold him back the first half mile. There was no holding back today. Her first concern evaporated in pure excitement as she watched him run. He was glorious, angry and unstoppable. It was as if the horse himself wanted vindication and perhaps revenge.

He clung to the rail, taking the turns hard and close. Travis's Apollo held back by a length. The Pentel colt, under a new rider, was coming up fast on the outside. And the crowd was on its feet. Erin was shouting, but was unaware of it even after the nurse came in.

As he came down the backstretch he poured on more speed, impossibly more, so that even the announcer's voice cracked with excitement. Two lengths, then three, then three and a half. He went under the wire as if he was alone on the oval.

"He never gave up the lead." Erin brushed her palms over her cheeks to dry them. "Not once."

"Congratulations, Mrs. Logan. I'd say you've just had some of the best medicine on the market."

"The very best." But her fingers curled into the sheets as she waited for the official announcement. In her mind she could picture it, the weighing in, the certification. It seemed to take forever, but then the numbers flashed on the board. "The very, very best. There's Burke." She gripped the nurse's hand. "He's worked so hard for this, waited so long. Oh, I wish I could be with him."

She watched the cameramen and reporters vie for angles as Burke and his trainer grouped in the winner's circle. Why wasn't he smiling? she wondered as she wiped another tear away. She saw him reach up and shake his jockey's hand but couldn't hear whatever it was he said.

"It's a good day for Three Aces." A reporter stuck a microphone in Burke's face. "This must make up for the disqualification last week, Mr. Logan."

"It doesn't begin to make up for it." He patted the colt's neck. "I think Double Bluff proved himself a champion here today and proved my trust in his team, but this race was run for my wife." He pulled a rose from the blanket covering his horse. "Excuse me."

"That was a lovely thing to say," the nurse murmured.

"Aye." Still, as Erin watched the jockey hold the cup over his head, she wondered why she felt so lost.

Chapter Twelve

They flew home as soon as Erin was released from the hospital, but she didn't feel like celebrating. Everything should have been right. Burke's reputation had been cleared, his prize colt had won the Derby with a track record, and she was safe. So why was it everything was wrong?

She knew Burke could be aloof, that he could be arrogant and hardheaded. Those were three ridiculous reasons to love a man, but they were reasons none the less. What she hadn't known was that he could be both withdrawn and distant. He never touched her. In fact, as the first few days passed, Erin realized he was going out of his way to avoid any opportunity to touch her. He came to bed late and rose early. He spent a great deal more time out of the house and away than he spent at home.

She tried to tell herself he was just gearing up for the

Preakness—the second jewel of the Triple Crown—but she knew it wasn't true.

With too much time left to herself to think, she began to remember the words she'd heard on her wedding day. *Men are easily charmed, and just as easily bored.*

Was that it? Was he bored with her? Trying to find the answer, she took stock of herself. Her face was the same. Maybe she was a little hollow-eyed, but those things came with worry and restless nights. Her body was still firm, though she knew that would change in a matter of weeks.

And what then? she wondered. When she told him about the baby, would he turn away completely? No, she couldn't believe that of him. Burke would never turn his back on his own child. But on her? If he was tired of her now, how would he feel when she began to round and swell?

She wanted to look forward to the changes in her body, to the signs that her baby was growing and healthy. But would those same changes push Burke only farther away? How could they not, if they didn't reestablish their intimacy? Since the physical change couldn't be avoided, Erin decided she'd better do something about seducing her husband now.

She chose the wine herself. That was something she was pleased to have developed a knack for. She wouldn't do any more than play at drinking it herself, but it was the atmosphere that mattered.

And candles. She set dozens of them around the bedroom, lighting them so that their scent would be as much a part of the mood as the flames. She chose the same gown she'd worn on her wedding night, the white lace that made her feel like a bride. He'd thought her lovely once, desirable once. He would again. She picked the Chopin he'd played on their first night together and wondered if he would remember.

Tonight would be another first, another beginning. When they'd loved each other, when they'd finally come back together as they were meant to be, she would tell him about the baby. Then they would talk about the future.

He'd taken himself to the wire before he climbed the stairs. Burke found it easiest to wear himself out before he slipped into bed beside her. That way it wasn't as difficult to stop himself from pulling her against him. It wasn't as difficult to ignore the fact that she was right there next to him, soft and lovely and incredibly sweet. It wasn't as difficult to will himself to sleep and pretend he didn't want her.

But it was all a lie.

It was killing him to be with her and yet not to be with her. Still, he knew no other way to wean her away, to give her time to make a choice. She had secrets she was keeping from him. He could see them in her eyes. There were times he wanted to take her by the shoulders and shake her until she told him. Then he would remember what she had gone through because of him, and he didn't touch her at all.

She'd been the perfect wife since they'd come back. Never demanding, never questioning, never arguing. He wanted Erin back.

Then he stepped into the bedroom and his limbs went weak.

"I thought you'd never come up." She crossed to him, holding out a hand. "You're working too hard."

"There's a lot to be done."

When he didn't take her hand, she curled her fingers into her palm but made herself take the final step. "There's more to living than horses and the next race."

Involuntarily he reached up to touch her hair. "I thought you'd gone to bed."

"I've been waiting for you." She brought a hand to his cheek as she rose on her toes to kiss him. "I've missed you. Missed being alone with you. Come to bed, Burke. Make love with me."

"I haven't finished downstairs."

"It can wait." Smiling, she began to unbutton his shirt. She was sure, almost sure, that she felt his response, his need. "We haven't had an evening alone in a long time."

It only took the feel of her bandages rubbing against his skin. "I'm sorry. I only came up to see if you were all right. You should get some rest."

The rejection stung her, and she stepped back even as he did. "You don't want me anymore, do you?"

Not want her? He was nearly eaten up with wanting. "I want you to take care of yourself, that's all. You've been through a lot of strain."

"Aye, and you. That's why we need some time together."

He touched his fingers lightly to her cheek. "Get some sleep."

She stared at the closed door before turning away blindly to blow out the candles.

Erin closed herself in the office and buried herself in columns of figures. Those, at least, she could understand. With numbers, when you added two and two, you could be assured of a logical answer. Life, she'd discovered, and Burke in particular, wasn't quite that simple.

When the call came from Travis that Dee was in labor, she found herself not only pleased for her cousin but for herself and the diversion. Scribbling a hasty note, she left it on her desk. If Burke bothered to look for her, he'd find it. If he didn't…then it didn't matter where she was.

She'd learned something else about marriage. Both husband and wife should stand on their own. In the best of worlds this was offset by an interdependence—a sharing, a love of each other and a contentment in each other's company. In the not-so-best, it simply meant survival. She was and always had been a survivor.

Still, she watched the house retreat as she drove toward the main road. Such a special place it was, the kind she'd always dreamed of living in. The grass was green now, and the flowers were in bloom. It was hard to believe she could finally have something so beautiful and still be unhappy. But it could be so much more than a place to live, she thought, just as her marriage could be so much more than an agreement between two logical adults. In time, Burke would have to decide how much more he would permit it to be.

He was dealing with his own devils when he came into the house. All morning and half the afternoon he'd been unable to erase from his mind how lovely Erin had looked the night before, how hard it had been to walk away from her and from his own feelings. He was no longer sure he was doing her a favor, and he knew for a fact he was killing himself.

Maybe the time had come for them to talk. Plain words, plain thinking. He didn't believe himself capable of much else. It hadn't taken him long to realize he was useless without her. How that had come to be, and why, didn't seem to matter. It simply was. But nagging at him, gnawing at him, was the question of what she would be without him. He'd never given her a chance to find out.

So they'd face off. That was something he understood. Now was as good a time as any.

He glanced in her office and, finding it empty, passed it by. In the atrium, Rosa was watering geraniums. He paused there, wishing he didn't continually find himself uncomfortable when he caught her going about her household duties.

"Rosa, is Erin upstairs?"

Rosa glanced up but continued her watering. "The *señora* went out a few hours ago."

"Out?" The panic was absurd. So he told himself even as it choked him. "Where?"

"She didn't tell me."

"Did she take her car?"

"I believe so." When he swore and turned away, Rosa moved to a pot of asters. "Burke?"

"Yes?"

She smiled a little and set down her watering can. "You have little more patience now than you did when you were ten."

"I don't want her left alone."

"Yet you do so continually." She lifted her brow at his look. "It's difficult to pretend not to see what's under my nose. Your wife's unhappy. So are you."

"Erin's fine. And so am I."

"You would say the same when you came home with a black eye."

"That was a long time ago."

"It's foolish to think either of us have forgotten. To have a future, it's necessary to face the past."

"What's the point in this, Rosa?"

She did something she hadn't done since they'd been

children. Crossing to him, she touched a hand to his face. "She's stronger than you think, my brother. And you, you aren't nearly as tough."

"I'm not ten anymore, Rosa."

"No, but in some ways you were easier then."

"I was never easy."

"It was the life that wasn't easy. You've changed that."

"Maybe."

"Your mother would be proud of you. She would," Rosa insisted when he started to back away.

"She never had a chance."

"No, but you do. And you gave one to me."

He made a quick gesture of dismissal. "I gave you a job."

"And the first decent home I've ever known," Rosa added. "Before you go, answer one question. Why do you let me stay? The truth, Burke."

He didn't want to answer, but she'd always had a way of looking straight and waiting for as long as it took. Maybe he owed her the truth. Maybe he owed it to himself. "Because she cared about you. And so do I."

She smiled, then went back to watering. "Your wife won't wait as long for an answer. She's impatient, like you."

"Rosa, why do you stay?"

She fluffed the leaves of a fern. "Because I love you. So does your wife. If you don't mind, I would like to pick some flowers for the sitting room."

"Yeah, sure." He left Rosa there, watering plants, and went back to Erin's office. It was the first time he'd asked himself or allowed himself to ask why he'd permitted Rosa to stay. Why he'd provided her with a job in order that she could keep her pride. She was family. It was just that simple, and just that hard to accept. She'd been right, too, when she'd said that Erin wouldn't wait so long for an answer.

He wanted Erin there, where they could sit down together. There where he could talk to her about his feelings. That would be a first, he admitted.

Restless, he began to push through the papers on her desk. She was a hell of a bookkeeper, he thought ruefully. Everything in neat little piles, all the figures in tidy rows. A man could hardly complain about having a conscientious wife. It certainly shouldn't make him want to gather up all the books and papers and dump them in the trash.

It was the doctor bill that made him frown. All medical expenses from her stay in Kentucky should have been addressed to him. Yet this one was clearly marked to her. Annoyed, he picked it up with the intention of dealing with it himself. He wanted her to have no reminders. But the doctor's address wasn't in Kentucky; it was in Maryland. And the doctor was an obstetrician.

Obstetrician? Burke lowered himself very carefully in her chair. The words "pregnancy test" seemed to jump out at him. Pregnant? Erin was pregnant? That couldn't be, because he would have known. She would have told him. Yet he had the paper in his hand. The paper stated "positive" clearly enough, and the test was dated almost a month earlier.

Erin was pregnant. And she hadn't told him. What else hadn't she told him? He sprang up again to push through the other papers as if he'd find the answers there. It was then he found her note, hastily scribbled. *Burke, I've gone to the hospital. I don't know how long it will take.*

As he stared at the note, he felt all the blood drain out of his face.

* * *

"Oh, I don't see how Dee can be so calm and patient!"

Paddy turned a page in the magazine he was pretending to read. "You can't hurry babies into the world."

"It seems to be taking forever." Erin paced the waiting room again. "My palms are sweating, and she looked like she could take a walk in the park. It's scary."

"Having babies?" He chuckled a little and sneaked a peek at his watch while Erin wasn't looking. "Dee's an old hand at this."

Erin laid a hand on her stomach. "Was she this way when she had the first one? I mean, the first one would be the scariest. It's like taking everything on faith that nothing's going to go wrong."

"Dee's a trouper."

"Aye." She prayed she would be as well when her time came. "It must make a difference, having Travis with her through it all." She'd seen the way he'd been with Dee, standing beside the bed, holding her hand, talking, making her laugh, timing her contractions. Total support, total commitment. "I wonder, Paddy, do you think most men would do that?" Would Burke?

"I'd say when a man loves a woman the way Travis loves Dee he wouldn't be anywhere else right now. Lass, you're going to wear a rut in the floor."

"I can't sit still," she muttered. "I'm going to go downstairs and see if I can buy some flowers. Have them waiting for her."

"That's a fine idea."

"I could bring you some tea."

"You do that. Won't be long now."

He waited until she was out of sight to get up and pace himself.

Downstairs, Burke burst into the hospital like a man possessed. In seconds he had pounced on the admissions clerk. "Where's my wife?"

The clerk swiveled her chair over to her computer. "Name?"

"Logan, Erin Logan."

"When was she admitted?"

"I don't know. A couple of hours ago."

The clerk began to punch buttons. "For what purpose?"

"I—" He wasn't sure he could deal with the purpose. "She's pregnant."

"Maternity?" The clerk continued to punch. "I'm sorry, Mr. Logan. We don't have your wife."

"I know she's here, damn it. Where—" Continuing to swear, he pulled the paper out of his pocket. "Dr. Morgan. I want to see Dr. Morgan."

"Dr. Morgan's in delivery with another patient. You can check at the nurse's station on the fifth floor, but—"

She shrugged when Burke raced away. Expectant fathers, she thought. They were always crazy.

Burke jammed a fist against the elevator button. He hated hospitals. He'd lost his mother in one. Only days before, he'd watched Erin lie in one, and now...

"Burke, I didn't expect you."

He turned to see Erin walking toward him with a huge arrangement of rosebuds and baby's breath. Her hair was pulled back and her cheeks were glowing. The flowers nearly tipped to the floor when he grabbed her shoulders.

"What the hell are you doing?" he demanded.

"Burke, you're crushing them."

"I'll crush more than a bunch of flowers. I want you to tell me what you're doing."

"I'm taking them upstairs. If they survive. I think Dee will appreciate them more if they're not mangled."

"Dee?" He shook his head but didn't manage to clear it. "What are you talking about?"

"What are *you* talking about?" she countered. "It doesn't seem so strange to me to buy flowers for someone who's having babies."

"Dee? You came here because Dee's delivering?"

"Well, of course. Didn't you see my note?"

"I saw your note," he muttered. Taking her arm, he pulled her into the elevator. "It wasn't very clear."

"I was in a hurry. I wish they'd had more roses," she murmured. "Seems when you're having twins you should have twice as many flowers." She buried her face in them a moment, then smiled at him. "I'm glad you came. It'll mean a lot to Dee."

Struggling for calm, he stepped out when the doors opened again. "How is she?"

"She's perfect. Paddy and I are a wreck, but she's perfect."

"You shouldn't be on your feet." He took the flowers because he was abruptly afraid for her to carry anything. "You shouldn't be getting yourself worked up."

"Don't be silly." She turned into the waiting room, not to find Paddy pacing but to find him dancing.

"One of each!" he shouted to both of them. "She's gone and had one of each."

"Oh, Paddy!" Laughing, she flung herself at him and let him whirl her around. "She's all right? And the babies? Everyone's all right?"

"Everyone's fit as a fiddle, so the nurse told me. They'll be bringing them all out in a minute so we can have a peek. A fine day to you, Burke. A fine, fine day."

"Paddy. Erin, why don't you sit down?"

"Sit?" She shook her head with another laugh and hooked her arm through Paddy's. "I couldn't sit if my legs fell off. Paddy and I are going dancing, aren't we, Paddy?"

"That we are." He put his chin up and began to hum. Recognizing the tune, Erin joined in as their feet began to move.

Burke stood holding a bushel of roses and watched them. He hadn't heard her laugh like that for too long. He hadn't seen her smile just that way. He wanted to toss the flowers aside and gather her up. Snatch her away, take her home. Hold her for hours.

"Here she is!" Paddy did another quick jig as Dee was wheeled out. "Here's my little girl. Look at this." He had to pull out his handkerchief and wipe his eyes. "They're beautiful, lass. Just like you."

"What am I?" Travis wanted to know. "Chopped liver?"

"You did a fine job." Erin moved over to kiss his cheek. "A boy and a girl." She looked down at the two bundles beside her cousin. "And so tiny."

"They'll grow quick enough." Dee turned her head to the right, then the left, to nuzzle them. "The doctor said they have everything they should have. Lord, they came out squalling, both of them. Didn't they, Travis?"

"They have their mother's disposition."

"It's lucky you are I've my hands full. Burke, it's good of you to come. This is the best time to have family around."

"Are you okay?" He felt both foolish and awkward as he passed the flowers to Travis. "Is there anything you want?"

"A ham sandwich," she said with a sigh. "A huge one.

But I'm afraid they'll make me wait just a little while yet."

"I'm sorry, we'll have to take Mrs. Grant now. Evening visiting hours start at seven."

"Paddy, bring the children back tonight."

"No children under twelve are allowed, Mrs. Grant," the nurse said as she began to push her away. Dee merely smiled and mouthed the request again.

"She looked wonderful, didn't she?" Erin mused.

"She's a Thoroughbred, my Dee. Always has been." Paddy stuffed his handkerchief back in his pocket. "Well, I'd better get home and think up a way to smuggle that brood in here tonight."

"Let me know if you need any help."

"That I will, lass." He kissed both her cheeks. As he walked down the hall, he jumped up and clicked his heels.

"You've been on your feet long enough," Burke said tersely. "I'll drive you home."

"I've got my car."

"Leave it." He took her arm again.

"That's silly. I'll just—"

"Leave it," he repeated, pulling her into the elevator.

"Fine." She bit the word off. "Since you're sure you can bear to be in the same car with me." She crossed her arms and stared at the doors. Burke stuck his hands in his pockets and scowled.

Neither of them spoke again until Erin stormed into the atrium. "If it's all the same to you, I'm going upstairs. And you, you can take your foul mood out to the stables with the rest of the dumb animals."

He wondered that her neck didn't break from holding her head that high. Burke gave himself thirty seconds to calm down. When it didn't work, he strode up the stairs after her.

"Sit down." He spit out the order as he slammed the bedroom door behind him. Erin simply narrowed her eyes and crossed her arms. "I said sit down."

"And I say to hell with you."

That was all it took. Before she could evade him, he had scooped her up and plunked her down on the bed.

"All right, now I'm sitting. Don't tell me you actually want to have a conversation with me?" She tossed her hair back, then slowly crossed her legs. "I'm all aflutter." She saw his hand close into a fist and angled her chin. "Go ahead, pop me one. You've been wanting to for days."

"Don't tempt me."

"It was quite clear last night I couldn't even do that." She pulled her shoes off and tossed them aside. "If you're so fired up to talk to me, then talk."

"Yeah, I want to talk to you, and I want some straight answers." But instead of asking, he shoved his hands back into his pockets and circled the room. Where to start? he wondered. His fingers brushed over the ring he'd carried for days. Perhaps that was the best place. Burke pulled it out and held it in the palm of his hand.

"You found it." Erin's first burst of pleasure was almost blanked out by the look in his eyes. "You didn't tell me."

"You didn't ask."

"No, I didn't, because I was sick about it. Dropping it in the stables was stupid."

"Why did you?"

"Because I couldn't think of anything else. I knew I couldn't get away from them. They were already tying my hands." She was looking at her ring and didn't see him wince. "I guess I thought someone would find it and take it to you, and you'd know. Though I don't know what I expected you could do about it. Why haven't you given it back to me?"

"Because I wanted to give you time to decide if you wanted it or not." He took her hand and dropped the ring in it. "It's your choice."

"Always was," she said slowly, but she didn't put the ring on. "You're still angry with me because of what happened?"

"I was never angry with you because of what happened."

"You've been giving a champion imitation of it, then."

"It was my fault." He turned to her then, and for the first time began to let go of the rage. "Twenty hours. You lay in the dark for twenty hours because of me."

The words could still bring on a cold flash, but she was more intrigued by Burke's reaction. "I thought it was because of Durnam. You've never seemed willing to talk it through, to let me explain to you exactly what happened. If you'd—"

"You could have died." There was really nothing else but that. No explanations, no calm recounting, could change that one fact. "I sat in that damn hotel room, waiting for the phone to ring, terrified that it would and there was nothing, nothing I could do. When I found you, saw what they'd done to you... your wrists."

"They're healing." She stood to reach out to him, but he withdrew immediately. "Why do you do this? Why do you keep pulling away from me? Even at the hospital you weren't there. You couldn't even stay with me."

"I went to kill Durnam."

"Oh, Burke, no."

"I was too late for that." The bitterness was still there,

simmering with a foul taste he'd almost grown used to. "They had him by then, where I couldn't get to him. All I could do was stand in that hospital room and watch you. And think of how close I'd come to losing you. The longer I stood there, the more I thought about the way I'd dragged you in with me right from the beginning, never giving you a choice, never letting you know what kind of man you were tied to."

"That's enough. Do you really believe I'm some weak-minded female who can't say yes or no? I had a choice and I chose you. And not for your bloody money."

It was her turn to rage around the room. "I'm sick to death of having to find ways to prove that I love you. I'll not be denying that I wanted more out of life than a few acres of dirt and someone else's dishes to wash. And I'm not ashamed of it. But hear this, Burke Logan, I'd have found a way to get it for myself."

"I never doubted it."

"You think I married you for this house?" She threw up her arms as if to encompass every room. "Well, set a match to it, then, it doesn't matter to me. You think it's for all those fine stocks and bonds? Take them all, take every last scrap of paper and put it on one spin of the wheel. Whether you win or lose makes no difference to me. And these?" She pulled open her dresser and yanked out boxes of jewelry. "These pretty shiny things? Well, take them to hell with you. I love you—God himself knows why, you thickheaded, miserable excuse for a man. Not know what kind of man I married, is it?" She tossed the jewelry aside and stormed around the room. "I know well enough who and what you are. More fool I am for not giving a damn and loving you anyway."

"You don't know anything," he said quietly. "But if you'd sit down I'll tell you."

"You won't tell me anything I don't know. Do you think I care you grew up poor without a father? Oh, you don't need to look that way. Rosa told me weeks ago. Do you think I care if you lied or cheated or stole? I know what it is to be poor, to need, but I had my family. Can't I feel sorry for the boy without thinking less of the man?"

"I don't know." She rocked him, but then it seemed she never failed to do so. "Sit down, Erin, please."

"I'm sick to death of sitting. Just like I'm sick to death of walking on eggs with you. I *did* nearly die. I thought I was going to die, and all I could think was how much time we'd wasted being at odds. I swore if we were back together there'd be no more fighting. Now for days I've held my temper, I've said nothing when you turn away from me. But no more. If you've any more questions, Burke Logan, you'd best out with them, because I've plenty more to say myself."

"Why didn't you tell me you were pregnant?"

That stopped her cold. Her mouth fell open, and for all her talk about not sitting, she lowered herself onto the bed. "How do you know?"

Burke drew out the paper he'd found and handed it to her. "You've known for a month."

"Aye."

"Didn't you intend to tell me, or were you just going to take care of it yourself?"

"I meant to tell you, but… What do you mean, take care of it myself? I could hardly keep it a secret when—" She stopped again as the realization hit like a wall. "That's what you thought I'd gone to the hospital for today. You thought I'd gone there to see that there would be no baby." She let the paper slip to the floor as she rose again. "You *are* a bastard, Burke Logan, that you could think that of me."

"What the hell was I supposed to think? You've had a month to tell me."

"I'd have told you the day I found out. I came to tell you. I could hardly wait to get the words out, but you started in on me about the money and the letter from my father. It always came down to the money. I put my heart on a platter for you time after time, and you keep handing it back to me. No more of that, either." She was ashamed of the tears, but more ashamed to wipe them away. "I'll go back to Ireland and have the baby there. Then neither of us will be in your way."

Before she could storm out of the room he asked, "You want the baby?"

"Damn you for a fool, of course I want the baby. It's our baby. We made it our first night together in this bed. I loved you then, with my whole heart, with everything I had. But I don't now. I detest you. I hate you for letting me love you this way and never giving it back to me. Never once taking me in your arms and telling me you loved me."

"Erin—"

"No, don't you dare touch me now. Not now that I've made as big a fool of myself as any woman could." She'd thrown up both hands to ward him off. She couldn't bear to have his pity. "I was afraid you wouldn't want the baby, and me with it when you found out. That wasn't part of the bargain, was it? You wouldn't be so free and easy to come and go if there was a baby to think of."

He remembered the day she'd come to tell him about the baby, and the look in her eyes. Just as he remembered the look in her eyes when she'd left without telling him. He chose his words carefully now, knowing he'd already made enough mistakes.

"Six months ago you'd have been right. Maybe even

six weeks ago, but not now. It's time we stopped moving in circles, Irish."

"And do what?"

"It's not easy for me to say what I feel. It's not easy for me to feel it." He approached her cautiously, and when she didn't back away he rested his hands on her shoulders. "I want you, and I want the baby."

She closed her fingers tightly over the ring she still had in her hand. "Why?"

"I didn't think I wanted a family. I swore when I was a kid that I'd never let anyone hurt me the way my mother had been hurt. I'd never let anyone mean so much that the life went out of me when they left. Then I went to Ireland and I met you. I'd still be there if you hadn't come back with me."

"You asked me to come here to keep your books."

"It was as good an excuse as any, for both of us. I didn't want to care about you. I didn't want to need to see you just to get through the day. But that's the way it was. I pulled you into marriage so fast because I didn't want to give you a chance to look around and find someone better."

"Seems to me I'd had chance enough."

"You'd never even been with a man before."

"Do you think I married you because you had a talent in bed?"

He had to laugh at that. "How would you know?"

"I doubt a woman has to bounce around between lovers to know when she's found the right one. Sex is as sorry an excuse to marry someone as money. Maybe we've both been fools, me for thinking you married me for the first, and you for thinking I married you for the second. I've told you why I married you, Burke. Don't you think it's time you told me?"

"I was afraid you'd get away."

She sighed and tried to make herself accept that. "All right, then, that'll do." She held her wedding ring out to him. "This belongs on my finger. You should remember which one."

He took it, and her hand. The choice had been given, to her and to him. It wasn't every day a man was given a second chance. "I love you, Erin." He saw her eyes fill and cursed himself for holding that away from both of them for so long.

"Say it again," she demanded. "Until you get used to it."

The ring slipped easily onto her finger. "I love you, Erin, and I always will." When he gathered her into his arms, he felt all the gears of his life click into place. "You mean everything to me. Everything." Their lips met and clung. It was just as sweet, just as powerful as the first time. "We're going to put down roots."

"We already have." Smiling, she took his face in her hands. "You just didn't notice."

Cautiously he laid his palm on her stomach. "How soon?"

"Seven months, a little less. There will be three of us for Christmas." She let out a whoop when he lifted her into his arms.

"I won't let you down." He swore it as he buried his face in her hair.

"I know."

"I want you off your feet." As he started to lay her on the bed, she grabbed his shirt.

"That's fine with me, as long as you get off yours as well."

He nipped her lower lip. "I've always said, Irish, you're a woman after my heart."

* * * * *

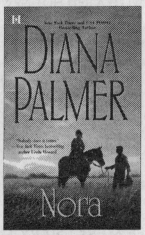

REQUEST YOUR FREE BOOKS!

2 FREE NOVELS
FROM THE ROMANCE COLLECTION
PLUS 2 FREE GIFTS!

YES! Please send me 2 FREE novels from the Romance Collection and my 2 FREE gifts (gifts are worth about $10). After receiving them, if I don't wish to receive any more books, I can return the shipping statement marked "cancel." If I don't cancel, I will receive 4 brand-new novels every month and be billed just $5.99 per book in the U.S. or $6.49 per book in Canada. That's a saving of at least 25% off the cover price. It's quite a bargain! Shipping and handling is just 50¢ per book in the U.S. and 75¢ per book in Canada.* I understand that accepting the 2 free books and gifts places me under no obligation to buy anything. I can always return a shipment and cancel at any time. Even if I never buy another book, the two free books and gifts are mine to keep forever.

194/394 MDN FELQ

Name	(PLEASE PRINT)	
Address		Apt. #
City	State/Prov.	Zip/Postal Code

Signature (if under 18, a parent or guardian must sign)

Mail to the **Reader Service:**
IN U.S.A.: P.O. Box 1867, Buffalo, NY 14240-1867
IN CANADA: P.O. Box 609, Fort Erie, Ontario L2A 5X3

Not valid for current subscribers to the Romance Collection
or the Romance/Suspense Collection.

Want to try two free books from another line?
Call 1-800-873-8635 or visit www.ReaderService.com.

* Terms and prices subject to change without notice. Prices do not include applicable taxes. Sales tax applicable in N.Y. Canadian residents will be charged applicable taxes. Offer not valid in Quebec. This offer is limited to one order per household. All orders subject to credit approval. Credit or debit balances in a customer's account(s) may be offset by any other outstanding balance owed by or to the customer. Please allow 4 to 6 weeks for delivery. Offer available while quantities last.

Your Privacy—The Reader Service is committed to protecting your privacy. Our Privacy Policy is available online at www.ReaderService.com or upon request from the Reader Service.

We make a portion of our mailing list available to reputable third parties that offer products we believe may interest you. If you prefer that we not exchange your name with third parties, or if you wish to clarify or modify your communication preferences, please visit us at www.ReaderService.com/consumerschoice or write to us at Reader Service Preference Service, P.O. Box 9062, Buffalo, NY 14269. Include your complete name and address.

NORA ROBERTS

28594	O'HURLEY'S RETURN	__ $7.99 U.S.	__ $9.99 CAN.
28592	O'HURLEY BORN	__ $7.99 U.S.	__ $9.99 CAN.
28590	SWEET RAINS	__ $7.99 U.S.	__ $9.99 CAN.
28588	NIGHT TALES: NIGHT SHIELD & NIGHT MOVES	__ $7.99 U.S.	__ $9.99 CAN.
28587	NIGHT TALES: NIGHTSHADE & NIGHT SMOKE	__ $7.99 U.S.	__ $9.99 CAN.
28586	NIGHT TALES: NIGHT SHIFT & NIGHT SHADOW	__ $7.99 U.S.	__ $9.99 CAN.
28583	WORTH THE RISK	__ $7.99 U.S.	__ $9.99 CAN.
28595	WINDFALL	__ $7.99 U.S.	__ $8.99 CAN.
28580	THE MacKADE BROTHERS: DEVIN AND SHANE	__ $7.99 U.S.	__ $8.99 CAN.
28575	THE MacKADE BROTHERS: RAFE AND JARED	__ $7.99 U.S.	__ $7.99 CAN.
28574	CHARMED & ENCHANTED	__ $7.99 U.S.	__ $7.99 CAN.
28597	LOVE BY DESIGN	__ $7.99 U.S.	__ $9.99 CAN.
28569	THE MacGREGOR GROOMS	__ $7.99 U.S.	__ $7.99 CAN.
28568	WAITING FOR NICK & CONSIDERING KATE	__ $7.99 U.S.	__ $7.99 CAN.
28565	TREASURES	__ $7.99 U.S.	__ $9.50 CAN.
28134	THE MacGREGORS: ALAN & GRANT	__ $7.99 U.S.	__ $9.99 CAN.
28137	PERFECT HARMONY	__ $7.99 U.S.	__ $9.99 CAN.
28133	THE MacGREGORS: SERENA & CAINE	__ $7.99 U.S.	__ $9.99 CAN.

(limited quantities available)

TOTAL AMOUNT	$ _____
POSTAGE & HANDLING ($1.00 FOR 1 BOOK, 50¢ for each additional)	$ _____
APPLICABLE TAXES*	$ _____
TOTAL PAYABLE	$ _____

(check or money order—please do not send cash)

To order, complete this form and send it, along with a check or money order for the total above, payable to Harlequin Books, to: **In the U.S.:** 3010 Walden Avenue, P.O. Box 9077, Buffalo, NY 14269-9077; **In Canada:** P.O. Box 636, Fort Erie, Ontario, L2A 5X3.

Name: _____
Address: _____ City: _____
State/Prov.: _____ Zip/Postal Code: _____
Account Number (if applicable): _____
075 CSAS

*New York residents remit applicable sales taxes.
*Canadian residents remit applicable GST and provincial taxes.

Where love comes alive™

Visit Silhouette Books at www.Harlequin.com

PSNR0711BL